Ring *of* Secrets

Ring of Secrets

ROSEANNA M. WHITE

HARVEST HOUSE PUBLISHERS
EUGENE, OREGON

Scripture quotations are from the King James Version of the Bible.

Cover by Garborg Design Works, Savage, Minnesota

Cover photos © Chris Garborg; Harald Biebel / 123rf.com; Anandkrish 16 / Bigstock

RING OF SECRETS

Copyright © 2013 by Roseanna M. White
Published by Harvest House Publishers
Eugene, Oregon 97402
www.harvesthousepublishers.com

Library of Congress Cataloging-in-Publication Data
White, Roseanna M.
   Ring of secrets / Roseanna M. White.
      p. cm.— (Culper Ring series ; bk. 1)
   ISBN 978-0-7369-5099-2 (pbk.)
   ISBN 978-0-7369-5100-5 (eBook)
   1. Women spies—Fiction. 2. New York (N.Y.)—History—Revolution, 1775-1783—Fiction.
I. Title.
   PS3623.H578785R56 2013
   813'.6—dc23

2012026068

Printed in the United States of America

13 14 15 16 17 18 19 20 21 /LB-JH/ 10 9 8 7 6 5 4 3 2

To those who can read my mind and love me anyway—
David, the other half of my heart. And Stephanie, the other half of my brain.

Acknowledgments

This book's journey has been full of amazing support and encouragement. I need first to thank my husband, David, who answered my question of "What was that spy ring thing called again?" with "The Culper Ring, honey," about five times before I finally looked it up for myself—and got the idea for the story. And, of course, my sweet little Xoë for always wanting me to tell her about Winter's story, and precious Rowyn for zooming around the house singing his "super spy" song. Then there are my parents and in-laws and sister and her family, whose support means the world.

Thanks to Stephanie, critique partner and best friend, who wouldn't let me give up on the idea at the first obstacle. Then comes my rock star of an agent, Karen Ball, who believed in this story enough to sign me after a single phone call. And, of course, the writing groups that answer all my questions and cheer me ever on: ACFW, HisWriters, and Colonial American Christian Writers, and my critique partners, Stephanie, Carol, Dina, and Amanda.

Finally, a big, mile-wide grin of gratitude goes out to my fabulous editor, Kim Moore, and the enthusiastic team at Harvest House. Ever since that first excited phone call an hour after I sent the proposal, this process has been one leap for joy after another. I'm so honored to be a member of the Harvest House family, and I am having such fun working with you guys!

He shall cover thee with his feathers, and
under his wings shalt thou trust:
his truth shall be thy shield and buckler.

PSALM 91:4

"Intelligence is the life of every thing in war."

Letter from General Nathanael Greene
to Major John Clark, November 5, 1777

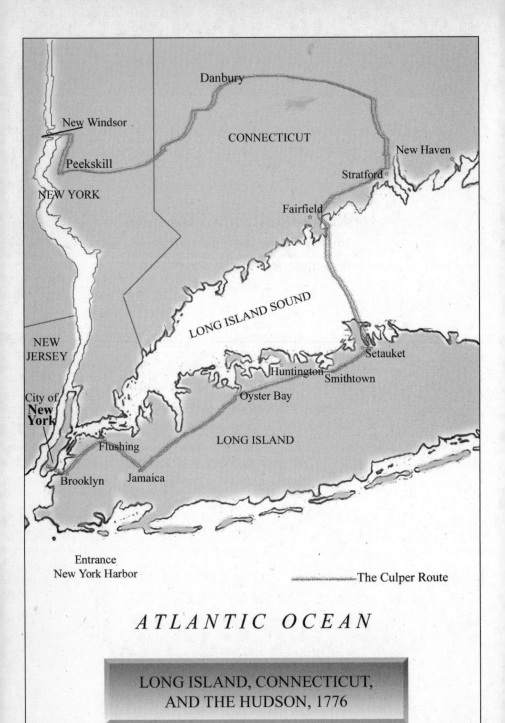

Danbury

New Windsor

CONNECTICUT

Peekskill

New Haven

NEW YORK

Stratford

Fairfield

LONG ISLAND SOUND

NEW
JERSEY

Setauket

Huntington
Smithtown

City of
**New
York**

Oyster Bay

Flushing

LONG ISLAND

Brooklyn

Jamaica

Entrance
New York Harbor

———— The Culper Route

ATLANTIC OCEAN

LONG ISLAND, CONNECTICUT,
AND THE HUDSON, 1776

One

City of New York
November 1779

L et innocence be your mask.
Winter Reeves swished her ivory lace fan and gave Colonel Fairchild the same practiced smile she always did. She squelched the response that wanted to escape, forbade her eyes from so much as flashing. Perhaps her gaze wandered, but he would only think her bored.

He thought her very easily bored.

"A stroke of luck, do you not agree, my dear?"

Despite the racing of her heart at the pearl of information he had just let slip, she made her nod a half-second later than it ought to have been. As if she were inattentive, paying no heed to his endless prattle. Why, after all, would she care about such a boring matter as paper? In his eyes—in the eyes of everyone here—she was naught but the pretty, brainless granddaughter of the Hamptons.

Let your beauty hide your heart.

Winter's gaze snagged on Robbie's, though she looked past him quickly. A successful business owner and newspaperman for the *Royal Gazette*, Robert Townsend was deemed acceptable company on a day-to-day basis, but Grandmother had higher hopes for her. At social occasions, she was not permitted to speak to him.

She didn't have to speak to him. A mere glance showed her his waistcoat tonight bore seven silver buttons. Seven—that meant he had slid a note into the bottom, middle drawer of the chest in the drawing room.

Feigning a yawn partially hidden behind her fan, Winter blinked. Slowly.

Colonel Fairchild interrupted his monologue with drawn brows. "Forgive me, my dear. You must be in need of refreshment by now. Allow me to fetch you a cup of spiced tea."

"That would be lovely, thank you." Winter injected her tone with relief and made her smile sheepish. "I shall just slip out for a moment while you get it, Colonel."

Fairchild bowed, though he kept his head erect. No doubt to stop his new powdered wig, more heavily curled than his old one, from slipping.

Winter dipped a short curtsy and headed for the ballroom's exit, her palms damp.

"Winnie!"

She forced pleasure into her face as she turned toward her grandmother. "Yes, ma'am? Can I get you anything?"

Grandmother narrowed her ice blue eyes. "Where are you going? The ball has barely started, and there is someone I want you to meet."

Winter lowered her gaze. "I will only be a moment, Grandmother. I must attend to a personal need."

The matron lifted her chin. No one would doubt Phillippa Hampton was the queen of this particular event. Her hair was an extravagant tower of whitened curls, ribbons, and gems. Her gown was a creation so exquisite, King George himself would have envied the craftsmanship.

Her glare could shrivel a thriving oak tree. "Return posthaste. Mr. Lane is awaiting an introduction."

Let your enemies count you a friend.

She pasted on an obedient, docile smile. "I will be quick."

"I should think so, knowing who awaits your return." The snap of Grandmother's fan of Spanish lace all but forced Winter's eyes to the right.

As if Mr. Lane were different from any other guest here. As if he were anything but another haughty, arrogant Loyalist. As if he were…

She drew in a sharp breath when her gaze collided with the stranger's. He stood beside her grandfather, his eyes locked on her. 'Twas nothing unusual, given the gilding her grandmother poured upon her. But the *way* he looked at her, the eyes that did the looking…

He was only passably handsome, if one examined his nose, his mouth, his jaw. Strong features, and sandy hair he hadn't bothered to powder or cover in a wig. Pleasant, not exceptional. But those eyes—they seemed to pierce right through her facade, down to the heart she'd been forbidden to have.

Penetrating. Stirring. Tugging.

No. She couldn't afford to let a man turn her head, and she certainly couldn't let one see her heart. No matter that a single gaze from him made her yearn for someone who might understand her.

God of my end, help me to focus upon Your will for me. Winter tore her gaze free and curtsied to her grandmother. "I shall be glad to meet him in a moment, ma'am."

Perhaps some other enterprising young lady would have laid claim to him by the time she returned. Eyes like that were far too dangerous.

Grandmother kept her a moment more. "You have heard of the recent fortune of the Manhattan Lanes, I presume."

If one could call it fortune when one's uncle's son died and one's father returned to England to learn to manage the family estates. Which Grandmother certainly did, being ever loyal to the Crown—no matter how hard the heel of His Majesty's army crushed the city.

Winter nodded.

Her grandmother pursed her lips. "Go, child. But hurry back before Mrs. Parks snatches him and forces him to dance with Theodosia."

To God's ear. Somehow she suspected Mr. Lane's gaze wouldn't unnerve Dosia at all. Her friend had no secrets to be discovered.

Winter made her escape from the ballroom. Guests filled the hallway too, and they would be in and out of all the main rooms in her grandparents' first floor. She followed a bewigged couple into the drawing room and traced a path along the chamber's edge until she came to the polished maple of the high chest of drawers.

The bottom center drawer was open a bit. Not so much as to be noticeable to anyone not looking, but enough that Winter could catch her sleeve on the knob as she walked by and make a show of looking irritated before freeing it.

She folded the slip of paper she'd recovered into her fan, shut the drawer with a scowl, and then headed out of the room, inspecting her sleeve as if the lace had torn.

No one stopped her as she darted up the stairs and headed for her bedchamber. That didn't keep a relieved breath from seeping out as she threw the bolt on the door.

Winter strode to the banked fire and stirred it enough to light a taper. She set the candle upon a table and pulled the slip of paper out. The message written upon it made her smile.

> My dearest lady, flame of my heart,
> How you make my day burn bright!
> With the smallest turn of your reddest lips,
> You are all that is beauty and light...

Winter snorted a laugh and checked the right top corner of the page. An "H" marked it. The real message, then, would appear with the application of heat.

Hands steady, Winter held the page close, then closer to the flame. Closer still until the smell of scorching paper filled her nostrils, until a faint sizzle reached her ears. Until the invisible ink filling the space between the lines of terrible poetry turned a golden brown.

Eleven o'clock tonight. The tulip tree behind the stable.

Eleven. She pulled the paper away from the flame and squinted to read the darkened face of the mantel clock. One hour more. Time enough to appease Grandmother, to bat her lashes and act the part of witless society lady for Mr. Lane. Then she could slip outside. She hoped Robbie would be there to meet her, and she could tell him what Fairchild had said. Though there remained the possibility that he had simply left another message for her.

This one could bring her trouble enough. If her grandparents saw it, they would place her under lock and key to keep her from eloping as Mother had.

Or worse, if Grandfather had meant the threat that still made her shiver. And she had no reason to doubt his sincerity, given the hatred he had never tried to hide from her.

Time nipped at the back of her throat, each tick of the clock telling her to hurry downstairs. But first she tossed the page into the fire. As the flames licked over the wisp of paper and then smoldered into glowing ash, Winter held her spot, watching the last ember die out. In her mind's eye, she saw another letter, another fire.

Why had she burned it? Why? The last word she had from her father, the last thing her mother had given her before she passed away.

A cloud must have raced over the moon, for deeper shadows cloaked her room. Winter spun for the door. Best to lock away the memories of Oyster Bay, of life before the war. Best to remember who she was now. Best to push down the longing to go back, even for one day, to the life she once knew.

That life was gone. She had come to terms with that.

Better a life among enemies than a noose around her neck.

Bennet Lane buried his terror in a glass of cordial and silently recited some Latin to calm his nerves. How had he ended up once more in a ballroom lit with crystal chandeliers, surrounded by batting lashes and swishing fans?

George jabbed him with an elbow—not exactly subtly—and smirked. "You look like I felt when expected to recite the opening of *Hippolytus.*"

"Give me Euripides above this any day." Ben forced a smile and stiff bow when a set of well-dressed young women glided by, simpering looks partially hidden by their fans.

His friend's chuckle held no sympathy. "You garner admiring gazes from them all."

"Because they all know my father just became the heir to considerable property. But the moment I try to talk to any of them… Women are baffling, George. Baffling. They complain if you treat them as pets but grow bored if you treat them as equals."

Placing his empty glass on the tray of a passing servant, George snorted. "Your idea of an 'equal' is a fellow from Yale. They are lost and bored with your constant references to Latin and Greek, but that does not mean they have no brains at all. Well, most of them."

Ben grunted a laugh and sent his gaze over the gathering. Young ladies abounded, all in imported silk and lace. Some had beauty to their faces that couldn't be hidden by the mountain of curls atop their heads; others relied on the fuss to bolster what nature had withheld.

"I have spent too many years in Connecticut, with its boycotts and homespun. All this luxury is confounding." He took another sip of his drink and let his gaze linger upon a young lady with pink powdered hair. She was pretty, but when they had been introduced, it had taken only a stuttered sentence from him for her eyes to glaze over. Perhaps she would be amenable to a suit, but he'd rather find a woman to court with whom he could have a full conversation every now and again.

George narrowed his gaze upon Ben's hair, tied back but otherwise unadorned. "You had better get accustomed to fashion again quickly, old boy. Gentlemen of Hampton's ilk expect you to dress appropriately when you come to their houses. Even I know that, and I would never have been invited if not for your request."

"Hmm." He hated powdered wigs—itchy and hot. But he would do what he must. Ben scanned the room again, looking for the angel in pale blue and gold he had seen leaving a quarter-hour earlier. Hampton's granddaughter, and hence the highest-bred young lady here. With her on his arm, he could secure invitations to all the elite's functions. His family's heritage gave him the proper pedigree for them, but he had been too long away from New York to know from where the invitations would come.

Access was crucial. Somewhere in this ballroom, or another as exclusive, a spy might lurk. Someone undermining the British cause, feeding information to the rebel army that they could only have learned from high-ranking associations. Either an elite themselves, or one of the bottom-feeders who catered to them.

He would find that someone, eventually. He must. And he was prepared to do whatever was necessary to achieve it.

Even if that "whatever" meant attaching himself to one of these terrifying, lace-bedecked creatures.

His expression must have shifted to betray his panic. George laughed. "If they befuddle you so, why are you determined to make a match?"

Ben shook himself and grinned. "It is like chemistry, George. You know well that combining certain elements might explode in your face, but you cannot resist pouring them together on the chance they will create something spectacular."

"'Tis talk like that which sends them running." George clapped a hand to Ben's shoulder and nodded toward the corner. "Now, look at that one—Miss Parks. She bears a striking resemblance to our old friend Charlie Mason, does she not?"

"Parks." Ben frowned. "Are they not cousins to the Masons?"

"Probably. Hence the resemblance, I suppose. Irrelevant. My point is, you could always carry on a conversation with Charlie, who lacked your excellent education, without confusing him. Do the same with Dosia. Talk of the weather, of the latest news, of *anything* not straight from your laboratory at Yale. Pretend she is Charlie."

Ben folded his arms over his chest and nodded decisively. "Charlie in a dress." An excellent plan.

"Right," George said on another snort of laughter. "Or, if you can wrest her from Colonel Fairchild, you might set your sights on Miss Reeves. She hasn't a spare thought in her head anyway, so she is well used to giving an absent nod of assent. Well, from what I have seen. I've never been introduced, mind you."

Bennet's gaze followed George's gesture toward the doorway, filled by the vision of beauty herself. Hampton's granddaughter—Miss Reeves, apparently.

Empty headed? That dug a furrow into his brow. When he had caught her gaze a bit ago, she had struck him as many things, but thoughtless was not one of them. Hers were not eyes that covered an idle mind.

Were they? *He* was not the type to be so blinded by beauty as to attribute to a lovely face nonexistent qualities, was he?

Well, time would tell. Hampton was even now striding toward Bennet, undoubtedly to make the promised introduction since his ward had returned. Which George apparently took as his cue to leave with a mumble about another drink.

Miss Reeves held her place in the doorway for a moment more, looking out at the ballroom as if taking stock of everyone there. A princess surveying her kingdom? Perhaps. Certainly she put all the other young women to shame, from the details of her gown to the powdered tower of hair, to her face, exquisite in its detail.

His pulse hammered. She was too beautiful for him. His tongue would twist into knots if he dared to open his mouth in her company. She would dismiss him in a moment, as every other girl did. He'd do better to find a more approachable lady to court, one common enough that she wouldn't actually distract him from his true motive for returning to New York.

Miss Reeves turned her head to her left and then moved toward Mrs. Hampton. Her every step was a dance, each gesture the epitome of grace.

Ben would be lucky to secure a minuet with her, much less any other sign of favor. And because he was not so superficial as to think a pretty face was all one needed, he certainly wouldn't mourn the loss of what would never be.

She kept her gaze down as Mrs. Hampton ushered her forward. Seemingly demure, but there was something else in the tension of her neck. Something that spoke of anxiety, perhaps conflict.

Interesting.

Hampton stopped at Ben's side and nodded at the approaching ladies. "My granddaughter has returned."

"Excellent, sir." He should have stayed home tonight. Settled in with a text. Montesquieu, perhaps. Montesquieu would be a fine companion for this blustery November night, far better than this present company—George excluded.

Hampton glared at the women when they arrived. "There you are."

Miss Reeves curtsied, her gaze on her grandfather now, though his granite face didn't soften in the slightest. "I trust you are enjoying your birthday celebration, Grandfather?"

"Quite." He looked as though *enjoying* wasn't a word in his vocabulary. "Allow me to introduce Mr. Bennet Lane, of the Manhattan Lanes. Mr. Lane, my granddaughter and ward, Miss Winter Reeves."

She didn't look at him, though she turned her face his way. When he held out a hand, she settled her fingers on his so lightly as to barely touch him at all.

Still, awareness coursed through him. She was even lovelier up close than from afar. A narrow bridge of a nose, lips of a perfect rose, brows that bespoke hair the color of his favorite mahogany chair—if one could see beneath the powder coating each lock, anyway.

He bowed over her hand. "It is a pleasure to make your acquaintance, Miss Reeves." Ah, not so much as a stutter. He would do his debate professor proud.

She drew in a breath too short, too sharp. And finally she lifted her eyes to his.

They were green. Deep as an emerald and not just in color. So many thoughts, so many needs seemed to swirl within those jewel-like irises for one fraction of a second—then it was as if a door slammed shut and they were only eyes. Pretty, empty eyes.

The strain was gone from her posture, and the turn of her lips looked half bored. "Likewise, Mr. Lane."

He let her fingers go but couldn't convince himself to look away from her perfect countenance. Not so much as a twitch revealed any thought at all, but he knew well he hadn't imagined it.

Winter Reeves was more than the face she showed this crowded ballroom. Why did she feel she must hide it? And what, exactly, was it that she hid? Puzzling.

One corner of his mouth tugged up. Ben loved nothing so much as a puzzle. "Mr. Hampton, may I have the honor of dancing with your granddaughter when the next set begins?"

Hampton glowered. "She would be delighted." Another word that seemed foreign to his frowning mouth.

Mrs. Hampton, however, beamed. As for Miss Reeves...if he weren't mistaken, that look of ennui upon her face was designed specifically to put him off.

Well, they would see about that. Any philosopher, be he political or scientific or abstract, knew that sometimes one must revise one's stated mission. His may have to become twofold.

Find the Patriot spy in New York.

And unravel the mystery that was Winter Reeves.

Two

Robert Townsend leaned against the cold, damp bark of the tulip tree and folded his arms over his chest. Shrouded by darkness, he watched the glittering assembly through the window and let himself shake his head at it all. He made a good living by selling imported goods to families like the Hamptons. A respectable family and his work for the *Royal Gazette* guaranteed him entry to any gathering he could wish to attend.

But the secrets...much as he believed in his cause, much as he knew he did right by helping the Patriots, the secrets gnawed at him until his stomach was a constant, roiling ball of dread.

At least all this business brought him closer to Winter. He watched her slip out the rear door of her grandparents' house and glide through the deep shadows at the side of the yard. Seeing her decked in such finery still gave him pause. In Oyster Bay she had been just another village girl. Pretty enough, in her simple way. Homespun dresses and a deep Congregational faith to do her Puritan ancestors proud.

Now he sighed each time he saw how little remained of sweet little Winter. What hadn't been snuffed out by the strong arm of the British, by her father's fleeing to take up the colors for the Patriot cause, by her mother's sudden death had been pressed upon and crushed by her grandparents.

When she stole up beside him in the protective blackness of the tree's broad trunk, Rob offered a lopsided smile. "So kind of you to slip away to keep tryst, fair lady. Seeing you in such glorious beauty has made my heart take wing—"

She interrupted him with a laugh, bright and free as it had been when they were children, if quieter. "Your poetry is atrocious, Robbie. But lucky for you, I shall forgive it. I have news." She stepped closer and rubbed her gloved hands over her arms. The night was icy, but she hadn't grabbed a wrap.

"Here." He shrugged out of his cloak and draped it over her shoulders. "You will freeze in half a second dressed like that."

"It would have looked strange for me to grab a cloak. And it hardly matters as this will only take a moment." But she pulled the wool close. The moonlight caught her face and painted her in silver.

She wore silver well.

"Colonel Fairchild mentioned this evening that they are counterfeiting—"

"We already know that." Any hope he'd felt deflated. He'd promised a correspondence to Woodhull—operating as Culper Senior to Rob's Culper Junior—but he would have nothing of substance to put in it.

Winter pursed her lips. "Would you let me finish? I know well they have been counterfeiting congressional dollars for years, but there has always been a flaw—"

"Their paper is too thick. Yes, we all know that. It has still succeeded well in devaluing the dollar."

"And it is about to succeed even better." She straightened her shoulders and raised her chin. "Fairchild said they've managed to steal several reams of paper from the last emission in Philadelphia."

Though Rob never traded in dollars in the British-held city, it still struck like a blow. "The very paper? Then there will be *no* telling them apart from the genuine articles, and the money will be totally without backing. And so—"

"Worthless." Winter nodded. "You must let them know. Congress can perhaps withdraw the bills from circulation before it is too late."

"Let us pray so." For a moment he stared into the night, and then at the windows spilling golden light. Couples danced, moving about as if oblivious to the war. Clad in their silks and velvets, their lace and jewels.

"Well." Winter took his cloak off again and held it out to him. "I have nothing else beyond the normal. We are swimming in luxuries and cannot get staples. Morale among the Tories wavers under the weight of the military's heel, but they all still consider the Patriot cause a futile one and doubt Washington will be able to muster another campaign."

"Unchanging." Rob slipped the cloak back on. Even after so brief a time around her, it smelled of Winter. Lavender and violets. "There is one thing more. I had a letter from my father the other day, who had heard from yours. A brief note to assure anyone wondering that he is well."

Moonbeams caught the tears that sprang to her eyes and turned them to diamonds. Lovelier by far than those dangling at her ears. "Thank you, Robbie. If your father writes him back, I would appreciate him including that I miss him—that he remains always in my prayers."

"Of course." He said no more, made no attempt to detain her when she spun back for the house. Even if the constriction of his chest insisted he was allowing her to return to a lion's den. Perhaps so, but it was not his place to shut the lions' mouths. The Lord Himself would have to do that.

Sighing, Rob turned toward the property's back gate—and nearly shouted in alarm when a massive shadow blocked his path.

"Mr. Townsend?"

"Freeman." Rob swiped at his brow and bade his pulse return to normal. "Did no one ever teach you not to lurk in shadows?"

Winter's servant grinned, the whites of teeth and eyes the only thing visible in the darkness. "No, sir. They taught me to use them well instead. Mr. Townsend, I worry for her. I help her much as I can, but I worry, and I would be lying if I said otherwise. This game you two play—"

"'Tis no game, Freeman." Pulling his cloak tight, Rob moved nearer to the man, and hence the gate. "'Tis the most serious matter in the world."

"Exactly, sir. Her daddy made me swear on the grave of mine that I would take care of her, that I would make sure no harm came to her because of his loyalties. But if she gets caught helping you in this—"

"I would never let that happen. Never." Rob craned his head up to look into the towering face of the son of a slave, the only other link Winter had to her family on Long Island. "No one will ever know how she helps me."

Freeman stepped aside. "See that they don't, sir. The Hamptons would toss her to the streets in a blizzard if they caught even a whiff of scandal. They hold her accountable for her mother's decisions and made it pretty clear that if she fails to atone for Amelia's 'bad' marriage with a brilliant one of her own, they will wash their hands of her."

He couldn't hold back the snort. "That may be the best thing for her. I hate seeing how they have stifled her spirit."

But Freeman shook his head. "You don't understand. The mister, he hates her. He hates her just for being, and he never would have let her step foot in his house if weren't for the missus wanting to redeem her reputation through Winnie. I heard him threaten to drop her off in Holy Ground if she doesn't behave herself. No good to come of that."

"No." Icy fear settled like lead in the pit of Rob's stomach. Sweet Winter, tossed in with every disease-ridden harlot in New York? Nay, it was too evil to even ponder. "It shan't come to that, Freeman. You have my word."

The man nodded, the movement barely discernible in the darkness. "You take care too, Mr. Townsend. No good to come of you getting caught, neither."

"Don't I know it." He slipped out of the gate, lifting a hand in farewell even though he doubted the older man would be able to see it.

The nausea churned, exacerbated somehow by the rows of mansions in this part of the city. True, many of them now housed British soldiers instead of wealthy families. The Hamptons had avoided that solely because of their connections with Governor Tryon and the favor they had incurred with Generals Howe and Clinton.

Rob's Quaker roots nevertheless thrummed within him at this obvious display of mammon. He had grown up in a home too affluent to earn the approval of the Friends, but even Father's taste for finery, even Rob's own focus on successful business ventures, had nothing on this kind of excess.

Yet only a few miles away, evidence of the Great Fire lingered. Hundreds of buildings, a third of the city's housing, still lay in ruins. Every month, it seemed, there was a new scare about the state of provisions. Would there be enough flour to last the winter? Enough firewood? Enough straw?

Would he live to see it even if there were? If he were caught...

Well, he mustn't be. That was all there was to it.

The blustery fingers of the winter wind snuck into his cloak as he hurried home, but Rob ignored them. Soon enough he climbed the stairs to his apartment. He roused the fire, and its warmth chased away the chill. Bathed in its orange glow, he picked up his quill.

On the newest paper he could find, he penned a simple note. A letter seemingly about mercantile business, any names mentioned the coded ones they had agreed on. He was careful to leave ample space between all the lines.

While it dried, he moved over to the bookcase. He had added two new tomes to his shelves that afternoon, and the promise of evenings well spent in their company made him smile. Rather than pull them out now, though, he removed the entire line of books and then the piece of wood on which they sat.

There, in the few inches of space between shelf and floor, he kept his most important tools. Vials of what they called in their letters "medicine," which the Misters Jay shipped to General Washington in crates marked as such.

He took out the ink and the special quill he used with it, and then moved back to his desk. He eased the cork from the glass bottle and then halted, squeezing his eyes shut.

What would this news he was about to impart mean to his country? How could a nation hope to survive with its currency diminished to nothing? With what were they funding their government? Their army? Never mind the expenses he and his colleagues incurred through travel and lodging.

"Dear Lord..." Not knowing what to pray, he settled for opening his spirit for a moment and submitting this business, yet again, into the hand of the Almighty. Then he opened his eyes and picked up his quill.

The substance dubbed "the sympathetic stain" by Washington was barely visible as he wrote with it, such a pale yellow, and it dried into nothingness. Only the sheen of candlelight on liquid showed him his letters and the dire message they formed. Careful to keep his quill strokes between the lines of regular ink so as not to cause any telltale runs, he penned the terrible news.

> They think America will not be able to keep an army together for another campaign. Everyone reasons that the currency will be depreciated, and that there will not be enough provision to supply the Army. The concern for the currency I am afraid will prove true, as the British are tireless in increasing the quantity of it. Several reams of paper made for the last emission struck by Congress have been stolen from Philadelphia.

There. When next Roe was in the city, Rob would deliver this to him. Roe would take it to Woodhull, whom Rob had come to know when they both boarded in the same house until a few months ago. From Woodhull it would make its way via the sailor Caleb Brewster to Benjamin Tallmadge, and from Tallmadge to General Washington himself.

And from Washington…well, Rob hoped it would make it to whoever could salvage what was left of young America's treasury.

He recorked the vial, put it and the quill away, and replaced the shelf. Then he stood for a long moment, leaning against the bookcase.

He must hope. Must hope and believe he could make a difference. Must trust that if one fought for the light, it could hold the darkness at bay.

He must.

Winter eased the door shut with nary a click. Warmth welcomed her, along with the muted din of many voices in the other rooms. In this back hallway, though, all was quiet.

"Felt the need to escape?"

Hand clutching her throat, Winter spun around with a gasp. Not that she had to turn to know who waited. When they were introduced an hour ago, Mr. Lane's voice had soothed like her favorite spiced tea. She wouldn't forget it anytime soon.

What was he doing back here, though? Had he followed her? Had he seen her with Robbie? Impossible. One couldn't see from the house into the shadows of the tulip tree at this time of night.

She swallowed back anything but expected alarm and willed herself into her usual role. "Mr. Lane, shame on you. You startled me."

That shrewd gaze of his narrowed, though his lips were turned up in a smile. "Does your given name lend you a predilection for such inhospitable weather as is to be found in your backyard right now?"

Though she wanted to grin, instead she blinked—as if confused but not wanting to admit it. The Winter known in these circles never would have been able to follow that question. "Pardon? No, I was not outside to predict the weather. I just needed a breath of fresh air."

The gentleman arched a brow. "In that chill?"

"My mother once said she named me well, given how much I like the cold."

Mr. Lane chuckled and straightened from where he leaned against the wall. "You are a clever one."

"Clever?" She gave him a surprised smile, even while mentally scolding herself. She ought not to have added that last part. Colonel Fairchild might smile when her presumed stupidity seemed to stumble into correct understanding, but Mr. Lane didn't know her mask well enough to make such assumptions yet. "Why, Mr. Lane, that is a most unequaled compliment. I shall have to tell everyone you called me clever."

His smile faltered as his eyes widened a tad. He had probably already heard enough opinions on her to realize that if he called her witty, it would speak to the opposite in him.

She nearly sighed at the need to resort to such strange threats.

Mr. Lane edged closer, challenge gleaming in his eyes. "Clever indeed. Is it not exhausting?"

Now he really did confuse her. "Is what exhausting, sir?"

"The need to hide your wit as you do, and reveal it only in ways so *very* clever that most cannot understand you."

Alarm bells clanged in the depths of her mind. How in the world could someone have seen that within an hour of meeting, when those who supposedly knew her well thought her superficial at best?

Father in heaven, protect me.

She blasted him with her most brilliant smile and strode forward, leaving him little choice but to turn and fall in beside her. "What a charmer you are. Your family is all from New York, are they not? How is it you only now come to our fair city?"

The light dimmed in his eyes. "Fair? What I have seen of it since coming home two days ago bears little resemblance to the New York I knew before the war."

"The current state of things has been hard on everyone, to be sure." She studied the wallpaper as she spoke, as if merely parroting what she'd heard others say and not sharing her own observation. As if she, in this golden world, had remained untouched. Oblivious.

"I imagine so." His voice was too soft, too understanding—but thankfully, he shook himself. "To answer your question, I have been at Yale. First as a student, and then I stayed on as faculty."

"Yale." Questions sprang up, but she covered them with her usual smile. "I know it, of course. Grandfather calls it 'a hotbed of Whiggish sentiment.' It sounds delightful. I should greatly like a wider selection of wigs, perhaps one of those with so many curls a servant must follow behind with a stick to hold it up."

He laughed. No polite chuckle or a chortle that he thought to be at her expense, but a genuine laugh of delight. Of understanding.

Or perhaps she was too tired, overwrought with all this business, and seeing things that weren't there. Surely that made more sense than a total stranger comprehending her so immediately.

His mirth quieted to a smile, and he proffered his arm. "Your grandfather has the right of it, to be sure. I found there were many opportunities for debate."

Somewhere deep inside, a kernel of warmth took up residence within the block of ice in her chest. Had anyone ever continued to talk seriously to her after one of her "misunderstandings"? Winter tucked her hand into the crook of his elbow. "You often debate on the fashion of wigs, then? Most intriguing. How many rows of curls do you prefer? Do you favor the gray powder or the white?"

He sent her a wink that ought to have scandalized her. "A good Yale man can debate any topic, Miss Reeves. For my part, I prefer no wig at all, as you can see. And powder makes me sneeze."

"'Tis a problem, I confess. Some enterprising chemist ought to devise a better recipe."

"Or perhaps some enterprising lady of fashion ought to make wigs a thing of the past, for the sake of our sensitive noses."

She made a show of debating that as they regained the ballroom. "I shall take it under consideration, to be sure. But I so enjoy the display."

Mr. Lane opened his mouth to retort, but before any words could come forth, another young gentleman walked up. He had brows closer to red than brown, a face well-dusted with freckles, and a cheerful gleam in his eyes. She recognized him but had never been told his name. All she knew was that he was considered beneath her.

"Ah, George." Mr. Lane grinned and slapped a friendly hand to the newcomer's shoulder. "Miss Reeves, allow me to introduce to you Mr. George Knight. He and I are childhood chums."

"Miss Reeves."

She held out her hand and measured her smile to the appropriate brightness, gauged according to what her grandmother would approve. "Mr. Knight. Are you one of the esteemed Staten Island Knights?"

"Ah." He'd barely bent over her hand before releasing it. With a glance toward Mr. Lane, he shifted his feet and grimaced—he probably intended it for a smile. "No, miss. No relation that I know of. My family are gunsmiths."

Those Knights? Far more interesting than the stuffy landowners her grandparents so admired. Not that she ought to be interested in such things, so she put on the patronizing smile that always felt so vile upon her mouth. "Oh."

Mr. Knight pursed his lips and turned to Mr. Lane. "Excuse me, Ben. I only wanted to find you to let you know I'm off. Do stop by sometime in the next few days. We have years to catch up on."

"Certainly I shall."

They clasped wrists, and the gunsmith bowed curtly to her. "Good evening, Miss Reeves."

"And to you, Mr. Knight." Her usual, absent smile would cover the pang snubbing him caused her. This was the part of life in her new society she would never get used to, this expectation to dismiss decent people based on their income.

Up until a year ago, she would have been the one dismissed.

The scowl that creased Mr. Knight's forehead as he turned away proved the success of her facade. How...excellent.

Exhaustion settled on her shoulders and sent her gaze toward the tall case clock in the corner of the room. Not yet eleven thirty. The celebration would continue at least until one.

Mr. Lane studied her again, his blue eyes like a torch seeking out an escaped convict. Thankfully Colonel Fairchild approached. She had already promised him another dance, which was surely about to begin. The perfect excuse to escape Bennet Lane. With a little luck, she would be able to avoid him the rest of the night.

With a little diligence, forever.

Three

December 1779

Ben chafed his hands together and anchored down the rolled paper with his inkwell and a book. His gaze traveled over the map yet again, though he'd memorized it even as he sketched it. Now to add a few more noteworthy locations.

He cast a longing look toward the fireplace, though he daren't build a fire yet. Fuel supplies were dwindling, and though he could probably bribe the right men to get a bit extra, he couldn't bring himself to do it, not when so many others needed it more than he.

Soon he'd have to be off anyway. They were expecting him at Hampton Hall.

With his quill dipped in ink, he set to work. On the map he had marked each affluent home—the ones where high-ranking officers gathered, where gossip was likely to venture from benign to sensitive. Hampton Hall. Barton House. The Felders', the Parks', the Masons'. Several others he'd managed to visit over the past few weeks. Enough that he now recognized which families moved in the circle he would scrutinize.

He'd ventured out into the city during the days too, to reacquaint himself. He wanted to get his bearings in a town depleted of so much of its previous self. Yesterday he had wandered over to the eastern side, where the burnt-out shambles from the Great Fire still stood black and forlorn, mile after mile. From the battery all the way to King's College, nothing remained but a charred memory of the New York he had known as a boy.

Part of him wished he had never come home. If only this quest had taken him somewhere else, anywhere else.

He drew a line around Rivington's Corner at the bottom of Wall Street, home of the *Royal Gazette*. Though the paper didn't have the stellar reputation of the *New York Mercury*, the newspaper's office was a meeting place of officers eager to pass along tantalizing tidbits for the *Gazette*'s owner to exaggerate before printing. They also had their favorite coffee shops, public houses, vendues...all of which he intended to frequent. Not so much to see who was speaking, but rather to discern who was listening.

Were it not a holiday, he would head out again now. But alas.

On a separate piece of paper, he made notes of the next places he intended to visit. The favored tailor of the officers, under the guise of needing a finer suit of clothes than his tenure in Connecticut had permitted. He'd stop in for coffee afterward at the shop owned by the same Rivington who ran the newspaper. Perhaps from there he would follow any gossip he heard to a few new locations, which he would then add to his map.

Explore, discover, document.

He rested his quill in its glass holder and flexed his frigid digits. His father's old, large house was as drafty as it was impressive.

"Hallo, there! You home, Ben?" The muffled shout came from outside his front door.

At least George was still in town. Smiling, Ben removed the weights to let the map roll back up and shoved his work into a drawer. He would take it all back up to his personal quarters later. "Coming."

"Well, hurry it up. My hands are full. Don't you have a footman?"

"'Tis Christmas, you dunderhead. I gave him the day off." Ben jogged to the entryway, wrenched open the door, and found his friend to be without exaggeration. He frowned at the stack of boxes and wrapped parcels in his arms. "What in blazes is all that?"

George arched his brows, incredulous. "'Tis Christmas, you dunder-head. I have brought you a gift, and Mother sent a few treats for your supper. Are you sure you will not join us?"

"Ah." He relieved George of half his burden and led the way to the table. "I cannot, but thank her for me. I will be at the Hamptons'."

He turned in time to catch George's sneer. "Calling on Her Lady of Oh again, are you?"

"Her lady of…George, where do you devise these things?"

"Didn't you see her face when I confessed I was not one of the Staten Island Knights? It was as if I ceased to exist. And never before in my life have I heard someone manage to contain a world of dismiss-als, disappointments, and judgments in a single 'oh.'" He folded his arms over his chest, the very image of stubbornness.

Ben loosed a long exhale, though a grin fought to burst forth. "You judge her too harshly."

Now George's arms flew up. "I? I judge too harshly? Have you both-ered to tell her ladyship that *she* judged *me* too harshly?"

"Her 'ladyship' did not judge you at all." And she hadn't given him the chance to tell her anything in this past month. Other than exchanging basic civilities, she wouldn't be budged from Colonel Fair-child's side whenever they were in company.

No need to let George know that, though.

His friend leveled an accusing finger at his nose. "Do you know what has happened to you? I shall put it in terms you can understand. You are Odysseus, and she is your siren. You had better lash yourself to your ship, my friend, or face destruction on the rocks of her island. She may look the part of an enchantress, but she has no heart within her, as most anyone will tell you."

"All this wisdom gained from seeing her across a crowded ball-room a few times and exchanging a single greeting. Your intuitiveness astounds me, George." Ben lifted the cloth on a particularly fragrant package. "Ah! Bread. Your mother has enough flour for this?"

"She had been hoarding it for the Christmas feast, apparently, and thank heavens for the freezing temperatures or it surely would have been weevil ridden by now." George leaned onto the table, bending over to catch his friend's gaze. "Ben. I grant hers is the prettiest face in the City of New York, but you have better sense than to get caught up in her game. If she *does* give you the time of day, it will only be because of your family's fortune."

And yet if that were in her mind, she would have obeyed those prods he'd seen her grandmother make toward him rather than avoiding him so adroitly. No, Miss Reeves was not interested in his fortune.

Though any observer would argue she wasn't interested in any of his other qualities, either.

He flipped open another parcel. "And bread pudding too. You know, I grew so accustomed to not celebrating Christmas as per New England regulation, 'tis hard to remember it is more than a quiet time of reflection for so many of my friends and family."

"Celebration became considerably louder when the British arrived, for certain. Their revelry helps me understand why our Puritan fore-fathers forbade such boisterous observance of the day." George tapped a box. "Your gift."

"Yours is there." He indicated the present, wrapped in calico, that sat on his side table. When George had fetched it, he untied the string on his own gift. And laughed.

George did as well, holding up the book Ben had selected for him. Alexander Pope's translation of *The Iliad.*

Ben held up his new *Odyssey*, courtesy of the same translator. "Your warning about Miss Reeves suddenly makes sense."

"I noticed you did not have your copy here. Perhaps you left it in Connecticut, but I know how you love to pass a winter night with Homer, so it seemed a lack in need of filling." George shook his head and smoothed a hand over the tome. "And because many of mine were lost in the fire, this one included, I greatly appreciate your thinking the same."

"Certainly." He waved a hand at the treats covering the table. "Would you like some?"

"I must hasten home. If my sister and her family get there before I do, I shan't hear the end of it all day. And since I cannot convince you to join me…"

"I do appreciate the offer, George. And the book. Shall I give Miss Reeves your felicitations?"

"I would prefer it if you gave her your own permanent farewells."

Chuckling, Ben saw his friend to the door. Then he sighed when silence smothered him yet again. He enjoyed quiet, even depended upon it much of the time, but he also relished a good debate, an evening spent in philosophical discourse. Things sadly missing from his current existence.

Well, he might as well head to the Hamptons'. He may not find any exhilarating conversation there, but perhaps he'd be able to corner Miss Reeves again. Another taste of her delightfully underhanded wit would be a welcome change from all these thoughts of spy-catching.

After donning cloak, hat, and gloves, he went round back for his horse and set off for Hampton Hall.

Minutes later he was doffing that which he'd just donned and following a servant into a parlor bursting with well-dressed merrymakers. A few of the officers looked to be in their cups already, their laughter loud and grating.

Was there no happy place between silence and carousing? Perhaps he ought to have gone with George after all.

"Ah, Mr. Lane. Welcome, and a happy Christmas to you." Mr. Hampton held out a hand in greeting, thunder in his brows. Did the man not know how to smile?

"Thank you, sir, for opening your home to me."

Hampton grunted and nodded toward a flock of young gentleman. "Wilkens and Prescott are over there. Friends of yours, are they not? There is still a good while until supper, though the ball shall begin soon."

Ben barely managed a nod before his host was off to welcome another guest, if "welcome" was the proper term.

"Bennet Lane, there you are. I thought you would never arrive!"

"Oh…ah…" He could feel his neck flush as he turned to find Elizabeth Shirley, one of the prettier young ladies he'd met, standing before him, her fan hardly covering the coquettish tilt to her lips.

"I…that is…" Blast. His tongue felt thick and boorish, to match his addled brain. *Think, man, think.*

Whom did she look like? Her nose—it was the same shape as Daniel Clifford's, and Daniel was a fair-minded fellow. He had a taste for the ridiculous, though, that could certainly reveal itself in a smirk not unlike Miss Shirley's.

Daniel. Daniel stood before him now, undoubtedly preparing for some hideous play, given the frippery he'd dressed in. That was it.

Ben cleared his throat. "I do hope you are enjoying a pleasant Christmas?"

Daniel swished his fan. "I am indeed. Mrs. Hampton has paired us for supper, you know. I look forward to it."

Daniel dissolved fully back into Miss Shirley, and Ben could manage no more than an "Ah...yes. Well, then." He nodded as he edged away.

He drew in a sharp breath. Deuces and blazes, why couldn't he act the part of a normal young buck? At least every now and again. But no, Providence had seen fit to reserve such gifts, which wasn't very Providential at all, now was it? Ben ought to do them all a favor and mire himself with the other gentleman, thereby sparing himself and every female in the house a goodly dose of embarrassment.

His gaze tracked to the corner of the room, where Miss Reeves stood at the window. Theodosia Parks and Emeline Barton sat on the settee beside her, but she seemed oblivious to her friends' chatter. She stared out the window as if the skiff of snow covering the gardens had some magical secret hidden within its crystals. For the first time since the night they met, he noted the stiffness of anxiety in her neck and shoulders.

Miss Parks directed a question her way, and yet again he watched her assume a facade of ease that obliterated the telltale tension. Her smile was of perfect brilliance, and whatever she said had the girls tittering, though the look they exchanged between them seemed to also say they thought her dimwitted, however delightfully. When Miss Parks turned from her again, Miss Reeves let her eyes slide shut for half a moment, and then she turned toward the door.

He was following before he could consider the wisdom of it. They had been at many of the same functions in the preceding weeks, but not since that first one had he seen her slip away from the gathering.

Perhaps Providence was with him today after all.

"Not running away, are you, my dear?"

Winter had to bite back tears at the unwelcome voice, though she pasted on a bright smile. "Colonel Fairchild. I will be back directly."

The colonel grinned and took her hand, pressing a kiss to it. "I am sure you will be. I have barely had a chance to enjoy your company this afternoon, so busy have you been with your friends."

Busy. With her friends. Those silly girls interested in nothing but fashion and beaux, who made an art of insulting her in subtle ways that they assumed she didn't understand.

She swallowed the sob that threatened her throat and prayed her grin was convincing. "They've been regaling me with descriptions of the lovely gifts their parents gave them for Christmas."

Concern flickered in Fairchild's eyes as he studied her. "Have you a headache, Miss Reeves?"

Regret mixed with the sorrow that had haunted her all day. For all his verbosity, for all his loyalties, he was a decent man. One who seemed to care for her. She owed him more than she gave him, for certain. The least she could do was convince him not to worry now. "Grandmother warned me against eating too many sweets, but you know I cannot resist them."

There, relief moved through his warm brown eyes, and a smile creased his face. A more handsome officer she had yet to meet. She ought to feel more for him than she did.

Perhaps she would, were he not her main source of information to be passed along to Robbie. But how could she ever love someone she saw mainly as a conduit of intelligence?

Though on the other hand, how could she ever attach herself to someone who couldn't help her with her cause?

He squeezed her hand before releasing it. "Are you going to rest for a few minutes? Have a nice cup of tea in solitude, and I imagine you shall be yourself again directly."

"Exactly my thoughts, Colonel." She dipped a curtsy. "I shall look forward to our dances and supper together."

"As shall I."

She had barely gained the sanctuary of the hallway when Grandmother's clawlike fingers gripped her arm. "Winifred Reeves, whatever are you doing?"

She gritted her teeth at the misnomer. Grandmother despised her given name and usually shortened it to "Winnie." But when in a temper, she deliberately chose to pretend Winter had been named after a distant Hampton cousin rather than Father's aunt.

Grandfather, on the other hand, always used her correct name. And oh, but he could convey in those two syllables how low he thought her. How much he despised her. That she was a blight upon his name and a reminder of what he deemed her mother's unforgivable betrayal.

Winter drew in a long breath to bolster her courage and seized the excuse Colonel Fairchild had provided. "I am sorry, ma'am, but I need a few moments of quiet. I have a headache coming on, and I know you would prefer I fight it off now rather than being forced to my room when the ball and supper are underway."

Grandmother released her grip, though her flinty eyes remained hard and biting. "You may have fifteen minutes, no more. And I have changed the supper arrangements. Mr. Lane has arrived, and you will dine with him rather than with Colonel Fairchild."

Panic snapped its jaws around her throat. "Grandmother—"

"I shan't hear a word of protest. No matter how partial you are to the colonel, Mr. Lane is the better match. I expect you to do your duty and try to win him. Obviously you must still keep Colonel Fairchild's favor in case Mr. Lane does not propose, but that is the union you will vie for. Am I understood?"

For a long moment, Winter stared at her matriarch. How had sweet, gentle Mama ever come from this harsh, ambitious couple? Then she inclined her head. "You are understood."

"Fifteen minutes." Proclamation issued, Grandmother stormed back to the gathering.

The tears wouldn't be held back any longer. Winter rushed down the hall and into Grandfather's study, the closest room she knew would be empty and could offer some solace. Her eyes burned, her throat felt tight as a fist. She tossed herself onto the window seat, pressed her forehead to the cold, wavy glass, and gave her emotions free rein.

Most days, it didn't bother her. Most days, she could pretend so well.

But it was Christmas. A day she should have spent with her family, her *real* family, those who loved her. A day of quiet, of somber reflection on all her Savior did for her by coming to earth as a babe, of how great was her heavenly Father's love, that He would send His precious Son to be born as a lowly human. It should have been a day of peace. Of joy.

Not of drunken laughter, mercenary comparison of gifts, and reminder after reminder that she was not, could not be the person who lived within her.

She wanted to scream. Wanted to pound her hand against the glass until it released her from this terrible place. No, she wanted to lock herself in her room and hold the rest of the world at bay until it was just her and her Maker, communing in prayer.

She could do none of that, not now. She couldn't even cry. Tears stuck in her throat, suffocating her.

Movement outside caught her attention, and she moved her burning eyes to seek it out. Freeman stood in the dormant garden, his dark brow creased as he watched her. Thumb and pinkie out, middle knuckle higher than the others to form a W, he tapped his chin twice in one of the gestures he and Father had devised for her deaf Grandmother Reeves. *What is wrong?*

A few drops trickled out of her eyes now. How she wished she could go outside, to Freeman's room at the back of the stable. How she wished she could spend the day with the closest person she had to real family. Instead, she splayed a hand over her heart, then pointed her index fingers at each other and twisted them. *My heart hurts.*

Free touched his chest, pressed his palms together in the universal symbol of prayer, and then pointed to her.

A few more tears broke loose. Winter touched her lips and lowered her hand toward the window in thanks.

Freeman nodded, offered a tight smile, and strode away. She watched him go with a sigh. When Father took up the colors and joined the Patriot army, she knew Freeman had wanted to go with him—and knew he stayed behind solely because Father had asked him to take care of her and Mother.

She'd never imagined he would take that oath so seriously as to come here with her too. He was treated no better than a slave in her grandparents' household, despite his technical freedom. *That* was family. That dedication, that loyalty, that fierce, protective love.

A throat cleared behind her, and Winter spun around on her seat.

Bennet Lane stood in the center of the room, his lips pressed together and careful curiosity lighting his eyes. She knew better than to hope he didn't notice the droplets on her cheeks.

He bowed in greeting. "Forgive me for interrupting, Miss Reeves. I just spoke with your grandmother, who informed me of the change in supper arrangements." Half a smile tilted his mouth. "I suppose that would make me cry too, were I you."

A laugh slipped out in spite of herself. She wiped away the tears. "Are you enjoying your Christmas, Mr. Lane?"

He tilted his head and shrugged. "'Tis not the kind of Christmas I grew accustomed to in Connecticut. I confess I have come to prefer quiet reflection on the day." Stepping closer, he arched his brow. "And you?"

Try as she might, she couldn't summon her mask, not fully. "I grew up on Long Island in a Congregational home. Our Christmases were quiet as well. This—" she waved a hand toward the house at large "—makes me miss my parents all the more."

"They are…?"

She focused her gaze on the bookshelf across from her rather than on his compassionate face. "I lost my father some three years ago." Her grandparents insisted she say he was dead—killed by the random fall of a roof slate, of all things—but she couldn't bring herself to lie on this holy day. "My mother succumbed to a fever last year, rather suddenly. Though she had time to write her parents so they could take charge of me."

"I am sorry for your losses."

Not so sorry as she. But she dug up a smile. "The Lord has sustained me." Though for so long she wondered why He had bothered preserving her, only to lead her to a place where she must deny all He had made her. It hadn't become clear until Robbie approached her six months ago about gathering intelligence. Now she could see the Father's hand in it all.

This was what she'd been created for.

Winter stood and smoothed a hand over her embroidered stomacher. "I ought to get back."

But Mr. Lane didn't move from her path, though he studied the floor as if its patterned wood were the most intriguing thing he'd ever seen. "Miss Reeves...your grandmother led me to believe she and your grandfather would fully approve if I were to pay you court. Would you...? That is, I realize I am...apart from my family and our recent..." He huffed to a halt, and then he lifted his gaze to her face. Whatever he saw seemed to bolster him, though she thought she'd emptied her countenance of any telling expression. "Is your heart already set on Fairchild, or have I a chance at winning your affections?"

Oh, how she wished he had phrased it in a more complicated fashion so that she could play her usual role and act the imbecile. But a question so direct could not be misinterpreted even by pseudo Winter. She cleared her throat. "If my grandparents sanction your court, then certainly I shall receive you when you call."

The set of his jaw looked at once amused and frustrated. "That is not what I asked."

Winter took a long moment to study his penetrating eyes, his pleasant face, the uncertainty in his posture. She took a moment to recall how endearing he was as he bumbled his way through all the balls they had both attended, how many smiles she had tamped down as he stuttered through each introduction to eligible females, yet spoke with eloquence to the gentlemen on topics of philosophy and science.

Her heart seemed to twist within her. She could like this man, could enjoy his company, but she dared not. He knew nothing that would interest General Washington; she would be beyond useless if she attached herself to him. She would be no more, then, than another Loyalist daughter, seeking her own merriment above the call of freedom.

That she could not do. She could not return to an existence without purpose.

"Mr. Lane..." Her voice sounded uncertain to her own ears, so she paused for a slow breath. "I am surprised you would ask about my heart. Surely you have heard the rumor that I haven't one."

He moved to her side and took her hand, tucking it into the crook of his elbow. All the while his gaze bore into her, measuring her. "I know you are not the empty vessel you pretend to be, Miss Reeves. With your leave, I intend to discover what lies beneath this lovely surface."

Let innocence be your mask.
Let your beauty hide your heart.
Let your enemies count you a friend.
And the most important of all her axioms:
Let no one see your true self.

Much as she might yearn to disregard that last one, she couldn't. She gave him her loveliest, emptiest smile. "Best of luck with that, Mr. Lane."

Four

Rob pushed through the back door of his store, unfastening his cloak with one hand even as he slid the now-empty crate onto a table with the other. His hands trembled. Most would think it a result of his hours out of doors in the cold—and he would let them think so.

Washington was always interested in the state of the British fleet, in the numbers of ships in the harbor and the number of soldiers and seamen. Tallmadge had warned him not to guess—*never* to guess—not to exaggerate, not to round down. He must, at all costs, represent the true situation so the general could properly strategize. Thus far, Rob's accurate information had earned him commendation and respect. He intended to keep earning it.

Hence his hours-long trek through the city to the harbor and around military headquarters. Ostensibly to deliver newly arrived goods that had been ordered, but he had also been counting. Making mental note.

And getting nervous. Being about such covert business while surrounded by scores of saber-wielding enemies…well, it was a relief to be back at the shop, where he had only to worry about his cantankerous business partner. And wonder again what in the world had possessed him to bring on a man like Henry Oakham the very summer he started spying for the Patriots. Of course, he and Oakham had already made the agreement before Woodhull had approached him about this business…

Ah, well. Rob hung up his cloak and followed the sounds of voices to the front of the store, where said cantankerous business partner stacked fabric bolts for one Hercules Mulligan.

Rob smiled and slid behind the counter. "Mulligan! How fortuitous. My father sent me back to the city with a message of greeting for you."

The older man chuckled and rapped a knuckle against stacks of fine worsted wool. "I thought you had gone to Long Island for Christmas, hence why I waited far too long to come in and unburden you of some of your stock. How is your sire?"

"Excellent, sir. Thank you for asking. And I am so glad you came by. I tried to squeeze any interesting goings-on from Oakham here when I returned, but he is, as always, too silent."

His business partner rolled his eyes and stalked away. "Thank you for your business, Mr. Mulligan. Now I shall leave you ladies to your gossip."

Mulligan's gaze went sharp, though his lips still held their easy grin. "I'm afraid I have no interesting gossip to share, Mr. Townsend. Though loud in revelries, nothing of note happened here while you were away."

He leaned in, down, as if studying the cut of Rob's waistcoat. "Atrocious work. I do hope none of my tailors made it. Now," he said in a bare murmur, "is there anything in particular you need me to keep my ears open for?"

Rob smoothed a hand over the new clothing. "My mother made it, sir," he said at normal volume. Then, quietly, "Not just now, no. Though if I receive instructions, I shall get them to you."

Mulligan straightened as he nodded. He had once been a tailor of middling ilk, but through an advantageous marriage and an excellent way with a needle, he had turned his operation into an emporium that outfitted the city's elite—which meant he was in position to overhear invaluable information. Information he passed on willingly to Rob, unlike the many who gave him help without ever knowing it.

The man looked ready to leave but then halted. "Ah! Buttons. I am in desperate need of gold buttons, if you can help me."

"Of course." Rob pulled out a box and then straightened when the bell over the door jingled. A vaguely familiar gentleman walked in. Rob recognized him from the rounds of balls and fetes as well as from the coffeehouse of which he owned a share, but they had not been introduced. Which would soon be remedied, it seemed, because the man's face brightened upon spotting him, and he approached the counter with a smile.

"Good day to you, gentlemen."

"Sir." Rob nodded. "Might I assist you?"

"I should think so." The man held out a hand. "Bennet Lane. You look familiar, though I cannot recall learning your name."

Ah, yes. Rob had heard of the Lanes' recent fortune, which made them desirable customers, indeed. He smiled. "A pleasure to make your acquaintance, Mr. Lane. Robert Townsend at your service, and Mr. Hercules Mulligan besides."

Lane turned his smile on Mulligan. "How excellent. I have an appointment with one of your tailors next week, sir."

"I saw your name in the book." Mulligan offered a small bow with all the aplomb he had learned through years of catering to his wife's well-connected family. "It will be my privilege to take your measurements myself, sir. I outfitted your father for some time before he departed for England."

Lane chuckled. "I wish I had known that before asking every officer and gentleman I could find whom they would most highly recommend. I am afraid I have been too long in Connecticut to know my way about the city these days."

"You can certainly do no better than Mulligan's," Rob interjected. "He and my father have been friends for decades as well." They had in fact known each other back in the days when one could confess one's politics without being beaten and dragged from one's house for them, or forced into the city with a blanket over one's head.

Rob took the buttons Mulligan selected and wrapped them up.

Lane turned and faced Mulligan. "Your name is bandied about with respect as well, Mr. Townsend. I am told I can do no better for my dry goods. And my not-dry goods, if I incline that way, though I confess I am not overly fond of rum."

"Nor am I, truth be told." Rob handed the package of buttons to

Mulligan, along with the cloth. "But I am happy to help you with your other needs. We received a new shipment of mushroom catsup." At the look upon his customer's face, Rob chuckled. "Spanish olives, perhaps? Some Gloucester cheese?"

Lane straightened, shaking his head. Unlike most gentlemen of his standing, he wore no wig under his hat. And was that cloak of homespun?

Yes, he needed that appointment with Mulligan, to be sure.

"What have you by way of stationery? I am in need of a good deal of paper, a new journal bound in leather, and some ink, if you have it."

"Certainly. One moment."

Rob moved to the aisle containing the requested goods.

"A good deal of paper, you say?" Amusement sounded in Mulligan's voice. "Writing a book, good sir? Or perhaps a pamphlet?"

The newcomer chuckled. "I am afraid I must plead guilty to all manner of scholarly pursuits. I am a professor at Yale in the subjects of chemistry and philosophy, and I have been known to fill many a winter night at work upon my treatises. Unfortunately, I left my home in haste and failed to bring adequate supplies with me."

"Upon hearing your family's news, I assume. With your father gone, your mother is no doubt pleased to have you home."

Lane released a breath that sounded of laughter. "She may have been, had she remained long enough to receive me. It seems she had little faith in my arrival and went to visit her sister upon my father's departure, as my brother is away on maneuvers as well."

Rob lifted a goodly amount of paper from its shelf, its color near white and its weight thick, and then he added the nicest of his leatherbound diaries. And, in case the man's cloak was a testament to his spending habits, poorer versions of the same. After adding a selection of quills, ink, and a pen knife for mending nibs, he returned to the counter.

Mulligan had gathered his notions together and nodded upon Rob's return. "I must be away. I thank you, Mr. Townsend, for yet again coming to my rescue. Do give your father my regards when you write him. And I shall look forward to seeing you next week, Mr. Lane."

"Likewise."

"'Twas a pleasure speaking with you, Mr. Mulligan." Rob smiled at the older man as he left, and then he spread out the writing supplies on the counter. "Here you are, Mr. Lane."

"Ah, thank you." With the exact expression children usually wore when perusing his sweet selections, Lane flipped through the paper and examined the writing instruments. "A most excellent stock of paper, sir. Very white."

"I always keep some of the highest quality on hand." Largely because the sympathetic stain worked best upon paper of pure white, though others oft preferred to buy it as well. Rob adjusted his spectacles and glanced at his partner's back at the end of a long aisle of goods. He had to watch his every move, his every thought whenever Oakham was nearby. Heaven help him if the man ever realized Rob was aiding the Patriots under the cover of their store.

The customer hummed in approval as he ran a hand over the leather of the expensive diary. "Exquisite. I will take both journals, this paper here—" he slid forward equal portions of the good paper and the lesser variety "—half a dozen quills, the knife, and this vial of ink."

Rob gave the man a smile. Obviously this was a fellow of sound mind and admirable intellect. "Would you like me to put it on your father's account, Mr. Lane?"

"No, no." Lane pulled out his purse. "I am unsure how long I will be in the city, and I despise the thought of leaving debts in my wake for my family to cover."

Yes, a most likeable gentleman indeed. Rob tallied up his purchases and read him the total. "Is there anything else I can get for you today?"

Lane leaned close, conspiracy in his eyes and a smile playing at his lips. "Well, what I have a true hankering for is apples. Have you any of those in stock, Mr. Townsend?"

Laughing, Rob shook his head. "I fear that for those particular luxuries you will have to try the London Trade."

Lane's face went blank. "Pardon?"

Rob motioned him closer, though any New Yorker knew this "secret" as well as he. "I am surprised no one has told you of this already. When you are in want of produce, you must go to those shops specializing in goods smuggled from rebel-held territory, where all the farms lay. There you will find your beef and poultry, your potatoes and apples. Those merchants will, in turn, take some of our silks and jellies and pastries to Long Island. This is known as the 'London Trade.' Strictly illegal, of course, but no one on either side much cares as they like their fruits and silks as much as any citizen."

With a glint of amused self-deprecation in his eyes, Lane straightened. "So that is where George has been getting his goods all this time. He always made me believe he was extraordinarily well connected and never once mentioned I could find such things without his help. If you could kindly point me in the proper direction, my friend?"

Rob accepted the coins for the purchase and wrapped up the more fragile items in a box of card paper. "Gladly. So long, of course, as you come here for your legally purchased goods." He handed over the box with a grin and held out a hand for the stack of paper Lane had picked up. "I shall tie that up with some twine for you, if you will."

The bell over the door jingled again, and they both turned that direction, Lane still clutching the stack of paper. In rustled a flock of gaily clad women, the elder ones leading the way as their daughters brought up the rear. And away flew the quiet of the shop into the brisk air out of doors.

Were these particular ladies not given to tossing their money about with abandon, Rob may well have groaned. He was glad he hadn't, though, when he spotted Winter wedged between Theodosia Parks and Elizabeth Shirley. She giggled along with the other girls over whatever so amused them, but her eyes, as always in such company, were blank.

At least Mrs. Hampton was nowhere in sight. Surely the freedom of that would soothe her, even if she daren't show it.

The frippery-laden flock made their way toward the counter—and were greeted by a shower of flying sheets of paper as Mr. Lane dropped his burden and made it worse by lunging for them and so sending them every which direction.

At least he had already paid for them.

Laughter rang out. Rob had to bite back a chuckle of his own, but he did so. Given the shade of red poor Mr. Lane's neck had turned, he needed an ally in the worst way.

"Oh, dear me." Mrs. Parks stepped backward, though she urged her tittering daughter toward the mess. "So sorry if we startled you, Mr. Lane."

"My fault. I was…that is I…my apologies, ma'am. Ladies. Clumsy of me."

Mrs. Shirley all but shoved her daughter forward too. "We shall help you pick it up, Mr. Lane, no fear. My darling Elizabeth can bring order from any chaos."

Her darling Elizabeth hiccupped and slapped a hand over her mouth, eyes wide with horror.

Under normal circumstances, Rob would have been quick to round the counter and restore order himself. But because these circumstances were far from normal, he merely caught Winter's gaze and silently shared the mirth she did an excellent job of covering. Though even her lips hinted at a smile in the corners. She had apparently caught one of the fluttering sheets and held it in her leather-clad hands.

The other young misses had already bent over to help, though Rob winced at the way they trod upon more paper than they rescued. Lane seemed oblivious to the dirt upon it. He took each offering thrust at him with an "Oh…yes, thank you. And you. Miss…very kind. So sorry. Again, I…"

After they had fluttered back into position behind their mothers, Lane heaved out a breath and stood to survey the lot. Rob watched the man's shoulders roll back when he spotted the sole remaining piece of paper in Winter's hands. "Miss Reeves, I do believe that belongs to me."

Rob quirked a brow. Not a stutter, not a blush. Indeed, it sounded as though the man smiled, though standing behind him as he was, Rob couldn't be sure.

Winter glanced at the paper with a good show of surprise. "Oh, I thought it a gift. Though I confess, when a man slips me a piece of paper, it usually has words of verse upon it." Somehow she made it sound as though such words confounded her.

Rob drew in a deep breath to keep his countenance schooled. Was he the only man to slip her notes, or did Fairchild and the like do so as they paid her court? Certainly, she would never laugh at any poem of the colonel's and insult his ability as a scribe.

'Twas the colonel's loss. For he would never know the true mind of the lady he sought.

Lane chuckled and held out a hand for the paper. "Were it appropriate, I would offer to return it to you with some clever poetry. Though my verses tend to expound on Descartes or Lavoisier, so I doubt how well they would be received."

How did she manage to convey such innocence and oblivion in a single blink? "Indeed, I have never received either of those gentlemen. Were they at any of the balls I have been to?"

Mr. Lane laughed, which made Rob's fingers grip the edge of the counter. Thank the good Lord he was not often allowed in Winter's company when she was with others. He could not have born hearing them find their entertainment at her supposed expense.

With a shake of his head, Lane set the paper upon the counter. "I daresay you have met Descartes in some form or another, Miss Reeves."

Miss Shirley frowned. "Is he not one of those dreadful philosophers, long since deceased? The one who said 'I am, therefore I think'?"

"Certainly I have never met anyone who spouts such nonsense." Gliding forward, Winter approached the counter. Finally, Rob could see the well-hidden twinkle in her eye. "My existence has never caused me to think."

A few snorts of laughter slipped from Winter's friends, though Miss Parks rolled her eyes at Miss Shirley. "'Tis 'I think, therefore I am,' you goose."

Winter stopped a couple of feet before him. "So if I do not think, I will cease to exist?" Terror, feigned to perfection, saturated her tone and widened her eyes.

Grinning like a fool—a lovesick one, no doubt—Mr. Lane slid his purchases to the edge of the counter to make way for the lady. "You are in no danger of blinking out of existence, Miss Reeves."

"Sometimes I wonder." Her low mutter likely went unheard by all but Rob, and perhaps Mr. Lane, though he surely wouldn't know what to make of it. She rested her hands upon the counter. "Now, Mr. Townsend. Have you the last order I placed?"

Rob snipped off a length of twine to tie round the soiled paper. At the niggling of his conscience, he added a few extra fresh sheets to the top of the stack, which earned him a grateful nod from Mr. Lane. As he bound them up, he glanced at Winter. "The lace of gold your grandmother wanted for you? Yes, I have put some aside."

Her eyes snapped like an angry flame. "I was referring," she said, voice low, "to the *other* item, sir. The special…perfume."

Rob pressed his lips together, his thoughts winging to the precious bottles of stain and counterpart he had received not two days ago. He had enough now to spare a bottle for her, yes, but what if he ran out before Tallmadge could ship him more? He would never dare send a message to Woodhull without using the stain. It was too dangerous.

Though no less dangerous for her to leave messages for him for any to see, she would argue.

But she could have found a time to question him about it when they were not surrounded by over-curious, fluff-brained females and a gentleman who watched her as though she were the very light of the heavens. Rob cleared his throat. "I have it, yes, though are you certain you want a new scent?"

A flicker of annoyance flashed through Winter's eyes. "I am quite certain, Mr. Townsend, otherwise I would not have asked for some."

A sigh leaked out. He could spare a vial of each for her. It would make their correspondence far more secure than the heat-developed inks, which anyone with a flame could expose. But how was he to give her the instruction on its use? He would have to visit her at Hampton Hall in the next several days and find a time to teach her. The stain was far too delicate to be applied willy-nilly. And the counterpart could as easily destroy the hidden message as it could develop it.

"That reminds me," Miss Shirley said, turning to her mother. "I am nearly out of rose water, Mama. We ought to purchase some while we are here."

"As soon as Mr. Townsend has finished filling Miss Reeves' order, dear."

Winter lifted her brows. Rob nodded. "Just a moment, ladies. I have not yet put this new perfume in the shop, so I must fetch it. Do browse my selection of ribbons while I am away, though."

Oakham appeared from the back, his smile pasted on. "I can assist the ladies while you step out, Townsend."

"Thank you, Mr. Oakham." That would guarantee his partner would not be standing over his shoulder seeing what he ought not see.

He couldn't resist another glance at Mr. Lane before he left. The young man—he must be in his mid-twenties, like Rob—kept his gaze trained on Winter, his expression announcing for all to observe that he was smitten.

Half the men in the City of New York would have to admit to the same.

But Winter did not so much as look at him. She studied her hands and then the shelves on the wall behind the counter, appearing for all the world as though her brain really were so empty that she might cease to be at any moment.

Rob moved into the storeroom with a shake of his head and indulged in a smile. Who would have guessed all that playacting she had once done with his sister Sally would turn out to be so useful?

Lines of crates and boxes cluttered this back room. Oakham had insisted on trying out a new system of inventory, and it had resulted in one inexplicable mess. But in this particular instance, the lack of order suited him fine. His partner hadn't paid any heed to that one spare box of "medicine" that had arrived, and he would certainly not note Rob slipping some of it into a small box marked "perfume." Nor would he know how fared their stock of perfume enough to realize he hadn't given any of that to Winter.

Even so, he must remember to take the remainder of the sympathetic stain home with him this evening. It wouldn't do for it to garner questions. Or, worse still, be put upon a shelf with the other herbals and vitriols by mistake.

He packed up the two vials for her but then hesitated. Would she try her hand at them without his advice? Quite possibly. He grabbed a scrap of paper and a pencil.

626 ycmm 298.

There. Tucking the paper in with the vials, he closed the box and carried it back into the shop in time to hear Mrs. Shirley say, "Certainly, dear, go ahead. I am still flush from the latest haul the *Royal Charlotte* brought to port."

For a moment, Rob feared Mr. Lane would toss his stack of paper again, given the shocked bulge of his eyes. "The *Royal Charlotte*? My dear madam, is that not a pirate vessel?"

Mrs. Shirley gave him a smile that would have been deemed coquettish on a younger woman. "A privateer, if you please, good sir. Several of my friends and I have invested in her, and a fine venture she is proving to be. Our stated goal is to humble the pride and perfidy of France and chastise the rebels of America—and a fine job we are doing too."

Winter delivered that slow, confused blink again. "How does one humble the making of holes, Mrs. Shirley?"

The older woman stared for a long moment before shaking her head. "Not *perforate*, Miss Reeves. *Perfidy*. The betrayal of trust."

"Ah." As if bolstered by the explanation, Winter smiled and reached for the box in Rob's hands. "Well, I should think perforation a handy skill for a pirate vessel to have as well. It would make for the easier sinking of enemy ships."

He held onto the stain a moment before handing it over, until she met his gaze for a fraction of a second. Long enough that she should realize he wanted her to pay attention, which would alert her to look for a note within. Then he released it into her hands with a nod. "Use it sparingly, Miss Reeves, for this particular perfume is hard to obtain."

"But not so sparingly that I offend, correct?" Challenge quirked her brow. "For 'tis certainly easier to obtain than my grandmother's pardon."

"Granted." Rob said no more on the matter, not when he felt the regard of Mr. Lane, who looked from him to Winter with obvious curiosity. Blast. The man might bumble socially, but he obviously had his wits about him in most cases. Best not to raise questions whose answers could not be easily obtained by all. Rob forced a smile. "Shall I tell my sister you send your usual salutations?"

Winter's smile was large and honest. "Yes, do. How is she enjoying married life?"

Lane's shoulders relaxed. "Your families are acquainted?"

"We are from the same Long Island town." Rob pulled out the lace he had put aside for Winter and handed that over as well. "And Sally has only good things to say about her new husband. Mary is set to wed this spring as well, and my eldest brother's family has grown yet again."

"Send my felicitations to all."

"Indeed I shall." But when Oakham appeared to tally up the purchases for the other ladies, nausea churned in his stomach.

He had handed off some of the most priceless, crucial materials

the Culper Ring possessed under the very noses of British sympa-
thizers—and Winter hadn't the good sense to look unnerved, even
when no one else watched her.

'Twas enough to make perspiration bead under his collar.

Five

Winter exited the shop before the others and let her eyes slide shut for just a moment, just a breath. The peace was short lived. A few seconds later the door opened again and the rest of her party laughed their way out onto Smith Street.

She couldn't decide if it were help or hindrance to her bid for reprieve when Mr. Lane stepped to her side and offered his arm. She wanted to return his smile, wanted to slip her hand into the crook of his elbow merrily, as any other girl would.

Wanted to run and hide to escape that delving gaze of his.

Under the jealous glares of her chaperones, who looked ready to push her away from Mr. Lane to make room for their daughters, Winter took his arm. When he held out a hand for her package, she relinquished that as well. It would have looked odd to refuse, though she could all but hear Robbie's outrage in her mind when she passed off the precious invisible ink.

Ah, well. Robbie must learn to keep his anxiousness in check if he wanted to succeed in this business while keeping up appearances.

A cold wind whipped down the street and did its best to rip Winter's hat from the pouf of her hair. She anchored it down with her free hand. If the hat came loose, it would undoubtedly pull her pins with it and leave her in total disarray.

Appealing as that sounded, her grandmother would fall into hysterics if she came home from town with her curls about her shoulders. She had scowled half the morning over Winter's insistence that she needn't powder her hair for a shopping trip with Dosia and Lizzie.

"Where are you headed now, Miss Reeves?" Mr. Lane asked.

She smiled. "Back to Hampton Hall, sir. This was our last stop."

Mrs. Parks tugged Dosia with her to Mr. Lane's other side. "Not that we will be on foot all that way. We had luncheon with the Shirleys and walked from there, though my daughter and I shall see Miss Reeves home in our carriage. We are happy to drop you home as well, as it is on the way."

Had he any idea how panicked he looked at that suggestion? A flush stole over his ears and into his cheeks, and his eyes went as wide as Grandmother's panniers. "I, ah...very kind of you, madam...of course I would...that is, if I hadn't...previous engagement, you see."

Winter's hand lifted of its own accord, ready to pat his arm in reassurance. She barely checked herself, covering her blunder by settling the thoughtless appendage on her arm rather than his. "A shame, that. Then I suppose we must bid you achoo."

Dosia's mouth fell open. "'Tis *adieu*, Winnie," she said in a fierce whisper, as if the correction would be able to reach Winter's ears but not Mr. Lane's.

She leaned across him toward Dosia and made her volume match. "Well, I'm sure he *does* have much to do. 'Tis why I was saying goodbye!"

"No need for that quite yet." Grinning at her, Mr. Lane shifted the stack of packages in his other arm. "I can walk with you as far as the Shirleys'."

Her gaze stayed glued to her box. "You have too many burdens, Mr. Lane. Allow me to reclaim mine. 'Tis light enough for me to manage."

"Nonsense. I have it."

At this moment, perhaps, though heaven forbid they come across any other ladies who might greet him, or it could go flying. "All the same, if you were to drop it—"

"Then I would replace it."

She sincerely doubted Robbie would give her more if anything were to happen to this batch. And Mr. Lane would need knowledge of chemistry to rival Lavoisier himself if he wanted to replace it otherwise.

But in the face of his continued boyish grin, unhindered by blush or nerves, she had little choice but to subside. With a sigh. *Giver of all, lend him Your steadiness, and see me safely home with this gift with which You have entrusted me.*

As if in answer, she became aware of the coarse, comforting texture of Mr. Lane's homespun cloak under her fingers. If she closed her eyes, she could pretend it was Father's arm she held. Could pretend the wind was gusting through Oyster Bay rather than the City of New York. Could pretend these were the Townsend girls giggling behind her, joking with her rather than about her.

Mr. Lane led her forward, but she squeezed her eyes shut for one moment more. She could imagine him strolling along the dirt roads of her hometown. He wouldn't bumble so much in the easy society to be found there, and he would enjoy settling in around the fire of an evening and talking philosophy with Father and Freeman.

Or perhaps he would be one of the kind who came pounding on doors in the middle of the night, torch in hand. He could be one of the men who demanded that all others believe as he did or pay the price for it. He could even be the kind to hurl rocks into windows and steal family heirlooms, all because of differing politics.

Winter opened her eyes again to the crowded, crowding buildings of Smith Street and Hanover Square. Much as she hated the city, Oyster Bay had become no better since the war began. Other parts of Long Island may be given to Patriot politics, but not their town. Father and Mr. Townsend had both been abused and threatened for their views.

Robbie's father had bent his knee to the Crown to avoid further problems. Hers had taken up the colors and joined the rebel army. If he hadn't, if he had been home when Mother died…

Then she would not be here now. Would not be surrounded by these people she could never call true friends.

Would not be able to help the cause she so believed in.

"I am so glad we ran into you today, Mr. Lane," Mrs. Parks said as they all turned the corner onto Queen Street. "I have been meaning to issue you an invitation to dinner at your earliest convenience. My husband and son would greatly enjoy your company."

A blush crept up Mr. Lane's face again. "Your…yes. The Misters Park. I would…sometime…"

The matron batted her lashes. "I suppose it is too much to expect that you would be free on such short notice as to join us tonight?"

"Ah…"

Clearing a chuckle out of her throat, Winter figured she could spare him this embarrassment easily enough. "I am afraid my grandparents have already claimed his company for us at Hampton Hall this evening, Mrs. Parks."

Mr. Lane nodded and pulled his arm—and therefore her—closer to his side. "Quite true. And tomorrow I have engaged with the Knights."

Mrs. Shirley sniffed, her brows arching toward her gray-powdered widow's peak. "I have seen you with the young Mr. Knight. Given your many years away, you may be unaware that his family is, shall we say, unequal to yours. In your mother's absence, I feel compelled to bring that to your attention, Mr. Lane."

His spine went straight, his shoulders rigid, and his arm tensed under Winter's fingers. 'Twas as if the lady's disapproval burned the nerves right out of him. "I cannot fathom what you mean, ma'am. The Knights are right respectable folk, abounding with charity and of an honest profession. Perhaps their means may not be as great as some, but who are we to judge anyone for such as that? Mine was not so great a few short months ago and could fall away again just as quickly if the tides of fortune pulled against me."

Mrs. Shirley didn't appear chastised. "Their means are not my grounds for complaint, good sir, but rather their loyalties. 'Tis a known fact that the elder Mr. Knight was of decidedly Whiggish bent before the British won New York, and he even tried to evacuate the city when Washington fled."

The muscle in his jaw ticked, as if he clenched his teeth hard before opening his mouth again. "I imagine I would have fled at that juncture too, Mrs. Shirley, had my primary residence burned as his did."

"But his opinions—"

"Opinions." He shook his head, his gaze so intent upon the matron that surely she felt it as physical force. "There is a very large difference, ma'am, between an opinion and its execution, especially an opinion several years old. Perhaps Mr. Knight would philosophize on what rebellion would mean—that does not make him a rebel. At Yale I was forced to debate both sides of many issues, occasionally even convincing myself of a false ideal for a time—am I to be ostracized for that? Judged for what I once said, whether or not I still believe it? I say nay. And so I will not judge the Knights for what they may have thought or said before the war, but only by what they do now. And they have *done* nothing deserving of your censure. If they had, I assure you I would not be in association with them. More, I would see that their actions met justice."

Winter felt as though she ought to applaud his eloquence, especially as it had been directed at ladies rather than gentlemen, which she had never heard him manage before. Certainly, his defense of his friend was worthy of praise.

But beneath her appreciation for his passion, her heart sank. Perhaps he saw more of her than anyone else in the city seemed to, but he must never see the truth. If his version of justice bore any resemblance to that of most other men she knew, it would land her at the end of a rope—or wishing for the mercy of one.

Mrs. Shirley gave him a tight smile. "Your loyalty is to your credit, sir. And certainly you are right. I have never heard of the Knights putting action to what they once voiced."

Whatever string had held him so tight seemed suddenly to fray. Mr. Lane relaxed again, all the way into awkwardness. "I…yes. Quite."

They plodded in silence for a few feet, and then the girls clustered together and resumed their usual chatter about sack-back gowns and brocade shoes, Spanish lace and British beaux.

Mr. Lane held Winter back half a beat, long enough for the others to get a few steps ahead. Then he turned his face toward her, his mouth in an uncertain line. "My apologies, Miss Reeves."

She did not have to feign the question in her blink this time. "Whatever for?"

"Well." Brows drawn, he pursed his lips. "Something, surely. Lapsing into argument with your friend's mother, perhaps."

"It cannot always be helped." She smiled, perhaps with more cheek than required. "Just this morning I had to argue with her myself when she dared to say that her daughter's hat had too many feathers—as if such a thing were possible!"

He glanced at Winter's hat, with its single plume, and his lips twitched up. As if he somehow realized she didn't favor the frivolous as much as she might claim. "I defer to you in such matters, to be sure. And I see thanks are in order. You have obviously taken pity on me and have begun your campaign to make powder a thing of the past."

Her hand flew to her hair. She hadn't considered that Mr. Lane would see her before she whitened it this evening. Had she anticipated this encounter, she would have given into Grandmother's prods in a heartbeat to keep from encouraging him. "Oh, how terribly out of ton I must look. Perhaps if I had Dosia's flaxen locks—but I ought not to have ventured out of doors with hair so dreadfully brown."

The twitching of his lips increased. "Are you fishing for a compliment, Miss Reeves? I daresay gentlemen enough have told you that your loveliness far outshines any other's in this city."

She dropped her hand, as fast as if her hair had burned her. "I most certainly was not."

"Ah, there we have a bit of genuineness."

'Twas obviously time for a deflection. And how better to achieve it than with a smile of blinding brightness? "Your genuineness was striking as well as you defended your friend. I do hope Mr. Knight realizes how blessed he is to have such an advocate."

"I daresay he would prefer not to be judged, so he would need no advocate." He studied her for a long moment. "He thinks you have a low opinion of him as well, Miss Reeves."

It took all her restraint to keep from wincing, and a second longer than it should have to dig up a smile to cover it. "Nonsense, sir. I have no opinion of him at all—only that of my grandparents."

Outside the Shirley house the ladies stopped, though their prattle did not. Mr. Lane pulled her to a halt several feet away from them and turned to face her. "We both know that is utter rot—both their opinion and your clinging to it instead of professing your own. Why do you do it, Miss Reeves?" He shook his head and lowered his chin, his gaze still arrowing into hers. "You are a true conundrum."

The way he said it, with such affection on the word *conundrum*, explained more of him than she intended to show him of her. That, then, was what he found so intriguing. Not the looks Grandmother had cultivated and polished, not the wealth or respect of the Hampton name. Only that he saw contradiction within her, and he was the type to want—perhaps even need—to resolve it.

He deserved credit for his skill in observation. But such an interest was no better than any other gentlemen's, who saw only her face. For what were her choices then? Either refuse to give him more than a glimpse, and so be forever exactly as she was now, or show him the true Winter under the facade and lose his interest.

As with every option in her life, there was no way to win—not in the long run.

Well, then. Best to send him on his way sooner rather than later, so Grandmother could put aside that hope and focus once more on Colonel Fairchild's suit. Winter rolled back her shoulders and tipped up her face so she could better look into his. "My grandparents have rules, Mr. Lane, that do not take into account Monsieur Descartes's observations. Perhaps I *am*—a fact which has always displeased them—but they will not suffer that I *think*."

There. A simple answer, and one for which he would no doubt have little respect.

His head shook, slow and contemplative. "How can *you* suffer *that?*"

She forced a small smile and reached to reclaim her package. "'Twas not so difficult a sacrifice, as thinking always led me to pain anyway."

His eyes dimmed. Because the mystery was solved, or because he knew she had layered her usual deception overtop the kernel of truth?

Either way, he would make excuses to himself hereafter and fade from her life. Exactly what she required of him. The box of stain cradled in her hands once more, she dipped a short curtsy and turned away. "Until this evening, Mr. Lane."

"Good day to you, Miss Reeves. Ladies." He tipped his hat to the group, made as if to say more, and then spun away, apparently thinking better of it.

Dosia sidled over to her with a smirk. "I cannot decide if I envy you his favor or not, Winnie. On the one hand, he is so very wealthy and not bad at all to look upon. But on the other, he is so very awkward and more than a little dull."

Lizzie appeared on her other side. "A boring, backward husband I could manage quite nicely, thank you, given his looks and amount of sterling. So if you are through with him, Winnie, direct him my way."

"Why should she be? She is the only one he seems able to converse with." Dosia huffed and folded her arms over her chest.

Winter pasted on the only grin of hers they knew. "If only I could understand any of what he said."

Giggles served to dispel any lingering tension, and a few moments later Mrs. Parks ushered her and Dosia into the carriage and they were headed toward Hampton Hall. Winter spent the ride with her eyes closed, allowing her companions to think her fatigued from the hours of shopping.

Once they had arrived at her grandparents' home, she gathered herself together, and, package in hand, she bade them farewell with profound relief and waved them back down the drive.

No one opened the front door. No one ever did, unless she knocked upon it like any other guest. Yet another of her grandfather's dictates, meant to remind her that Hampton Hall was not, nor would ever be, her home. In this instance it suited her fine, because she had no desire to enter the mausoleum of a house anyway. Once the Parks' carriage was out of sight, she skirted the perimeter and ran across the back lawn, not stopping until she'd gained the shadowed interior of the stable.

Freeman looked up from the stall he was mucking out, a broad smile creasing his face. "Did you bring me a present, Winnie?"

For the first time since her last visit here two days ago, she really, truly grinned. "Indeed, Free—for 'tis another level of safety."

He glanced all around before motioning her toward the hidden door in the floor of one of the stalls. After checking over her shoulder to be sure no one watched, Winter stole down the dark, narrow steps and into the forgotten cellar that had been a mass of cobwebs when they first discovered it a year ago.

Now it smelled of citrus and wax, and the lamp she lit glowed rich and warm upon scavenged, scarred tables and once-broken chairs. Winter moved to the largest of the tables and set her box down, and then she removed her hat pins so she could toss that away too.

Freeman, hunched under the low ceiling, peered over her shoulder as she opened the box and pulled out the two priceless vials. "Is it that stain you told me about?"

"Indeed." She uncorked the first of the bottles and held it under her nose. No distinct odor, though it was the color of pale straw. "I wonder what it's made of."

Freeman shook his head and sniffed the second vial. "Vitriol, perhaps, in this one?"

Winter smelled it too. Mostly odorless, though there was a faint hint of sulfur at the finish. "Could be, in part."

"What is the paper there?"

She drew out the note and huffed at Robbie's handwriting. Naturally, he would never dare entrust her with anything without some warning.

626 _ycmm_ 298.

I will instruct.

The slip of paper she slapped onto the table, the vial she handed to Freeman. "Of course he will."

Her friend lifted a dark brow. "Will what?"

"Instruct me. For a man who swears up and down he could not fulfill this duty without my help, he trusts me not a whit. He probably thinks I will waste the entire vial upon a single experiment if left to my own devices."

Freeman chuckled and slid the corks back into both vials. "Now, Winnie, don't be cross with him. If the situation were reversed, you would insist upon the same." He shook his head and exchanged the stain for the note. "Have you the whole code memorized now?"

Arms folded over her chest, she shrugged. "I've little else to fill my time with, and 'tis only seven hundred words."

"Well." He returned the piece of paper to the table and motioned toward the stairs. "Back up I go before my neck complains too loudly. Are you coming?"

"I shall store these somewhere first." And bask in the comfort of her little sanctuary a while longer.

Once Freeman nodded and plodded up the steep steps, Winter loosed her pent-up breath and took the stain and counter liquor in hand. Her fingers itched to open them again, to find a quill, perhaps a paintbrush, and see how they worked. And if it took Robbie too long to make his way out here to show her how to use them properly, she might. But for now, she would forgo curiosity for the sake of peace.

The shelves Freeman had built for her already held a variety of homemade invisible inks. Lemon juice dilute was her top choice, both because of its fragrance and because it developed under heat more quickly than the others. But she had also tried the onion juice dilute, as well as honey water. These new additions she placed on the top shelf, in the position of honor.

A layer of dust had accumulated, so she grabbed the rag she kept handy for such purposes and cleaned each surface with care, ending at the rather hideous desk that held her beloved contraband. The book of Puritan prayers, copied in Father's own hand from a manuscript he had found of his grandfather's. Mother's diary, filled with words of love for her husband, home, and daughter. *Common Sense*, which Father had read aloud to her and Mother three years prior, when the pamphlet had first been printed.

She pulled out the prayer book and opened it to a random page. *Lord, high and holy, meek and lowly, Thou hast brought me to the valley of vision, where I live in the depths but see Thee in the heights.*

"Help me to see Thee, Lord," she whispered into the cellar.

Let me learn by paradox that the way down is the way up, that to be low is to be high, that the broken heart is the healed heart.

Tears stung her eyes. She had been pulled so far down, trodden so low, broken to slivers. But praise to the God of her fathers, He was always there. Cradling her spirit, lifting her again.

She pulled another forbidden book from its place and smiled at the embossed name of the author. Rene Descartes. She opened it too, flipping not to the familiar portion that had been quoted that morning, but rather to a place a bit beyond it. "I am, therefore God is."

That, in her opinion, was the true epiphany the Frenchman had hit upon. Not that one proves one's existence by merely wondering about it, but that the existence of a rational man demands the existence of a God to have created him.

"Winnie!" Panic permeated Freeman's voice as he stuck his head down the stairs. "Mr. Hampton is coming!"

Six

A muted squeal slipped out. Winter dashed for the table, grabbed her hat, extinguished the lamp, and vaulted up the stairs. Freeman was pulling the door closed and pushing hay back atop it even as she flew from the stall toward the horse they had brought with them from Long Island. Old Canterbury nickered in greeting—she could only hope it covered the sound of her galloping pulse.

When Grandfather stomped into the stable, 'twas as if the light of the sun fled his presence. Any hope she had that his business here would have nothing to do with her evaporated when he strode her way and yanked her forcibly from Canterbury's stall.

She knew better than to make any sound of protest, in spite of the pain. He gave her a shake, lightning flashing in his eyes. "What in thunder are you doing out here again, you worthless chit? I told you not to step foot in this place unless it be with my instruction."

She pulled her arm free of his grip and backed up a step. If the reddening of his face were any indication, rebellious fury sparked from her eyes in that way he so hated. "You have told me many things, Grandfather. What I may wear, what I may eat, what time I may rise and go to bed. With whom I may socialize, what opinions I might express in society. Who among my family is allowed to live in my conversation. How am I, stupid girl that you think me, to keep it all straight?"

He growled, inched forward with hands balled at his sides. "You are nothing but a low-born wench, better suited for mucking out stalls than dancing at balls."

She folded defiant arms over her chest. "You will hear no argument from me."

Such agreement only made him growl the louder and fling out an accusatory finger toward Freeman. "You will not spend your time with that Negro, not so long as you are eating at my table and clothed in gowns paid for with my coin!"

Fire burned deep inside, scorching and consuming until it blackened every crevice of her being.

No, not blackened. Purified. Rid her spirit of the chaff to refine the gold within. She lifted her chin and let the fire blaze. "So be it. I will change back into my homespun and leave your table for good."

His roar filled her ears, joined a moment later by a strange ringing, one that shot arrows of pain through her face, over her skull, and down into her shoulder. Not until she saw his hand fall did she realize he had struck her.

She felt Freeman charge even before she heard his "Winnie!"

"No." Arm up to stop him, she prayed he would obey. Free or not, her grandfather considered him a slave, and if he dared retaliate it would mean a whipping. Unto death, knowing Grandfather.

He halted, his chest heaving. His rage pulsed from him, compounded with fear and love.

It bolstered her, shored up her spine when the pain in her face and the anger radiating from Grandfather would have doubled her over.

Slipping into her social mask, she lifted a hand to the corner of her mouth and dabbed at the blood there with all the concern she would have given a stray dollop of jam. Then she wiped it on the detestable gown he had purchased with his precious coin.

His eyes narrowed to two frozen slits. "How far do you think you can push me?"

A question she had asked herself time and again over the past year, as he twisted and bent her into his mold, uncaring how many times she cracked or broke. Always, she came back to the knowledge that she must walk a careful line to protect Freeman, to preserve her own life so there would be a Winter left when Father returned. And then, so she could aid Robbie and the Patriots from the safety of this house.

But there would be nothing to preserve, no way to pass along any information, if she let him take this last shred of her past from her.

She settled her hat back on her head. "One might ask you the same question, sir. I obey you to the letter in everything else. I do only, exactly, what I am instructed when in company. But you will *not* take from me the only family I have left, the only moments of peace I can steal."

His lips curled back from his teeth. "Or what?"

"Or," she said slowly, lowly, with a sugar-sweet bat of her lashes, "I will let all of the New York elite know every secret, every hidden shame of the Hampton family. Simple Miss Reeves would certainly be believed if she accidentally let slip, for instance, that information I stumbled upon last month about a certain affair with your friend's wife."

Though his fingers fisted again, the bob of his Adam's apple said he took her threat seriously. After clenching and releasing his jaw a few times, his nostrils flared and he relaxed his hands. "You have six months from today to decide on a husband and get out of my house. Or I swear to you, Winter, you will take up residence with all the other harlots in Holy Ground, and I will tell the world you are dead."

He stalked away. Only once he was gone did she let her sobs rise up. Only then did she lift a hand to her throbbing cheek. Only then did she collapse into Freeman's waiting arms.

He folded her in and bent his head over hers. "Father of mercies, hear me for Jesus' sake."

The familiar words soothed over her like a balm, interrupting her tears with gasps of solace. "Giver of all graces, I look to Thee for strength to maintain them in me, for it is hard…" Her voice broke, but she swallowed and forced the words out around the tears. "For it is hard to practice what I believe."

Freeman held her tight. "He shall sustain you, Winter. And if that man ever raises a hand to you again—"

"It hardly matters." She pulled away, sniffed, and lifted her chin. Not because she felt ready to do so, but because Freeman needed to see she could. "I will have to be away from him within six months anyway."

He shook his head. Strange how eyes dark as midnight could shine brighter than the sunniest day. "Your daddy will never forgive it if I let you marry some Tory you cannot even like all because he isn't here to protect you from it."

"I see little help for it." Though her shoulders wanted to sag under the weight of a future that hardly seemed worth living, she held them straight. And, cheek still shooting with pain, she strode toward the house.

She could only hope that she looked purposeful, determined. That he couldn't see the new fractures upon her spirit.

She could only pray the Lord would show her some safe path through this field of briars and snares.

Ben surveyed the coffeehouse from what had become his usual seat over the past five weeks. In this dim corner he could watch the comings and goings of the shop's patrons, enjoy a cup of strong coffee, and hide behind his books and newsprint like many another man here.

All of the usual customers he now knew by face, and most by name. Passing conversations with them had told him that most were either well-respected members of society or, as their red coats declared so boldly, officers in His Majesty's service.

And where there were officers, there was gossip. Sometimes sensitive enough that they ought not bandy it about so carelessly.

The two men at the next table over were talking of the condition of the fleet. But for the life of him, Ben could detect no one but himself paying undo attention—and he was fairly certain *he* was not the one feeding information to Washington.

He didn't seem all that good at finding whoever was, though. Perhaps he ought to have left this clandestine task to someone else. Which he may have done, had he known anyone else he trusted enough in these matters.

Movement ahead of him caught his attention, and his eyes focused upon two sets of boots descending from the private rooms above stairs.

The first man to come into view was a rough-looking character, not at all the usual clientele of Rivington's Coffeehouse. He wore trousers of coarse, stained linen, topped with a patched jacket rather than the waistcoat and greatcoat or cloak that was to be expected in this establishment.

A sailor, Ben would guess, given the style of hat and the scent of brine and fish that wafted his way. A whaleboater, perhaps? The idea made him sit up straighter. Now that warships occupied the harbor, the fleet of whalers had turned to pirating and smuggling more than honest fishing. Everyone he had spoken to with cause to travel across the sound told him of the terror wrought by these maritime menaces.

And his information said it was highly likely that a whaleboater took the messages from the ring of spies in the city to Long Island. Could it be this very man?

The sailor stepped to the side, and the second man came into view. Ben's breath stopped mid-inhale. George? What the deuce was *he* doing with such a companion?

As the two bent their heads together again and exchanged a few words too low for him to hear, Ben's knuckles whitened on the table's edge. He had come here almost daily, but rarely had George ever darkened Rivington's door. Upon being asked why, his friend had informed him with no little distemper that some of them must spend their days at work rather than at play.

Yet there he stood, speaking with a miscreant and having been in a private parlor with him.

No. Ben forced his fingers to relax, his breathing to resume. There was no cause to assume the worst. This could be an honest fisherman, one in need of a weapon to protect himself from the whaleboaters.

Why, then, would he not have gone to the Knight's Arms like a normal customer?

Blast it all. He would not suspect his dearest, oldest friend. 'Twas utter rot to even consider, and he would never had done so had Mrs. Shirley not planted questions about the Knights in his mind.

Still. He hid behind his *Royal Gazette* until George had strode by him and left the coffeehouse. Then rested his forehead in his palm. He ought to have hailed him and let the man explain himself.

But then, what would be the point? If George really were involved in espionage and meeting with a contact at a place such as Rivington's, he would have a lie prepared for anyone he came across.

And for that matter, why the blazes would he set up a meeting in the establishment of a loudly Loyal newspaperman?

On the other hand, where better? No one would ever look for traitors here.

Other than Ben, of course.

Disgusted with himself, he slapped the *Gazette* onto the table and stood, gathering his books and the sack of contraband apples he had purchased earlier. He never should have let himself get involved in this ridiculous spy hunt. Who did he think he was, anyway? A master agent of espionage? A dedicated code breaker, to find and solve the most sophisticated ciphers?

Hardly. Unless the code were a chemical formula, he'd have no idea how to manage anything he *did* find.

He tossed a few shillings on the table to cover his coffee and slung his cloak over his shoulders. It settled upon him like a weight of lead. If only his day were done, and he could escape from all the lies surrounding him. If only he could go home and not have to wonder about George, or whaleboaters, or loose-lipped officers.

But no. He could return home only long enough to change into appropriate dress and head to Hampton Hall, where another of New York's finest liars would smile sweetly up at him, dangle a hint of intriguing truth under his nose, and then snatch it away again.

"Well, well, well. If it isn't Mr. Bennet Lane."

The voice was not familiar, but when he turned, Ben recognized Colonel Fairchild easily enough. He was without question one of the most noteworthy officers in the city, what with his educated speech and height that overshadowed other men. The way he stood now, one hand on his hip holding back his brilliant coat, his bearing shouted his aristocratic heritage.

Ben had never been more aware of his homespun cloak. "Good day to you, Colonel."

"I would ask you to join me in a cup, but I see you are on your way out. No doubt to prepare for your evening with the Hamptons." Oddly,

Fairchild's words rang not only with mild challenge, but with amusement, and he gave Bennet a friendly enough smile.

Blast it, the man had dimples. Perhaps that was what made the
females swoon so over him. He probably didn't even consider Ben a
threat to his suit of Miss Reeves.

Well, and perhaps he wasn't. Perhaps he didn't want to be. Perhaps,
if she expected him to believe that she cared nothing for thinking,
then he would cease giving her any of his thoughts, and so cease to care.

'Twas about as likely as creating gold from lead. Possible in theory,
but it would require a bit of magic to achieve it.

He dug up a returning smile. "I am afraid you are correct, sir.
Though another day I would be delighted to join you."

"A shame. I have met your brother, you know—and despite that, I
look forward to becoming better acquainted with you." Fairchild took
a seat at the table Ben had just vacated and hooked an ankle over the
opposite knee. "Perhaps tomorrow then, an hour earlier."

The insinuation about his brother hardly even struck him, so keen
was the relief that stole through the tension wracking Ben's shoulders.
Tomorrow seemed a fine time to deal with this. "Excellent. I shall await
you here."

"Until then, Mr. Lane."

Well, that had not been so bad. Ben smiled, nodded, and turned.

"Oh, Mr. Lane?"

And sighed. He ought to have known better. "Colonel?"

Fairchild pushed the other chair out with his foot. "One moment,
if you please."

Rather than looking petulant through hesitation, Ben simply sat,
making sure his expression was affable. "Certainly."

Shoes planted on the floor, now, Fairchild leaned in. "At the risk of
sounding like a jealous suitor," he said, voice a low thrum, "I must question whether you are earnest in your pursuit of Miss Reeves."

Ben arched a brow in the same way he did when a student proposed
mixing saltwort with vinegar. "Pardon?"

Fairchild spread his hands. "Forgive me, but while you seem to
spend as much time in company with her as you may, I must admit you
don't strike me as a man who can truly appreciate her."

His arms folded over his chest of their own volition. "Oh? Prithee, why is that?"

"Isn't it obvious? You are a Yale man. A scholar, an academic. I have even heard you dubbed a wit among the gentlemen."

"Usually I take such words as compliments, sir, and yet I have the feeling I ought to consider them an insult in this case."

Fairchild straightened a bit, his expression combining apology with concern. "Not at all, I assure you. It is only that...well, sir, I cannot think you superficial, nor mercenary, given your family's late windfall. But you cannot possibly find in my dear Miss Reeves a companion who will provide you with scintillating conversation, and I daresay that is something you require in a wife."

Were it not for that genuine concern on the man's face, Ben would have taken offense on Miss Reeves' behalf. But given the soft light in his rival's eyes... "Colonel, forgive me, but if that is the opinion you have of her, why do *you* pursue her? For surely a man so quick to assume the best motives in me harbors no ill ones himself."

Half a smile possessed Fairchild's mouth. "Mr. Lane, I spend my days among bickering, foul-mouthed soldiers, dealing with problems and complications. When evening comes, my greatest desire is to relax beside someone who sees the world through a lens of simplicity, who finds delight in every event. Who listens—just listens—without complaint or ambition." His gaze went distant. "I would consider it the highest honor to provide for her all her days, to protect her from those who would abuse her gentle spirit."

Those like him? Compared to Fairchild, who seemed to love her as she was, who had the purest of intentions, Ben felt small and dirty.

What did he even hope for? Marriage was not in his immediate plans, at least not to some fine lady of New York who would then wrinkle her nose in distaste when he took her home to Connecticut. He had set his sights on courtship for solely underhanded reasons.

And yet, Miss Reeves was not the creature Fairchild supposed her, Ben was sure of that. The colonel loved only a mask, while Ben strove to discover the creature behind it. He wanted to know who she truly was, not who she appeared to be. Did that not make *him* the better man?

Or just the one destined for disappointment?

He drew in a long breath and let it slowly out. Then he stood. "I thank you for speaking with me, Colonel, as it has assured me you deserve the highest esteem. And I promise you, I have no ill intentions toward Miss Reeves."

Fairchild leaned his chair back on two legs. Somehow the pose of relaxation made him all the more authoritative. "I will be keeping an eye on you, sir, to be sure you have not."

Ben nodded and left, but once he was out of doors, he paused to pinch the bridge of his nose. Lovely. An officer of the Crown watching his every move, ready to pounce if he made a mistake.

It gave him the feeling of being a beaker over too high a flame, in danger of fracturing from the heat and pressure.

Seven

B ennet's fingers were painfully cold by the time he reached the house. Flexing them as he went in the door, it took a moment to realize that all was not as he left it. In place of the all-but-empty tables and skeleton crew of staff, boxes and trunks littered the entryway, and servants dashed this way and that.

Which could only mean one thing.

"Bennet Ellsworth Lane. I hardly believed it when Hutchins said you were here."

Ben slid his burdens onto a table, bit back his sigh, and held out his arms for his mother. "I came as soon as I received Archie's and Father's letters. I was just speaking of you to the tailor this morning about how sad I was to see you gone when I arrived."

Caroline Lane arched her brow in that way that said he fooled no one, especially not her. "And why would I wait for you to come? We all know, Bennet, that had your father and I not traveled annually to New Haven for a visit, we would have gone these eight years without so much as glimpsing you."

"But as you were always happy to come, I still managed to rejoice in your company." He offered his most charming smile. "'Tis good to have you home, Mother, though I confess I was headed out again to a dinner engagement."

"Yes, I know, Hutchins informed me." The arch of Mother's brows shifted into one of omnipotent accusation. "The Hamptons', of all places. I already took the liberty of sending a note around letting them know your brother and I have arrived back in town—"

"Archie is here too?"

"Just, yes. As I was saying, Mrs. Hampton was quick to invite us along as well, so I have accepted." Now her eyes went flinty. "Though for the life of me, I cannot fathom why you are dining with the Hamptons."

"Well, they...I..." He turned from her to pick up his books before again meeting his mother's unwavering gaze. He had no reason to feel awkward. She had been after him for years to settle down. "I have been paying court to their granddaughter, Miss Reeves."

Yet rather than the overjoyed speech he half expected, a breath hissed from between her teeth. "You jest! You cannot be interested in that stupid girl."

Was he the only person in all of New York who saw that something more lurked behind her empty countenance? Or perhaps George was right, and he saw something he wanted to see rather than what was there.

No. He could not believe that. So he shook his head and swept by his mother. "She is not stupid, Mother."

She scoffed and trotted after him as he headed up the stairs. "I never thought to see the day when my Bennet fell prey to a pretty face. I expect it of Archibald, but not *you*, dear. You have too much sense than to saddle yourself with a brainless minx like her for the rest of your days. We must keep tonight's engagement, of course, but afterward I expect you to succumb to better sense. You are now the heir to a sizable English estate, and you must consider a woman's ability to manage it before you make any commitments."

"Mother." He pushed into his sitting room and set his books onto a table. "I daresay when out from under her grandparents' influence, she will have no trouble rising to any task."

Huffing to an angry halt once inside the door, she planted a hand on her pannier. "Her grandparents are hardly the problem, Bennet. Have you any idea the disgrace her mother brought upon them?"

He paused with a hand on the fastener of his cloak. "Disgrace?"

Mother rolled her eyes and came in far enough to take a seat on the settee. "It never ceases to amaze me how you can retain absolutely any information you read in some dusty tome and yet rarely remember what goes on with our neighbors."

Ben fought the twitching of his lips with admirable aplomb. "I must say, Mother, I have often wondered how you manage the opposite."

"Impudent boy." But she smiled. Briefly. "It caused such a scandal that it was talked of for years. The Hamptons had only the one surviving child, Amelia. She was a few years my younger, and your father and I were already married by the time she entered society, but she was without question the toast of New York. Until *he* came to town."

Shrugging out of his cloak, Ben arched his brows. "He? Mr. Reeves?"

"A nobody. A penniless farmer from some backwoods town in Long Island."

"Oyster Bay."

Her mouth already open to continue, Mother stared at him. "Well, you can apparently retain *some* information on our neighbors. Did Miss Reeves actually admit to the filth from which she came?"

"'Tisn't a secret, apparently. If you still recall her parents' story, I daresay everyone else does as well. And Oyster Bay is a fine community from what I have heard."

"Humph." She patted the whitened curls resting atop her head. "If I were her, I should do my best to make them all forget. Amelia shamed the entire family by running off with that man, and who knows if the marriage was even legal? Certainly it was not performed in the Church of England, and she was too young to have wed without her parents' permission. Undoubtedly she lied about something, or else they never married at all but lived together by common law."

If she expected that to shock him, she had obviously never read the bawdy tales of Rabelais. Which of course she had not. Neither her father nor his ever would have let them soil her delicate female mind.

But she expected some response, so he shrugged. "'Tis hardly Miss Reeves' fault what her parents did or did not do. I see no reason to judge her for their actions."

Mother's lips thinned to a line of blotchy red paint. "'Twill suffice to judge her on her own. She is an utter ninny. I know not how Phillippa tolerates her. And be forewarned. The girl will flirt with anything in breeches, but her sights have long been set on Colonel Fairchild, with the Hamptons' blessing." She blinked in that way that spoke of an epiphany she didn't much care for. "Or it *had* been. They would no doubt prefer you, though, now that you are heir to Clefton."

"Mother…" He drew in a breath and shook his head. "Please, give her a chance."

For a long moment, she stared him down. "Why do you argue with me, Bennet? Everyone knows I am an excellent judge of character."

Ben held her gaze without flinching. "But all agree I am an excellent judge of wit, and I am sure Miss Reeves has more of it than she shows."

The slam of a door below saved Mother a response to that. She smiled. "Archibald must be home."

Ben didn't know whether to grin or sigh. He always so looked forward to seeing his brother, younger by a mere eleven months. Unfortunately, they seemed to get along better from a distance these days.

Feet pounded, and then Archie's voice called out, "Where is everybody?"

Mother stood and poked her head out the door. "Up here, darling, in your brother's sitting room. Do tell me you cleaned your boots before stomping your way through my house."

"Of course, Mother." When his brother entered, it was with a mischievous grin—and soiled footwear. He gave their mother a loud kiss upon the cheek and then turned to Ben, arms outstretched.

The grin won out. Might as well enjoy the reunion. Ben flicked at the gold fringe on his brother's red army jacket. "Look at you, with epaulettes on both shoulders now. Major Lane."

Archie chuckled. And then lunged.

Ben couldn't recall the last time his brother greeted him with something other than an attempt to wrest him to the ground. It had been this way since they were tots, the slight, wiry Archie determined to prove that strength rested not in Ben's bulk but in his own determination.

And since they were tots, Ben had obliged him. When his brother's arms closed around him, he put up just enough fight to be convincing before he allowed Archie to capture him in a headlock.

In all likelihood, Ben would not have to let his brother win anymore. Archie had filled out a bit and ended up the taller. But he still felt like a stocky bear in comparison to his brother's lithe frame, and he still feared injuring him. If not physically, then his pride—if by chance Ben *did* win a tussle.

"Oh, boys, do stop this childish display." Mother stayed beside the door. "And now that we are all here, we had better dress for dinner. We are going to Hampton Hall to dine, Archibald. Your boots had better be polished by the time we leave."

Archie released Ben's neck, though he caught him on his way up for an actual squeeze of greeting. "The Hamptons', eh? Excellent. It has been entirely too long since I have enjoyed the particular scenery to be had in their hallowed halls."

Ben didn't much care for the gleam that entered his brother's eyes.

Mother must not have either. She arched her brows and leveled a finger at Archie's nose. "None of your nonsense, young man. Miss Reeves hasn't the brains to recognize the wolf beneath your sheep's clothing, and we cannot afford a break with her grandparents over something as shifting as your affections. Besides." Her gaze swung to Ben, probing and not without challenge. "Her family has apparently decided your brother can offer the alliance they seek."

"Benny? With Miss Reeves? You jest." As if to prove it, Archie loosed a loud guffaw.

And why was that absolutely everyone's reaction? Ben planted his hands on Archie's back so he could send him helpfully toward the door. "I fail to see the humor. Now, if you please, I must dress."

Archie skidded into the hall behind their mother, though he turned back once out there, grin in place. "I had not thought you capable of this, Benny. I am impressed. To think that you, the most intellectual man I know, being led by far baser inclinations...well, this is wonderful. I cannot wait to see it for myself."

Ben took great pleasure in shutting the door in his brother's face.

But it festered, the accusation Archie hadn't the sense to make sound accusing. Ben couldn't ever recall an instance where George and Archie had been in agreement before, and the fact that they were now...a wise man did not dismiss such things. A wise man would entertain the possibility that the rest of the world was right and he was mistaken.

Maybe it *was* only her looks that drew him. Maybe Fairchild saw the true her, a gentle spirit clothed in simplicity of mind, and Ben had fabricated any idea of depth. Maybe what he had taken to be her admittance that she hid a brain beneath the beauty was really only a momentary serious side to a girl otherwise happy with her frivolity.

Maybe he ought to heed his mother's advice and make this engagement his last at Hampton Hall. Leave Miss Reeves to the honest, upright affections of Colonel Fairchild and find himself another excuse for frequenting balls and soirees.

Uncertainty brewed within him as he dressed and slid on the itchy powdered wig, and it only increased as he climbed into the carriage alongside his mother and brother. He ignored their prattle during the short drive, focusing instead upon his inner questions.

He must examine himself tonight and gauge every reaction to her to determine whether it was only a physical attraction he felt. He must watch her with the thought in mind that he could be mistaken about her and see which theory her actions upheld.

The winter skies were cold and clear as they exited the carriage and went through the open doors of Hampton Hall, but Ben could have sworn a storm brewed, so electric and thunderous were his thoughts. Lightning pierced him when the Hamptons greeted them in the drawing room and he had his first glimpse of Miss Reeves.

She curtsied to his family. "So good to see you again, Mrs. Lane. Oh, and I did not know you were back in the city, Lieutenant."

"'Tis 'major,' now," Mother corrected.

"Oh!" Miss Reeves' eyes went wide, her gaze upon his brother's right shoulder, where the second epaulette now resided. But her blink was empty. "I can never keep these things straight. But congratulations, sir. Mr. Lane, I cannot believe my good fortune, getting to greet you twice in one day."

Confound it, his tongue felt verifiably twisted. "I…yes…that is… the fortune is mine."

She wore cosmetics tonight, more than he had ever seen on her before. Perhaps she had, in the past, dusted her nose with rice powder, but he had never seen her wear rouge. Indeed, when he bent over her hand in salutation, he caught a whiff of the beet juice used to color the powder for cheeks and lard for lips.

Her smile was small and halted rather abruptly. Pain flashed through her eyes, though it was quickly doused.

His gaze focused on her right cheek again. Was it swollen? Without question—and the rouge did not quite cover an edge of bruising.

As the rest of the party moved to the furniture, a few of the knots smoothed out within him, though a couple of different ones took up residence. He did not release her hand. "Would you take a turn about the room with me, Miss Reeves?"

"Very well, sir." She sounded far from enthusiastic and moved to his right side. Undoubtedly so that hers was turned away from him. "I trust you passed a pleasant afternoon?"

He kept his gaze upon her as he led her to the edge of the chamber so that they might walk its perimeter as far from their families as possible. In a low voice he said, "More pleasant than yours, from the looks of it. What is wrong with your cheek, Miss Reeves?"

She turned wide eyes on him, filled with outrage and a grain of amusement. "Mr. Lane, perhaps you are yet unaccustomed to seeing ladies wearing paint, but I assure you, 'tis the height of fashion. I resent being told it looks wrong."

He may have been tempted to smile, had it not been a matter of her welfare. "It is not the rouge to which I refer, Miss Reeves, as you well know."

"In which case I have no idea…" Her gaze shifted beyond him, and her smile went completely false and stunningly beautiful. "Lieutenant."

His brother stiffened. "Major."

"Oh! Yes, do forgive me." Her lashes fluttered, but to Ben's eyes she looked far from repentant.

It made a man wonder what had passed between Miss Reeves and Archie before Ben returned to New York. Knowing his brother's habits with females as he did…well, whatever it was, Miss Reeves seemed to know how to handle him.

Still. "Archie, I am about to say something with all fraternal love." Ben smiled too and clapped a hand to his brother's shoulder. "Go away."

The major laughed. "Nay, I cannot. Having conversed separately with both of you, I cannot resist listening in on what you talk about together. I mean only to lighten the discussion for Miss Reeves, as she cannot possibly find anything of import in your talk of scientists and philosophers, Benny."

She joined her hands together on Ben's arm and moved a fraction closer to his side. She had that look of amused stupidity on her face again. "Oh, you are most correct, Lieutenant. Your brother never speaks with me of imports, neither of jams from England nor silk from Europe. Yet I know not how I could ever survive without them. Can you imagine an existence with only fresh produce?"

"'Tis 'major.'" He put a bit more rebuke in the correction this time. Then his lips melted back into their usual smile. "And prithee, brother, how could you have neglected such riveting conversation with the lovely Miss Reeves? You must bore her to tears."

Her grip on his arm tightened a bit and then relaxed. "Not at all, sir. I find your brother's company quite singular. He is the only person I have ever met who called me clever."

"Did he?" Genuine confusion joined the mirth in the gaze Archie turned on him. "He is usually quite stingy with that particular compliment."

Mother lifted a hand from her chair. "Archibald, do come tell the Hamptons what you told me of General Clinton."

Archie sent his gaze to the ceiling, bowed to Miss Reeves, and then spun. "Coming, Mother."

"Thank you, Mother," Ben muttered.

Miss Reeves chuckled. "Are you not on good terms with your brother?"

For a moment he stared at the bright red of his brother's jacket. Archie had grown into the sort of man who made friends wherever he went, though often left a few enemies behind him—generally in the form of irate fathers. His features were finer than Ben's, his hair a few shades lighter, his form fashionably slender. But for once he was in the company of a young lady whose head didn't seem to be turned by him.

Amazing.

"On the contrary, Miss Reeves, we are on very good terms—when not together." He turned his head toward her again and smiled, pitching his voice once again to a quiet level. "I have discovered that Archie and I make the best sort of correspondents and the worst sort of companions. We care for each other greatly, but we are too different."

She nodded, her expression finally absent the layer of performance. "You ought to be glad of that, Mr. Lane. I certainly am. Your brother is… tiring, let us say. Or parrying his advances is so, at any rate."

He could follow that line and get a few answers, and maybe he would at another time. But there were more pressing concerns to address in the few minutes of semi privacy they enjoyed. "And what is it you failed to parry today, my dear, that resulted in the bruise upon your cheek?"

Her chin lifted. But still it trembled ever so slightly. "Mr. Lane, it is quite rude to draw attention to my clumsiness."

"It may be, were it a result of such." Yet 'twas not embarrassment that colored her eyes, but something darker. Something that made fierce instincts clamor up inside him.

Someone had done this to her in the few hours since they had parted ways at the Shirleys'. Someone, no doubt, beneath this roof. If he were a betting man, he would have staked his fortune that the someone *owned* the roof.

She looked deep into his eyes for a few moments and seemed to see the thoughts rioting within. Her fingers soothed over his forearm. "If you think it not a result of my running into something, then you must imagine…well, that is absurd, of course. Though if it *were* the case, you would still have no cause to worry."

"Would I not?" He led them to the window and halted, so close to the panes that he could feel the cold radiating from them. Better that than being any closer to the rest of the group.

"Indeed not." Her voice was the barest of whispers, scarcely making it to his ears. "For you see, Mr. Lane, though I can tolerate the order not to think for myself, there are some things I will not suffer. And so you can be sure that if this bruise were the fault of anyone but myself— which, of course, it is not—then it is the first time such a thing has happened. And will without doubt be the last, lest such a perpetrator— who does not exist, mind you—finds his secrets all spilled."

That eased his mind for only a moment. He had no doubt Hampton possessed his share of secrets he would not want society to be privy to. But a man who would strike his granddaughter on the face was surely not one to let her threaten him in response. He shook his head. "I do not want to see you hurt, Miss Reeves."

"Nor do I, I assure you." Brightness bullied its way into her smile.

It made the room feel all the darker. This place, this family, was not where she belonged. Yet he was not the one to rescue her from it, not when his own life would offer her none of what she thought it would. "Miss Reeves…has Fairchild proposed? Or would he, do you think, with the proper encouragement?"

Her hand fell away from his arm as her face went completely blank. "Pardon?"

Ben sighed. "He loves you, you know. He wants to care for you and protect you. With the proper urging, I imagine he would make an offer, and you ought to…he would keep you safe and do all in his power to make you happy."

Now she folded her arms over her torso. Try as he might, he could not determine what emotion filled her eyes. Not quite contemplation, nor realization. Not exactly disillusionment.

She swallowed. "Is that what you want me to do, Mr. Lane? I must say, 'tisn't what I expected, given your speech on Christmas."

"It is not what I want, no." The truth of that pierced him like his brother's sword. "But I want, above all, for you to be safe and well."

Her lips parted, but apparently she could think neither of truth nor inanity to say. Her gaze fell to the ground, she curtsied, and then she glided her way to the couch to sit beside her grandmother.

Ben stayed at the window and wished for a rousing thunderstorm to shake the panes and match his mood. All he got was his mother's company a minute later.

She touched his arm and drew in a long breath. "You actually care for her, don't you? I cannot understand why. But if that is where your heart is inclined, I will be reasonable. We will host a few dinners and balls, and I will get to know her better to see if she can at least be molded, or else will be willing to let others do her managerial duties in her stead. Will that please you, Bennet?"

Would it? He leaned into the window's frame and stared out at the gray street. "I don't know, Mother. I don't know."

Eight

Frost etched lace onto the pane of her window. Fragile beauty, as deadly as it was short lived. Winter traced its outline with a lazy fingernail, looking more at it than the icy world outside. January was well on its way to February, and these past weeks she had rarely been permitted out of the house. 'Twas too cold, they said. The streets too messy.

She thought it more because they wanted no one to see the mottled bruise upon her cheek, and it had taken a dreadfully long time to fade. Grandmother forced her to apply concealing cosmetics whenever they had company, but the Lanes were the only ones she invited. No doubt, bruised or not, her grandmother didn't want to risk Bennet Lane forgetting her. They had come often enough to keep her thoughts in turmoil.

Her breath of mirthless laughter fogged up the window. His reactions to her seemed to oscillate like a pendulum. One moment all concern, the next determined to keep his distance. Frustrated with her for not laying bare her soul, amused by her supposed misinterpretations. He liked her—but he didn't seem to want to.

Ah, well. Winter touched a finger to her cheek. The pain had gone, finally, as had the discoloration. Grandmother had at last deemed her passable for other company, so tomorrow she would entertain Dosia

and Lizzie. After weeks of nearly unbroken solitude, Winter was actually looking forward to an hour or two with her supposed friends.

Much of the past weeks she had spent remembering winters in
Oyster Bay. How she would love to strap on her ice skates and glide
over the pond in their back field again. To spin round and round with
Sally and Mary Townsend until they were so dizzy they fell, laughing, to their bottoms on the ice. To have nothing more to think about
than the mulled cider that would be heating over the fire when they
returned.

And if she were dreaming, then she would put Mother there, awaiting her return. Reading, perhaps, or spinning wool onto the spool of
her walking wheel. Forward and back, round and round, onto the skein
until the weasel popped after the one hundred fiftieth revolution.

Temple against the cold glass, Winter closed her eyes. "God of my
end," she whispered, "hear the cry of my heart. I feel as though You
have put me on a path with no one to walk beside me. Yet I know You
are there. If this journey has been given me so that I might draw closer
to You, then help me, my Father in heaven, not to squander the opportunity. Help me to seek You in every moment of solitude, to hear Your
voice in every echo of silence. And strengthen me for what lies ahead,
for I know there are rapids coming upon this river."

Something pinged against the window. Her eyes flew open, and
she spotted Freeman on the lawn below, smiling. He motioned that
she should come, nodded toward the stable, and made their sign for
Robbie.

Finally. Winter sprang up from her seat and sneaked into the hall.
Spotting no one, she dashed down the servants' back stairs and outside, not stopping to grab her cloak. Moments later she gained the hay-
scented haven of the stable, where Freeman waited with a grin.

"I showed him down."

"Thank you." She checked to make sure no one else was about and
then descended into the hidden room herself.

The candles were lit and a lamp burning, and her old friend sat
at her table, a book before him. His smile was warm, but his cheeks
seemed hollower than the last time she'd seen him, at his store. Winter frowned with concern and sat beside him. "Have you been ill, Robbie? You look a bit peaked."

He waved it off. "No, nothing to speak of. Just the stress of the times, which eased considerably when I got a note of thanks from Washington himself for the information about the stolen paper."

"Did you?" That made her smile. Such a letter would certainly put his mind at ease—always appreciated, as he tended toward bouts of melancholy and dark moods.

"I must share the acclaim with you, of course. Privately, at any rate." He grinned, though it faded as he studied her. "And you? How have you been? I thought to see you again by now, but you have been nowhere. I began to fear something had happened."

Not knowing how long they would be able to stay down here, Winter gathered up the stain and counter liquor along with some paper and a new quill. "A bit of a disagreement with my grandfather, is all. I have not been allowed out, and no one has been invited but the Lanes."

"Not Fairchild?" He reached for a sheet of paper but then halted, eyes wide. "Winnie, is Bennet Lane courting you?"

A chuckled slipped out. "Sometimes I think so. Sometimes I think he is only studying me as he would one of his scientific experiments."

Robbie's nostrils flared, and he shook his head. "But he laughed at you. In my store, two weeks ago."

"No, not like you think." Why did defense of him come so quickly to her tongue? She shook her head. "He is not convinced by my display of witlessness and thinks me quite clever when I spout mindless babble."

"He…Winnie." Robbie slapped a hand to the paper and leaned closer, eyes wide. "You mustn't let that go on! Had I realized…I hate to see them laughing at you, but it is safer than if they know the truth. No one must know you are more than you seem. 'Tis too dangerous for you."

"You worry too much."

"Nay, you worry not enough."

She covered his hand with her own. With most young men she knew she would never dare be so forward, but he had been a friend all her life. Practically a brother. "Robbie, Mr. Lane is nothing to worry about. He thinks me more intelligent than I pretend to be, yes, but he also thinks I hide it solely because of my grandparents' dictates— which, if you recall, was the truth until six months ago."

He took off his spectacles and rubbed at his eyes. "I ought never to have gotten you involved in this."

"Oh, stop speaking nonsense." She punctuated her command with a playful slap on his arm. "You have given me purpose, and I thank you for it."

"A purpose far too perilous. I believe in our cause with my whole heart, but 'tisn't worth our lives."

Her eyebrows stretched upward. "My father seems to think it is. As do thousands of others."

"That is different." Turning in his chair to better look at her, he shook his head. "Taking up the colors has honor to it. If soldiers are captured in uniform, then they are treated as prisoners, not traitors. But spies, Winnie—there is no honor in what we have taken upon ourselves. If we are caught, we are executed. There are no second chances."

The chill of the room finally struck her, and she shivered. She wrapped her arms about herself. "I know all that, Robbie, but we are not mercenaries, selling information to the highest bidder. That sort of spy deserves ill regard. We are only trying to do our part for our country. Quietly, where the Lord has placed us."

"They will not see it that way."

"They will not have to because we will not get caught. All that matters is that we have the respect of those we work *for*. Washington, Tallmadge—they know we do this out of love for the Glorious Cause. Certainly we must be careful, but the point remains that what we do is worthwhile. Worth the risk. Now." She sat up straight and tapped the paper. "Teach me how to be careful."

He sighed and put his spectacles back on. "Very well. First, you must always use the whitest paper possible, as the stain is temperamental and develops best on good stock. Washington has recommended we use books where necessary, writing in the margins, or between the lines of an innocent-looking letter." A smile finally emerged. "I have been writing about false orders of merchandise to a fictitious customer. Always signing, of course, with Samuel Culper, Junior."

Winter pushed aside the older yellowed paper and pulled forward the best she had available. "This will have to do for now, though I will find better."

He nodded and uncorked one of the vials. "This is the sympathetic stain. It is difficult to make, I understand. Woodhull told me in our last meeting that the brothers Jay have requisitioned gallic acid from hospitals to create it. So we must use it wisely. We have already run out once."

"Certainly. Do we use it as regular ink, with a quill?"

"Yes." He picked up the fresh one she had brought over, dipped, tapped, and wrote. Other than a slight glint from the flame, she couldn't make it out at all. "As with the homemade invisible inks, you must be careful not to let it overlap your false text, as it will cause telltale runs."

She leaned forward to try to see whether it formed any waving in the paper. Minimal, so far as she could see. It would be easily disguised by that of the visible ink. "Are the letters containing messages in stain still marked?"

"With an A for the acid counterpart rather than an H for heat." He sat back in his chair and clasped his hands over his stomach. "We must let it dry thoroughly before applying the counter liquor. Tell me more about this disagreement with your grandfather."

Rather than look at him and risk him seeing too much truth in her eyes, she kept her gaze on the paper. Spots of ink had already dried completely, invisibly. "He tires of my presence, I think. No doubt I remind him too much of Mother and what he deemed their failure with her."

Robbie loosed an exasperated breath. "Your mother was happy and well cared for, well loved. Why is that not enough for them? 'Tisn't as though your father were a pauper or ill respected."

One corner of her mouth pulled up. "Respected in Oyster Bay, yes, and comfortable enough there, but we both know Father was nothing in the City of New York, which is all that matters to them."

"So he tires of you." His gaze bore into her. "What does that mean for you, Winnie? Ought you to leave? Go back home to Oyster Bay?"

Her head was shaking, her heart pulsing with a deep ache. "Would that I could, but there is nothing left for me there. I have no one, and I cannot stay on the farm alone."

"You could stay with my family. They would take you in happily. You know they would."

They may at that. The Townsends were a fine family. But they were not *her* family, and so she would feel like an imposition there as much as here. And if she were going to impose, she would rather be an inconvenience to the grandparents who, frankly, deserved to be put out after their treatment of Mother.

Robbie rapped a knuckle on the table. "I see you will dismiss that idea. What, then? You cannot compromise any more of yourself— there is little enough left. What will pacify him?"

She wove her fingers together. Not so long ago, her hands were calloused from hard, honest work about the farmhouse. Now they were as soft as a babe's, lily white, and mostly useless. Winter squeezed her eyes shut for a moment and then met his gaze again. "My marriage."

"Winnie." He rested his forehead in his palm. "To whom?"

She lifted one shoulder. "He did not specify, though Grandmother has said she wants it to be to Mr. Lane, or, if he does not propose, Colonel Fairchild."

Shaking his head, slowly and contemplatively, Robbie looked pained. "Perhaps they are both nice enough men, but Winnie—they are both bound to England, and likely bound *for* it soon enough. Have you considered that? That if you accept either of them, you will have to leave the country you love so well?"

"I know." Her voice sounded so small to her own ears, so uncertain. "But what am I to do, Robbie? My grandparents are my guardians. They must approve any match, at least until I have gained my majority at twenty-one, and Grandfather will never suffer me for another three years."

"Forget them. They may share your blood, but they are no family. Go home." Earnestness saturated his face.

Baffled, she shook her head. "And do what? I cannot run a farm on my own, so I would be forced to marry anyway, and everyone else in Oyster Bay is as loyal as Lane and Fairchild. I may not end up in England, but I would still be wed to someone with whom I could not share my beliefs. And at home I cannot help the cause."

He muttered something unintelligible, but whose vicious tone made her think it a curse. "What then? You will marry one of these men just so you can keep sending me information?"

Of their own will, her shoulders rolled forward. "If I must marry one of them, it might as well be the one beside whom I can do some good. Which would mean Fairchild."

"Fairchild thinks you an idiot. You will *not* resign yourself to playing that part for the rest of your days."

"But Mr. Lane is not…" She could find no words to put to the turmoil he churned up within her. How could she explain that he left her without the comfort of her pretense, that she enjoyed his company too much to allow herself to enjoy it at all? And that he seemed every bit as confounded by her? In all likelihood, he would never pursue her to the point of marriage anyway.

At least Fairchild was a career man. Winter would do better in those circles than as mistress of an estate like Clefton.

"I agree. He is no more suited for you. So marry neither of them. Find a better option."

"There is no better option, not if I want to keep helping you."

His hand settled on her shoulder. "Winnie, be reasonable. One of these days the war will be over. What will you do then as wife to one of them?"

"I…" She had no answer. How could she? It seemed the war had been brewing all her life. Perhaps fighting had only broken out a few years ago, but they had been long, earth-changing years. How could it ever end?

It couldn't, not until England released them from her grip. If the British managed to squash this campaign, then it would be only a matter of time before the Patriots rose again.

If that happened, she would be there. Ready to help.

But if Washington's army won, if these United States gained their freedom…well, she would have served her purpose. Perhaps then she could live her life with contentment, whatever life she was given.

A shadow seemed to settle deep within her. Contemplating the future had been nothing but peering into a dark tunnel ever since Mother died. Contentment seemed little more than an illusion, a flicker of light so far distant she knew she would never grasp it.

Why torture herself with such thoughts? She nodded toward the paper. "It is dry."

Robbie sighed, but he pulled forward the counter liquor and

extracted a small paintbrush from his pocket. "You will need this to apply it. Not much or it will be ruined. Here, try."

She took the brush, dipped it into the acid, tapped the excess off, and then slid it over the page where he had written. After a moment, words began to appear in a pale green.

In the beginning, God created the Heaven and the earth.

Winter smiled. "Amazing. No scorched places. It all develops evenly. 'Tis rather faint, though."

"Keep watching. It darkens with prolonged exposure. But put more on the last word here, so you can see what happens with too much."

Nodding, she dipped the brush again and didn't tap this time. The script was now blue, edging toward the color of a naval jacket. When she applied more acid to the word *earth*, it ran and smeared into an illegible puddle. "Ah. Yes, that could make it a bit difficult to read."

Robbie chuckled. "The rest of the words will darken to near black after a few more minutes."

"Amazing. You need this exact counterpart for it to develop? None other will do?"

"Precisely." He put the corks back in both bottles. Apparently her instruction was complete for the day. "Our code may be breakable, but this is not. When we combine the two, our correspondence becomes as secure as is possible."

"I will use it sparingly."

"Good. You are the only one of my contacts to whom I have given any, which ought to tell you how highly I value your information." A grin won possession of his mouth. "It seems Washington values mine quite highly as well. He has asked me to find a more direct route for our letters to take, to bypass Woodhull and reach him the faster, to go through New Jersey rather than Long Island and Connecticut. I have my cousin out searching for a safe passage."

Winter frowned. "Which cousin?"

"James."

She undoubtedly looked every bit as incredulous as she felt. "Could no one else be found to do this?"

Robbie waved her concern away. "Washington recommended a few names, but I am unacquainted with them all. And as my neck is on the line, I will not trust anyone I do not know."

"But Jamie?" She sucked in a slow breath, unsure how best to convey her reservations. "He is only sixteen, Robbie, and as of last year not entirely dependable."

"Nonsense. He is a good lad, if a bit adventurous. Which will serve us well, I should think." He stood and then stared down at her. "Winnie, promise me you will not make any rash decisions. Your father may be willing to give his life for the cause, but I daresay he wouldn't like the idea of you risking yours. I will never mention you, never even hint that I have a contact in your position, but—"

"I daresay you don't mention any of your contacts." She hoped her smile would distract him from his warning. "That would be a bad idea, I should think."

His face remained unamused. "I will let it drop, but think on what I have said. The war cannot last forever. You must consider your place once peace reigns again."

She nodded and pasted acceptance onto her face. But even when the state of the world had changed, her grandparents would not have. So really, what did it matter?

Nine

Ben seemed to have a knack for setting himself up for discomfort. He stood in a corner of the drawing room, his arms folded over his chest as he watched the collection of young people flirt and laugh, bat their lashes and puff out their chests. True, it had been Mother's idea to have such a large gathering tonight, but he had been the one to recommend inviting Fairchild.

He knew the colonel would be drawn to Miss Reeves' side as iron to a lodestone; he had even wanted it that way. Until he then was forced to witness the adoration on the man's face and the pretty little smiles Miss Reeves sent him. It may indeed be best for her to marry the colonel, and sooner rather than later. But recognizing that didn't mean he liked it.

Perhaps she felt his glare, for Miss Reeves glanced his way. An amused grin mixed with a challenging tilt of her brows creating an amalgam of reactions within him. Frustration and satisfaction, jealousy and hope.

Confound it, he missed his laboratory. He may not always know what two elements would do when he combined them, but he could be sure they would do the same thing each time. They would not create an inert mixture one day and an explosive one the next.

Oh, to have such certainty when it came to Winter Reeves.

For that matter, to have it with George. His friend shifted beside him, glancing at the clock. Again. Ben did not want to keep entertaining doubts, but… "Have you somewhere else to be, George?"

"Hmm?" His friend snapped to attention and grinned. "Anywhere but here. No offense intended, old man, but I tire of watching you glower at them. If you don't intend to relinquish Lady Oh to Fairchild, why did you invite him?"

"Because he looked so woebegone when I had coffee with him the other day. Mrs. Hampton has not let her granddaughter see anyone but my family these weeks, and apparently the colonel felt her withdrawal acutely." Ben, on the other hand, had been allowed to watch her bruise change color under the rouge. Each shade proved a twist to the knife in his gut.

Yes, it would be better for all if Fairchild were given the chance to declare himself.

George clapped a hand to his shoulder. "Well, cheer up, my friend. If his expression is any indication, he may propose tonight, and then you will no longer be plagued by indecisiveness, what with him removing all decision from your hands."

"Indeed." Blast it.

His friend chuckled again. "In the face of such good spirits, I imagine you will forgive me if I abandon you in favor of sweeter company. Miss Parks looks at loose ends."

Ben waved him off. Then he moved off himself, out of the room altogether. He had already suffered through the meal, and any moment dancing was likely to begin. 'Twas more than he could endure.

He spotted his mother in a corridor with one of her friends and started toward her for lack of a better plan.

She was motioning toward their back garden and giggling. "That ought to suffice, don't you think?"

Her friend chuckled too. "Quite. I daresay if the colonel has any intentions, he will not hesitate to make them known out there. You have created a lovely little scene for a proposal."

"And if he takes that brainless girl away before my son can be any more addled by her, then I will deem it worth the effort."

The women moved off in the opposite direction, never noting him at the corner. Ben rubbed his temples. Then, curious, he headed for the window overlooking the garden.

Lanterns glowed along the winding path throughout it, twinkling lights that cast their shine off the snowflakes gliding lazily down. Benches, which he knew for a fact had been stored away for the winter, now sat before the blooming witch hazel bushes with clusters of Christmas roses around them.

His breath fisted in his chest. How very thoughtful of Mother to create such an enchanting place for Fairchild and Miss Reeves to discover.

He had better get a few minutes of fresh air himself if he wanted to escape this peevish temper that plagued him. He stormed toward the back door, snatching his dark cloak of homespun on his way out.

When the first touch of breeze brushed his cheeks, some of the anxiety melted away. Drawing in a long breath of the witch hazel's heavy perfume, Ben let the peace of the night waft over him.

Snowflakes drifted and danced, quiet and magical in the glow of the lanterns. His feet still felt far too heavy for copying nature's cavorting, but he followed the path toward the back of the garden and the stone wall he had scaled as a child so he might spy on the neighbor's youth.

He pressed his lips together. It had seemed an innocent sport then. How different the word *spy* sounded now.

The corner beckoned, as it always did. As a boy he had inevitably ended up here, behind the thick trunk of the oak tree. Father had ordered it cut down once when its roots threatened to destroy the stone wall of their fence, but Ben had talked him out of it. He had presented every argument he could think up, whether it be foolish or practical, until his sire had laughed, slapped a knee, and promised to leave the tree intact.

It had been eight years since Ben last slid into the tight space, and he barely fit these days. The tree had grown, as had he, but he managed to get his back against the oak, and the stones were still set so that he could position his feet upon them and brace himself, suspended above the ground.

A grin stole onto his mouth. He folded his arms behind his head, tilted his face up, and stuck out his tongue to catch a crystal of snow.

Hear, ye deaf; and look, ye blind, that ye may see.

Ben's shoes hit the ground with a thud. Gooseflesh prickled his neck at the words, unbidden, that filled his mind. Shaking his head did nothing to dislodge them, so he instead closed his eyes, thinking to place them.

Isaiah. Chapter forty-two, he thought—from a portion he had memorized in a class at Yale. That, then, was how he knew the verse, though he couldn't think why it would leap into his mind so randomly.

Hear. Look.

Footsteps, stealthy ones, moved along the garden wall. He must have heard them before he realized what they were, which in turn called to memory the appropriate instruction.

That must be it.

Slowly, silently, he eased from behind the tree. In all likelihood, it would be a couple set on taking advantage of his mother's arrangement. Or another guest merely seeking a moment's solitude.

Or…George?

Ben's brows pulled down. His friend glanced over his shoulder and then trotted toward the corner opposite Ben, where the gardener's shed resided.

Ben slid from his spot and eased along the wall. The shadows of the hedges would conceal him, but perhaps George sensed him, for he kept turning his head this way and that. Once at the door to the shed, he hunched his shoulders, pulled down the brim of his tricorn, and opened the rickety wooden door.

There was a reasonable explanation. There must be. One that did not involve his oldest friend being involved in espionage. He could be merely…or perhaps he intended to…

What? Check the gardener's equipment for rust and wear? There could be no good reason for anyone to seek that building under cover of darkness. Ben would not rest easy until he knew what in thunder George was up to, and the only way to discover that to his satisfaction was through firsthand knowledge. He must follow him. He had no choice.

He slid his way along the wall until he could press himself to the splintering wood of the outbuilding. It possessed no windows but was poorly enough put together that he could see between the unchinked boards.

A candle burned within. It provided enough light to reveal two figures inside, though angled in such a way that he could make out no faces.

If George had greeted the second man by name, it had been before Ben could hear him. Now a gravelly growl sounded from the chest of the stranger. "How can I be sure I can trust ye?"

George's sigh sounded exasperated. "I might as well ask the same of you. For all I know, you could be setting me up for arrest."

"Me?" The man sounded genuinely surprised by the suggestion. "Nay."

"Well, then. You got my name from someone. Presumably someone you trust."

The nameless one snorted. "The word of one desperate man to another. And since I be desperate enough to take a risk…"

George nodded and bent down, into the shadows. Ben heard the scraping of something upon the rough floor of the shed and then the creak of hinges.

Another snort, this one of incredulity. "Is that all ye have to offer?"

"What do you want, man? You call for a meeting at a neutral place with only a few hours' notice. If you are unwilling to take what you can get, then by all means seek someone else to help you."

The man spat out a curse as he toed the box. "You have me in a hard spot, to be sure. And I haven't much to offer you in return."

George shook his head. "I am not doing this for the adventure, my friend. How much have you?"

The sound of jingling silver came through the crack. Ben watched George reach out, count, pick up a few, and leave several coins in the man's hand. "That will do, sir. And now I will—"

"Shh." The man stiffened as his hand lifted to silence George. "Someone comes."

Had Ben breathed too loudly? Snapped a twig?

"I hear nothing," George whispered. But the candle was extinguished, and the other man shushed him again.

Then laughter sounded—from the direction of the house, but outside. Ben looked toward the rear door and had to bite back a curse.

Fairchild led Miss Reeves into Mother's winter paradise.

Winter's head thudded as Colonel Fairchild took her hand and guided her into the garden. The look in his eyes, the particular curve of his smile, the way he didn't release her fingers...she ought to be feeling joy. Or excitement, at least, at being brought outside for a moment of stolen privacy by a man as handsome and yet trustworthy as the colonel.

Only anxiety banded her chest. Keeping her smile in place was a challenge, but she refused to let it waver. "Colonel Fairchild, whatever are you up to? We ought not to be out here without a chaperone."

He tugged her along the snow-dusted path with a grin and then paused to reach for her other hand as well. "It would be a shame not to enjoy this lovely spot. Look how much trouble our hostess went to, and why would she have done it if she did not mean it to be enjoyed?"

Why indeed? She renewed her smile, though she had to wonder if perhaps Mrs. Lane had set the garden up for this specific purpose. Given that Winter wasn't as stupid as the lady assumed, she hadn't missed the many times Caroline Lane's eyes rolled the last few weeks whenever Winter said something particularly misinformed. "But, Colonel—"

"Isaac." He stepped closer, so close she could feel his warmth. Lantern light glinted in his eyes...at least she hoped it was lantern light and not the flames of ardor. "I would like you to call me Isaac."

She packed as much oblivion into her blink as she could manage. "Why would you like me to call you that, Colonel?"

He chuckled and reached to rest his gloved fingers against her cheek. "Because it is my name, my sweet."

"Oh." Tears wanted to clog her throat, which made it difficult to smile innocently. "It is a very nice name. You must be pleased with it."

"Do you know what would please me more?"

He leaned in, his eyes definitely glinting with feeling more than firelight. How she wished it kindled a like response in her, something more than this conviction that she could never really make him happy. She shook her head.

His thumb stroked over her cheek. "If you allowed me to call you Winter."

How long had it been since someone other than Freeman had used her given name with such affection? Since someone had made it sound like an endearment rather than an accusation? She drew in a shuddering breath. Grandmother might not like her to grant him such liberty, but… "'Tis only fair, I suppose, if I am to call you Isaac."

"Good." His fingers trailed their way down her neck, halting at her cloak. "I have missed you so these last weeks, Winter. I felt as though a light had gone out of my life."

"I…" Her throat closed over any response. So much promise shone in his eyes—a future together, security, love. All things she craved.

All things that would rest on a lie. And so, what would they really be worth?

He lowered his head as he pulled hers nearer. Gently, tenderly. Actions to perfectly match the expression on his face that said he would cherish her forever.

Or at least until he discovered that his Winter was only a figment.

Her heart raced, confliction building upon anxiety. Ought she to let him kiss her as he obviously wanted to do? Perhaps. After all, if she planned to marry him…but somehow, his were not the lips she envisioned bestowing her first kiss upon her. Handsome as he was, as kind and good, the arm he slid around her waist felt strange. Unfamiliar, though she arguably knew him better than any other gentleman in New York.

Father of my fathers, lead me in Your ways. Guard my decisions. Show me Your will.

Something squeaked in the corner of the garden, and Colonel Fairchild paused, a frown marring his brow. "What was that?"

Relief surged through her at his retreat, though it was tinged with guilt. She shook her head. "It almost sounded like a door."

A crunching came next, subtle but there, like a foot upon the deeper snow off the path.

Fairchild urged her aside, his brow still creased. "Stay here. I will see what it is."

Probably only a squirrel or a rabbit. Perhaps a servant trying to remain unseen. But she made no objection to him striding away toward the garden wall. Indeed, she loosed a quiet sigh and meandered in the opposite direction.

One step outside the circle of lantern light, she halted. The shadows along the wall here felt different. A chill swept her spine, and she spun back toward the colonel.

An arm clamped around her neck, pulling her backward and down a bit until she collided with a solid form. She managed only the start of a scream before the cold edge of metal convinced her to be silent.

"Winter!" Fairchild came running, though he halted abruptly when her captor forced her to step back into the light.

"Not a step farther or I will slit her throat." The man's voice was a raspy rumble against her temple. "You stay where you are, sir, while I slip out this gate here. Your lady will come with me that far."

Winter relaxed, though Fairchild certainly didn't. He stretched out an arm. "Release her, please. You are free to go."

"Aye, and I shall be making sure of that."

The colonel took a step toward them. "But—"

"Halt."

Fairchild obeyed, and Winter let her captor pull her out of the light again. "Slow and steady," he whispered in her ear.

Winter gripped his arm to keep from tripping and matched her murmur to his. "Silas, what on earth are you doing here?"

The farmhand's arm loosened abruptly. "Miss Winnie? Gracious, child, I did not know ye with all this fancy costume."

"Never mind that." She continued to slide backward with him, careful to keep her voice too low to be heard by Fairchild. "Why are you in the city? And here, of all places?"

"Had to get me a weapon, miss. I cannot let them catch me unarmed again, and they destroyed everything else."

Her fingers tightened on his arm. "'They'? What has happened?"

Silas sniffed and halted. The fumbling sounds behind them indicated they had reached the gate. "Sorry I am to tell you this, miss. I had intended to get word to the Townsend boy while here so he could let you know. But they burned it. The house, the barn—gone. Just last week it happened."

The lanterns doubled, dimmed in her wavering vision. "Wh–what? My house?"

"Aye. A pile of rubble it is now. I did me best to save it, but one man against a mob of Tories…I tried, indeed I did. I am sorry for failing. But I must go, miss, before that officer of yours loses patience. If you would kindly distract him?"

She could manage only a jerk of her head in acquiescence. When he released her, her knees buckled and she slid to the cold, snowy ground.

Gone. Her home, her father's house. Would anyone get word to him? Or would he return from campaign one day not knowing that only charred remains would await him? The house his father had built, wife and daughter…all vanished.

She had known she couldn't go back, at least not until Father returned, which would likely be too late. But now? Knowing she had nothing to which to go at all?

"Winter!" Fairchild's hands gripped her arms and pulled her up. "My darling, are you injured? If that villain put so much as a scratch upon your throat—"

She shook her head, but the motion made the world sway again. All she could focus on was the red of his coat.

"Here." He moved her, round and seemingly round, and she couldn't think what he was pointing her toward until a different arm encircled her. 'Twas warm and solid and held her aright. "If you would get her inside, Mr. Lane, I must…"

If he finished his sentence, Winter was unaware. With a flash of movement his red coat vaulted over the gate and disappeared into the darkness behind it. How very odd. He moved so quickly, and she couldn't seem to budge at all. Couldn't lift a hand, couldn't open her mouth, couldn't even step away from Mr. Lane.

"Miss Reeves." The smooth spice of his voice bade her look up at him. It took her a long moment to convince her head to turn, to meet his questioning gaze. When she did, she found his face etched with worry. He brushed a fallen curl away from her face. "Do not faint on me, I beg you."

She had to shake her head again and swallow before her tongue would cooperate. "I am not the fainting kind."

A snort sounded from beyond Mr. Lane's shoulder, though she lacked the energy to look for its owner.

Mr. Lane's face went taut, as did the arm still around her. Though both relaxed again in moments. "Come, Miss Reeves. Let us get you inside, where you can warm up and put this fright behind you."

He tried to urge her toward the path, but she held her spot, shaking her head again. Perhaps a bit too wildly, as the curl tumbled onto her cheek once more. "Not yet, please. I beg you. They will make a fuss, crowd around. I cannot...I cannot suffer that just yet."

All those faces, sympathy mixed with curiosity, colored with disbelief. Nay. 'Twas quiet she needed. Peaceful quiet, so this fresh loss could seep in slowly.

That snort came again. "I have never known you to mind a fuss being made over you, Miss Reeves."

"George Knight, I ought to..." Mr. Lane's voice tapered off, and then he lifted an accusing finger. "This is your fault. What were you doing meeting with such a man in my garden shed?"

Mr. Knight shifted, which put him in the circle of light. His face bore all the feeling of a granite sculpture. "What I always do, Ben. I was selling a gun."

Mr. Lane's eyes went wide. "Here? *Now?*"

His friend shrugged. "He made it sound urgent, but I already said I would be here, so..."

"So you bring a criminal onto *my* property—"

"He was cornered," Mr. Knight said, his voice even, "not criminal."

"How can you know that? He could be a rebel, an outlaw, any number of kinds of miscreant!"

Mr. Knight rolled his eyes and pivoted, though he didn't walk off as Winter half expected. "What care is it of mine whether he favors blue or red? I am concerned only with sterling."

Mr. Lane's nostrils flared. "What have you brought upon me, George?"

"He did not harm her." But contrition finally snuck onto the man's face.

His friend seemed unimpressed by it. "Physically, perhaps, but she is obviously suffering from the shock."

Mr. Knight snorted a third time. "How can you tell? She looks no more dazed than she ever does."

Tears surged to Winter's eyes, but she spun away to keep him from seeing them. Cold closed around her when she left the shelter of Mr. Lane's arms, though. She stalked toward the house. She would find an empty room and hide herself away until the choking sensation left her throat, until the waves of pain ebbed away.

Still, she heard Mr. Lane's biting, "Get out of here, George."

And Mr. Knight's low, "Ben. I did not mean—"

"Later. Tomorrow. Just go for now. Please."

Winter broke into a run, praying she could reach the door and somehow disappear before Mr. Lane could catch up with her. Solitude, she needed solitude. To curl into a ball and let the tears come.

She wrenched the door open and even made it two steps inside before his hands closed over her shoulders. Gently enough that she could have pulled away, but all her energy was spent in trying to stem the sobs heaving their way upward. As he spun her around, she squeezed her eyes shut so she wouldn't have to see the concern upon his face. It would surely unravel her.

"Winter—Miss Reeves. I am so sorry. To think that this happened to you in my house because of the poor business decisions of my friend—"

"'Tisn't your fault, nor his." She ought not to have spoken. Once she'd opened her mouth, a sob escaped and wouldn't be stemmed no matter how hard she pressed her hand to her lips.

When he urged her to her right, she went blindly, unable to see through her tears. And because the room he opened was draped in silence, she didn't much care where he'd taken her.

He led her to a sofa and sat beside her. "There now, Miss Reeves, take a moment. I…bother. I've no experience dealing with distraught females."

And she despised being one. But trying to blink away the tears and look around only made it worse. Rather than a receiving room, he had brought her into what must have been a more intimate family environment. Embroidery sat, in progress, on one of the chairs, newspapers and books lay open upon the table. Pipe tobacco lingered in the air, and the furniture was well-worn and comfortable.

Images of home filled her vision. The dark beams and white chink, the stone fireplace, with its stove top and iron oven box. "I can't believe it's gone. Even thinking I would never see it again, I knew it was there. But now—Mother's spinning wheels. Father's favorite chair. The wooden horse he carved for my doll when I was a girl. Gone, all of it."

Mr. Lane caught his breath. He wore panic on his face. "Deuces. Are you delusional, Miss Reeves?"

A laugh tangled with her tears.

His panic amplified. "I will go fetch someone. Perhaps call for an apothecary and obtain something to calm your nerves."

"No! Please." She reached out to stop him. "Grandmother will come, and I…please, not yet."

He sighed. "At least let me see if the colonel has apprehended the villain."

She shook her head. She certainly hoped not. And suspected he wouldn't. Silas had always been sly.

Mr. Lane frowned in that probing way of his. "What is this? Surely you want the man caught. I cannot conceive why you would not after he put a knife to your throat."

Did nothing escape this man? Winter swiped at her cheeks. "I know him, Mr. Lane. He was a hand on our farm before…before I came to live with my grandparents. I left Silas in charge. He didn't recognize me at first, of course, but…but when he did, he told me it had burned. The house, the barn. Everything within." She had to swallow past more rising tears. "I was allowed to bring so little here with me, and now—it's gone, all of it. All the things of my childhood."

Mr. Lane's hand covered hers. She ought to pull away, but he looked so concerned, so desperate to help. And strangely, that small touch gave a good deal of comfort. "I am so sorry. I cannot imagine how you must feel. How very odd to be accosted like that, only to discover…" He paused to pull in a long breath. "Do you want me to go make sure the colonel has *not* apprehended him?"

How was it that he always managed to pull a laugh from her in her darkest moments? "No need to worry for Silas. He is a wily sort, though loyal as can be once one has won his trust."

Mr. Lane nodded as he studied her. His face relaxed. "Your color is returning. I must say, I'm all relief you are not hysterical, Miss Reeves."

She dug up a smile and pulled her hand from under his. "Oh, no. Not at all, Mr. Lane. I have no head for history whatsoever. Such a dull subject."

He grinned and chucked her on the chin as her father used to do. "There you are, yourself again. Come." He stood and held out a hand to assist her up. "We had better return to the group before we are missed."

Though their hands had touched mere seconds before, she hesitated before putting her fingers back in his now. And once she had, once he had helped her to her feet, she wasn't surprised when he didn't relinquish her or when he lifted his other hand to wipe away a tear she must have missed. "Winter, you must promise never to frighten me like that again."

Eternity stretched through a few ticks of the clock, during which she couldn't tear her gaze from the blue depths of his eyes. 'Twas all she could manage to whisper, "I shall do my best to avoid it, Bennet."

"See that you do." His smile bloomed.

Had one of them moved? They seemed closer, and his fingers had somehow woven through hers when she paid no attention. Perhaps he leaned down now, or perhaps she strained up. She couldn't say. She knew only that this was where she wanted to be, away from the crowds, in this quiet, welcoming room. With him.

Commotion in the hallway shattered the peace and dispelled most of the pulse-thumping tension. Fairchild's voice filtered through the door, followed by feminine exclamations.

Winter sank back down upon her heels, though still Bennet held her gaze. He gave her a rueful smile, and then he leaned forward and pressed his lips to her forehead. He tightened his fingers, touched his forehead to hers, exactly where he had kissed her, and sighed. "He will be a good husband to you."

And with that nonsensical declaration, he let go of her hand, stepped away, and hurried out the door. Winter held her spot, at least until her breath regulated, and lifted a hand to her flushed cheek. Two near kisses in one night.

And it seemed she was longing for the wrong one.

Ten

Ben stood for a long moment in the street, staring up at the sign that swung from its iron fastenings as a stiff wind gusted by. *The Knight's Arms*. Inside, George no doubt sat at his bench alongside his father and younger brother, putting a weapon together. Combining the skill of a craftsman with the eye of an artist, not to mention the scientific mind of an engineer.

All to create a method to kill.

He drew in a long breath but still did not move toward the door. He knew well the Knights had ongoing contracts from the British military—no better weapons could be found in all New York. But if George's words were true, he would sell his guns to those in blue coats as quick as to those in red, if they had the coin.

Thirst for silver had certainly led men enough into dangerous business. The London Trade, with their apples and beef and other items otherwise impossible to find, proved that smuggling was alive and well in the city, and perfectly acceptable. But if George were caught handing over a weapon to the wrong person…well, it didn't bear thinking about. 'Twas as perilous as if he *were* a spy.

Which was still a question in Ben's mind. Try as he might to extinguish it, the doubt Mrs. Shirley raised about the Knights' loyalty continued to smolder. Did a person's politics ever really change…or did they merely lessen in volume?

His fingers flexed. Why had he not seen *that* before? When Washington still held New York, many of its residents considered him an oppressor—many, but not all. Plenty were sympathetic to the rebel cause, and some left with him when he fled. But many stayed behind, from what he had seen, and adjusted to life under the British.

Adjusted…but did their thoughts ever alter? Especially after seeing the corruption the English military machine brought with them? Ben had heard enough grumbling to know the Redcoats' boots were hard upon the necks of the city's inhabitants. Even the always loyal were eager for the army to leave. So it stood to reason that those already inclined toward the Patriot cause would be all the *more* eager. And perhaps willing to help it along.

Excitement sang through his veins. That was how he would find his spy. He would discover the former Whigs among all the Tories, those who had put their names to any of the many documents demanded by the new American Congress and which still floated around the city, if one knew where to look. Perhaps many of those had since bent their knee to the Crown and retracted said allegiance, but they would have retained their ties to other Whigs. It may be too vast a list to be helpful, at first sight, but there must be connections. To Washington himself, perhaps, or to those he had put in charge of endeavors of espionage.

Would that tack lead him straight back to George? Ben drew in another long breath and stepped toward the door in search of his friend. He could only hope it would not.

When he entered the shop, he bypassed Mr. Knight at the front with a wave and headed for the workshop in back. George sat at the table, a length of metal before him. His younger brother was nowhere in sight, which Ben considered a blessing.

His friend looked around, brows raised. "Good morning, Ben. You're out and about early today."

"Morning, George." He sat in his usual place at the end of the long bench. "A Brown Bess?"

George ran a hand down the metal. "It will be."

He didn't want to ask. But he must. "And to whom will you sell that one? Or do you even care?"

"I knew you wouldn't let it pass. Yet, strangely, I hoped you would." Not meeting his gaze, George kept at his work. Though for the life of him, Ben never could figure out what it was the Knights did to turn metal and wood into a gun. He understood the theory, of course, but the execution was beyond him.

"George." He leaned close, voice low. "How can I let it pass? You were hidden away on *my* property, selling a weapon under cover of darkness. Do you even know who the man was?"

George shrugged. "A farmer from Long Island, one who had to get back this morning. It is only business, Ben."

"Business? George, your business is not hurting, what with all the military contracts you must fulfill. Do you mean to tell me you care so much for a single sale that you would go to such extraordinary lengths to achieve it?"

Now his friend sighed. "Perhaps my love of sterling was colored by sympathy a bit. He was obviously in dire straits."

"You didn't seem terribly sympathetic in my gardener's shed."

"You were listening." Sounding resigned, George pinched the bridge of his nose. "I wondered. All right, I shall be forthright with you. I don't ask a man about his loyalty before I sell him a weapon. I could get in trouble for that, I know, but I have had enough of politics. Frankly, both sides have their tyrannies as well as their valid points. The way I see it, my job is to make and sell guns. 'Tis no great concern of mine who buys them."

"George."

"Don't lecture me, Professor. Last night may have gone poorly, but I swear to you that particular man was not the threat he seemed, only a desperate farmer." Yet his quick glance showed some concern. "Did Fairchild catch him?"

"Nay." Which made a grin tickle Ben's mouth. "The man apparently led him into an unsavory area and then vanished."

"Did he—Fairchild, I mean—ask about our presence?"

Ben measured his friend. He supposed, even if the sale had been as innocent as he claimed, he would worry about Fairchild's questions. Frankly, Ben had felt some anxiety about that himself, and he had nothing at all to hide when it came to his presence in his own garden. But no gentleman ever wanted to be caught seeing what he ought not.

"I informed him that we came out when we heard Winter scream. He accepted that without consideration."

"Winter?" His hands paused in their busy task, and his gaze finally held Ben's. Though now he wished it wouldn't. "You are calling her by her first name now?"

Oh, bother. Ben scrubbed a hand over his face. "No. That is, not really, I just…" He rested his head in his hand. "Seeing a knife to her throat like that, the fear in her eyes, and then the blankness—"

"Which I maintain was nothing new."

"Then you're a dunderhead, George." He looked up, wondering if he appeared as foolish as he felt. "I fear I…I think I'm in love with her."

Metal thudded onto the table, and George spun to face him. "You cannot be serious."

How he wished he weren't. But seeing her first in Fairchild's arms and then in that stranger's, a blade so near—he had never felt such jealousy, followed by such terror.

Apparently his silence proved answer enough, for George groaned and slapped at his leg. "Confound it, Ben, you are too intelligent to be so stupid. 'Twas bad enough when I thought you merely infatuated by her beauty, but *love*? You cannot be such a fool."

Ben tried to rub a hand over his head, which resulted in knocking off the hat he'd forgotten to remove upon entering. After leaning over to pick it up, he dropped it on the table. "I wish you could see in her what I do. Then you would understand."

"Terribly sorry, old man, but I can't see what isn't there."

"It *is* there!" Ben stood, paced to the wall, and pivoted back again. "She puts on a good show, yes, but it is only that. A show, with her as her grandparents' puppet. Saying what she must to please them, or at least to keep from angering them. Hampton struck her, you know. That was why she was out of society the past two weeks. I saw the bruise upon her cheek."

George looked at him as though he were an unfortunate soul bound for the madhouse. "Ben, she probably ran into something."

"Have you ever seen her lacking in grace?"

"Well, perhaps she was trying to hold a thought in her head while walking. I imagine that would make her trip and stumble."

Ben huffed to a halt. "George Knight."

Hands spread, George shook his head. "What do you want me to say? I've never much cared for Hampton, but he is a respected man. And Miss Reeves is…"

He folded his arms over his chest. "She is what?"

Rather than finish his thought, George held his hands up in surrender and turned back to his work. "What an unbelievable conversation. But since we are having it, it must be asked—does she even like you? I don't mean to be insensitive, my friend, but you are not notorious for your ways with women."

He couldn't be insulted by such an obvious truth. Indeed, it made him chuckle. Ben settled on the bench again. "I know I'm not, but it's different with her. I think she *does* like me, actually. She defended me to Archie, and she made no objection when I tried to kiss her last night."

"When you what?" Hands still again, George turned wide eyes on him. And grinned. "If she made no objection, then why only 'tried to'?"

He had spent several hours lying awake last night, asking himself that question. Even after Fairchild returned, he could have kissed her. No one knew where they were, and the moment had lingered long enough. He could have ignored the hubbub in the hall, leaned down… but it would have changed nothing and only given him more cause for hopeless longings. "She is practically engaged to Fairchild."

George cocked a ginger-colored brow. "And…?"

"And I am not my brother."

"Ah. Say no more." But his friend studied him intently before releasing a veritable gust of breath. "I cannot believe I am about to say this, but you obviously care for her a great deal, in spite of all good sense. So why do you not propose before the colonel can?"

He had considered that too during the long, sleepless night. But he barely knew her. Certainly he had not discovered the full scope of her depths. The fact that she hid herself so well from everyone, that she constantly threw up another wall whenever he discovered a crack in one…an intelligent, amazing woman lurked under the beauty, he was sure of it. But he had met many an intelligent, amazing woman with whom he would not want to spend his life. How could he be sure she wasn't one of those until she let him see her in her fullness?

None of which George would understand, given that he denied

such fullness existed. So he shook his head and opted to share another, no less valid, reason. "What can I possibly offer her?"

George's mouth fell open. "Do you jest? A certain estate called Clefton springs to mind."

"Yes, it springs to everyone's mind—except mine." He rubbed his eyes and leaned into the table. "I was raised with Colonial understandings of ownership, George. That you build your own legacy and then pass it to whomever you please. I feel no tie to the land in England, no obligation or duty toward it and its tenants. I should, I suppose, but... frankly, I don't want to move to the other side of the Atlantic. I want to go back to Connecticut, conduct my experiments, teach my classes, and so pass a contented life."

For a long moment George just looked at him, his gaze absent its usual teasing and filled with what could only be termed new understanding. "Is it entailed?"

Ben shook his head. "Father was the only logical heir for Uncle Milton to name now that his son is dead, but it needn't be me that inherits from him. Archie could as well—though I doubt Father will see it that way."

"Would you..." As if unable to grasp the words he was about to say, George shook his head, repositioned himself on his seat. "Would you refuse it? Tell your father you don't want it?"

Assuming the choice weren't taken from him, he would still in good conscience have little choice. "It would be the best thing. Archie has traveled there, and he loves the old place. There has been some talk among the family lately of him inheriting the property here in America now that I'm the presumed heir of the English estate, but I think the reverse would suit us all better."

George breathed a laugh. "And yet you go about in society letting everyone think you are landed gentry in the British sense. Ben, I did not know you had it in you."

"Well, it's hardly the business of society at large what I may eventually work out with my father, is it? Besides, they assume what they will. I have never said a word about it one way or another."

Grinning, George turned back to his work. "I agree wholeheartedly. And I applaud you for knowing what you want. Even—or perhaps especially—if it means the Hamptons wouldn't then approve a match with their granddaughter."

Ben stood again and picked up his hat. He had done what he came to do. He had gotten George's story and had then let him think Ben was distracted from it by his own woes. Now to prove he had not been. "George, whatever you are involved in, promise me you will be careful. Had it been Fairchild who overheard you, or even Archie…they may turn a blind eye to much that goes on in the city, but I daresay weapons are of the utmost concern to them."

"You have no need to worry, Ben, I assure you. I am involved in nothing for them to take issue with." But he did not look up. And though his fingers moved, they accomplished nothing.

He was involved in *something*, Ben was sure. But he would say no more without knowing exactly what. "Well, I must be on my way. I will see you tomorrow as planned?"

Now George tossed him a smile. "The whole family is looking forward to it, myself included."

"Excellent." Ben positioned his hat on his head and nodded. "Until then."

He headed for the door, pushing these concerns aside to make room for others. He had some documentation to dig up, and it brought a smile to his lips. This kind of search he was actually good at.

Much as Winter loved her below-stable sanctuary, she had to admit that she preferred it with light. The scent of melted wax continued to tease her nose even after she had hurriedly snuffed out her candle, and she waved away the smoke toward the ventilation cracks at the end of the room. She hoped the telltale whiff wouldn't go straight up toward the trap door.

No light seeped through the portal, which meant Freeman had covered it when the servant approached. She inched her way through the darkness toward the stairs, barely suppressing a squeal when a cobweb caught on her cheek. She swiped it away, flapped her hand a few times, and scrubbed at her face to make sure a spider hadn't joined its web.

Yes, illumination made all the difference when one was in a hole with no way out.

"I can take it no more. I have to get away, Free. I must."

Winter frowned and rested her hand against the cold earthen wall as she tried to place the voice. One of the slaves from the house?

"Percy." Freeman sounded tired and anxious. "I know he treats you poorly, but you can't run away. If you get caught—"

"I'll join the army. The British have promised freedom to any slave who joins them."

Freeman's sigh came through the floorboards without difficulty. "Any slaves of *Patriot* families. They have not extended the offer to slaves of Loyalists."

"Well, maybe the rebels have. I'll join with them, then."

"How will you get to them?" Freeman no doubt shook his head in that way that insisted on reason. "You would more likely be caught than make it to rebel-held territory, and if you are then brought back to Mr. Hampton...it's not worth the risk."

"How can you know that? You, who were born free?"

Winter heard shuffling and then settling. And another of her friend's long sighs. "I was blessed in that, yes. Blessed to spend most of my life with a family like the Reeves, who offered me and my parents respect and even friendship. But am I any better than you now? The Hamptons and those like them—they don't care if I'm free. To them, I'm worthless."

It sounded as though Percy toed the stall wall. "Come with me, then. We can claim I'm your son, and—"

"No, boy. I cannot leave Miss Reeves here unprotected. They hold her in no higher esteem than they do us."

She had a feeling the slave wouldn't see it that way, and Percy's scoffing laugh verified it. "You think I'm a fool? The way they dress her up—"

"They dress up Thomas too, to open their doors and polish their silver."

Another incredulous snort. "What ties you to her, Free?"

Winter smiled into the darkness. There could be no simple answer to a question like that. Eighteen years of shared circumstances, shared toil, shared fear and loss. She shut her eyes to focus on his words, whatever they may be.

He chuckled, soft and quiet. "I had a wife once, Percy. A fine woman I loved with all my heart. We were set to have a babe, and my Nan took to her childbed the same time Mrs. Reeves did. Neither Nan nor our little girl made it. But Mr. Reeves, he took little Winnie from her cradle while Mrs. Reeves slept, he put her in my arms, and he said, 'I can share your pain, Freeman, and you can share my joy.' So you see, from her first hour of life, she was my little girl as sure as she was her daddy's, the gift the good Lord gave me to ease the pain of losing my own child and my sweet bride."

A few tears trickled from beneath her lashes. He had called her his girl often when she was younger, and she had known, of course, about the terrible loss of his wife and daughter. But she had never heard this story before. It may not make sense to the young man who stood directly above her now, who wanted only to be away from this terrible place, but for Winter it proved they had done right by staying together. It demonstrated why he mourned the destruction of their home as keenly as she did.

Percy made a noise that combined the disgusted with the dismissive. "You must be daft, staying here when you could leave. But I ain't. Better to die trying to find freedom than to live out my days tied to that man."

Winter leaned her head against the wall. She could understand that sentiment. Terrible as her grandparents were to her, they were worse to many of those who served them. But Freeman was right. The military might accept slaves from Patriot families and offer them their freedom in exchange for their service, but they had been forbidden from offering the same to Tory slaves—and making it out of British lines would be difficult indeed for a black man traveling alone. Even with the right passes, he would be stopped, searched, and likely sent back.

And Grandfather wasn't kind to those who had attempted escape.

Percy moved off, and Freeman sent a farewell after him. Winter drew in a deep breath and waited. One minute, two, until the coast would be clear.

In the darkness, her mind conjured up an image of fire and of the letter she had tossed into it in a fit of anger. The words that she so wished she still had in her possession, to reread when she felt alone.

I know you do not understand fully why I left, sweet Winter, her father had written. *But I hope someday you will see that I fight for you. For your right to live free.*

Freedom…sometimes it felt like an illusion. One for which men like Percy were willing to risk a flogging, one for which men like Father were willing to leave their family.

She hadn't understood that then, when Mother had first fallen ill and she had just wanted Father *there*, beside her, making it all well. She had resented his cause, his conviction, his duty to country above kin.

But his words had burned into her mind as they were consumed in the flames, haunting her as she sat by her mother's deathbed, as she waited for the arrival of the grandparents she had never met. As they brought her here, forced their wills upon her, and made her wonder if she would ever again be free to live how she wanted.

That was when she realized freedom and faith were so inexplicably linked. The Lord had granted mankind an amazing gift when He allowed them to choose for themselves how they would live. He had surpassed even that when He freely offered forgiveness for choosing wrongly.

How could they who loved Him and His precepts not want to extend that right of freedom to everyone? To their children and their neighbors?

Winter breathed in the damp darkness and hoped Father somehow knew she understood now.

When the door was raised and precious light flooded down, she flew up the stairs and wrapped her arms around Freeman's waist. "Why is it that neither you nor Father ever told me that story of the day I was born?"

He chuckled and patted her on the back. "Never needed to be told. It just was. But knowing how you worry for me, and how I worry right back for you, it seemed a fine time to remind you that we are family, Winnie girl. Sure as if my blood flowed in your veins."

A statement so true it needed no other words. So she stepped away and smiled. Matched both pointer fingers to thumbs in a circle, touching, and then drew them apart into a larger circle. *Family.*

Freeman nodded, and then he jerked his head toward the house. "Get on back inside before they miss you, now."

Miss her…a laughable choice of phrase. They may note her absence, may grow angered by it, but they certainly would never miss her when she was gone. Still, she said her goodbyes and left the stable, hurried across the lawn, and entered through the kitchen door.

The cook greeted her with wide eyes and a frantic whisper. "Where you been, Miss Winter? Colonel Fairchild done come and asked to speak with Mr. Hampton. Your grandmother, she be looking everywhere for you."

Her heart couldn't seem to decide whether it ought to race or thud to a halt. So her chest banded up instead, nearly suffocating her. The colonel had never before come to seek Grandfather's company. And there was only one reason he would do so now.

"Thank you, Cookie." She managed a nod before sprinting up the back steps and into her room. The moment she gained it, she kicked off the shoes soiled by the stable and slid on fresh slippers.

Then sank onto the edge of her bed and stared into nothingness.

So then. Fairchild had asked for her hand. Grandfather would have granted it, happy to be rid of her so soon after his ultimatum. The colonel would probably propose to her in the next day or two, Grandmother would launch into a flurry of wedding plans. Perhaps tsking a bit over her not landing Bennet—Mr. Lane, that is—but she would be satisfied. 'Twas a fine match.

A fine match indeed. Colonel Fairchild was handsome. He was good, honest. He came from one of the best families in England, his bloodline impeccable. At his side, she would always be privy to sensitive information, which she could pass to Robbie. He would cherish her. Love her.

So why did panic join forces with dread inside her? Why did the feeling strike, even stronger than last night after Silas's news, that she would never be *home* again now?

Her door burst open, and Grandmother blew in like a tempest. Her eyes glinted—not with excitement, not with pride, not even relief. Yet not with anger and frustration, either. She stopped in the center of the room and raised her chin as she emptied her countenance of all expression.

Winter had learned that particular tactic from the best.

"Colonel Fairchild was here," Grandmother said.

Thinking it safest, Winter only nodded.

"He asked for your hand. I expected this would come soon, given his fervor last night, so your grandfather and I had already discussed our response. He has been refused."

In spite of the panic of a moment before, this brought no relief. Only great, deeper dread. "Pardon? But…why?"

"Do not be a fool, Winifred." She waved a hand and sailed to the window. "Fairchild may have the better blood by far, but his fortune is nothing compared to Lane's, and think not for a moment that I missed the looks *he* has been sending your way. You will wait for his offer."

"Grandmother—"

"Not a word of protest. Our answer was gentle, of course, and left him with the freedom to continue his courtship. We just indicated we were not ready to marry off our *darling* granddaughter quite yet." A regal sneer turned the words into a threat. "Not to him."

Winter stood, though she had no idea what she intended to say, what plea she could make. What plea she even *wanted* to make. "Grandmother, you cannot even be sure Mr. Lane will propose. He… he…"

"He is an awkward, bookish bore. Yes, I am well aware. But even bookish bores can be persuaded to make declarations with the proper encouragement." She took two steps back to Winter and glared directly into her eyes. "Encourage him."

She straightened her spine. Slowly, so it would not look like a show of will. "I am afraid he is not as easily led as you might think. We have talked enough that I can be quite certain he hides an iron resolve under all his scholarly words. I don't think I can push him where he wants not to go."

When Phillippa Hampton arched a brow in that way, the earth seemed to tremble. "Then get imaginative, Winifred. He is only a man. One who obviously delights in your beauty."

Her stomach turned. "But—"

"I have made quite sure you have wiles at the ready." With a click of her fan, Grandmother pivoted back toward the door. "Use them."

Winter shook her head as the woman blustered out of her chamber.

Grandmother obviously knew not what she asked. Bennet—Mr. Lane—had demonstrated last night that he had no great difficulty in holding to reason above passion. And she suspected that if she tried to use any womanly wiles on him, his reaction would be opposite what Grandmother intended. He would not be tricked or persuaded into marriage. He would flee and force her into Colonel Fairchild's arms. Again.

She sat and fell backward onto the mattress, flinging an arm over her eyes. Perhaps she ought to obey. Let the facts prove her suspicions true. Let him turn away from her once and for all. Let Grandmother see that some men rose above her expectations and could not be lured in by simpering smiles, batted lashes, and coquettish words. That they were in fact repelled by them.

Let him be repelled. Let him reject her. Let him be purged from her mind and shorn from her heart.

Tears had the audacity to burn at the thought, but she squeezed her eyes shut against them. She would be the better for it.

Eleven

March 1780

Winter could scarcely take pleasure in the first bloom of spring. A warm breath of air had finally descended upon the city, and when cooped up in Hampton Hall the first half of the morning, she had wanted little more than to be out enjoying the fine weather. Now, strolling through a small park on Bennet Lane's arm, it was all she could do to focus on the chirping of birds.

His gaze was locked on some nonexistent point before them, contemplation writing an epic of thoughts upon his countenance in a language she had yet to learn. He had grown increasingly distracted over the past month and a half. Pushed away by the flirtation Grandmother insisted she employ? Perhaps. Yet still he went to all the gatherings she did, escorting her in. Still he came, at least once a week, to visit with her privately. Still he sat, often silent, in their drawing room.

She must be a fool to miss the probing glances, the leading questions. Was this not what she wanted? For him to lose interest, to be less of a danger to her? Yet here she was, strolling through the first beautiful day of the season, missing the perilous exchanges of winter.

A child's shout came from the other side of the park, something to the effect of "Catch it! Catch it!" It brought a smile to her lips. Indeed, this was a day to be caught with both hands and enjoyed. She might as well forget about serious things for an hour and bask in the sunshine.

Repositioning her hand on his arm, she turned her face toward his. What a strong jaw he had—one it seemed he hadn't bothered to take a razor to in a couple days. Somehow, the oversight on his part made her grin, as did the sandy hair tied at the nape of his neck. Barring the most formal occasions, he still refused to wear a wig. "You have become so quiet of late, Mr. Lane. Your mind must be hard at work on some scientific treaty."

Light kindled in the gaze of blue he swung her way. "Treatise, you mean? Nay, unfortunately. Without my laboratory I am afraid I have had little chance to explore my theories in chemistry."

"You miss it." 'Twas so obvious even empty-headed her would have seen it.

"Very much."

"And do they miss you at Yale?"

He chuckled, looking a bit more like the Bennet she had first met. "So say the letters from the president, who also happens to be a friend. He begs me to assure him I will return when the next school year commences."

The thought brought an unwelcome lump to her throat. She smiled past it. "And will you?"

"I…" His mirth faded back into contemplation. "I cannot say. I hope so, if everything here is adequately resolved by then."

If Grandmother were here, Winter would be expected to make some comment about duties to one's family and then to nudge the topic into his need for a wife.

But Grandmother was not here, only Freeman trailing a fair distance behind. So instead she grinned up at him. "You know, Lizzie and I were reading a bit of science the other day."

At that his brows arched and his eyes went sharp again. "I am all amazement. You and Miss Shirley? Together?"

"Mmm. She wanted to be able to discuss it to impress…someone." As little attention as he had paid Winter lately, he had paid less to any other young woman. Not that any of the mothers of said young women had given up hope, given his lack of proposal to Winter. "'Twas by that being-and-thinking fellow."

Bennet's lips twitched. "Ah, him. Whatever *is* his name?"

At least he was playing along. It proved such a refreshing change that she nearly ruined the game with a chuckle instead of a wide-eyed stare. "Something to do with cards, I believe. He must be a terrible gambler."

He loosed a laugh. "Descartes may not like your inference, Miss Reeves."

"Ah, yes! That is his name. At any rate, we were reading about his thoughts on collisions. Small bodies and large bodies and whatnot."

"A popular topic with physicists, to be sure. How hard bodies react to one other, what becomes of their momentum..." He looked to be suppressing his smile again. "Did you learn anything?"

She pasted epiphany onto her face. "Indeed I did! He said that a small body can never, under any circumstances, move a larger body. This was quite enlightening, Mr. Lane, for I would have sworn I moved my bureau last week, having put some force into it. But it is larger than I, so obviously I was mistaken."

"Oh, yes. Obviously." He put his fingers over her hand on his arm, affection at last in his eyes.

Which shouldn't please her. Nay, she ought to chide herself for inspiring it so deliberately. Yet his smile sent a thrill of contentment through her veins.

He gave her fingers a squeeze. "For the life of me, I cannot fathom why he printed such rot. Did the man never do an actual experiment? He should have stuck with philosophy."

"Oh, but surely he is right. He thinks it, therefore it must be."

His laughter now scared a few robins to wing. Yes, she was a fool for it—but she had missed this.

"Why have we not had these conversations of late, Winter? It seems that..." His smile faded as his words trailed off and his brows knit. He nodded beyond her shoulder. "Is that Townsend rushing this way?"

Robbie? She craned her head around and sucked in a breath at the distress that pulsed from him. "It is. And he looks upset."

"He does indeed." Bennet was already pulling her toward her friend. "I would guess it is you he seeks in this part of town. I do hope nothing has happened to his family."

"As do I." She lifted her skirt a bit so she could traverse the muddy path with a quicker step.

Robbie's rush had him aimed toward the house, but their movement must have caught his attention, for his stride changed abruptly, and he shifted his course toward them. The way he flicked his gaze from Winter to Bennet as they neared and then pressed his lips together made her stomach quiver. What if this were not about his family at all? What if whatever news he carried had to do with Culper business? He could hardly share that with anyone else present.

God of all, let the road of our cause remain clear.

"Good morning, Townsend," Bennet said, concern in his voice.

Robbie nodded, though his frown didn't lessen. "And to you, Mr. Lane. My apologies. I did not mean to interrupt your outing."

"'Tis only a walk, given the fine weather." Winter withdrew her hand from Bennet's arm so she could reach for Robbie's hands. "Robbie, whatever is wrong?"

He glanced at Bennet again before drawing in a deep breath and blinking rapidly, shaking his head. "It is my cousin. He has been arrested."

In spite of the thaw in the land, something inside her froze. "Which cousin?"

His gaze fell to their clasped hands. "James."

James? As in the cousin whom Robbie had tasked with finding a new route by which they could send their information to Washington? The cousin she had cautioned him not to trust with such a task? *That* James? "Robbie."

He released her hands and turned away, nearly knocking off his tricorn when he rubbed at his forehead. "He was traveling through New Jersey on his way to visit family in rebel-held territory and hoping to recruit men for the British army."

That was the story Robbie said they had devised for the boy, yes. Winter bit her tongue to keep from asking anything that would give away the falsehood of the claim. "Is New Jersey not heavily Loyalist?"

"Aye, but..." He faced her again, countless emotions warring across his face. Frustration, anger, concern. "It seems he was in his cups and bragging about this goal of his a bit too loudly in the wrong place to a couple of lovely young lasses. As it turns out, the family of these girls are secretly Patriot and turned him in to the local rebel authorities as a British spy."

She could only stare. His cousin—a Patriot pretending, too loudly, to be a Loyalist—had been arrested by other *Patriots*?

On the one hand, 'twas far better than if the British had discovered his true purpose, for it would be an easy task to trace him back to Robbie. But what must Washington have thought when he got the news that a spy by the name of Townsend had been arrested?

"Poor Jamie," she murmured, though she felt no sympathy for him. What had the boy been thinking by letting his tongue get so loosened by drink while out on covert business? "Had he any condemning documentation about him? Or is there a chance he will be released?"

"He had…" Robbie cleared his throat before answering. "He had nothing condemning. Just a, ah, poem I had written."

It no doubt contained an invisible message as well, but that was secure. He would have written it in the stain. She pasted on a grin for his benefit. "No wonder he was arrested then, for your verse is a crime in itself."

The jest did nothing to lighten the shadows in his eyes. "I have hope he will soon be released. He is only a boy, after all, and was all bluster besides."

"I will pray." Relentlessly, and for far more than James himself. For the situation he had brought upon them and the consequences that tormented Robbie's gaze.

"I know you will. 'Tis why I rushed over here." Again, he flicked his gaze in Bennet's direction. "Though I must reiterate how sorry I am to have interrupted your pleasant excursion with my news. It is only…he was with me not two days before his arrest. We discussed his trip and the possibility of recruiting others to join the army with him. I cannot help but feel responsible."

"I can imagine." Bennet gave his head a sad shake. "Is there anything I can do? Having come from Yale, I've some friends with ties to Patriot circles. Perhaps one of them knows someone who could help secure your cousin's release."

An offer probably unnecessary, but so very gallant. Winter looked to Robbie to see how he would parry it.

Her childhood friend's smile looked strained. "I do thank you, Mr.

Lane. I suspect the matter will work itself out, but it is good to know you have such connections if I need them—and that you would be so kind as to call upon them on our behalf."

"Of course I would." Bennet looked sincere as could be, his brows drawn in sympathy. "Charges of espionage cannot be taken too seriously. I am sure we all remember what became of Nathan Hale in seventy-six. I would think the Patriots eager to return the favor and execute a British spy after losing their scout to us."

Robbie went pale, and Winter knew it was not really for fear of his cousin. Washington or Tallmadge would surely intervene before any execution could take place, but the reminder of the price of espionage sent a shiver up her spine, so it would affect Robbie even more. He cleared his throat. "Ah, but Hale was caught in the act. My cousin may have boasted of recruiting, but I daresay they shan't charge him with espionage for such foolishness."

"Let us hope not. I knew Hale from our days at Yale, you know. I was very sorry to hear of his fate in spite of his sad choice in politics."

She could tell Robbie would flee soon. He kept shifting from foot to foot and tugging on his greatcoat. So while he answered Bennet, she turned to where Freeman stood a few strides away and made a series of quick gestures. *Tell Robbie to return later.*

Freeman nodded, obviously not needing to ask why. She had questions that could not possibly be asked in front of Bennet.

A moment later Robbie offered a quick bow and backed up a step. "That is all I wanted. Again, my apologies, and I hope you have a lovely stroll. Miss Reeves." He met her gaze, saying far more with that action than he would with words. "Those prayers of yours are much appreciated."

Freeman walked with him a few steps as he strode away, which she didn't imagine would look too odd. But to ensure Bennet paid it as little heed as possible, she looped her arm through his again and loosed a sigh so blustery it could not be ignored. "I do feel badly for the Townsends."

He patted her hand. "As do I. He is taking it very personally. Should I contact my friends at Yale? I know he refused, but he seems so anxious about it."

Again, his skills of observation could have been a bit more lacking and she wouldn't have complained. "Robbie has always been prone to anxiousness." 'Twas both a convenient explanation and a very inconvenient truth. "He is aware of this tendency and tries to offset it by being otherwise clever and witty, but nerves and black moods have plagued him since childhood. I daresay his words are right, however, though his countenance may disagree. Jamie will surely get out of this scrape, and Robbie will bring his nerves under control again."

He nodded and then his gaze arrowed into her in that way she should have had the good sense not to think she'd missed. Nor should she have found the quirk of his brow so endearing. "And what was that you did?"

She blinked, perhaps exaggerating her confusion but not fabricating it entirely. "What was what?"

"This"—he imitated, poorly, the signs she had made at Freeman.

Fighting a smile, she widened her eyes. "I don't recall doing *that*, Mr. Lane. I would say I must have been swatting at a bee, but I have yet to see any so far this year. Could you demonstrate it again?"

He narrowed his eyes, though his lips curved up. "I did a poor enough job the first time, but you know of what I speak. What was it?"

She saw no reason to lie. Admitting its purpose wouldn't teach him the language. So she smiled. "Signs. My father's mother was deaf, you see, so Father and Freeman developed a system of signs and gestures to communicate with her. I learned them as a child before Grandmother passed on, and the family continued to use them for the joy of it since."

"Fascinating." He led her along the path again, though his eyes remained locked on her face. "I have read of such systems. Did your father base it on the Spaniard's book? Bonet, was it?"

"Well, now. That name does sound familiar, but then he came into possession of a French text when it was published in fifty-five. This one was written by an abbot."

"L'Epee?"

"You know of him?" She was too surprised to feign stupidity.

Bennet chuckled. "Of him, yes, though I never read his work. So what did you say to your servant?"

She glanced at Freeman, who was now following them again. "I asked him to speak a bit more to Robbie. He did seem quite anxious, but I daresay he would not have appreciated me asking him about it in front of you."

"You said all that with a few gestures? A request, a comment about his anxiousness, your reasoning?"

Looking back at him, she saw he had put on what he probably intended to be an imitation of her confused expression. She couldn't help but laugh. "And much more besides."

"Astounding." Mischief entered his gaze. "You should teach this language to me, and then we could communicate covertly."

She grinned in response. "Not only that, but right under the noses of my grandparents, without them ever knowing what we said."

His laugh thawed away the ice inside that Robbie's news had brought with it. "That too. What say you, then? Teach me something."

"Very well. Let me think of something you would often have cause to say." She tapped a finger to her chin and then grinned. "Ah, I have the perfect thing. This is 'interesting.'" She splayed both hands over her chest, right hand above her left, and then moved them out.

He mirrored her. "All right. 'Interesting.'"

"And this…" She put her palms together and then opened them as if they were pages. "This is 'book.'"

Though he scowled, amusement still tilted up his mouth. "And why would that particular phrase have to be said secretly?"

She made sure to add an extra dose of innocence into her smile. "Well, good sir, you will find my grandparents disapprove of many books. No doubt at some point you will want me to know that you like one they do not."

He chuckled, reclaimed her hand, and then tucked it back into the crook of his arm. "And you will find, good lady, that my opinion of a book is the one thing I have no qualms sharing with any and all who care to listen, even if it involves disagreement. I love a good debate on a text."

"I suppose you are right." One shoulder lifted, eyes wide, she said, "Shall I teach you a few greetings and niceties, then, for you to use in the presence of young ladies? You seem to have a few qualms about those."

"Cruel creature." But still he grinned, and he pulled her a bit closer. "'Tis unforgivably rude of you to point out my awkwardness."

She ran her gloved fingers over the texture of his homespun cloak, which he still wore for day-to-day activities, though he donned his new, elegant one for social gatherings. Yet another thing she could never admit was her appreciation for how stubbornly he clung to the simpler ways he had known in Connecticut. 'Twould be unfashionable of her to think so, and therefore out of her supposed character. "Oh, but I find it so interesting. I have heard you say such bafflingly clever things to other gentlemen, yet you can scarcely string two words together in the presence of the fairer sex. Tell me, Mr. Lane, what is it about females that befuddles you?"

That befuddlement showed on his face now. "I simply cannot grasp the workings of the female mind, Miss Reeves."

"Ah." She forced relieved understanding into her expression. "That, then, is why you seem to have no such trouble with me. I always knew not thinking was the answer to life's woes, in spite of what Mr. Gambler may have to say on the matter."

His lips twitched at her name for Descartes, but his eyes went thoughtful. "On the contrary, my dear, I believe I am comfortable with you because you, above any female I have ever met, put me in mind of my scholarly friends."

She halted, stared at him. "What an odd thing to say."

"Nay, 'tis perfectly reasonable. For you are quick tongued and of deep intellect."

"We have been through this." She leaned slightly forward. "My grandparents disapprove of independent thought, and so I have given it up. I know not what you think you see, but surely 'tisn't that."

Bennet lifted a brow. "They obviously approve of flirtation, though. Until today, it seemed the only thing to fall from those lovely lips of yours were ridiculous comments about finding one's match and how well suited you thought yourself for life in England."

Arguments that always left her feeling nauseous. "And what is wrong with such talk?"

"What is wrong with it?" Genuine frustration seeped into his tone, and he tossed his free hand into the air. "It is inane!"

"Mr. Lane." She blinked rapidly, as if injured by such a declaration. "How dare you? I am no lunatic. Perhaps you find flirtatious talk to be insignificant or empty, but it is hardly mad."

Though obviously amused at the play on insanity and inanity, he turned to face her and looked deep into her eyes, far deeper than a jest would allow. "You know what signs I would like you to teach me, Winter? Those that would allow you to share with me your real thoughts."

She could summon only a ghost of a smile. "What thoughts do you possibly think I have that are worth sharing?"

"If I knew the answer to that…" He sighed, faced forward again, and set a course for Hampton Hall.

His hopelessness echoed within her. It had been foolish to resort to the banter they both enjoyed. She ought to have known better than to torment herself, and him, so. She could not give him what he wanted; he could not offer her what she most needed…why waste any more time on each other?

"Bennet…" Yet she couldn't look at him as she said it, and she had to pause to keep undue emotion from clogging her thought. "We are not suited. That is so obvious even I can see it. You would do better… you ought to shift your attentions elsewhere."

When she glanced at him, she saw that he kept his gaze straight forward as he shook his head, jaw clenched. "I am afraid that is not feasible, Winter. You are the only young woman I have ever met to whom I can talk."

"But I cannot talk to *you*." She didn't dare.

His head turned and his gaze burned into her before moving to her cheek. "Has he struck you again?"

"No." But her six months were halfway over, and just yesterday Grandfather had cornered her and reminded her of that. If she were not betrothed by the tenth day in July…part of her thought he hoped she wouldn't be so that he would have an excuse to carry out his threats. She couldn't shake the feeling that the hatred roiling inside him would not be satisfied until she was punished for her mother's perceived sins. Not just out of his house, but *gone*.

As if reading far more than an assurance in that "no," Bennet drew in a long breath. "I will not give up."

But he would, eventually. He was too much the scientist to chase a theory when it gave him no new data to consider. Eventually he would find someone new to hypothesize about, and he would stop frequenting Hampton Hall. Only then would Grandmother give up hope and allow other suitors a chance.

Winter just wasn't sure the stubborn man beside her would give up in time—or if his determination would get her tossed into the bowels of Holy Ground.

Twelve

Ben entered what had once been a prosperous house, and which had since been converted into offices for Colonel Fairchild and those who worked directly under him. A glance at the clock against the wall told him he was a few minutes early, but he saw little point in dawdling at the end of his walk with Winter. The moment they reached Hampton Hall, she reverted to her flirtations and empty glances, so he had hastened away.

Best to move to his next appointment and try not to think of how he wished she would give what she so staunchly refused. A glimpse, just a glimpse of her true mind…but nay. 'Twas always her grandmother's words that spilled from her lips lately. The cleverness disguised as its opposite was far preferable, but even that was naught but a well-decorated mask.

He strode toward the room Fairchild used most often and caught sight of him at his desk. Another man was on the other side of it. Fairchild looked up, smiled, and held up a hand to signal he would be only a minute more. Ben nodded and moved out of the way.

A painting caught his eye, so he positioned himself in front of it. Though after a moment, he gave it no thought. Would Winter persist in her stubbornness indefinitely? Until he gave up?

Yet how could he? Even as she dismissed him, her conflict had shone through. She did not *want* to be what the Hamptons made her, but obviously she did not want to be honest with him, either, or she would let down her walls when they were alone.

The way she had done so briefly on Christmas. Or on the night she had learned of her home's destruction. Those times he had gotten a tantalizing glimpse of the mind beneath the mask.

Where had that Winter gone in the past three months? He had begun to think she had died away entirely. Begun to despair. But then the jesting today...

"I'm telling ye, Fairchild, something must be done about those blazing whaleboaters." The voice from Fairchild's office was unfamiliar and bore the cadence of a lower-bred British man. "They attack rebel and British ships alike, which makes it nigh unto impossible to carry out our missions on the sound."

Fairchild sighed. "Would that I could solve this dilemma, but I am at a loss as to how. You have more experience on the sound than I do—"

"Aye, but little good it does me. I no sooner think I have an enemy in my sights than those pirating scoundrels descend."

The sound of fingers drumming on wood came into the hall. "You have had no luck of late determining who may be ferrying messages to Long Island?"

Ben's ears perked up.

The other man let out an exasperated breath. "For all the good it does me. I be all but certain one Caleb Brewster of Setauket is involved, but the man's a slippery fish. I no sooner get a tip that he is at sail than he has disappeared again or the blasted pirates get in me way."

Brewster...the name struck a chord in Ben's memory. Not an uncommon one in New England, to be sure, but *Caleb* Brewster. He pressed his lips together and called to mind all the many documents and correspondence he had chased down in the past few months.

Caleb Brewster, if he recalled, had gone from whaleboating as a profession to an active member of the Patriot military. One who was suspected of seeking out information up and down the coast—and for what purpose but to pass it to Washington?

The question to Ben's mind was whether the man acted as an independent scout or if he had ties to the secret organization operating in the city. He had yet to find anything supporting a theory of more involvement, but something niggled.

Setauket, that was it. Nothing but a small Long Island town. But he had read its name just yesterday.

A fellow by the name of Tallmadge came from the same town, a high-ranking aide in Washington's army. Ben had yet to discover much about him, but he would seek out any information on the Long Islander he could find.

Not that two men in the Patriot army coming from the same town was any great coincidence.

Who is my neighbour?

Ben scowled at the painting, for lack of being able to scowl at the words that had invaded his mind. What business had these Bible verses to hit him at strange moments? First that bit about watching and listening from Isaiah, in his garden—now this, from the story of the Samaritan? Nonsense, utter nonsense. The whole point of that passage was that a true neighbor was not one who lived near, but one who demonstrated godliness and did right by one. Whereas he was now wondering about *actual* neighbors.

And yet…how many from Setauket had joined the rebel army? Would doing so have created a bond that turned them from neighbors only thanks to location to true friends? Or had they perchance already been such, hence why they made similar decisions? If in fact they were neighbors in a deeper sense of the word, could it prove a link useful to his search? Would Brewster have passed his information to his high-ranking friend rather than directly to Washington, for instance?

He clasped his hands behind his back and directed a mental grunt toward the part of his mind that had come up with the verse. Perhaps it would be helpful after all, but couldn't his brain have found some other clever literature to quote to him? The Bible was a fine manual for instructing man in how to behave properly, and certainly he had the utmost respect for the Creator, but he had little use for those who referred only to it for every detail of their lives.

The Creator, after all, had endowed them with reason so that they might use it. No doubt intending they not then bother *Him* with their problems all the day long.

If any further speech were exchanged between Fairchild and the second man, Ben must have missed it, for a chair scraped across the floor and a soldier hastened out. Fairchild followed soon after, putting his hat upon his head. "Is the weather as fair as it promised to grow this morning?"

Ben smiled. "Quite tolerable. I dropped my cloak at home on my way here. But also brisk enough that we will enjoy a respite with a hot mug of coffee at Rivington's."

"Perfect." Fairchild led the way toward the exit, and a moment later they were in the warm sunshine. "Ah, lovely indeed. You were out already this morning?"

"Yes, I went…" He cleared his throat to cover his hesitation. 'Twould surely be thoughtless to share the whole truth. "For a stroll."

But Fairchild sent him a knowing sideways glance. "With Miss Reeves, I take it? How is she? I have not seen her in more than a week, and then only a glimpse across a ballroom."

Ben frowned. He had obviously not lost interest in her, so… "Why is that?"

A sigh gusted from Fairchild's mouth and joined the refreshing spring breeze. "I was told when I came to visit last week that she was not at home. And her grandfather informed me at the ball that she was not feeling well and ought not be bothered with more dancing, and when I tried to make my way over to her, her grandmother intercepted me."

"Sounds like a blockade."

Fairchild nodded, looking like a dog that had been kicked. "I have been thinking the same."

"But why?"

He turned that mournful expression on Ben. "I daresay it is because I am not you, Mr. Lane."

Ben could only stare at him for several paces. "Ought that not be a mark in your favor?"

Fairchild laughed, though the light left his countenance again a moment later. "Apparently not, my friend. For though—and I mean no offense—I come from a family superior to yours, I cannot boast the same pending fortune. My mother is a daughter of a duke, my father an earl, but I am a third son, and both my older brothers have heirs already. The second will inherit my mother's estates, which leaves me with what I can earn myself. And apparently the Hamptons prefer wealth to pedigree. Again, I mean no insult to your family. They are not lacking in good blood by any means."

Ben grinned to assure him he took no offense. "But we have no duke in our immediate ancestry. You need not apologize, Fairchild. I know I am no aristocrat."

"You are a perfectly likable man, though, and immensely wealthy besides. I recognize that. Still, to be barred from her presence as I have been…"

The poor fellow looked downright haunted about it. "I had no idea they were acting that way. Frankly, I assumed you visited on the days I do not."

"When I can, but they turn me away as often as they let me in."

Ben paused at a street corner for a carriage to rumble by, and then they strode across together. "Knowing how much you care for her, that must be painful. I feel as though I ought to offer to step aside so that they will not hold my family's fortune against you."

Fairchild sent him a crooked smile. "While I appreciate the thought, I know you care for her too. So please, make no such offers on my account."

"Speaking of offers…forgive me if I am prying, but I am surprised you have not made one for her already."

The colonel sidestepped a child sprinting down the street. "I did. I was informed by a sour and dour Mr. Hampton that they were not ready to part with their precious grandchild quite yet. Which I took to mean they would not grant permission to me until they knew whether you intended to propose."

Ben stopped short and then waited for Fairchild to turn around from a step ahead. "When was this?"

Eyes on the ground, he seemed to debate his answer for a moment. "In January."

"What?" Ben could scarcely fathom that. He and Fairchild had met at least once a week for coffee since then, and the man hadn't said a word. "Why did you never mention this?"

"It is hardly something one shares with one's rival suitor, no matter how good a friend he has become. You must grant me my pride."

"Yes, but…" Ben huffed to a halt. "Had I realized—"

"You would have done what? You are trying to make up your own mind, Lane. I ought not to factor into your decision." Looking uncomfortable with the conversation, Fairchild straightened his red jacket and turned.

Ben would have fallen in beside him again, had another man in a red coat not come barreling toward him yelling, "Bennie!"

He nearly groaned. "Archie, don't—"

Too late. His brother attacked him with all the exuberance he would have had they been in their own home. And he had the gall to laugh as he locked an arm around Ben's neck.

For the first time in his life, Ben was tempted to put up a real fight to avoid being "bested" by his little brother. Instead, he put up none at all, but just said calmly—or as calmly as one could manage when stuck under a man's armpit—"All right, Archibald, you have now embarrassed me in front of all the City of New York. If you are quite satisfied…"

Archie laughed again and released him. While bent over, Ben collected his hat from the puddle it had fallen into and shook his head over the dripping stain. When he straightened, he found his brother staring, open mouthed, at Fairchild.

"You must be jesting." Glancing at him, Archie shook his head. "You and Fairchild? Out and about together? What in the world do the two of you have to talk about other than Miss Reeves, and why in the world would you want to talk about her to each other?"

Fairchild glared at Archie with all the superiority his ducal grandfather likely would have used on a wayward tenant. "And a good morning to you too, Major Lane."

"Colonel." Archie's too-polite smile fell away after a mere heartbeat. He turned to Ben again. "It's no wonder you have become duller than ever if you willingly spend your time with this—"

"Do watch your tongue, *Major*," Fairchild said, sounding bored. "In spite of your recent promotion, I still outrank you."

Archie rolled his eyes. "You see? All seriousness, all the time. Perhaps it is no wonder the two of you get along, actually. Neither one of you knows how to be anything but dull."

"Archie." But he had no new admonition, so Ben shook his head and sent a look toward Fairchild that he hoped conveyed his apology.

Archie reverted to his usual grin. "On second thought, it may be quite entertaining to hear the two of you converse. Fairchild with his constant stream of upstanding British this and most excellent British that, and Bennie with his Monsieur le Chemist did such-and-such and have you read what no one ever has."

Ben shut his eyes, though there was no hope his brother would go away until he had been thoroughly embarrassed. "Archie, *really*."

"And then do you both get all dewy eyed over Miss Reeves? That would be most entertaining of all, two sound-minded men gone daft over a brainless—"

"Watch yourself, Major." Fairchild's tone brooked no argument this time.

If only his brother ever noticed such things. But no, he crossed his arms and lifted one finger to wag at the colonel. "You see, that is a fine example. She cannot even remember to call me major instead of lieutenant."

Ben let a laugh slip out before he could stop it. "Actually, Archie, I believe that's intentional on her part."

His brother's arms fell and his face went serious. Or somewhat serious, anyway. "Why would she blunder intentionally?"

"Because…" Unable to think of a gentle way of phrasing it, Ben shrugged. And yes, grinned. It served the pup right. "She does not like you."

Archie looked genuinely shocked. "Nonsense. Everybody likes me."

Fairchild made a show of fussing with the gold braid at his cuff. "Not everyone."

"Well, *you* don't count, Colonel, and neither does that friend of yours who is off besieging Charleston with General Clinton. He only dislikes me because I stole that pretty redhead out from under his nose last year."

Ben had to give Fairchild another measure of credit. The man had the patience of a saint. His face betrayed not the slightest annoyance as he redirected his gaze to Archie. "André is too good a man to base his opinions on personal slights, Major. And though I fail to see why *my* opinion counts for nothing, it is hardly to the point. You surely have business to be about, as do your brother and I."

"Business." Archie lifted a brow, but he stepped away, hands up.

"Coffee, no doubt. Well, have at it, good sirs. I surrender you both to the soporific company of the other."

Ben waited until Archie had jogged across the street before turning to Fairchild. "My apologies for my brother, Colonel. And so you know, your company has yet to put me to sleep."

Fairchild grinned and jerked his head toward Rivington's. "Nor yours, me. And you have no need to feel responsible for your brother. I am only grateful you are not like him."

Nearly verbatim what Winter had said…but he wouldn't mention her again. No need to cause the colonel any more upset on the subject.

Rob paced the confines of the garden path, his stomach so twisted he felt he might double over at any moment. When he passed by the bench, Winter's hand came out, but he ignored it. He refused to look at her. He would see only pity on her face, combined with frustration, and he could not suffer that right now.

"Robbie, please." She kept her voice low, but it was long with pleading. "Please sit. You will gain the attention of the entire household pacing around like this."

"Well, had we been able to meet elsewhere—"

"You came to the front! It would look a bit odd if we disappeared now."

Oh, yes. All his fault. He came to the wrong door, he employed the wrong cousin…had he ever made a sound decision? Perhaps even talking to her was a mistake. Perhaps he ought to close himself into his room and save society from his unforgivable errors.

She drew in a shuddering breath. "Please, sit. Talk to me."

Well, he was here now. He pivoted and all but tossed himself to the wrought iron bench beside her. He still did not dare look at her face. "I have failed, Winnie. Seven-one-one—you remember?"

"Yes, I remember." Her tone was all patience, but he wasn't fooled by it. Of course she would remember their code for General Washington, and she would resent his insinuation that she did not.

Yet another thing he could never get right. "He is furious with me. Furious. The scathing letter I received from him this morning..." He had to stop and shake his head. He clasped his hands between his knees and stared at his white knuckles. "Culper Senior is angry that we were trying to bypass him, and John Bolton—" He paused but stopped himself before asking if she remembered their code name for Benjamin Tallmadge. "He is upset that my actions have made seven-one-one doubt the entire ring. I have gone from their favorite to their bane with a single misstep."

"Robbie." Her voice, soft as a mother's touch, soothed over him. Yet could bring no comfort. Not now. "Unfortunate as this is, it does not negate all the good you have done. Why, I have heard that Congress recalled all the new dollars based on *your* information. They will remember that."

"Will they?" He tried to dredge up a smile, but it wobbled into a grimace. "I have my doubts about that, Winnie. This is too much."

"Nonsense." She scooted a touch closer and leaned in a bit more. "They will forget it with the next bit of useful information we pass along."

He shook his head. "I cannot. I cannot continue."

"Robbie." Now her voice was a low pulse, incredulous and desperate. "Don't say such things. I know you are upset. 'Tis perfectly understandable, but we cannot give up after one setback."

"A 'setback'?" Finally he looked at her, at her perfect, earnest face. How could she not see that it was so much more than that? "Winnie, this could have been my ruin, *our* ruin. Do you not realize that? That we could, even now, be swinging from a tree had things gone differently? If my idiot cousin had not been so deeply immersed in his story, if he had shared the *truth* rather than a lie with a different set of pretty faces...how difficult would it have been to trace him back to me? Hmm?"

Her expression changed—to peaceful. She even smiled. "I thought of that. And yes, it frustrated me and then scared me. But the fact that it did not happen that way is proof that the Lord is with us. He holds us in His palm. When things could have gone in the worst possible way, He instead led your cousin to friends rather than foes. And while the consequences still come with a cost, they are far less steep than they could have been. Perhaps…perhaps it happened to teach us caution. Or to urge us to our knees more faithfully."

He breathed a laugh and stood again. "Or perhaps it was to tell us to get out while we still have our lives." Seeing her distress, the objection ready to spill from her lips, he held up a hand. "At least for a while. I cannot…I cannot, Winnie. Not now. I need to lie low and let things settle. Perhaps, if they decide to trust me again enough to ask direct questions, I shall endeavor to find the answers for them. But to be out seeking intelligence randomly…" He shook his head. "I will not invite calamity. It seems all too willing to visit my door."

She looked at him as though he had stolen the last ray of her hope. "You are making a mistake, Robbie."

"I am not. This is best, for both of us." Forcing down a swallow, he waved a hand at her concerns. "I know you think it your purpose, but it is coloring your decisions too much. You have enough to contemplate with your grandfather's ultimatum. This ought not factor into your decision of a mate. So I will remove it for you, and you can evaluate Fairchild on his merits rather than his loose tongue."

She dropped her gaze to her clasped hands and seemed to be struggling for control. After a moment, all emotion fell away from her countenance. The tension left her shoulders and emptiness reigned.

He nearly broke then, seeing her slip on her mask because of him. But nay, he couldn't be swayed. 'Twas too critical.

She turned a hollow gaze on him. "What if I hear something of the utmost importance?"

He sighed. "Then obviously you ought to get word to me, but we will take no more risks."

A nod, curt and dismissive, was all he received in response. Which was just as well. He backed up a step and tried to dig up a parting smile for her. "I will still stop by to visit. Keep you abreast of news from Oyster Bay."

Unable to suffer seeing her without feeling for another moment, he spun and strode away. He would go home, close himself into his room with a book, and try to beat back the wings of despair.

This time, though, they seemed to smother him.

Winter watched Robbie stride away, his shoulders hunched against the beast of anxiousness. Tears surged to her eyes. She hated seeing him like this, in the claws of his dark mood, and never had she seen it quite so bad, seen him give in to it so fully. Usually he would try to jest it away. He would never indulge it in her company for more than a few moments.

She squeezed her eyes shut. *Father in heaven, pour out Your succor upon him. Help him…help me…please, Lord. I know not what to pray but "please."*

A familiar movement made her open her eyes. Freeman knelt beside her. He also followed Robbie's retreating form with his gaze. "Maybe this is for the best, Winnie. He's right that this business should not influence your decision in a husband."

Shaking her head, Winter let a wisp of a laugh escape. "I don't seem to *have* a decision to make about a husband, Free. And now I have no purpose besides."

His big hand settled on her shoulder, instilling decades of love and encouragement in a seconds-long touch. "Your purpose rests not with this, child, but with the Lord. We shall do what we have always done, and trust in His guidance. If He leads us to information that will not allow for silence…well, we will know then if this is still in His will."

Intellectually, she knew he was right, and so she nodded. But her heart still bled. The tunnel of the future seemed to close in on her again, with no light at its end. Nothing but an ominous threat and choices that would leave her forsaken of what truly mattered.

No parents. No home. No friends.

No hope.

Thirteen

July 10, 1780

Never in her life had Winter dreaded every moment of a day as she did this one. When her father had left, the sorrow had been outweighed by pride and hope. When Mother had died, she had thought, up to the very last minute, that it would not—*could* not—happen. There had been no dread, though devastating grief followed.

But today. Each ticktock felt like a spike through her mind. Each creak of the floorboards sounded like canon fire. Each open door loomed wide and vast as the ocean.

She was out of time. And she dared not hope Grandfather would forget it, not given the dark, menacing satisfaction that had been gleaming in his eyes recently.

"Are you well, Miss Reeves?"

Bennet's voice made her jump, and the overreaction set her nerves that much more on edge. She forced a smile, though she hardly dared to look at him lest she then do something foolish, such as toss herself upon his chest and beg him to marry her. "I am quite fine, Mr. Lane. Just off in my own world today, I suppose."

A world of shadows and devouring darkness. A world of foul stenches and painful moaning. A world of sickness and depravity.

Colonel Fairchild straightened from where he had bent at the waist to smell a yellow rose. He turned a questing gaze her way and sent it over her face. "You do look a trifle peaked. If we are taxing you, my dear, you must let us know."

"Oh, but I am very well, Colonel. And so glad you all could come visit today." She made sure her gaze included Dosia and Lizzie where they sat on the bench, though the girls were far too busy tittering behind their fans and batting their eyes at Major Lane and Mr. Knight to pay any attention.

It at least served as a distraction. Grandfather surely wouldn't toss her to the streets with guests present.

But later…how would she survive in Holy Ground? For surely nothing good could ever exist in that den of iniquity, no matter if the church owned the land. The stories she had heard…nothing but harlot after harlot, in their dank, disease-ridden hovels. If Grandfather took her there—oh, how she prayed he hadn't meant that threat.

Yet she dared not put any hope in that prayer.

The sun beat down with an intensity that made winter seem a decade away, though a refreshing breeze blew through the garden. Winter swished her fan and tried to focus on Bennet and Colonel Fairchild.

The former regarded her as intensely as the sunshine. Her hand betrayed the tremble it caused, so she fanned all the faster and smiled at Fairchild. "Colonel, I have not seen much of you lately. You have been dreadfully busy. I do hope no campaign is underway that will take you from New York."

He smiled in return. "There has indeed been much afoot. I confess part of my time has been spent catching up with my friend Major André since his return to New York last month. But more, I have been assisting General Clinton in quietly mustering the forces."

Though she kept the motion of her fan from so much as hitching, her pulse kicked up. *Life*. She had scarcely felt it in three months. She made sure her smile was only mildly curious, partially bored. As he would expect. "Oh? Has a new shipment of mustard arrived? I do hope you saved some for us, Colonel, and did not give it *all* to your soldiers."

While Bennet chuckled and shook his head, Fairchild gave her a fond smile. "Muster, my dear. We are assembling troops and lining up transport. It seems the French have arrived and intend to join forces with the rebels. They think to surprise us, but the general has known for nearly a month now and has taken every necessary step to turn the surprise around on *them*."

How fortunate that the summer heat disguised the sweat that broke out on her brow. The French, here—and the British had known a month already. Had been making plans and seeing to provisions all this time.

Would Washington be counting on catching them unawares with his newly swollen fleet?

She must get word to Robbie. He said Washington had officially shut down the Culper Ring some two months ago after going to considerable trouble to extract Jamie from prison, but this was surely news enough to justify reopening the lines of communication.

However, she couldn't think quite yet about the information she would convey with the stain the first moment she was alone. First she must respond. She widened her eyes and turned them on Bennet. "The French! Mr. Lane, perhaps that gambler fellow has come. Or the apothecary you so admire. He is also French, is he not?"

Bennet arched a brow and gave her a crooked smile. "Descartes is long since deceased, Miss Reeves." The *as you well know* came through in his gaze. "And Lavoisier is not a chemist in the sense of an apothecary, but rather a nobleman who expounds on the history and philosophy of chemistry."

"I suppose he will be no help at all in developing a hair powder that does not make you sneeze, then." Careful to keep the teasing from her tone, she turned back to the colonel. "We do not like the French, do we?"

Such affection shone in his eyes that new guilt sprang up. He motioned her toward a second bench. "England and France have long been enemies, my dear. They only help the rebels as a slap at us."

"How terribly rude." She sat, positioning her skirts around her. "We must slap back at them, then."

Fairchild sat beside her and smiled. "We will indeed. General

Clinton has an agent in Rhode Island who sent him a map and detailed numbers and positions of the French fleet. We likely know more about them than Washington does."

She hid the swirling of her mind behind a nod and then lapsed into her usual faux boredom as he spoke of his dealings with the general and various aides, and then how glad he had been to welcome his friend home along with Clinton in June.

"And really, 'tis no coincidence that this informant got his news to Clinton when he did. André has been put in charge of intelligence and has come up with a brilliant way of keeping it all organized, as well as getting messages to sources covertly."

Her stomach clenched. It sounded as though this friend of Fairchild's was the British equivalent of Tallmadge, who handled such matters for Washington. Could the name be somehow useful? She would note it too and pass it along to Robbie. Beg him to get a message out somehow.

She glanced at the angle of the sun, trying to gauge how much longer she would be expected to entertain. Another hour, perhaps. Then they would all leave, probably together, and she could slip out to the stable and down to her room. Get a message written and send Freeman with it to Robbie.

Avoid Grandfather that much longer.

For now, she concentrated on looking bored and witless, which became much easier to accomplish after the others joined them a few minutes later. Listening to the endless flirtation and gossip was nearly enough to put her in a coma. But thankfully, 'twasn't long after that the group prepared to depart.

All but Bennet, who stood at her side and waved off his brother, Mr. Knight, Colonel Fairchild, and the ladies with a smile.

Oh, bother. She had forgotten that Grandmother had invited him to stay and dine with them. It may provide her safety from Grandfather, but how, then, would she find the time to write her note? She barely had time to rush up to her room and have her dress changed for the meal, and her maid scurried about too much to grant her any privacy then.

Bennet, looking uncomfortable in a powdered wig, awaited her in the downstairs hall. Her grandmother received them into the drawing room with a smile some may have mistaken for welcoming. "Ah, your friends left just in time, darlings. The meal is ready."

Winter looked around the room and saw no one but the three of them. Her pulse accelerated. "Is Grandfather not joining us?"

"Oh, no. He had already agreed to dine with a friend of his newly arrived in town. We mentioned it at breakfast, Winnie dear. Don't you recall?"

At breakfast she had been in a daze of fright, certain her grandfather would refuse her entry into the room. Or that, at least, his ultimatum would come up during the meal. Strange how his silence had not brought her an ounce of relief.

Her smile wobbled even now. "Of course. How silly of me to forget. Well, then." She tucked her hand into the crook of Bennet's arm and tried not to wonder if it was the last time she would do so. When she was seated across from him, she tried not to dwell on the thought that if he did not toss aside the previous months of near silent attention and propose, she would never eat at this table again.

Tried not to hope when she knew well it would lead to disappointment.

Still, her hand shook as she spooned up her soup. For the first time in a year and a half, she was grateful for her grandmother's constant stream of meaningless gossip, as it kept Bennet's attention away from her. If he looked her way, he would surely see that something was the matter. And what would she tell him if he asked what it was? She could hardly confess the truth.

Oh, why hadn't Robbie tried to put things right with Washington and company months ago? Then the ring never would have been shut down, and she wouldn't have been doomed to day after mindnumbing day of nothingness.

No friends.

No purpose.

No promise.

Stagnant—that was what life had become. The same dinner parties, the same balls, the same silks and laces and curls. The same man sitting in the same place by her side, refusing to leave but refusing to take another step forward until she gave what she would not.

Could not.

"Winifred."

Winter started at the low, furious command, and dropped her fork with a clatter. Which made her frown. When had she exchanged spoon for fork? How had they come to have the sweet before them already?

If Grandmother's scowl were any indication, her inattentiveness had not gone unnoticed. Winter cleared her throat. "I am sorry, Grandmother. Did you say something?"

"No. But Mr. Lane did." How did she convey so much censure in such a simple sentence?

"Oh." Winter looked to Bennet, who studied her with eyes narrowed in concern. "What did you ask, sir?"

He shook his head. "It hardly matters. Are you quite sure you are not unwell, Miss Reeves?"

"I…" Was she unwell? She certainly felt it. Perhaps nothing was the matter with her body, but oh, how her spirit ached. "I've a touch of the headache, is all."

Grandmother put down her fork. A motion that had no sound yet rang with finality. "Then you ought to take a few minutes of quiet in the drawing room before we join you. Come, dear. I will make sure you are comfortable. Do excuse me a moment, Mr. Lane."

Feeling as though the drawing room housed a gallows, Winter managed a tight smile for Bennet and followed her matriarch out of the dining room, down the hall, and into the receiving chamber.

Grandmother pulled the door closed behind them and then spun on her. "What are you thinking, you stupid little chit? You know well your grandfather intends to forbid you from our home after today. Will you waste your final hours with this nonsense?"

"I…" She could put her tongue on no words. The trembling possessed her so fiercely she would have crumpled to the ground had Grandmother not dug her talons into her arm and forced her upright.

"You listen to me." Giving her a shake, Grandmother leaned in close. "I will *not* be disgraced again. Mr. Lane is obviously interested in you, otherwise he would not still be paying you court after seven months. Any girl with half a brain would have convinced him to propose by now. But you! You have wasted month after month and have nothing to show for it."

"It isn't my fault." Her voice came out wispy, far from certain. "I warned you he was not the type to be won by flirtation, but you insisted I—"

The harsh sting of Grandmother's hand striking her cheek silenced her. "Enough. You can blame this failure on no one but yourself. Had you fully listened to me, you would be Mrs. Lane by now, likely carrying his heir and perhaps even on your way to England."

Her nostrils flared, her chest heaved, but Winter bit her tongue. There was no use arguing. Grandmother's advised method for achieving a proposal was simply unthinkable. She would not throw herself at him, would not grant him any liberties.

Grandmother must have read her mind. "You think your virtue will do you any good if you have not secured a promise from Mr. Lane by the time Hampton returns? I have stayed his hand this long, but I will not be able to any longer. Do whatever you must, Winifred, but get it done."

After tossing her away like a tattered rag, Grandmother pulled open the door and stormed out. Winter sank to the nearest surface at hand, the arm of the sofa. How had it come to this? What more could she possibly lose?

Words from the prayers copied in her father's hand filtered into her mind. *I am nothing but that Thou makest me. I have nothing but that I receive from Thee. I can be nothing but that grace adorns me.*

She needed His grace. Needed His strength, for she had none left.

She must stir herself. Escape before Grandmother could send Bennet in. Go to her underground sanctuary, where she could pray and then send one last message to Robbie. And if after that she was consigned to the fearsome fate her grandparents had in store for her…well, the Lord would either deliver her or sustain her.

Course plotted, she stood and raced for the door—where she collided with Bennet's solid chest.

He greeted her squeal of surprise with a chuckle and steadied her with gentle hands upon her arms. "Going somewhere?"

"Apparently not." She turned her face up to see his smile. Perhaps it would fortify her.

Instead, it faded as he studied her, and he lifted his fingers to turn her head. To present a full view of the cheek Grandmother had slapped.

"Winter." He filled her name with boundless concern. "Your grand-mother is striking you now?"

Why was he always the one to discover such things? She tried for a smile, though she managed only half of one. "I am apparently a very frustrating girl."

He matched her crooked grin. "Sometimes, yes. But that is hardly cause for such treatment." Sobriety took him over once again. "You said you would not suffer another instance of it."

"I have not." Though it was hardly relevant at this point.

"Then why now? What is wrong today? It is as though…" He shook his head as he caressed her stinging cheek. "I have watched you fade away this spring, but I have never seen you like this, starting at shadows. You seem to be in terror, but I cannot think why. Please, Winter. Tell me what troubles you."

What would he do if she obeyed? If she told him that her only hope of a future rested in his hand, that if he didn't offer it to her, she would be on the streets by morning?

As if she really had to wonder. He had too noble a soul to deny her help when it was within his power, but she would not force him to action with such a terrible truth. She would not trick him into it. She would not weigh him down with a burden like that.

His thumb stroked over her cheek, much as it had done six long months ago, the night she learned her home was destroyed. Now, like then, the tenderness broke something inside her. Her breath came out in a shudder.

"What wears you down so?" He pulled her a little closer, only to then ease away again with a frown. "Is it Fairchild? I ought to have asked you before. He intimated that they refused him because of me. If you are in love with him, I will step aside. You only have to say the word—"

"'Tisn't that." She covered his fingers with hers before he could pull them away, and then she dropped her hand. What was she thinking? Such behavior made her every inch the creature her grandmother wanted her to be.

He tipped up her chin, forcing her to meet the blue depths of his gaze. "What is it then? Winter, I daresay it is no secret by now that I care for you. You can trust me. Please, tell me what burdens you."

A tickle of happiness danced through her at his admission. Of course she knew he must care, but he had never said it. Hadn't shown it lately but through his continued presence, which could as easily have been habit. But it wasn't enough. And it didn't change the reality that she could not, in fact, trust him.

"There is nothing to tell." Still, she could not bring herself to pull away.

"Mmm, yes. Much like you can't remember Descartes' name and think 'muster' is something one applies to meat. You know well you don't fool me." His smile shed a hint of light on the darkness crowding in. "I suspect you may even care about me as well, though I cannot be entirely certain."

"I...yes. I do." That much she could grant him before she disappeared from his life.

And she was glad she had when she saw the joy spring up in his eyes and spill onto his lips in a pleased, teasing smile. "There now. Was that so hard?"

A chuckle surprised its way out. "You've no idea."

"An unfortunate truth." When his smile faded, he looked no less happy, though. He urged her head toward his until their lips touched, brushed.

A well of longing overflowed. For the first time in so long, homecoming swept through her and made her want to stay right there, in his arms, forever. Was it an illusion? Possibly—for surely one soft kiss could not set the world to rights. But it certainly proved he had burrowed deeper into her heart than she wanted to admit.

Bennet pulled her closer, but she turned her face away before he could deepen the kiss and her longing with it. His warm chuckle sounded directly in her ear and sent a shiver up her spine. "What is it? Do you fear your grandmother would disapprove?"

How could she want to smile and cry at the same time? Perhaps she ought to be used to such conflicting feelings when in Bennet Lane's company. She settled for shaking her head and then resting it against his shoulder. An indulgence she intended to hold close to her memory through the dark days ahead. "The opposite. She would approve far too much."

He rubbed a comforting circle over her back. "You know, my dear,

I am not opposed to you having your rebellions against them, but it seems a bit misplaced when you are thereby going against your own desires as well."

"That is not why I…" Winter sighed and closed her eyes. "Oh, Bennet. She would have me use such things to manipulate you into marriage."

"Shocking." Amusement rang through his tone. Then he urged her away enough to tilt her face up again and locked his gaze to hers. "Winter, we both know I will not be manipulated, but I think we also both know things could progress that direction if you let them. I must know your mind before anything can change between us, though. And I confess, I have oft wondered over these past weeks if your refusal to share any honest thought with me is your way of telling me you have no interest in…more."

If only it were so simple. If only she could decide to be open, and then be so without any risk but to her own heart. Impossible. Not with all the secrets she must keep to stay out of harm's way. Even with the closing of the ring having effectively taken that out of her reasoning… "It is more complicated than that, and…and too late, anyway."

"Never." He said it with calm assurance and punctuated it with another kiss so featherlight she couldn't say why it turned her limbs to mush. Then he pulled away and smiled down at her. "It is never too late, Winter. I may be lacking charms aplenty, but patience I have in abundance."

A glimmer of hope shone through the shadows. So faint she could scarcely identify it, but too beautiful to be denied. She smiled. "Your so-called lack of charm is my favorite thing about you."

"Now I will have to kiss you again. Although…" Mischief sparked in his eyes. "Three times would make it a habit. And if you will oblige me by naming the philosopher who said as much, I will make sure your grandmother sees. That would pacify her a bit, wouldn't it?"

She chuckled, though for once she didn't know what he referenced. "That one couldn't be simpler—*you* said it."

He narrowed his eyes and pursed his lips. "Aristotle. Don't tell me you are unfamiliar with the Greeks."

Well, that explained it. She never much cared for Aristotle. "I have never met a one, no."

He shook his head with a grin but then sighed. "I feel as though I have made this entreaty a thousand times, but I must ask you once more. Please, Winter, speak frankly with me. At least consider it. I cannot know what holds you back, but if it is not lack of affection… well, I have never met another young lady who likes my awkwardness. And it would seem the other young gentlemen fail to see the wit you adeptly hide. We could suit so well. I would like nothing more than to learn if we do."

Gazing into his eyes, she couldn't convince herself he was wrong. Maybe their secrets weren't worth risking their futures for, like Robbie said. Maybe she could be content in England if she were at Bennet's side. Maybe raising a family with him would be purpose enough, and she would cease to miss the intrigue and the weight of responsibility it brought with it.

Maybe a chance with him was worth fighting for.

"You are thinking about it." The corners of his mouth tugged upward, though he seemed to fight the smile into submission.

She let out a slow, long breath. "I must also pray about it."

He lifted a brow. "If that is such an important step, why have you not done so over the last seven months?"

She wasn't about to confess her prayers about him had all been focused, instead, on keeping her distance. "And why do you say that as if you doubt its importance?"

He held up his hands in surrender. "I certainly did not mean it to sound that way. A life of prayerful contemplation is to be desired."

She could not resist a playful grin. "I would prefer a life of contemplative prayer."

"And one of verbal sparring is an excellent way to go, as well." He chuckled and then cradled her face in his hands. "Think, pray, whatever suits you. I will leave you to it. But I will return tomorrow, Winter. Hopefully to *talk*. Truly talk."

He leaned over and pressed a kiss to her forehead. Again, an action he had done before—but this time he didn't follow it with an absurd order to marry Fairchild. "Good night."

"Good night." She made sure her smile was the last thing he saw before he went out the door. But then she moved to the window, arms folded over her middle.

Eighteen months she had lived by someone else's rules, going against all she believed, all she knew in her heart was right. So long. So long to be who she was not. Was it any wonder she hadn't been able to see, until now, when it was time to take a stand?

But she could ignore it no longer. She was done with being the whipping boy, taking the punishment her grandparents intended for her mother. Done with doing what she was told when it led nowhere but to pain and emptiness.

Grandmother wanted her to marry Bennet Lane? Then she would inform the mighty Phillippa Hampton that she would go about it her own way, *his* way, and then they would see if it was what they wanted.

Grandfather wanted her out of his house? Then if he would not extend his hospitality while she got to know Bennet, she would stay with the Parkses or—which would annoy him far more—the Townsends on Long Island. She had a feeling Bennet wouldn't mind escaping from the city for a while for a less-public courtship.

If Washington had dismissed the Culpers, then she could accomplish no more good here anyway. Better to do right by Fairchild and let him know her heart inclined elsewhere rather than keep him dangling solely for information.

None of them, be they family or stranger, friend or enemy, ought to determine her worth. None of them ought to decide what she could contribute. She would leave that to the Lord. Spine straight, she made ready to turn and seek out Grandmother.

An arm clamped around her neck, cutting off her air. The scent of Grandfather's pipe tobacco filled her nose a second before he appeared in front of her. She clawed at the arm over her throat, noting the coarse fabric the servants wore.

Grandfather smirked. "You didn't think I had forgotten our agreement, did you?"

A crack, and then a slicing pain in her head. The world faded to gray.

Fourteen

Rob flipped a page in his book and took a sip from his cup of tea. The weather was too hot for the stuff, but he needed the ritual. He had to shake this mood soon. He could scarcely tolerate himself, so he could only imagine how his friends felt.

But a new book would help. 'Twould give him something to think about, to talk about. Allow him to focus on the intellectual rather than whatever part of him this anxiousness came from. He never could pinpoint it. Perhaps that was the problem. Perhaps if he better understood the tendency, he could better control it. Perhaps—

Bang, bang, bang.

For a moment Rob assumed the knocking was on his neighbor's door. Who, after all, would come here? But another *bang* convinced him otherwise. He put a marker in his book and moved over to the door, unlocked it, and pulled the latch.

And blinked. "Roe."

Austin Roe pushed past him with a nod of greeting. Which was odd indeed. The Culper courier hadn't been to the city in months. Or if he had, he hadn't bothered visiting Rob.

Not that he could be depended upon to show up on time even when he was scheduled to come.

"Townsend, we need you."

Those four words were enough to set his heart to pounding, though Rob had no intention of letting it show. He motioned toward his cup. "I was enjoying a nice pot of Chinese tea. Would you like some?"

Roe looked fit to throw something. "Do you think I came all the way across the sound for a cup of *tea*? I was just to see Woodhull—"

Rob cleared his throat. "Culper Senior, if you please."

"Yes. Sorry. Culper Senior is abed, ill. So I pressed on to seek out you. Wa—seven-one-one is activating the ring again. I was sent to see if you would be interested in employment."

"Employment." Rob chuckled, mostly to keep from shouting out agreement here and now. "Seven-one-one has shown little enough regard for us in the past, treating us as if we contributed nothing of worth. Culper Senior was quite hurt by his insinuation that we acted only in the interest of payment."

Roe helped himself to a seat. "I have already addressed that with him. All is forgiven, but the point remains that he is not well enough to provide the information we need, not as fast as we must have it. It seems another fleet of French has arrived."

"Ah." Though he had been set to pour a second cup in spite of the protest, Rob halted with his hand halfway to the pot. "Well, that makes sense, then."

"What? What makes sense? Do the British know this already?" His expression earnest, Roe leaned forward. The man did such an excellent job looking like a farmer, Rob had to wonder how he would appear in his military garb.

"I think they may. It would explain some things I have noticed. Nothing overt, but there has been a steady building…but I will have to check with a few sources to be sure." Winter—he needed to talk to Winter. Fairchild would know, and what Fairchild knew Winter could discover easily. "You must give me time."

Roe surged to his feet. "There *is* no time! Even now we are sending scouts along Long Island to try to determine the numbers and position of the French fleet, but any strategy made to include Rochambeau depends on if the British are already aware of his presence."

Rob folded his arms over his chest. "Perhaps the general should have thought of such possibilities before cutting us off." It was hardly relevant that Rob hadn't intended to send information anyway until the disaster involving his cousin had blown over. While an unfortunate situation, he still didn't think he had deserved so scathing a dismissal as Washington had sent two months ago.

"Townsend." Roe drew it out into four syllables, each one a plea. "Come, man, be reasonable. If you were about this business for the right reasons—as you always insisted, and which we always believed—then you cannot dismiss them now. Your country needs your help. Can you not forgive the rash words of an overwrought man?"

"Of course I can forgive him. But going about this, counting ships and men and provisions with Redcoats looking over one's shoulder all the while—"

"If you ask for more compensation, you will throw your motives into suspicion."

Rob unleashed a breath of exasperation. "We have never asked for more than the expenses we accrue—and seven-one-one is always in arrears to us. That is obviously not my motive. I merely meant to point out this is a very taxing employment, and respect is paramount."

"You have it. You have *his*. He asked specifically for you to be brought back into communication. Can we depend upon you?" Roe's face was so impassioned, for a moment Rob feared the man might make some demonstration, like clasping hands to both his shoulders.

Thankfully, he didn't. Which allowed Rob to maintain an unaffected demeanor, to smile peacefully. To pretend General Washington's respect didn't mean the world. "Of course. Give me a day to get all my information together and written out."

Roe surged forward and gave him a friendly smack on the arm. "Welcome back, Junior. I will return tomorrow for the letter."

Rob only nodded until the courier was out the door. Then he rubbed a hand over his face. Back in the business, back in the game. Back in the fire.

What were the chances that Winter could get him what he needed by tomorrow?

The darkness throbbed, pulsed. And smelled. Rotting food, human waste, perspiration, and a few things Winter could not—and did not particularly want to—name. The pain was fierce and scattered. Her head felt as though someone drove a spike through it with every beat of her heart, but after a few seconds of that, she became aware of other, smaller pains. Her ankle, her leg. And something digging into her back. A groan slipped out.

"Shhh, there now." The voice was young, nearly silent. Nothing but a murmur brushing over her.

In its wake Winter became aware of other sounds. Ribald laughter, a few bawdy songs. Arguing. Bartering? And noises that, much like the smells, she had no intention of identifying.

Lord help her—he had done it. She was in Holy Ground.

Maybe she should sink back into the darkness to hold it all at bay a few minutes more. Perhaps it was a nightmare holding her in its talons, and if she ignored it, it would fade.

A cool touch on her damp brow brought her eyes open. She expected to have to blink at an onslaught of light, but no. Not here. Barely enough came in from what she assumed were lanterns outside and one lone candle within for her to make out the outline of a girl bending over her.

Strange, though. The girl's smile she saw easily enough. "You are awake. You must be in terrible pain. I managed to staunch the bleeding of that wound on your head, miss, but I had no clean cloth to bandage it with."

Winter pushed herself onto her elbows. Her head responded with a stab of agony so fierce her vision blurred, and she nearly fell back again. Small arms caught her and helped her lean against a stack of pillows. Once settled, she blinked her eyes clear again. "Thank you. Where…?" No, that was a silly question. She knew where she was, more or less. "Who are you?"

The girl smiled again. She couldn't be more than fourteen, surely. What was she doing in this place?

As if oblivious to her surroundings, the girl tucked a strand of straggly hair, its color indeterminate in the low light, behind her ear and sat back on her heels. "I'm Viney. When I saw that man dump you in the alley, I brought you here quick as I could manage, before anyone else could see. 'Tis obvious you don't belong here, but there are others aplenty who would choose to ignore that."

A shudder coursed up her spine. "I am in your debt."

"Nonsense." Viney reached to a small, tottering table against the canvas of the wall and picked up a cup. "Here. A little watered wine."

She may have refused it had Viney left her with a choice, but the girl held the cup to her lips for her. Winter swallowed to keep it from spilling. "Thank you."

"I've a little bread if you are hungry."

"No, I...I ate not long ago." Hopefully her stomach would make no complaint to prove she had ignored her dinner more than eating it, but she had no intention of taking food from this girl's mouth. "My name is Winter. Winter Reeves."

Viney nodded and studied her for a long moment. "I have never before felt the need to ask this question when a new woman arrives, but why are you here? A fine lady such as yourself."

Winter's fingers balled in the silk of her skirt. She was almost surprised Grandfather hadn't made her change into her homespun before he brought her here. He must have valued being rid of her quickly above the cost of the dress. "I am not so fine a lady, Viney. Just a farm girl who has been dressed up."

A look of concern flashed over the girl's face. "You were that man's mistress?"

"No! No." She raised a hand to her pounding head. "His granddaughter, much to his dismay."

"Family has treated you so?" Viney set the cup back down, a frown on her dirty brow. "How very sad. It is loss of family that delivers most of us to this place. I lost my mother in the Great Fire and had nowhere else to go."

Winter couldn't battle back the horror. "So you came here four years ago? You couldn't have been more than ten."

Viney offered a crooked smile. "Fourteen. I am eighteen now."

"My age." She seemed so young, while Winter felt ancient. Should it not have been the other way around?

"Really?" Delight lit Viney's countenance. "I wouldn't have thought we had even that much in common."

A particularly loud shout came through the canvas walls, one delivered with slurring tongue and including phrases Winter had never heard before.

Viney winced and turned to tug the makeshift door closed a bit more. "Sorry about that, Miss Winter. I wish I had real walls, a real door to keep it all away from you."

"Walls and doors don't change anything."

The girl greeted that cynicism with a cheerful grin. "True enough. Only we can do that, with the good Lord's help."

Faith rang in that pronouncement, belief coloring every word. And as she spoke, Viney looked even younger.

No, not younger. Indeed, Winter now detected lines and creases on her face that one expected of a harsh life. 'Twasn't youth she saw in her after all. It was innocence.

Innocence—the very thing Winter had made a mask of, had falsified for her own protection. How did she come to find a genuine form of it in this, of all places?

Viney scooted closer and leaned in to examine Winter's head. "I cleaned it best I could while you were unconscious, miss, with wine and water, but you would do well to get yourself to a physician so it might be closed up properly. And I cannot shake the feeling that you must leave the minute you are able. Your place is not here."

Conviction rose, overtop the pain, leaving Winter no choice but to nod in agreement. "Yes, I must." Had she not determined in the drawing room that she would not accept this fate? That had not changed. And yet… "What of you, Viney?"

"Me?" She looked surprised by the question. Then she smiled, sure and bright. "No need to be concerned for me, miss. I've only a few months left before the consumption takes me home, I suspect. I shall do whatever good I can here. Care for the other girls."

"But…" Winter would have shaken her head, had the continued thumping not warned her against it. "How can you survive in this place?"

"Let us see if you can stand, shall we?" Viney scooted to her side and supported her with an arm around her waist. She did indeed feel frail and small. "They are only circumstances. The men out there may define me by them, but thank the Lord, He does not. Are you ready?"

She wasn't sure. The pain still throbbed, her heart as well as her head. And mad as it seemed, she hesitated to leave this dark, noisome hovel with its soft, invisible light. But urgency nipped at her, a still, small voice saying she must hurry. She must go back to Hampton Hall.

No. First she must go to Robbie and give him the information about the French. Beg him to send it to Washington. *Then* she must return to her grandparents' home and lay out a few facts for them. That she was not a rag doll to be tossed about on their whim. And that she was perfectly capable of living her life without their interference. If they wanted her gone, so be it. But it was not their right to determine where she would go.

God of my end, strengthen my spine and fortify my spirit. I feel You pulling me up from the mire, out of the pit I'd let them pull me into. I want to do Your will; I want to go where You lead. But I cannot rise on my own. I can be nothing but that Thou makest me.

Her head steadied. The pain eased from the forefront of her mind, though it didn't really decrease. Still, she could nod without agony. "I am ready."

Viney moved to a crouch and helped her get to her knees and then to her feet. "Slowly, now, miss."

After a gradual straightening Winter stood upright and found she stood several inches taller than Viney. "How did you manage to get me in here?"

Viney chuckled. "I wondered that myself, once I had you lying down. I suspect a few angels lent me their strength. Though you are a bit worse for the wear." She frowned and swiped at a streak of something dark on Winter's skirt.

"It hardly matters, when one considers how blessed I am that you found me first."

But the girl still frowned. "I had to rinse all the lovely powder from your hair and take out the style to get at your wound."

"Good. I detest the stuff." And if this night had proven anything, it was that such vanities were indeed like the wind.

An idea struck, and she reached up to unfasten the pearl necklace from her throat. Then she took Viney's hand and lowered the strand into it.

Viney's eyes went wide. She shook her head. "No, miss, I cannot. 'Tis far too dear for me."

"I want you to have it. You can untie the strand and sell each pearl as you have need. And 'tis nothing special to me. My grandparents bought it for me solely to create an appearance for which I don't care. There was no affection behind it."

Trembling fingers closed over the gift, and Viney blinked back tears. "I thank you, miss. My pride wants me to refuse it, but I cannot. I think this may be the Lord's way of providing the protection for which I have been praying. If I am careful, it can keep me until the end, and I will not have to..."

Winter smiled and patted the girl's hands. "Then let us thank the Lord I was brought here tonight. For it resulted in two of His daughters being blessed with the opportunity to help one another, and make a friend besides."

Viney nodded, slipped the necklace into a pocket, swiped a tear from her cheek, and held out her hands. "We must pray before you go."

Winter clasped her hands and closed her eyes.

"Father in heaven," Viney whispered, "we thank Thee for leading us in this unlikely situation. For bringing me outside at that very moment so I might see Winter be tossed from the carriage, and for her faithfulness in generosity. We thank Thee for seeing beneath our surfaces and to our hearts. And now we ask Thee, Lord my God, to spread over us Your wings of protection, this night and in the trials to come. Guide our every step and direct our every way. Get Winter safe to wherever Thou would have her go. Sustain my spirit as my body fails. Let this night be one we remember for the surprising blessing rather than the pain that could so easily overwhelm. For Thou art our shield and buckler, our truth and light. We praise Thee for all Thy ways, and ask these things in the name of Thy holy Son. Amen."

"Amen." As Winter opened her eyes, determination flowed through her. Her grandparents may be done with her, Washington may not think he needed them anymore, but her purpose was not complete. "I will pray for you every day, Viney."

"And I you. Let me..." Viney pulled the canvas back a bit and peered outside. "We are on the outskirts of Holy Ground here. Barclay Street is directly across from us. Granted, this part of it is hardly reputable, but it is best you get out of here quick as you can. Do you have somewhere to go?"

"I do." She knew not how to get there, but that small detail seemed insignificant given the strong feeling that she must make all haste. "I am ready."

"One moment…there." Viney held back the canvas flap and motioned to her right. "That way, hurry. Go with God."

"Thank you." Winter ducked through the opening and stepped out into a town of similar tents and lean-tos, a more permanent looking building here and there. Row after row, far as she could see, all covered with shadows that clung in spite of the lanterns that made a path through the village of harlots.

Women stood outside many of the hovels, some dressed in filthy rags, others in clinging silks that they had arranged in ways the seamstresses had surely never intended. Calling, all of them, to the men who ambled by.

Most of the men wore the red coats of the army, though a few she spotted were in common dress. And they laughed together, joked with each other and the females, as if this were a fair instead of a finger of hell itself.

Go.

She gripped her skirt and took off at a run across the empty street. Though her ankle protested and her head felt trapped in a vise, she could not slow down. She made it across the street and tried to recall the sketched map she had seen of the city, to determine where she likely was and where she must go now.

"Miss Reeves?" The voice was familiar and incredulous.

She turned around to find Major Lane standing in the middle of the road with a slack jaw. Her stomach clenched, but she ignored it and put on a small smile. "Oh, good. I seem to be lost, Lieutenant."

He only stared at her for a long moment, and then he shook himself and strode to her. "What the devil are you doing here?"

The devil was surely involved, but the Lord had outwitted him, as usual. So she smiled again. "Did I not just say I was lost?"

"But…" He shook his head and looked her up and down. Perhaps he saw the filth upon her dress, the now-bare neck that usually had some bauble or another fastened around it. And, of course, her hair, hanging free and dark down her back. "But how did you get to be lost? And as far from your home as you could possibly get within the city?"

Eyes wide, she shrugged. And touched a hand to the side of her head. "I have an injury. Perhaps I wandered and was unaware of it."

Bennet's brother didn't seem to find that idea plausible. Funny how his eyes, which she knew well were the same shade of blue as Bennet's, conveyed none of the same warmth. "You would have had to wander for hours. And I find it hard to believe anyone allowed that to happen."

Again, she shrugged. "'Tis a mystery, to be sure. Now, am I going to have to wander for hours in the direction of home, or are you going to be a gentleman and offer to drive me?"

He stared at her and crossed his arms over his chest. For a moment she feared he might make some lewd comment, but then he shook his head. "Does my brother know you are here?"

Of all the ridiculous... "How could he, when *I* didn't know? Though while we are asking questions, does your brother know *you* are here?"

A light of amusement entered his gaze. "I daresay he wouldn't be surprised, if none too pleased. Though I fail to see why anyone should judge me for it. Even the most sanctimonious of men end up here at some point or another, it seems."

As if her stomach needed to churn any more. "If you don't intend to help me—"

"Oh, calm yourself. My driver is waiting around the corner."

He offered his arm, but she shied away from tucking her hand into its crook. "Lead the way, Lieutenant."

"Touchy, are you not?"

She sent him a hard glare. "Oh, I am sorry. I cannot think *why* I would be so."

"Hmm." He started toward the corner, his gaze on her with every step. "Blast it, I do think Benny was right all along. You are not as stupid as you make yourself seem."

"Such flattery warms me to the core."

He grunted and motioned toward a small carriage parked before an empty lot. "I think I prefer you brainless."

"Typical of you." She paused before the familiar conveyance. "You rode in your mother's carriage in pursuit of your unholy entertainment. She must be so proud."

Major Lane rolled his eyes as his footman opened the carriage door.

"Head injuries do not agree with you, Miss Reeves. They make you terribly cross. Try to avoid them in the future, will you? At least when in my company?"

"I shall endeavor to oblige." She climbed in with the servant's assistance and settled on the seat. Really, she was grateful Mrs. Lane's vehicle was here—in fine weather like this, the major could as easily have ridden his mount or even walked, which would not have been much help to her at all. The Lord must have whispered in his ear, though she suspected Major Lane may disagree.

"And now you are grinning." The major took the seat across from her. "You are a bizarre creature."

He certainly stared at her as if she were, his gaze lingering on her hair. With a huff, she tore the ripped lace from the bottom of her sleeve and used it to secure the locks at the nape of her neck.

He sighed. "To Hampton Hall, then."

"Nay." Satisfied her hair was under control as much as possible for now, she lowered her hands again. "With all due gratitude and respect, Lieutenant, I do not intend to roll up to my grandparents' house with *any* man after nightfall. I'm sorry to deprive you of the laud of heroics, but I would prefer it if you would drop me a few streets away." Namely, a bit closer to Robbie's.

His brows arched upward. "I must object, Miss Reeves. 'Tisn't safe for a young lady such as yourself to be walking the city streets in the dark."

Not all of Grandmother's lessons were without their place. Now, for instance, she appreciated being able to project regal command with a single glance. "I will either get out at Queen Street or I will walk all the way from here, but I will *not* arrive at Hampton Hall with you."

For a long moment he stared, as if unable to grasp what she said. Then at last he shook his head, muttered a curse, and leaned his head out the window. "Queen Street, Johnny." When he sat back again, amusement had crept back into his face. "Does my brother realize what a stubborn female he is pursuing?"

A small smile pulled at her lips. "Oh, I daresay he does, Lieutenant. I daresay he does."

Fifteen

Winter waited until the Lane carriage had turned the corner before she made a dash for the side street that would deliver her to Robbie's door. She had never had cause to visit him at home before, but she had made sure she knew where said home was in case a time arose when she needed to get a message to him and Freeman could not assist her.

A time such as now.

"Winnie?"

She nearly shrieked at hearing her name when she was still a good minute from Robbie's, but after slapping a hand over her racing heart, she spun to face her faithful servant. "Freeman! What are you doing here? I was just thinking of how you were not around to help me."

He emerged from the shadows that had concealed him and folded her into a tight embrace. "I saw him cart you off, but he had me locked in the storeroom of the stable. Took a while to get out, and I thought I would see if Mr. Townsend would help me look for you." He drew back enough to put a hand to each cheek and tilted her head this way and that, examining and tsking at what he saw. His hands shook. "He did this to you?"

"I…cannot say. He had someone strike me with something, I think, but I am not certain the main injury is from that. It could have been from when he tossed me from the carriage to the street."

Even through the depths of night, the rage in his eyes burned hot and clear. "I could—"

"I know." She patted his forearms and pulled away from him. "But the Lord had me in His hand. I will tell you all about it as we walk home, but first I must speak with Robbie."

"Come, then. I would like to see you in the light, anyway."

She offered up a prayer of thanks as they walked, feeling completely safe for the first time all day. Freeman was by her side, the Lord's wing was above them, decisions had been made. When she knocked on the door, 'twas with undeniable peace.

Robbie pulled the door open so quickly she wondered if he had been standing directly before it, though the surprise in his eyes told her he hadn't spotted them as they walked up. "Winnie, Freeman. The Lord must have heard my prayers. I was about to sneak onto the Hampton grounds and rouse you, Free."

Excitement brimmed in his voice. Winter hadn't seen him so happy in months, which, strangely, nipped at her peace. To be sure, she had prayed for his black mood to end. But leaping straight from it to this...

Though when she stepped inside, his joy dissolved into an interjection she had never heard fall from his lips before. He took her gently by the chin to angle her head toward the light. "What happened to you?"

"Is it that bad?" Shying away before he could probe the wound, she moved past him in favor of the mirror she spotted on the opposite wall. When she tilted her face down to see the place from which the pain radiated, she found an unmistakable gash. Though it surely would not be so obvious had Viney not parted her hair there to clean it.

"What happened?" Robbie demanded again from behind her.

"A bit of an altercation with my grandfather, but that is not why I have come." She untied the lace at the nape of her neck and reparted her hair to hide the injury—she had to do so very carefully, as it screamed at her with the shift—and set about braiding her waist-length locks. "I learned something from Fairchild today that it is imperative we pass along. I know you have—"

"Is it about the French?" He stepped in front of her, eyes gleaming again. "Austin Roe stopped by to enlist my—our—help again on behalf of seven-one-one. Specifically as concerning the arrival of the French. I suspect the British forces are aware of them and was hoping you could get some information on specifics."

She paused, hands still up at her shoulder. "We…he…the Culper Ring is active again?"

"Yes, the general expects we will be most useful once more." He grinned, though it quickly faded. "I know you have still been taking note of anything of interest. I am preparing a packet for Roe to take tomorrow, so anything you have of import I will include, but especially about the French."

Winter went back to braiding as she told him what she had learned from Fairchild that afternoon. Then, lace tied at the end of her braid, she asked the question that made her head thump anew. "So this is not a one-time request for information? He expects us to report regularly once more?"

"Indeed. As you wanted us to continue doing all along."

Yes…until a few hours ago. When she had finally resigned herself to a life free of secrets, when she had finally decided she would be open and honest with Bennet. When she had finally resolved to take a stand before her grandparents.

What was she to do now?

Robbie went still. "This is what you want, is it not? You are still willing to cooperate? If you are unable, I will carry on without you. Use my other contacts."

Perhaps that would be best. Perhaps this mantle had been lifted from her shoulders. Perhaps she had…

No. Drawing in a long breath, the calling settled over her again as it had the first time he mentioned this business. She must still do what she could to help the Glorious Cause. To ensure that her father came back to her alive.

Nevertheless, things had changed today, things that could never be shifted back. She could and would press on, but a new balance must be found, for a new tightrope stretched before her.

For now, she summoned a smile. "Of course I will help, Robbie. Which means I must go smooth things over with my grandparents."

And she would have to keep Colonel Fairchild at hand, which may mean rescinding the words she had spoken to Bennet that evening.

She made her face as bright as she could as she moved back to the door. "I had better hurry home."

To the house that had never been home and the family that despised her. Where she must find a way to make her position clear, yet win a second chance. All so she could put country above heart and risk her neck.

Hardly waiting for his farewell, she followed Freeman back into the night. And wished, prayed, this day would end.

Ben straightened from where he'd been stooped over his desk and looked at his handiwork. He was no cartographer, but a second map had become necessary. This one, rather than containing places of interest in the City of New York, was on a grander scale. At the top was where Washington had made his headquarters in New Windsor. Technically, it was directly up the river from the city, but traversing the distance between was far more complicated, especially if one assumed his scouts, couriers, et cetera, would stay within Patriot-held territory as much as possible.

In all likelihood, their route of communication went through Connecticut to the east. For all he knew, New Haven could be a stopping point. But from Connecticut they would have to cross the sound at some point and then cut through Long Island. The other alternative would take them directly through massive British fortifications—highly unlikely.

But Long Island stretched for more than a hundred miles off the coast, and as loyal as some of the towns were in the western side, most of the east was sympathetic to the rebels. There were towns aplenty that would have citizens willing to help the Patriot cause by taking in spies or conveying messages.

His gaze kept returning to one Long Island town in particular. Setauket. Home to the Caleb Brewster he had heard mentioned in Fairchild's office last spring. To one Austin Roe, who had taken up the colors. And most notably to Benjamin Tallmadge, who had, so far as he could tell, become a favorite of General Washington's.

A favorite rumored to have been delegated the task of managing Patriot intelligence.

Was it a coincidence that Washington's intelligence man was from the same small village as a sailor wanted by the British for his activities on the sound? Ben had his doubts. If he were going to put together a ring of spies, he would start with those he knew he could trust. His friends.

Hence the list at his side of other Setauket residents. He had stared at it half the evening but couldn't quite determine which, if any, Tallmadge may have recruited. His suspicions kept settling on Abraham Woodhull, a noted schoolfellow of both Brewster and Tallmadge. But Woodhull had been arrested by the Patriots for smuggling. Would he then express his gratitude for release by becoming a spy, an endeavor far riskier than ferrying vegetables to the London Trade? Perhaps. But not necessarily. He could as easily harbor resentment for the arrest.

Some things paper could not disclose.

And he then had to discover their city connection. Without question, there was at least one man operating here. But who? So many Long Islanders had family in the city, and so many city residents had fled after the fire…but he had been making a chart. He had gotten his hands on a List of Associators—those so fervent about the rebel cause that they put their names to it before they even declared their independence. By comparing that to the lists he had obtained of residents of the various towns and what family history he could find, he was crafting a picture of loyalties and connections.

Footfalls in the hall prompted him to shuffle his maps and charts together and shove them into a drawer. He did that a great deal, it seemed, every time he heard Mother or Archie or, from time to time, a servant. And generally the person passed by without disturbing him.

Not tonight. The footsteps stopped outside his door, and the knock was followed immediately by the door opening.

Ben was glad he had hidden his work. All that remained on his desk was his volume of *The Odyssey*, on which he kept his gaze. "Usually one waits for an answer to one's knock before entering, Archie."

His brother chuckled. "I don't intend to bother you long. Did you, ah…spend the evening with Miss Reeves as planned?"

Ben paused with a page halfway turned. He let it fall and then pivoted on his seat. Her name was enough to make his heart rate increase. After he had left her, it had taken him a full hour to clear his mind of thoughts of her enough to get to work, and he could only hope it wouldn't take him another hour to get back to it. "I did, yes. I departed shortly after supper." After receiving, at long last, promise. After feeling the surge of rightness that accompanied her kiss. "Why?"

"I…" Archie sighed. Unusual for him. He rarely had difficulty stringing words together.

Discomfort squirmed within Ben. "Is something the matter with Miss Reeves?"

His brother shook himself. "I only wanted to say that I…well, I have revised my opinion of her. You were right. She is more intelligent than she lets on. But, Benny, do you really want that in a female?"

Ben laughed and turned back to his book. "Go to bed, Archie."

"I only want to be sure you know what you are getting yourself into."

"I am well aware." More or less.

Archie tapped his palm against something, likely the doorjamb. "But you could find a simple girl. One who is uncomplicated. Who will not question your every word."

"Where would the fun be in that?" Ben traced a finger down the edge of the page, eyes unfocused. A grin took over his mouth. "I like complication."

"You are as bizarre as she. Very well, then. I consign you to your fate."

Fate…a strange thing to contemplate when one was reading the ancient Greeks. If Winter was his fate, then nothing could keep them apart in the end.

But that wasn't to say there wouldn't be years of challenge and pain in the middle.

The house loomed like a monster with glowing yellow windows for eyes, its door a mouth waiting to devour her. For a long time Winter stood in the middle of the drive, Freeman waiting patiently beside her, as she tried to gather courage enough to face the beast.

Did she really want to go back in? To reenter that life? Perhaps she should sneak into the hidden stable cellar, gather those items most dear, and then slip out again. Go...somewhere else. Anywhere else.

Thou preparest a table before me in the presence of mine enemies.

Winter drew in a slow, quivering breath. The long-ago memorized psalm offered up that sentence as a promise kept. That even when surrounded by enemies, the Lord had a feast prepared. A head anointed. A cup overflowing.

She was no David, but the Lord had preserved her, especially tonight. He intended her to follow this path of peril that Robbie had set out.

Must she do it from Hampton Hall? Could she not somehow achieve it from another place?

Let innocence be your mask. Let your beauty hide your heart. Let your enemies count you a friend. Let no one see your true self.

Her fingers tangled into the soiled silk of her skirt. She had thought herself so clever when she devised those rules for herself, rules on how to survive in a world gone mad, rules for a game that meant death if she lost.

Perhaps they kept her alive. But they didn't allow her to live.

Father above, I want to be Yours above all. I want to follow Your will, Your way. You have called me here, but all this time I have played this game according to my own rules. Show me Yours. Please, Lord.

She must find a way to be like Viney. 'Twasn't enough to keep from being found guilty in the eyes of man. She must focus on remaining innocent before the Lord, no matter how others may judge her.

With one last, deep breath she paced up the driveway and nodded to Freeman that she would be fine. Then she opened the door wide enough to slip in and eased it closed behind her.

Raised voices came from Grandfather's study. Winter walked in that direction and took up a position outside the door, able to see in but confident they wouldn't see her.

Grandfather stood beside his favorite chair, gripping its back.

Grandmother paced before the unlit fireplace, waving a hand. "It is insufferable, Hampton. *You* are insufferable!"

"I warned her. I warned you. I have had enough of the whelp. Every day she was under my roof it was a slap across my face, a reminder of what her harlot of a mother did to us. How you could possibly abide her I cannot fathom."

Winter swallowed down the pain. She had long known how he felt, and he had certainly proven it tonight. Why did the words still slice?

Grandmother muttered something sharp but unintelligible as she strode out of sight. A moment later she appeared again, her finger pointed at Grandfather. "You are an idiot. A loathsome, bitter idiot. She had a proposal. You could have sent a note to Fairchild telling him we had decided to allow the marriage, and she could have been gone in a way that would have brought us good connections instead of more vile gossip."

His knuckles turned white before he abruptly released the back of his chair. "We will tell everyone she is dead. That we went for a picnic by the water and she fell in."

Grandmother hissed out a breath. "Which will be believed only until one of our gentlemen friends sees her in Holy Ground. You stupid, blind fool—"

"Enough!" His roar was so loud, reverberating with ferocity, that Winter half expected the windows to shatter. He picked up a vase from the table and sent it to its death against the wall. "This is all your fault, woman! First you parade our daughter around like some light-skirt, inviting the eyes of every male in the state. Then, rather than learn your lesson from your failure with her, you bring her illegitimate chit into our home."

Grandmother looked as if she might explode into a million pieces. "You are as slanderous as every other tongue in New York. Stupid Amelia may have been, but she was not immoral. They married."

"Clasping hands like a Quaker does not equal legal marriage when one was raised in the Church of England." He punctuated his words with a kick to the bookshelf. "You never should have—"

"*I* never should have? Yes, this is all my fault. *I* am the one who tossed our granddaughter to the streets for all my friends to make a harlot, when the richest man in New York has all but declared himself!"

With a growl, Grandfather stomped to the window. "'All but,' is it? He has no intention of marrying the chit or he would have proposed well before now. Obviously the man has better sense than to burden himself with her."

Another day, hearing those words may have brought tears to Winter's eyes. But after everything else she had suffered in the last few hours, they could only add another layer of glossed-over sorrow to the shell around her heart.

Grandmother snorted an unamused laugh. "You know so little of what goes on in this house. He kissed her tonight, and I have never seen such a besotted fool as he looked when he left."

Grandfather turned his back on his wife, his arms folded as he stared out the window.

Grandmother strode to the center of the room and halted. "You listen to me, Bartholomew Hampton. I will not endure another scandal as I did with Amelia. I will not stand there pretending I don't hear all the speculation when it comes out that Winifred is in Holy Ground, when everyone I respect wonders about our family. You will go there and fetch her home, or I swear to you I will leave you."

He grunted. "You think I will mourn you?"

Winter's breath caught when she saw Grandmother's wicked little smile. "I will leave you…and go to Simon De Wite."

Winter squeezed her eyes shut. She didn't even know who this De Wite was, but the implications were obvious. She knew her grandfather had been unfaithful, but Grandmother too?

Grandfather spat out a curse. "That is how you avoid scandal?"

"If I am going to be subjected to it, it might as well be for something from which I get some pleasure."

Winter feared she might be ill. She forced her eyes back open, though, and saw that her grandfather's fingers twitched in measure to the tic in his jaw.

"Even if I fetch her back, 'twill be too late. She will not be a maid. You will not be able to marry her off, not be able to redeem through her the reputation you lost with Amelia."

Grandmother laughed. "Oh, Hampton. Come now. You think we females have no tricks to cover this sort of thing?"

His eyes narrowed, but he held his silence for a long, interminable minute. Then his hands clenched. "Have it your way. If I can find her, I will bring her back."

Well, Winter knew a cue when she heard one. She stepped into the door's opening with all the calm she could muster. "That ought not to be too difficult."

Both Hamptons spun to face her, both with shock on their faces. Grandmother's colored with relief, Grandfather's with fury.

"Winifred!"

"My name is *Winter*, Grandmother. I will not answer to 'Winifred' anymore."

The relief gave way to anger in the matriarch's eyes. "Now see here—"

"You have both said your fill this evening. 'Tis my turn now." She looked from one to the other. Should she feel some bond to them? Some affection or loyalty that ought to have flowed through her veins because of shared blood? They seemed like nothing but strangers. "I came with you to the city because I was devastated and lost, and I believed you when you said it was the only way to survive. I let you strip me of all I am and became all you insisted because the thought of losing the only connection I had left to my mother was unbearable."

Winter shook her head, and then she had to clutch it when it throbbed. "I see now that there is nothing of Mother here, not in the two of you. Question their vows all you like, but the truth is that it is *you* who know not the meaning of marriage, nor of family."

Grandfather stepped forward. Fire smoldered in his eyes, but 'twas banked. "Hold your tongue, chit, or—"

"Or what, Grandfather?" She managed a mocking smile. "Will you toss me back to Holy Ground? Go ahead and try. I have faith, wits, and strength enough to pull myself from whatever ditch into which you would throw me. Perhaps thanks to the blood of generations of farmers."

His face mottled red. "You hateful—"

"I am not." Her voice broke and her eyes burned. The truth of her claim settled over her heart like a soothing balm. "You have hurt me and threatened me and tried your best to break me. And I have resented you and fought you and wished I were anywhere but under your roof. Yet...yet I don't want to be at odds with you. I don't want to carry this burden another day. We will never see eye to eye, and perhaps there will never be warmth between us, but can we not be civil? Can we not live peaceably?"

Grandmother scowled. "Not if you persist in shows of disrespect."

Much as she wanted to argue, wanted to be done with them, it *was* their house. She needed to respect that. She nodded again, more carefully this time. "I realize that, and I apologize for any such incidents. But respect must be mutual, Grandmother. I will give you what you are due as my matron and my hostess, but I cannot tolerate being treated as a slave and denied my right to think for myself. Let me be who I am. I promise you I will not shame or embarrass you."

Grandmother narrowed her eyes. "You think to present a new picture to society all of a sudden, and for them to accept it?"

She opened her mouth but could think of no retort. Another good point. If she showed a different face, she would invite attention and questions that could lead to danger for all of them. "At least at home, then. Without your rebuking me for it."

Nose in the air, Grandmother sniffed. "Very well. You may stay."

Resignation tinged her relief. Winter nodded. "Thank you."

Then Grandmother's eyes narrowed. "Where are your pearls?"

She raised a hand to her neck as if only just noticing its bare state. Then she dropped it again and looked at Grandfather. "I suppose one cannot expect to leave Holy Ground without paying *some* price."

Grandmother smirked. "I will go order a bath for you."

As apologies went, a bath was a good one on this night. But when the lady swept past, out the door, Winter felt fingers of ice slide up her spine.

Grandfather took a few slow, even steps until he was beside her, his gaze on the door. "I underestimated you, Winter. I will not do so again. Next time you misstep, I will not waste any time and effort on teaching you lessons. I will have you killed and be done with it."

Winter held herself upright and still until he had gone. Then she breathed a dry, tired laugh. If ever she misstepped so greatly, he would have to wait in line for that privilege.

Sixteen

Ben smiled at the footman and stepped into the cool entryway of Hampton Hall. "Morning, Thomas."

"Mr. Lane." The man smiled in return. "Miss Reeves is out back, I believe. If you will have a seat in the drawing room, I shall send someone to fetch her."

Though the servant had been reaching for his hat, Ben dropped his hand at that news. "No need for that, Thomas. We would undoubtedly end up in the garden anyway. I shall go find her out there."

"As you like, sir."

Ben hummed as he traversed the familiar corridors of the stately house, relieved when he gained the back door without running into either of the Hamptons. He wanted to see Winter. Needed to see her to determine if she had taken their talk last night to heart, but he could do without her grandparents today.

Pushing open the door into the garden, the sound of hammer upon slate met his ears. Given the intensity of the sun beating down, Ben did not envy the workman the task of roof repair, that was for certain.

He paused for a moment in the shade of the eaves to look about for Winter. She was nowhere, so far as he could see. Not near the roses, not on the bench beneath the arbor, not under the tulip tree, where she sometimes reposed. Had Thomas been mistaken?

Finally he caught sight of her graceful movements at the stable door. He frowned at first, unable to imagine her grandparents allowing her to spend time out there. But then he saw Freeman behind her, and it made sense. Of course she would be at his side whenever she could manage it, he being the only tie she had left to her Long Island home.

He took a step forward but paused when she came more fully into view. She wore a dress plainer than he usually saw on her, a light color appropriate for summer but unadorned, so far as he could tell, and her hair was in a braid. The vision made him smile. Perhaps it was wishful thinking, but *this* seemed more like the Winter who lived beneath the mask. And if so, there may be hope for them yet. For this Winter, more beautiful than ever in simplicity, may get on quite well in Connecticut.

She headed his way, spotted him, and lifted a hand in greeting. He saw that she smiled but wished they were closer so he could discern the flavor of it. Was it genuine? Perhaps embarrassed, after their gentle embrace last night? Regretful?

He hoped not regretful. He didn't know if he could suffer it if she chose, yet again, to keep her heart hidden.

But as she drew nearer he couldn't help but think that hers was not an expression of a woman floating on a cloud of romance. She looked tired, pained. And her smile seemed uncertain at best.

Blast. He might as well turn and leave. What was the point of going through this yet again? The progress, the hope, and then the disappointment when she reverted back to her old ways.

He had thought it would be different this time. He truly had.

Winter halted halfway to him, her eyes wide and turned upward. He heard the curse from above and the *chink* of breaking slate at the same moment he heard her scream, "Bennet!"

Each fraction of a second expanded, so that it seemed a multitude of observations whirred through his brain all at once. How horror took possession of her face, the sound of the slate accelerating as it slid down the roof, the knowledge that he must be directly under it, to alarm her so. He tried to send his limbs the command to move, but they seemed unable to respond.

Finally his knees bent, he came up on his toes. His arms stretched out before him, as if pushing the air out of the way so he could get through. But already the slate had gone silent, which meant it had left the roof. Already Winter charged toward him.

The slate knocked off his hat and caught him on the shoulder, though with the momentum he already had working in his favor, his fall took him out of its continued path. Still, its shattering on the stone patio came just as he hit the same unforgiving ground with a grunt. He had to wonder if he, too, had cracked something vital.

"Bennet!" Time came back into alignment when Winter dropped to her knees at his side, her hands flying over his shoulder and head. "Bennet, speak to me. Are you injured? Can you move? Should I call for a physician?"

It took him a second to force air back into his lungs. "Not the way I envisioned the morning going, but I seem to have emerged in one piece." He winced, though, when he tried to push himself up, his shoulder protesting the action.

"Everyone all right down there?" an anxious voice called from the roof.

"Fine. Fine." If one ignored the searing pain.

"Stay still." Winter's voice shook to match her hands, which attempted to hold him immobile.

Ben got himself to a sitting position. "No need for that. Hurts like mad, but I don't think I'm terribly injured. Bruised, no doubt, but that is all."

She shook her head, her lips pressed together as if afraid to speak. Her eyes wide, as if they may fill with tears at any moment. And her hands continued to tremble as she dropped them to her lap.

He must have given her quite a fright. Ben smiled and took her fingers in his. "There now, I am well."

Rather than answer, she squeezed her eyes shut and lifted their joined hands to rest her forehead upon them. Her breath came in unsteady heaves.

Concern eclipsed the fiery ache in his shoulder. "Winter, really. I am fine."

"I know." Yet her voice sounded unconvinced. "I know, and praise the Lord for it. But had you not moved those few inches…"

He grimaced at the thought. "'Tis a good thing you warned me. Nasty stuff, slate—at least when falling. Why, I have even heard of people being kill—" He cut himself off with a hiss. Hadn't Mother said Mr. Reeves was killed by a falling piece of slate? No wonder this reaction then. Confound it, what a dunce he was. "Winter, I am sorry. Your father...what are the chances that I...my poor darling. Come here."

She scooted closer and let him wrap his arms around her as she rested her head against his shoulder. Her hands curled into the fabric of his waistcoat. "I thought I had lost you," she whispered against him. "When I saw that slate coming straight for you—"

"But you did not. I am here." He slid a hand under the thick braid at her neck and urged her head up enough that he could touch his forehead to hers. "I am here."

"That is what Mother said. After my father..." She sniffed as she smoothed out his waistcoat where she had rumpled it. Ben tried to concentrate on her words rather than the yearning that surged through him at her gentle touch. "She said she was there, would always be there. Then when she fell ill...I was so angry, Bennet. Angry at Father for leaving us. Angry at Mother for falling ill."

"Understandable." And honest. Open. Something she surely didn't share with just anyone, something unmarred by her mask. Perhaps it was odd to find hope in her dismay, but how could he not, when it was proof of her affection? "I cannot promise nothing will happen to me. I would be a fool if I tried. But, my darling, while we may not be able to escape the hand of Providence, we can make the most of the time we are given."

"I do not want to escape Providence. His hand cradles, Bennet. It does not strike. But your larger point holds true." Her smile wobbled, but its appearance nevertheless made his heart take wing. "I am done with wasting our time."

The ache in his shoulder was suddenly sweet as a promise. "If you follow that with another order that I find someone else to court..."

She chuckled and rested her hand on his cheek. Which served to remind him that he had rushed out before his valet could fetch the razor this morning. "Not unless you proceed to order me to marry Fairchild."

"Nay," he said on a light laugh. "In fact, I am grateful you are a disobedient little thing."

Her grin shone forth. "I will remember you said that and remind you of it at the most inconvenient moment I can find. I hope you realize that."

"I have no doubt." He turned his head enough to kiss her hand.

Her smiled faded, and again he noted what had struck him when he saw her walking his way. Circles under her eyes, and an echo of pain within them. Yet she didn't pull away. "Bennet, I'm glad you are here. That I have not scared you off as I meant to do."

Another admission that surely cost her. "When I awoke this morning, I nearly disbelieved what transpired last night. I thought you may have decided not to…"

"I did." Her eyes slid shut, but her fingers remained on his cheek. "Not at first. First I decided to do whatever was necessary to ensure we had a chance to get to know each other. Then I…let us say I remembered all the reasons I had not done so to begin with. But now…"

He covered her fingers with his. "Hmm? Now?"

Her breath shuddered out and she opened her eyes to look into his. "I do not want to lose you. Certainly not to what is beyond our control, but how much worse would it be if I chose it? I cannot. Perhaps I still should, perhaps that would be the wise thing, the fair thing. But I cannot."

"Who would have thought 'I cannot' would be the most precious words in the world?" He smiled and reached to smooth back a stray wisp of hair from her cheek. And regretted it when his shoulder screamed. He barely stifled a word not fit for female ears. "Forgot it that quickly."

She sent him a glance that combined rebuke with amusement and dropped her hands to hold his—no doubt as much to keep him from raising it again as for the sentiment. "Bennet—"

"Don't fuss, my love. I will be more careful." Not to mention that he had no desire to call for a doctor, thereby interrupting this time with her. And he had logic enough to think that if he was more concerned with that than the pain, then the injury could not be so terrible.

Sighing, she shook her head. But a smile teased her mouth again, tempting him to lean in and give her that third kiss he had withheld last night. Make it a habit. He settled for stroking his thumb over her knuckles. "Did you truly not know my Aristotle reference last night?"

That earned him a laugh that banished a few of the shadows from her eyes. "Aristotle was never my favorite. Descartes I liked. And Lavoisier."

His pulse galloped. "You've read Lavoisier's papers?"

The gleam in her eyes said she knew how much that meant to him. "Those that reached us before I came here, anyway. My father enjoyed chemistry, you see, and he loved to read scientific papers with me during the winters. I find Lavoisier's new theories on the elements quite intriguing."

He raised their joined hands to his heart. Perhaps he ought to propose here and now. Just think of it—a beautiful young woman he admired, and who admired Lavoisier. Perhaps they could be like them, even, with her assisting him in his laboratory as Madame Lavoisier did her husband. Dare he dream such? Hope such?

He had so much he wanted to ask her, now that she may actually answer. Questions of literature, of her family, of her dreams. What she hoped for from life, what she feared.

Why she had given in so long to her grandparents' demands on her.

And she smiled at him as if she knew every bookish thought in his head and still wanted to converse with him. Why, then, did it have to fade again, all the way into a frown? "Bennet," she said, voice quiet. She squeezed his hand. "There are still things…I cannot…" She sighed to a halt.

He raised her hand to his lips and pressed a kiss to it.

'Twas apparently an encouragement. Her expression softened again. "You said last night you have patience aplenty. I pray that is true, because it will not be easy for me to emerge from this place into which my grandparents have put me. To step from the darkness of the cave into the light."

He chuckled. "You are unfamiliar with Aristotle, yet you have obviously read Plato's *Republic*."

Her lips quirked up. "With all the talk flying around of independence and new governments, Father thought it a wise idea to see what some of the great minds had to say on the subject."

"I should have liked to meet your father, I think."

A strange mix of emotion surged through her eyes—hope, fear, uncertainty. It settled on caution. "I can imagine the two of you getting along famously."

Perhaps he ought not to have reminded her of that loss, given the slate incident. But soon enough her expression moved back into sweet, and they fell to staring at each other in that way he had always scoffed at when he saw other couples doing it. Little had he known how fulfilling it could be to simply study the woman one loved.

Or how frustrating it could be when a clearing throat interrupted them. He looked over toward the noise, expecting Mr. Hampton or perhaps Freeman, who seemed to be her usual guardian. But it was Robert Townsend who stood at the corner of the house, frowning as he looked from one of them to the other.

"I seem to have a knack for interrupting the two of you. My apologies. I can return later."

Why, then, hadn't he simply turned around and done so without making his presence known?

Perhaps that was uncharitable.

"Robbie." Winter squeezed Ben's fingers and then reclaimed her hand as she pushed to her feet. "Mr. Lane had a bit of scuffle with some falling slate."

Townsend's gaze felt cold upon him. "I do hope you are not injured, Mr. Lane."

Ben pushed carefully to his feet as well. "Probably a bruise on my shoulder, but I was fortunate enough to have gotten my head out of the way in time."

The newcomer nodded. Given the pulsing of his jaw, he looked to be clenching his teeth. He turned that harsh gaze on Winter again. "I came by to check on you. See how *your* head was faring."

Ben's brows drew together. "Yours?"

Winter sent Townsend a look loaded with meaning Ben could not discern. Then that empty smile of hers took possession of her mouth. "Just a bump. Freeman told you about it when he came to your store this morning, Robbie?"

Townsend stared her down a long moment. What in the world were all these wordless messages? Ben tried to convince himself not to be bothered by it, but...

At last Townsend nodded. Curtly. "I was worried."

"'Tis nothing. Still sore, but Grandmother had the physician in last night, and he assures us it will heal nicely."

"Physician?" Ben had been trying to discreetly brush off his posterior but halted at that. Somehow he couldn't imagine Winter agreeing to a physician over nothing. "What exactly bumped you? And why did you not say anything?"

Her smile turned genuine, if a bit too mischievous. "I hardly had the chance, Bennet, what with you stepping into the path of falling slate and all the moment you arrived."

He lifted his brows. "An injury that only *could* have been should not take precedence over one that *is*."

Townsend cleared his throat again. "So you are feeling better?"

Her grin faded when she looked back to her old friend, the contemplation in her eyes making Ben think he was not the only one confounded by the man's tone of voice. "Better, yes. It still aches. But the physician stitched the gash closed—"

"Gash?" Ben went tense as he tried to find the wound on her head. She must have hidden it under the mass of mahogany hair...though that probably explained why she wore it differently today. "How did you get a gash upon your head?"

"I...I'm really not sure." She shrugged, and while she seemed to be truthful in her statement, he suspected 'twasn't so simple as that. "I must have fallen, though I cannot remember what happened between turning around after you left, Bennet, and waking up with a pounding head."

His hands clenched at his sides. If he were a betting man, he would have wagered on her grandfather having something to do with it. And if he were a violent man, he might toss aside respect for the man's age and station and challenge him.

Because he was neither, he contented himself with thinking up a few formulas that could make Hampton as miserable as he made Winter. Not that he intended to use it, but a little spirit of salt could cause serious pain. An acid burn was surely deserved if he indeed injured her so severely.

"Well." Townsend jerked his head again in a move too cold to be called a nod. "I am glad to know you are on the mend. Good day to you both."

When he pivoted and strode toward the corner again, Winter frowned and went after him. "Robbie, wait."

Ben held his ground, clasped his hands behind his back, and prepared to watch their interaction. The concern upon Winter's face was genuine, but of a different sort than what she had shown him earlier. Warm, but with a more muted kind of affection. Ought he to be jealous? He thought not.

And yet he couldn't help but think that the same observation was what had put Townsend in such poor spirits.

Ben rubbed his shoulder and halfway wished he had fallen for a homely girl who did not have so many other young men in love with her. Or perhaps he ought to wish he had the good sense not to make friends with those who were. Not that he and Townsend were particularly close, but they always got on well enough when in company.

Then there was Fairchild. Ben dropped his hand back to his side. He didn't want to think of how Fairchild might respond if Winter made known her preference for Ben.

Confound it. It would be simpler if he tossed to the wind all his lofty ideas about getting to know her fully and ran off with her. Got her out from under the Hampton roof and neatly avoided anyone who might not like the match.

But no. He couldn't do that. For the obvious reasons, and because of the mission that had brought him to New York to begin with. Time was surely running out. He must find the Patriot spy soon, or all these months of work would have been wasted.

Winter caught up with Townsend at the corner and stopped him with a hand upon his arm. "Robbie, are you all right?"

Ben barely caught the quiet question, but Townsend's scoffing chuckle reached his ears without problem. "No need to worry for me, Winnie. Go tend your darling Mr. Lane."

Winter looked so shocked when Townsend sped away that Ben had little choice but to go to her and take her hand in his. "Another manifestation of his black mood?"

She frowned as Townsend's figure disappeared down the drive. "I thought he had pulled out of it, but he sounded as though he were—"

"Jealous?" Ben fought a grin with what he deemed admirable determination. "That is the simple answer."

Her gaze swung his way and her mouth fell open. "That would not be *simple*. He is the closest thing I have to a brother."

Ben gave her hand an encouraging squeeze. "Does he realize that?"

Winter worried her lip and glanced toward the drive again. "I had thought so. Now I am not certain." She sighed and leaned into him a bit. "Could you suggest to my grandmother that a trip with me through the shops in town would be just the thing and then let me have a few moments to speak with him? I know it is a strange thing to ask—"

"Nonsense." He smiled, honored that she trusted him enough to ask it. "He is a longtime friend. Of course you want to smooth things out. I will gladly be your conspirator."

Loosing a long breath, she turned them toward the back door. "A dangerous word choice in this day and age, Bennet. But I thank you."

Dangerous indeed. Conspiracy was as reviled as espionage.

And so he had to wonder if she would instead run in the other direction if she realized his true purpose for returning to the city.

Seventeen

Never in her life had Winter been less pleased to find herself in the gaggle of her so-called friends. Perhaps the Lord was trying to teach her patience, for while her mind screamed that she must speak with Robbie and root out, at once, what had been behind his icy tone an hour ago, circumstances did not allow her to slip away. Bennet had tried to extract them from the group, but he had been outnumbered.

So now he stood a few feet away, chatting with the amiable and handsome Major André, who, she suspected, had been enlisted to engage him in conversation so that Colonel Fairchild might maneuver her in the opposite direction.

Perfect, just perfect. Barely an hour ago she had been hit with the force of her love for Bennet Lane, and now she must deal with Fairchild—and Robbie besides. 'Twasn't fair. Shouldn't the first strike of love be gentle? Beautiful? Warm and secure? But when she had seen that heavy piece of slate headed straight for him...

She couldn't lose him. She couldn't. No matter how difficult it would be to balance her feelings for him with her dedication to her country, she must find a way. Because the thought of carrying on without him was too much to bear.

As for how she could in good conscience proceed with that

courtship and yet somehow keep communication open with the colonel…

"You look deep in thought, my dear," Fairchild said.

Putting on her usual smile had never felt so false. "Oh, no, I assure you. That look of discomfort comes only from this ghastly heat."

He chuckled and covered with his fingers the hand she had obligingly placed on his arm. "Are you longing for winter? I know the feeling."

Though his meaning was clear and made her heart sink, she performed her usual absent blink. "I thought you disliked the cold, Colonel."

Why couldn't his interest fade on its own? She didn't want to hurt this man. He was too good. Too caring. Too oblivious to how ill she had used him all this time.

Fairchild chuckled again. "It depends entirely upon the company I'm in when out in it. I have very fond memories of a few moments in a winter garden."

She opened her mouth to respond, but then her attention was snagged by Lizzie and Dosia, who were moving away from their mothers and toward them. Though given the viperous glance Lizzie sent Winter's way, she somehow wasn't surprised when the girls steered for Major André and Bennet rather than her with a particular nonchalance that bespoke a plan.

Dosia positioned herself between the two gentlemen and directed such a bright smile at the major that he surely went half blind. Lizzie moved in as well and dropped her handkerchief directly before Bennet.

Winter barely kept from rolling her eyes. *That* was the best she could come up with to get his attention? He didn't even seem to notice the fluttering square of white cloth, so attentively was he listening to whatever the major was saying.

Which earned a pursed-lipped scowl from Lizzie. She made a face at Dosia, which must have had some predetermined meaning to it, for Dosia cleared her throat and said, far too loudly, "Oh, Lizzie, you have dropped your handkerchief." Then she gave Bennet a pointed look.

Poor Bennet. He seemed only then to notice he had been flanked by the girls, and he gave a visible start to complement the shade of red his ears turned. "Oh…ah…good day. Miss…and miss…"

Dosia cleared her throat and motioned toward the handkerchief.

But Lizzie must have thought it a lost cause, for she rolled her eyes and bent down to pick it up herself. Which was, of course, the very moment Bennet jerked into action.

"Oh, dear," Winter murmured as she watched what was sure to be a disaster unfold. Fairchild chuckled again beside her as the two somehow managed to avoid collision on the way down. Though after a brief tussle over the handkerchief, Bennet released it to Lizzie and must have bumped her as she rose—she squealed, windmilled her arms, and staggered backward. Unable to find her footing, she landed with a flop upon her bottom, in a puddle.

Winter winced. It hadn't rained in more than a week, so she dared not contemplate of *what* it was a puddle.

Dosia squealed too and lunged forward to help Lizzie just as Bennet spun around, presumably to offer his assistance as well. Yet another recipe for disaster. From where Winter stood, it didn't look as though Bennet actually made any contact with her, but rather that she shied away from him so enthusiastically that she got her heel caught in something. She rocked backward, overcompensated, and lunged forward.

Bennet caught her, his face crimson by this point, but that seemed to offer no comfort to Dosia. She probably feared he would toss her into the same puddle as Lizzie. "Unhand me!"

Poor Bennet. He muttered a string of things like "um" and "oh" and "so sorry" as he tried to ease her back onto her feet. But silly Dosia slapped at his arms and pushed off, thereby sending herself the other direction too forcefully.

Luckily Major André was on hand and steadied her before she could join Lizzie on her posterior. And Mrs. Parks and Mrs. Shirley rushed forward to help the unfortunate girl up, all the while dubbing Lizzy as the clumsy one and trying to assure Bennet it wasn't his fault.

He looked as though he wished for an earthquake, a tempest, a cyclone—anything to distract everyone from him.

Winter pressed her lips together to hold back her smile. Oh, how she loved that man. Loved every blush, every stutter, every panicked look. Loved seeing him move from perfect ease in one discussion to total bafflement in another. Loved the way he looked over at her and seemed to find some comfort in her presence.

"Ought I give up hope, then?"

Winter started and turned back to Colonel Fairchild. The cheer
had drained out of his face, which made her wonder what exactly had
been upon hers. She lifted her brows. "Pardon?"

Fairchild's fingers tightened over hers as he nodded toward Bennet. "Has he proposed?"

Not trusting herself to speak, she shook her head.

The colonel pursed his lips. "I know he cares for you, and it appears
you care for him as well. And your grandparents prefer him."

All true. But seeing the hurt in his eyes, she still could find no words.
She drew in a deep breath and moved her hand a bit on his arm.

He surprised her with a warm smile. "But I have not gotten where
I am today by giving up at the first obstacle. Or the second or third. I
will not relinquish you so easily, my love. Until you are his betrothed
wife, I will be at your side every moment I can manage it, trying to convince you that, excellent man though Mr. Lane is, I will make you happier than he could."

Guilt wove through the relief that welled up. She smiled, though
it probably looked a little sad. "I do not deserve such devotion from
you, Colonel."

"Nonsense. You are all that is bright and good in my life."

Those words made her feel the opposite. "I...I thank you, Colonel. For both your devotion and your patience. 'Tis a hard thing for
me, this deciding on a future. It requires far more consideration than
to what I am a customer."

"Accustomed." As always, his correction was given with a smile.

Mrs. Shirley huffed, loudly enough to draw Winter's attention that
direction again. "Well, you are a fright now, Lizzie. We shall have to
go home so you can change. Mrs. Parks, dear, let us meet at the milli-
ner's in half an hour's time, shall we?"

"Dosia and I will head that way now." Mrs. Parks arched a brow
Winter's way. "Will you join us, Winnie?"

"Perhaps shortly, ma'am. I must drop by Mr. Townsend's store first."
She waved a hand at the storefront directly across from them. She had
nearly made it there before running into the gaggle.

Colonel Fairchild tucked her hand more firmly into the crook of
his elbow. "Allow me to escort you, Miss Reeves."

Not good. But she could do little but agree with thanks, and then send a glance Bennet's way. His smile assured her he would help her, somehow or another. He and Major André both followed them across the street, and the moment they were safely over, Bennet said, "Did you see the *Royal Gazette* this morning, Fairchild? I was hoping you could tell me a bit more about that article on rebel movements. Have they really scattered so much?"

Undoubtedly not, but Mr. Rivington always exaggerated the bad luck of the Patriots for the ease of mind of his British readership. And it served to distract the colonel enough that she could free her hand and say, "I shall leave you men to such talk, if you will excuse me but a moment."

Not waiting for an objection, she hastened into the store and then sighed when a quick look around did not show her Robbie.

"Can I help you, Miss Reeves?"

She pasted on a smile for Robbie's partner. "Good day, Mr. Oaktree. I am only looking for Mr. Townsend."

"Oakham." The man made an obvious effort to put patience in his smile. "And I'm afraid Mr. Townsend is reorganizing stock in the back and asked not to be disturbed."

"Excellent. I shall see him back there." She headed toward the door to the storeroom with all the confidence of the spoiled chit she pretended to be. Yet she still wasn't surprised when Oakham jumped into her path.

"Miss Reeves, I can hardly allow you into our back room. 'Tis full of boxes and crates and is a veritable mess. It's no place at all for a lady."

"Nonsense." She gave a look as if *he* were a slow child. "Robbie is an old family friend, and I must speak with him of family business, that is all. I will pay no attention at all to my surroundings, I assure you."

Oakham folded his arms across his chest. "Why don't I bring him out here, hmm?"

Thankfully, Robbie appeared at the door, having apparently heard her. Though he looked far from pleased to see her. "It is all right, Oakham. I promised to share the latest news from my sister, is all, and I might as well do so while working. Come on back, Miss Reeves."

Oakham relented with a roll of his eyes and retired to the counter. Once past him, Winter let her smile fade and ducked through the curtain, which Robbie pulled closed behind her. He led the way silently to the rear of the storeroom and indeed got to work pulling items from a box rather than facing her.

Winter twisted the strap of her reticule between her fingers. "Robbie—"

"Please don't." He took a handful of bottles from the box, their contents a mystery, and shoved them onto a shelf. "You ought not to have wasted your time in coming here. Go home, back into the arms of Mr. Lane. Or Fairchild, or whoever your choice beau is this afternoon."

The censure in his tone struck her so forcefully that she drew in a quick breath to try to combat it. "You make it sound...Robbie, I did nothing wrong. Bennet was injured, and it scared me so much—"

"Bennet now, is it?" He halted and spun on her. "I know you feel you must marry one of them to escape your grandfather's threats, Winnie, but I didn't think...you are surely running out of time, right? Are you only trying to hurry him along?"

She expected such thoughts from Grandmother, but from Robbie? "You know I would not—"

"Do I? Frankly, I cannot say what you might do. In spite of all reason, all logic, you are set on marrying one of those pompous, England-bound men."

She drew in a long breath in an attempt to steady her temper. There was no use fighting with Robbie when he was in one of his moods. It would only make things worse. "I came to see if you were well, Robbie. You looked so upset, and I feared..." She couldn't say it. It sounded too ridiculous. Too arrogant an assumption.

He halted in the middle of reaching into the box again. Straightening, he let his hands fall and stared at her. "You fear for me? And I fear for you. Why not resolve it all, Winnie? Why not be done with the family that is bent on terrorizing you? Be done with their expectations?"

Her stomach clenched, dread settling in it like something sour. "How?"

"'Tis simple." His smile barely flashed before disappearing. "Marry me."

And now her eyes burned. "That is not simple, Robbie."

"It is." He took a step toward her, though he halted again two steps away. He didn't reach for her but just looked long into her eyes. "You can join the Friends, and we can marry in Quaker fashion, so your grandparents' disapproval will mean nothing. And you know your father would approve. I may not be wealthy, but I am well enough off."

Her throat was so dry she could hardly force a swallow. Hardly dared to move. "But then I...the Culpers..."

"I don't care." Now his voice came out low, quavering. "I thought I did, Winnie. I thought last night that it was all I needed to shake off this dreadful mood of mine. But it isn't. It cannot. Only you can help me."

"No, I can't." Why must he do this to her, put this burden upon her? She shook her head, wishing she in fact *could* make his troubles go away so easily. If she thought she could manage it, if she thought she could make him happy...well, maybe she would have proposed this course of action months ago.

But the sorrowful truth was that she had no such power over him, no more than any other outside force. His melancholy came from within. She moved forward, took his hand, and squeezed his fingers. "I wish I could, Robbie. I wish I could offer something, do something, that would help. But I would not be enough. My presence always irritates you as much as it soothes."

He gripped her hand. "Because there is always conflict within me, born of my feelings for you. I love you, Winnie. I have loved you so long."

Blink as she might, tears still welled.

Robbie sighed and let go of her fingers. "But you love Mr. Lane. I saw it clearly this morning, and now...even if you agreed, it would only torment me. I would always wonder if it was him of whom you dreamed."

"I am sorry." An ache wrapped itself around her, squeezing until she thought she might crumble within it. Part of her wished he had spoken long ago, before she had ever met Bennet. She would have been happy enough to join the Townsend family, to live in the modesty she best liked. To try to be what he needed. But another part wished he had never spoken at all. Wished he hadn't made her love for Bennet so bittersweet. "I never realized...had I known how you felt, Robbie—"

"An irrelevant hypothetical." He waved a hand and turned back to his box. "If you were ever going to love me, you would already. I should never have spoken. Just…go. Go back to your grandparents. Marry your Mr. Lane. Be happy."

That command came out so miserably that she had to press a hand to her lips to stop the cry that wanted to escape. "Robbie, you are important to me. One of my only true friends—"

"'Tisn't enough anymore, Winnie." He pulled out another bottle and gazed into it as if it contained a serum for everlasting youth. "Not now, with you knowing how I feel. Please, spare me this embarrassment. Leave."

She spun but only took a step before pivoting back. "But what of—"

"I don't know." He raised a hand, and though his back was still to her, she suspected he rubbed his eyes behind his spectacles. "Send Freeman whenever you must pass something along."

"Robbie."

He shook his head and somehow made his stance seem as though he turned his back on her anew. Perhaps because of the way he straightened his shoulders. "Go away, Winnie. I beg you."

Disobeying would have been too cruel, so she left. Slowly, with every step feeling as though she had a weight strapped to her ankles. She managed to avoid Oakham in the store and slipped out the door as silently as she could manage, given its bell.

The gentlemen had moved a few steps away and didn't notice her. Major André was speaking, his face sober. "I admit it is worrisome. My source is quite adamant that Washington has placed a ring of spies within the city, though he has been unable to learn the specifics."

Winter's limbs, already heavy, froze into ice.

Bennet frowned. "Unbelievable. Espionage is not only a risky endeavor, but one so very base—and the cost is so high. Why would anyone attempt it when they know well they will pay for it with their life?"

André shrugged. "In all likelihood, it is about money. It usually is. That is how we are enticing this high-ranking source."

The ice of her being cracked, a few shards splintering off.

Of course she knew the opinion of spies, how hated they were, how reviled. How dangerous it was. But to hear these men discussing it, discussing *her*, and ascribing to her motives so very low…

Bennet now smirked. "From what I hear, the Patriots have no funds with which to tempt anyone to espionage. Surely 'tis something else."

"Perhaps." Colonel Fairchild shrugged. "But it hardly matters why. The point remains that it must be stopped."

"Well, of course it must. And seeing the quality of officers looking into it," Bennet said with a grin, "I am certain it shall be resolved soon."

André breathed a laugh. "I wish I had your certainty. From what I am told, this ring has been operating for more than a year already, and we are no closer to finding its members now than when we intercepted their first letter."

That, at least, was a relief.

Bennet nodded. "Well, if by chance I stumble across anything helpful, I will pass it along."

Fairchild sighed. "I hope you will, Lane, and I hope you will not have to. But I must caution you to caution your friend. If he is seen again in such company, we will have no choice but to arrest him so that we might question him. Frankly, I would have the other day had I not known how close the two of you are."

Looking as though his smile caused him pain, Bennet clasped his hands behind his back. "I thank you for coming to me first, Fairchild. And I assure you I will speak with George and remind him that we are no longer in the days when one might converse with whomever one wills so freely."

Winter frowned. George Knight? Was he suspected of disloyalty? She could not fathom that they would long suffer such questions of a gunsmith. Yet she happened to know that he was in fact not a member of the Culper Ring, so surely he would escape any charges if he *were* questioned.

"Indeed. Sad as it is, we must—Miss Reeves!" Spotting her, the colonel's face lit up. "When did you come out? I do hope we were not boring you with our talk of rebels in disguise."

Winter blinked and let the familiar, false innocence settle over her face. "Oh, no. I only just stepped out. But what of disguises? Are we planning a masquerade?"

The gentlemen laughed and changed the subject, but even as Winter tucked her hand into the crook of Bennet's elbow, her mind went back into the shop. Was there really a high-ranking Patriot official feeding information to the British? If so, Robbie must alert Washington at once.

But she couldn't go back in there now, and with Robbie feeling as he did...well, she would send Freeman the moment she arrived home, and then Robbie could include it in the package of information for Roe.

Even as she thought it, a man rushed into the store matching the description Robbie had given her of the courier he found so unreliable. If that were Roe already...but surely they could impress on Robbie the importance of passing along this other information in the next correspondence.

'Twas too critical to be kept to themselves.

Eighteen

September 1780

Rob trudged along the waterfront, trying to work up the nerve to care about the fleet in the harbor, but everywhere he turned, red coats taunted him. Every time he planned to meet with a source, someone else lurked where they ought not. Every time he tried to secret a note out of the city, soldiers appeared.

The risk seemed to rise every day. The noose seemed to loom. And no matter how grateful Washington had been for the information about the British's knowledge of Rochambeau, appreciation made his job no safer.

"Please, Mr. Townsend." Freeman strode beside him, face neutral but tone pleading. "You must get this merchandise to Mr. Bolton."

All the code names made him grit his teeth. Yes, maybe Tallmadge—Bolton—would want the information. But it was vague at best, so what good would it even do? How often had he been told not to pass along conjectures and suppositions, but only facts?

Chilling as it was to consider that a Patriot officer might defect, he could offer no information on whom, where, or when. And who was to say it would even happen? No, it was not worth the risk of getting a message out. He had sent off intelligence about the ten sail of the line and other warships that left New York under Admiral Rodney two weeks ago, but that had represented clear and unquestionable danger to the American fleet. Not some specter of a threat like this.

'Twasn't worth the risk, not without more details than Winter could offer him.

"I am sorry, Freeman."

The older man tugged his hat lower. "Sir, she is adamant that—"

"Tell your mistress that I have endured trial enough with all this business. I will not needlessly invite more. So please stop coming every week on her behalf. 'Twill do nothing to convince me."

And he could do without the constant reminders of her. He hadn't spoken to Winter since July and had done his best to avoid the need to see her. Oh, he had caught glimpses of her at social events now and then when he must attend for the newspaper. One time, in August, he had even slipped a note into a drawer for her, to pass along the thanks from Washington about the French information. Another time she had signaled she had information for him, so he had taken her note home and uncovered it with the counter liquor.

But he must get used to doing what was necessary without her aid. She would marry Lane soon, and be off to…somewhere. If he intended to persist in this business, he must do so without her.

Rob should have spoken months ago. A year ago, when they first met up in the city. He had known then that she was the only woman he could ever admire enough to marry, so why had he dawdled? He should never have recruited her into the Culper Ring. Instead, he should have run away with her and made her his wife. Perhaps then the help she would have offered would be different, but still she could have assisted him.

Freeman came to a halt, his expression now beseeching. "Mr. Townsend, you know she does all she can for the good of the business. Please don't cut her off. Already you will not speak to her, but if you now refuse to speak to me…"

"It has nothing to do with you, Freeman." He tried a smile, but it felt foreign to his lips. "I am merely focusing on different aspects of the business for now."

Freeman opened his mouth as if to reply, but then a frown wrinkled his forehead as he looked at a point beyond Rob's shoulder. Rob turned to see what had caught his attention and found himself frowning too. "Is that George Knight?"

He had kept his voice low, but still Freeman shushed him. With a roll of his eyes, Rob subsided, content to cast another glance toward the wharf, where an ill-dressed Mr. Knight was helping a few fishermen load crates aboard a small rowboat.

Curious. Knight may not be the wealthiest man in the City of New York, but he could certainly afford better than the patched-up breeches and coarse shirt he wore now, not to mention the slouchy, filthy-looking hat. What was the man up to? Surely he wasn't assisting the fisherman for social purposes or out of a deep desire to heft what looked like heavy crates.

Freeman pressed his lips together and turned away. "Excuse me, Mr. Townsend. I had better get home to Winter. You have a good day."

He nearly told Freeman to give Winter his greetings but stopped himself in time. No use in keeping even that much communication open between them. 'Twas time to sever ties. Time to admit he hadn't a good disposition for this work, at least right now, and resign himself to a life of quiet.

Alone.

"Townsend!"

Rob jumped when a red coat blazed to a halt in front of him, and then he forced a smile at the always-exuberant face of Archie Lane. "Good afternoon, Major."

The young man grinned. "I was headed next to your shop to see how you fared on grog."

Rob cleared his throat. "I was down here checking on my next shipment, but alas, no new supplies arrived for me today. Perhaps tomorrow."

"A shame." Major Lane nodded and turned away. "I shall check with you tomorrow then. Good day."

"And to you." Rob loosed a long breath and turned inland. Perhaps the major's inquiry was innocent enough—or rather, safe enough—but it also proved Rob's point to Freeman. One never knew when a British officer might all but jump upon one.

Just as one never knew when an acquaintance would serve to put one in mind of things one had no desire to think about. From Major Lane to his brother, and from Bennet Lane to Winter.

Winter, with her courageous heart and deep faith. Winter, with her gleaming eyes and brilliant smiles. Winter, smiling always at someone else.

Blast. He may as well go home, pull the drapes, and lock himself in for the night. Perhaps wallowing was unhealthy, but it was a far sight better to do it in private than before the eyes of all of New York.

Winter let another candy melt on her tongue and grinned. She exhaled an exaggerated sigh of pleasure and batted her lashes at Colonel Fairchild.

If she had to eat one more marshmallow, she might lose her dinner. Sweets had been an unaccustomed treat when she first arrived in the city, and she had indeed partaken of more than she ought, but at this point she craved only the vegetables from the farm. Carrots and potatoes sounded like heaven.

But then, carrots and potatoes didn't make for very romantic gifts. Anything made primarily of white sugar, however…

She wondered if Colonel Fairchild knew the long and ancient history of the confection. Of the many medicinal uses of the root of the marsh-growing mallow plant, or how the Egyptians once combined it with honey and offered it to their gods. She suspected not. And suspected too that if she were to educate him, he may think she had lost her mind.

"I knew you would like them," he said as he watched her indulge with a warm smile. "Do save some for later though, my darling, for I shan't be by to bring you more for several days."

Praise the Lord for a reason to put the box aside. She did so with another supposedly happy sigh, sliding it onto the bench beside her. A cool breeze blew through the garden, toying with her hair and teasing her nose with the scent of autumn leaves. "Will you be away, Colonel?"

He pursed his lips. "Not I, but I want to be at the ready. André has set up another meeting with the Patriot defector as last week's did not work out as planned. And he says that Washington may visit him while he is in the area, so we may even...oh, I dare not hope for that much. 'Twill be enough to gain the general and his post, however many men he brings with him. The rebels will not be able to recover from such a coup. This blasted war may be over soon, my love."

The marshmallow churned in her stomach. She smiled brightly. "That is certainly welcome news. I do so tire of all the tinfoil."

It took him a moment. "Oh, you mean turmoil. Yes, it wears on us all."

"Although..." She pulled forward a whitened curl and twined it around her finger. "What happens when it is over? Do you return to your family in England?"

His shrug looked so peaceful that her heart had no choice but to worry all the more. "Perhaps, or perhaps I will receive a grant of land here or in Canada. I do like this continent, I confess. I shouldn't mind making a home here." He took her hand and kissed her fingers. "Of course, such decisions must also take into account the preferences of the one with whom I intend to build this life."

"That is very gracious of you, sir. Many men take no such interest in the preferences of their families."

He arched a brow. "Mr. Lane?"

"Oh!" Bother, she hadn't thought of how he would interpret that. She had only been thinking of her grandfather. "We have not talked much of his plans beyond returning to Connecticut soon. He does so miss his classes. And his lavatory, of course."

Fairchild choked down a laugh that time. "You mean laboratory, my darling."

Well, she had to do something to entertain herself. "Yes, of course. That is what I said."

"Mmm." He smiled and stood. "Well, I suggest you talk with him about these matters soon, my dear. While Mr. Lane is a man of many admirable qualities, he can be absentminded about some things. You must be sure you can suffer whatever future he envisions, if you intend to accept his proposal, which will surely be coming soon."

She gave him a small smile. He had taken hope from the fact

that Bennet hadn't yet made an offer, she knew, but she could hardly tell him that they had spent the past two months sharing whispered details of their hearts and had been enjoying it too much to rush through it.

Nor did she want to think of all she could *not* tell Bennet. The truth of her father, of her loyalties. Of how she prayed that what she did share—her faith, her intellect, her love of simpler ways—would somehow be enough.

"Well, I must be going. I imagine I will see you, if only briefly, at the Shirleys' ball tonight, and I will try to come by again on Sunday."

She rarely spent time with any gentleman but Bennet at social gatherings these days. Fairchild usually stayed close to André's side and stared at her half the night. Tonight would they be talking of this upcoming meeting?

Her spirit weighed heavy within her, making her smile waver. "I shall look forward to it, Colonel. Do caution the major to be careful."

He looked surprised by the serious admonition. "Of course. Good afternoon, my dear."

"And to you."

The moment he disappeared into the house, she ran toward the stable. "Freeman!"

He waited in the empty stall and motioned her down the stairs. A light already burned. "Mr. Townsend wouldn't budge, Winter. I did my best to convince him, but I fear he is losing his heart for it again."

Thanks to her. She squeezed her eyes shut, that weight only growing. "We must keep trying. André is leaving tomorrow for a meeting with this general who has promised to defect. A *general*, Freeman. One who has just traveled into the area. Surely Tallmadge and Washington would know who it is with that much information. We must get word to them. We *must*."

Freeman motioned toward her stain and paper. "Write him, then. But, Winnie girl, I rushed home for another reason."

She hurried to the shelf and pulled down the invisible ink, her regular ink, two quills, and a sheet of white paper. "What is it?" Onto the table by the lamp she spread out her tools.

Freeman leaned against the table. "I saw George Knight at the wharf. Dressed as a fisherman and helping load crates onto a small vessel."

Easing onto her chair, Winter kept her gaze on Freeman. "Was he with anyone else? Did you recognize them?"

Freeman nodded. "A few other fishermen from the looks of them. I think…I could be mistaken, but I thought I recognized them from Long Island. Patriots."

Once before George Knight had aided a Patriot—Silas, from her farm. And then in July, Fairchild had warned Bennet that his friend was seen in dubious company. Was it possible that Mr. Knight was friendly toward their cause? "Were they crates of weapons, do you think?"

Though he shrugged, Freeman's eyes gleamed. "Looked heavy enough to be, though of course I could not investigate it. Winter, is he—"

"I cannot say. I did not think so." She sent a whoosh of breath through her lips and focused her gaze on nothing. "He always makes himself sound simply mercenary. Yet to be smuggling crates of weapons in the middle of the day…he either has great love of every coin he can find, or something else driving him to such risky actions."

"There remains the possibility that they were not weapons, and the risk therefore not so great."

Then why disguise himself? Winter shook her head and turned to her paper. "A possibility, yes. But if you thought that were the case, you would not have rushed back here." Angling a smile his way, she opened the inkwell and dipped in her quill.

They would be at the Shirleys' tonight, where Winter had attended enough balls that she and Robbie had designated a few locations to slip notes to one another. She would use the bureau in the hallway. And so the logical thing to write in her visible message was a laundry list.

Freeman chuckled. "True enough. It struck me, for certain. If a gunsmith of Knight's ilk is making weapons for the Patriots, he could be a friend indeed."

Tension made her stomach clench again. "I cannot say if he is *our* friend—but he is Bennet's, and *he* has said on several occasions that if he catches Mr. Knight in dubious enterprises again, he will turn him over to the military."

Freeman held her gaze as he rested his hand on her shoulder. "And so if he knew our secret…"

"He cannot. 'Tis as simple as that." A realization she came to anew at least once a week, and which never failed to pull her spirits down into the abyss. It seemed every day she loved him more, wanted more to reveal every crevice of her being to him. She wanted to believe he loved her as much.

But these were strange times they lived in, when family members turned against one another for their loyalties. If Bennet would really offer up his oldest friend to the authorities, then he would certainly do the same to her, whom he had known for less than a year. His reason would rule his heart.

It always did. And she could hardly resent him for one of the things she loved about him.

Pushing that aside, she finished her visible writing, put a tiny A in the top corner, and took the cork from the vial of sympathetic stain. She held it up to the light with a frown. So little left—and with the way things were going, Robbie was unlikely to give her more. But she must use it tonight. There was no help for it.

Freeman was silent as she penned her true note, but once she put down her quill, he cleared his throat. "Winter, I know you love Mr. Lane. And from what I can see, he loves you as well. But if you really fear he would hand you over to a lynch mob, you must ask yourself if this is the match the Lord has planned for you. I cannot think our heavenly Father wants you to hide this part of your heart for the rest of your life."

"I don't know, Free." She squeezed her eyes shut as another wave of need washed through her spirit. "I cannot give up my cause, not when I know it's what the Lord has called me to. Yet I have never loved like this, and I cannot fathom why the Father would have given me such an attachment if it is doomed. How to reconcile the two, though…"

"I have been giving it daily to prayer." His hand settled on her shoulder again, warm and familiar. "An answer will come when the Lord is ready to provide it."

She nodded and held the paper up to the light to see if it was dry. No ink glistened, so she folded it, carelessly so it would look like an ordinary household list. Then she put the cork back on the few precious drops of stain that remained. "I had better go prepare for the evening."

"Be careful, Winnie girl." Freeman smiled, but it was small. "I cannot shake the feeling that we walk a narrower plank than ever before."

She nodded as she stood. "I feel the same." And so, when she regained her room after leaving the stable and reclaiming the marshmallows, the first thing she did was drop to her knees beside her bed.

Lord of all, I seek Your assurance, for You are the only one with the answers I need.

Eyes squeezed shut, forehead resting upon the feather ticking of her bed, she clasped her hands and poured out every fear, every hope, every goal, every need before the Father. Concern for André's endeavors, for what this treachery could mean to the Patriot cause. The discomfort she still felt every time Fairchild came to visit. Her love for Bennet she gave over to Him yet again, along with an earnest beseeching that a way would be made clear for the obstacles between them to be removed.

Winter didn't rise until a maid came to help her dress for the ball, and even then her stomach still felt as though a stone rested within it. She knew the Lord had the entire situation in His hand, but she also knew that sometimes He called His children to what seemed like failure, even destruction. That His greater plan often included what man deemed setbacks.

And, oh, how she prayed she were not on a course for one of them.

Grandmother had already given her instruction on what gown she was to wear, a sack-back creation in rose and gold. Only her accessories were ever left to her own choosing, and so she chose the ones with meaning.

Her fan of ostrich feathers, the sign to Robbie that she had left a message for him. A long string of pearls, wound thrice around her neck, to impart it was in their third location at the Shirleys', the top drawer of the bureau in the hall. A bright, silken rose tucked into the tower of her curls—her signal for urgency.

O Lord, let him take heed. Let us not be too late.

With one last, long breath, she determined she was as ready for the evening to come as she could hope to be.

Nineteen

Ben gazed at the dancing couples without really seeing them. Had Mother not come knocking on his door, he would have forgotten about the ball this evening and remained mired in his maps and notes, his charts and lists.

He was close. So close he could all but taste it, and his nerves leaped at every interruption. He was all but certain that Woodhull was the agent in Long Island who served as liaison between Tallmadge and their man in the city. It felt right; it made sense. He had little by way of solid proof, but then, he didn't need it. He wasn't going to try anyone in a court of law.

A group of tittering females swept by, and Ben took a step back, nodding to them but otherwise not attempting a greeting. Perhaps one of these days he would cease bumbling like a nincompoop in fair company, but until then he would content himself with the knowledge that Winter provided a perfect buffer between him and all of her lady friends, and that no one really expected him to pay attention to anyone but her.

When she was by his side, anyway. Which made him wonder what was keeping her. She had excused herself some fifteen minutes ago to see to personal matters.

A quick survey showed him she had been stopped by a few young women near the door. She stood with her usual expression of semi-boredom, her plumed fan waving before her.

His insides did that strange little twist they always did upon first sighting her. And they added a flip when she glanced his way and sent him a small, private smile.

How had he managed to claim such a magnificent creature? Not that she was officially his, of course, but everyone assumed he would propose soon. He assumed it too, if only…if only he could be sure all their advances in honesty would not fall away when she learned the truth about his goals, his very purpose for being here. If only he could be sure all their ideals matched as nicely as he hoped.

But he could hardly share the details of his spy hunt with her. 'Twouldn't do to get her involved. The dangers were too great. The military from both sides would likely toss him happily into prison if they knew what business he had been poking his nose into. Neither would much care for his reasoning. The point remained he was a citizen about work that could be construed as interfering with theirs.

Winter's fan fluttered again, and her gaze flicked to another corner of the room and then back to her companions. Ben turned his eyes toward the corner and sighed.

Townsend. There was no question why Winter would look his way and then away again so quickly. Her old friend still refused to speak to her, and Ben knew it caused her no little grief. He could hardly blame the fellow for that.

But seeing him brought up a whole host of other questions that sent Ben's mind back to the papers locked in his desk.

One of the primary reasons Woodhull emerged as a key suspect in the ring of spies was that his sister and her husband had taken up residence in the city. After the Great Fire, they had opened their doors to boarders. Woodhull reportedly stayed with them frequently a year and more ago, and then his visits tapered off.

It had taken weeks of subtle questions, but Ben had eventually discovered who else had been boarding with this couple during the months when Woodhull had frequented their home.

He was regarding one of them now.

Townsend must have felt his gaze, for he looked Ben's way and nodded. No smile, but Ben hadn't expected one.

But he smiled at Townsend before looking elsewhere. He didn't much like the picture that presented itself when he entertained the notion that Winter's childhood friend may be involved in espionage, but it made all too much sense. Townsend's father had been loudly Whiggish until he was arrested in seventy-six for his politics. Townsend had bent his knee to the Crown along with the rest of his family, but a little digging had turned up that, before that happened, he had attempted to help in the recruiting and organizing of Patriot troops back when Washington occupied the City of New York.

The Townsends were Quaker, and so ought to have been peaceful. To have broken from that enough to gather troops, Robert Townsend had to have felt pretty strongly about the rebel cause.

But now there he stood, mired in Loyalist society. A partner with Rivington, one of the loudest Tories in the city. At all the balls, all the dinners, all the fetes under the guise of a newspaperman. Doing business with nearly every officer in the British military through his store.

If anyone could obtain sensitive information, it was surely Townsend. And he certainly had the friends to get that information out of British territory and into Patriot hands.

Still, it was only supposition. A hypothesis. He must test it somehow. He could not afford to tip his hand until he was without doubt. If he spoke up only to discover he had made a mistake, then he would be forced to leave town and hence would not be able to correct his error.

Better to bide his time. Watch. Listen. Wait. If Townsend were his man, he would find him out soon enough.

He could do nothing now, though, so best to put such thoughts aside. Ben made his way around the edge of the ballroom, his goal to blend into the wallpaper until he made it safely to Winter.

She stepped away from the flock of her friends with a smile in which he had no trouble detecting the gratitude. Tucking her hand into the crook of his elbow, she made him feel instantly more comfortable. "Did you miss me, Mr. Lane?"

Odd how he didn't mind the flirtation, even enjoyed it, now that it wasn't all she offered him. He grinned. "The lights dim when you are not by my side, Miss Reeves. And as I tend toward clumsiness in the dark, I thought it expedient to find you again at once."

Winter grinned. "We certainly can't have you tripping over everyone in a ballroom this crowded."

"My thoughts exactly." He nodded toward the room's exit. "Shall we step out for a bit of refreshment? A lemonade, perhaps?"

"That sounds delightful." She cast another glance at Townsend's corner, though.

Miss Shirley followed her gaze and frowned. "Mr. Townsend has not left that corner all night. I do hope his article still reflects well on us. 'Tis hardly our fault he refuses to budge, after all."

"He will be fair, I am sure." Winter's smile was as bright and oblivious as ever, but Ben saw the concern in her eyes.

All he could do was cover her fingers with his and think it could be a blessing Townsend refused to speak with her. If he were indeed involved in this spying business, she would be better off having nothing to do with him.

Not that such reasoning, of which she would remain unaware anyway, could soften the blow of losing one's longtime friend.

He settled for steering her out into the hallway, away from the dour-faced reminder. "Have I mentioned how lovely you look tonight, my darling?"

Winter seemed to shake off the anxiety and grinned up at him. "You have, and I thanked you for it. Have I mentioned how nice *you* look? I like this suit of clothes nearly as well as the one you wore yesterday."

He chuckled and smoothed a hand over the silk waistcoat of his best clothing. Yesterday he had arrived at Hampton Hall in homespun again. "Perhaps I should have worn that tonight then."

Her laugh sounded free and bright. "I doubt your mother would have permitted you into her carriage."

"You do have a point." He pulled her closer as they drew even with a bureau. "Careful, there. Someone left a drawer open."

Winter turned to see what he had nearly run her into and made a tsking sound. "Here, let me close it before someone bruises a rib." She pulled her hand away and grasped both rings, glancing in as she shut it.

Ben stifled a grin. Always curious, his Winter, even when only an empty drawer greeted her gaze.

When she turned back to him, that tension possessed her shoulders as it had the first night they met, and the same emptiness filled her gaze. Ben frowned. "Are you well?"

A smile broke free for only a moment. "Sorry. 'Tis only Robbie. He will not speak to me even when I come into the store, but rather always sends Oakham to help me."

He hummed his understanding and drew her close again. "I wish I could make it better for you, but I'm afraid all I can do is fetch you that lemonade. And offer to risk a dance afterward, if it will cheer you up."

There. She relaxed again and grinned. "My toes still ache from the last dance we shared, my dear Mr. Lane. I think I would prefer it if you regale me with your thoughts on whatever book you have been lately reading."

Was it any wonder he loved this woman?

Winter paced before her open window, unable to be soothed by the fragrant air floating in or the spiced tea that sat, barely touched, on her table. She had hardly slept the past two nights—couldn't. Every time she drifted off, fierce need awoke her and sent her to her knees in prayer.

The world was unraveling. Major André had not yet returned, which meant that his meeting had taken place as planned, as best as she could tell. Somewhere upriver a Patriot general walked about amid his army, ready to deliver their lives to the enemy.

And she could do nothing. Worse, what she had attempted had gone terribly wrong.

Robbie had not left the ballroom after she slipped her note into the bureau Wednesday night—but the drawer had been empty when she walked past it with Bennet.

Reason told her she need not fear. She had written her message in sympathetic stain, so it could not possibly be discovered by anyone outside the Culper Ring.

Still. Why would anyone have taken what looked like a laundry list unless they saw her slip it in and were curious as to why she would? But she had taken care. She had been so sure no one noticed her covert movements as she opened the drawer upon arriving and slipped the paper in half an hour later.

But if someone had…if someone were watching her…

Nausea gnawed at her stomach, and she halted in front of the open window to draw in a breath of calming, cool air.

That was hardly the most pressing concern. More urgent was the fact that Robbie had refused to hear Freeman out when she had sent him yesterday, other than to verify he had not retrieved the note—and to add that he had not intended to at any rate.

She rubbed at her eyes. They ached, felt gritty and heavy, and yet she knew there was no use in trying to nap. Not until this weight lifted from her spirit.

If only she could get a message out without Robbie's help. She knew the route they took, knew the names and code names of all the agents of the ring along the way, but unless Roe were scheduled to arrive, or Woodhull, she had no way to start a message on its journey. Besides which, it took a week for anything to get from the city to General Washington.

'Twould surely be too late by then. And so this knowledge meant nothing. Could accomplish nothing. A general would defect, and for all she knew, he could hand her father over to the British when he did so. She was powerless to stop it.

"No." Her hands fell away and then balled up in her skirt. No, she was not helpless, not powerless. She was not just a secondary agent of the Culper Ring. She was a child of the Most High. Even if she could not get a warning to the Patriots, she could rouse help from the heavenly warriors.

With new determination, she strode to her bedside and took to her knees yet again.

"Father God," she whispered into her coverlet, "I come before You in praise, to thank You for all You have done for me and my loved ones. I thank You for preserving my father's life in these past years of war, for providing for my needs, for leading me to a man with whom I can envision a future. I praise You for seeing all, for knowing all, and for taking the care to direct our paths. Though I cannot see around the next bend in the road, I know You can. Though I may feel only the enemy nipping at my heels, I trust that You are by my side, for You have promised it."

She paused, drew in a long breath scented with the lavender tucked into her sheets. And listened to the chords of anxiety that sounded within her spirit. "Father, I do not know what Your plan is for this country, for the brave men fighting on both sides of this war. I know only that You have called me to help where I can. And today, this is where You have put me. Lifting up my cause to You and relinquishing it. My Lord, I cannot pray that You take the decision out of this general's hands, though I wish I could. He must have his will, I know. But I ask that You minister to him where You can, and urge him not to commit this crime against those who trust him."

Her voice shook to a halt, and a cloud must have passed before the sun, for the warmth across her back vanished, as did the soft, glowing light. "But, Father, though You cannot take his decision from him, and though he may follow through on his plan, You can speak to the hearts of Your followers and give them Your wisdom and discernment so that they might recognize the enemies among them. Please, Lord, open the hearts and minds of Your children. Urge them to pray. Protect them from this treachery. Deliver them from the traps likely set for them."

The cool breeze kissed her neck, and a measure of calm finally trickled over her spirit. "Deliver them, Lord. Deliver us." She let her words lapse away, content to breathe in the whisper of the Lord and pour her heart out to Him without such constrictions.

A gentle hand shook her back to awareness, and the face of her maid greeted her gaze when she opened her eyes. "Yes?"

The girl frowned. "Mr. Lane is waiting for you in the garden, Miss Winnie."

"Already?"

"'Tis afternoon, miss. You did not come down for the meal. Should I tell him you are unwell?"

She had spent that much time in prayer? Perhaps she had dozed off for a bit too. Winter straightened herself. "No, of course not. I will be right down."

"But…" Pressing her lips together, the maid seemed to debate a moment before saying, "You *look* unwell."

"Do I?" It was no wonder, given the lack of sleep. Winter stood and went to her mirror, nearly laughing at the picture that it revealed. Her hair was still in its nighttime braid, frizzing every which way. Circles ringed her eyes, and her skin looked pale otherwise. At least she had dressed well enough to receive company, if simply.

It took only a few minutes for the maid to school her waving locks into some semblance of order. There was little to be done about her face, but a few splashes of cool water at least made her feel more awake. And Bennet would not mind her lack of fashion.

She hurried down the stairs and out to the garden, where he waited on the bench as usual.

He stood and frowned much like her maid had. "Are you feeling ill, Winter?"

She smiled and put her hands into his outstretched ones. In truth, it was a blessing to have someone who cared about such things. Grandmother always acted as though the slightest discomfort on Winter's part were a huge inconvenience. And Grandfather probably took joy in her every pain. "No, I am well enough. I just have not slept well the past few nights."

"Why is that?" He urged her onto the bench beside him and kept their joined hands between them.

Winter drew in a deep breath and savored it before letting it out. Though she couldn't tell him all of what bothered her, she could share its source. "My spirit has been troubled. Every time I fall asleep, I awake again with the need to pray."

The need pressed again at the new frown to possess his brows. "Have you had so much on your mind?"

In hopes of restoring his smile, she grinned. "'Tisn't my mind, Bennet. 'Tis my spirit. You are a Yale man. Surely you know the difference. You attended chapel daily."

His grunt did little to ease that new burden upon said spirit. "Of course I did. The penalties were high if one missed chapel. And certainly I understand the philosophical distinction. But I cannot say as my spirit has ever kept me up at night, though an overactive mind certainly has from time to time."

'Twasn't just the tone of his words that made exhaustion sweep through her. He let go her fingers. Under the guise of repositioning his tricorn, but she suspected the action had deeper roots. She tried to keep her expression free of any negative feeling. "Yes, I have experienced that aplenty too, but this is different. This is the voice of the Holy Spirit."

He sent her the same gaze he used to do upon calling her on her feigned stupidity. "Come, Winter. The Lord has better things to do than interrupt your sleep."

Realization settled upon her. "You are a deist."

Bennet rolled his eyes. "It is an apt enough description, I suppose, though I don't see why we must label my theology."

"Because you have a theology instead of a faith." She bit her lip to keep from spouting a too-harsh opinion that he obviously was not interested in hearing.

"Winter." Each movement looked considered as he pasted patience onto his face and took her hand again. "You were raised Congregationalist. You said your father's family was Puritan. You have, therefore, different ideas about God and His involvement with mankind than I, whose family belongs to the Church of England solely because it is fashionable. And I do not mind your opinions. Faith, as you call it, is a becoming thing in a female."

"In a *female*?" She stood, knowing well her outrage shone. "Would that I could chalk this opinion of yours up to your usual misunderstanding of the *female* mind, but you ought to know better. Tell me, did *females* teach your classes at Yale that dealt with these matters? Did *females* give the sermons in chapel? What exactly is so very feminine about faith? It seems to me we talk of the patriarchs and *their* faith more than the few women mentioned in the Scriptures."

He took to his feet too and moved his hands in a quieting motion. "Calm yourself, please. I did not mean to imply...I was only going to say that I respect your opinions, even admire them in you, and so I hope you can respect mine as well."

A throb took up cadence behind her temples. She was far too tired to adequately debate anything with him right now. She would yell and then cry, which would only convince him of how unreasonable her opinions were. And really, it had nothing to do with a lack of respect. More a sorrow. The same she felt whenever she realized one of her friends hardly knew her father, who lived under the same roof. While she counted hers as one of the dearest beings on the planet, yet she could not even send him a letter in her own hand.

She drew in a deep breath and steadied herself. "You know I respect you. I am sorry for speaking in such a way, but it saddens me to think you do not understand this thing that is so important to me. Have you never heard the voice of the Lord, Bennet?"

He opened his mouth and then halted. His brow creased, first in thought, but then it deepened into a scowl. She watched as, muscle by muscle, his face hardened into a determined wall. "No."

Laughter and tears vied for a place in her throat. She swallowed both down. That was the face of a man denying the truth if she had ever seen one. And someone so determined to ignore the gentle whisper of God would not want to listen to her prod him about it. "Then I shall pray you will."

At least the stubbornness melted away, replaced by the amused arch of a brow. "Are you saying that to agitate me, my love?"

"Only in part." She gave him her most mischievous smile and made no objection when he motioned to the path that meandered through the garden.

The greater part was pure honesty. She must pray. Not only for her country, her father, her friend, her cause. But also for the man she loved.

Twenty

Today if ye will hear his voice, harden not your heart.
Ben scowled at the snippet of the psalm that battered his mind every time he looked over at Winter. That same verse had plagued him for days, ever since she had posed her ridiculous question.

"Have you never heard the voice of the Lord, Bennet?"

Of course he hadn't. The very idea was preposterous. Providence had no need to speak to him, and these verses that sprang to memory at key moments were little more than the workings of his own mind. A mind perfectly capable of directing him, one the Lord had created with the ability to reason and make decisions. *That* was the role of God.

An argument he had no desire to bring up again with Winter, seeing how worn she still looked and knowing well what she would think of his position. He had never dreamed his words the other day would upset her so acutely. But then, she was overtired.

He stole a glance at her out of the corner of his eye. Shadows still circled her eyes, but she seemed to be enjoying the book he had brought her. Mrs. Hampton had pursed her lips in disapproval of his choice, had made a comment about how different his gifts were from Fairchild's. Her tone had covered snideness with sugar.

Ben had only grinned. Winter had confessed how tired she grew of candy and confection, and he was far more set on pleasing her than her grandmother. She enjoyed Shakespeare, he knew, and so the book of sonnets would entertain her well.

Mrs. Hampton made an annoyed sound and slanted a hard gaze at her granddaughter. "Why do you not read that after our guest has left, Winnie?"

Winter put a ribbon in the page and offered a peaceful smile. "I wanted him to know how much I appreciate the gift."

The elder lady lifted her chin. "Appreciation ought not to be expressed by neglect. Do forgive my granddaughter, Mr. Lane. Tell me, have you heard lately from your father?"

"Indeed, ma'am." Ben nodded and cleared his throat. He wished the letter from Father hadn't left him with such bittersweet feelings. "He has acquainted himself well with Clefton, which greatly pleases his uncle, whose health is fragile."

Mrs. Hampton nodded. "I am glad to hear he has settled in so well. And I imagine he wishes you to join him soon, as you too will have to acquaint yourself with the estate."

Hence the bitter side of his feelings. Bennet loosed a long breath. "He did indeed express such a desire, but I have no intention of leaving New York yet." And when he did, he had every intention of heading back to Connecticut, not across the Atlantic.

An argument he intended to put off until he had finished his business here.

The lady smiled, smug. "Of course not. But Winnie and I were talking before you arrived about how she longs to see England."

Winter sent her grandmother a questioning look. "Were we? I believe, Grandmother, that you were saying how much *you* would like me to see England."

Ben grinned at Winter. "And what of Connecticut, my dear? Would you like to see that?"

"Indeed." She flashed that mischievous smile he so loved. "It sounds terribly exotic. So very unlike New York."

He chuckled even as her grandmother scowled. If she kept this up, she would soon rival her husband with her dour glances. "Winnie darling, do not be impudent. Really, sir, I don't know what has come over her of late."

"No need for apologies." Ben cleared his throat again, wishing he could rid himself of all anxiety with so simple a motion. But so long as his father had expectations he did not intend to fulfill, he knew well the discomfort would bind him. He caught Winter's eye. "In truth, ma'am, I am not so eager to cross the Atlantic myself. My home has always been here."

Something shifted in Winter's face and relaxed. While Mrs. Hampton stared at him with mouth agape, Winter raised her hands and arched one finger from her mouth outward, one of the signs she had taught him. *Really?*

He made a discreet knocking motion. *Yes.*

Mrs. Hampton huffed. "When it comes to family responsibilities, Mr. Lane, our personal desires must be put aside. Surely you realize that. Why, to think of all those for whom you will be responsible! 'Tis unthinkable that you would let them down."

"Unthinkable indeed." But Archie would rise to the occasion. Ben had long thought that all his brother needed to shove him into maturity was direction. He had hoped the military would provide it, but the army ran too amuck in New York. A British estate, though, would be all Archie's dreams come true. His current attitude may in fact be due to being denied what he so wanted.

Winter looked ready to respond but was stayed by the opening of the door. The butler walked in, concern upon his face. "Colonel Fairchild, ma'am."

Mrs. Hampton frowned, but the colonel gave her no chance to turn him away. He burst into the room with heaving shoulders and agony in his expression. "Forgive me for barging in, but I must—I am sorry. It is Major André. He has been captured."

Ben and Winter both took to their feet. She slowly, as if dazed. Ben felt like a cannon exploding from the sofa, so forceful was his incredulity. "Captured? But how?"

Fairchild shook his head, nostrils flaring. "I have tried to piece it all together from various reports. So far as I can tell, the meeting with General Arnold went according to plan. The price for his defection was decided on, and he promised to turn over West Point."

Ben started, eyes going wide. Benedict Arnold was the turncoat? He never would have guessed. Given her quick, startled breath, Winter was taken aback as well.

Fairchild paced to the window and clasped shaking hands behind his back. "The general was supposed to have already made provisions for André's return through the Patriot territory. Supposed to have sent out messages letting his men know that a 'Mr. Anderson' would be traveling through and stating that he was sympathetic to their cause."

Winter took a step toward Fairchild but then halted. Ben had never seen an expression quite like the one on her face, some strange variation of horrified disbelief. "When was this?"

"Saturday, the twenty-third." He lifted a hand to his face and rubbed at his eyes. "From what I can gather, he was stopped by Patriots...or perhaps locals out to make some coin. He must have misspoken to them, though I cannot fathom it. André always knew what to say. I would have thought he could talk his way out of any situation."

Ben could scarcely fathom it himself. A hard knot cinched tight in his stomach, and the words he had spoken to Townsend about his cousin came back to him now. The Patriots were still seeking recompense for the hanging of their scout Nathan Hale nearly four years ago. If they had captured André, who was indeed about covert business out of military uniform, then they would have no choice. He would be hanged.

Much as he hated it, Ben understood that. But why did another young man he dared to call a friend have to get caught up in this? Hale, and now André. Perhaps he was not exceptionally close to either of them, but both he knew. Both he had talked and laughed with.

Both deserved grieving.

Mrs. Hampton snapped her fan shut. "What terrible news, Colonel. Perhaps he shall escape. Or be released."

"I fear not, ma'am." Fairchild's hand fell to his side and dangled as if he had no fight left in him. "His execution is set for the second of October."

"Oh, Colonel." Winter moved over to him and rested a hand on his arm. "I am so sorry."

"I know." He covered her hand with his but kept his gaze out the window. "We are all sorry. I have to think that even his executioners will be sorry if they take a moment to converse with him over the next week. Never have I met anyone so charming and likeable as John

André. And yet that can change nothing. He played a game too dangerous, and he lost."

Ben's fingers curled into his palm. "What of General Arnold? Was he captured as well?"

Fairchild spun around, eyes narrowed. Then he relaxed. "I called him by name. Well, it hardly matters now. Our scouts have reported a flurry of activity that indicates they discovered his involvement, but that he escaped West Point before he could be captured. I expect he will arrive in the city any day."

"Good." Mrs. Hampton sniffed and made her posture more regal than ever. "I'm of the opinion that a man, once a traitor, can never be trusted by anyone, but it will be a welcome blow to the rebels."

Winter drew in a long breath. "I will pray for the major. And for you, Colonel."

"Thank you, Miss Reeves." Fairchild offered a wavering smile. "I appreciate your every prayer, for both myself and André. I ought to get back. I had to see you, though. To let you know. To…"

To get what comfort he could from the woman he loved. Ben sighed and wished there were some formula to simplify a situation. Or, while he was dreaming of such alchemy, to right the wrongs of the world. But all he could do was send an understanding, encouraging smile to Winter when she clasped Fairchild's hand between both of hers. And, when the colonel nodded and turned, dejected, toward the door, clap a hand to his shoulder to stay him. "I know there is probably nothing I can do. But if there is…"

Fairchild nodded. "I do appreciate it, Lane. Perhaps we could plan an outing for the second. To keep me busy. I will not be good company, I know, but—"

"I shall come up with something. 'Tis the least I can do."

His gaze straight ahead and lips pressed together—no doubt to quell rising emotion—Fairchild exited without another word.

"Well." Mrs. Hampton huffed and smoothed out her skirt. "That was certainly unexpected news. I am sorry for Major André. He struck me as a fine young man. But then, such is always a possibility when one opts for military life. I am of the mind that if one sends one's kin off to war, one might as well as assume they are marching to their deaths."

Winter spun to face her grandmother, two blooms of scarlet

bringing life back to her wan cheeks. "Grandmother! What a dreadful thing to say."

For a moment, Mrs. Hampton wore an expression of belligerent victory that made no sense whatsoever, but then she glanced over at Ben and her eyes widened. "Do forgive me, Mr. Lane! It slipped my mind that your brother is in the army."

He forced a smile and returned to Winter's side. When he took her hand, he found her trembling. From the shock of André's fate or anger? "Think nothing of it, ma'am."

But he would not be able to put it so easily from his own mind. Why had the woman said such a thing, with such a pointed expression? An expression pointed at Winter?

He drew in a deep breath as they took their seats on the sofa once more. It would seem they knew something he didn't. Which was one of his least favorite states in which to be.

A gust of wind sent spikes of cold rain into Winter's face as she all but ran down Queen Street, Freeman keeping pace with her. Earlier that day she had breathed in the scent of autumnal leaves with a smile, had taken solace in the cool breath of the air. Had spent an hour of prayer in the garden and had enjoyed every moment of silent communion under blue September skies.

Now the biting rain was welcome. Her concealing cloak didn't look out of place, and no one would think anything of her pulling it low over her face. Assuming anyone else was fool enough to be out in the building storm.

With each footfall, her heart galloped ahead. Her fingers curled tighter into her cloak's fabric. Her spirit cried within her.

All those hours on her knees this past week. So much supplication. Moment after moment of undulating urgency, chased by fleeting peace. Times when she thought others must have taken up her prayer, times when she felt she was the only one in the country who knew to pray for its protection from betrayal.

But this—this was not what she had wanted. Why did it have to be Major André who was caught, Colonel Fairchild's closest friend? He did not deserve this fate. He was guilty only of doing his duty, and much as that duty opposed Winter's cause, he still ought not to have been handed such a punishment. Why could it not have been the traitor himself who was intercepted? Whose execution was scheduled?

Benedict Arnold. One of the highest-ranking men in the Continental Army. In charge of West Point. Privy, no doubt, to countless Patriot secrets.

O God, the Eternal All, protect us.

What if he knew of the Culpers? What if Washington had confided in him, and he intended to have a few lynchings of his own when he reached the city?

What if her days, too, were numbered—not just by God, but by man? She choked down a sob.

Freeman drew a bit closer. "I know this isn't what we wanted, and I'm right sorry for the major. But, Winnie girl, our prayers have still been answered. Try to look at that. Had they not caught him and discovered the plot, Arnold would have turned West Point over to the British. That would have been the end of the Glorious Cause."

"I know. And praise the Lord for that." Yet it lit a fuse of guilt within her. When she prayed for discernment for the men around the traitor, when she prayed that Providence would waken His children to prevent such disaster, she had never stopped to think that the answer may mean death to one she knew, one she liked.

And yet her father's life could have been forfeit had Arnold had his way, as Grandmother had so nastily hinted at after Fairchild left. Any battle, any accident, any illness could snatch Father from this world before they could be reunited, and the chances would certainly have increased with treachery.

How could she weigh one life against another? How could she rejoice in the sparing of her allies and yet still mourn the loss of an enemy?

An enemy who was a friend.

She swiped away rain and tears and risked a glance up to see how much farther they must go. Only a few more buildings.

And praise be to the Father that He did all the weighing, all the judging. She would never, could never understand His ways. And so she would always be conflicted.

Freeman caught her elbow. "Hurry. He is locking up."

Winter broke into an outright run, but Robbie had still made it nearly to the corner before she caught him. She whispered his name once she was close enough for him to hear.

Robbie spun around with a startled frown and tugged his collar up to meet his hat. "Winnie! What are you doing here?"

"Shh." She motioned him into an alley. A roar of thunder ripped through the sky.

Taking what cover could be found beside a stack of crates, Robbie looked from her to Freeman. "Again, what are you doing here? If you mean to try to get me to warn seven-one-one of this possible defector again—"

"Have you not heard?" She forced herself to take a deep breath, though her throat wanted to close off. "André has been arrested by the Patriots, and so they have discovered General Arnold's intentions."

Robbie drew in a sharp breath. "Arnold? Nay, say you jest. And Major André?"

No nod had ever felt so painful. "He will be hanged next week."

"Nay." This time his denial came out as no more than a murmur. "It cannot be. He is such a fine man, so friendly and well liked by all."

"'Tis as true as it is terrible. Fairchild came to tell me as soon as he found out."

He squeezed his eyes shut as he made a visible effort to keep his breathing even. Freeman reached out and rested a hand on his shoulder. "We thought you would want to know."

Robbie didn't open his eyes. "I should have sent your message. I should have warned them weeks ago, and then this meeting never would have taken place. Arnold would be the one arrested, and André would be free and safe."

For a moment Winter just looked at him. 'Twas the first time in months she had been so close to her old friend, had exchanged words with him. Why must they be words so laden with death? With implications so very unmistakable?

If it could happen to André, it could happen to them.

And she didn't even know, anymore, how to try to comfort him.

He was no longer a friend whose hand she could clasp. No longer the brother to whom she could offer a shoulder. Yet still so much a part of all she had become, one of the few who knew from whence she came.

She must do *something*. And so she drew a bit closer and rested her gloved fingers on his arm. "I daresay they would not have believed it of General Arnold even if we *had* sent a message. They cannot deny it when they intercept the man who has turned him, but on mere rumor and hearsay?" She shook her head. "He did not manage to deliver West Point, which had apparently been his plan. So all is not as disastrous as it could have been."

Brilliant light arrowed through the gloom, charging the air with a snap and sizzle. Thunder pounced and rolled. Robbie's lips turned up, but it could hardly be termed a smile. "How can you find hope in circumstances like these?"

What was it Viney had said when Winter asked her something similar? *They are only circumstances. The men out there may define me by them, but thank the Lord, He does not.*

How true those words were. Perhaps man and man's justice doled out death and defeat. But the Lord's hand was still outstretched with life and victory. Winter patted his arm. "It may seem impossible, but our faith is founded on what mere logic says cannot be."

Perhaps that was why Bennet seemed not to have made the leap from knowledge to belief.

Emotion washed over Robbie's features as sure as the deluge of rain, affection as piercing as the lightning. "You can always...how I wish things were different." Shaking his head, he drew away from her hand. "In addition to faith, we also need caution. Tread with care, Winnie. Promise me."

"I will. And you must too, even more so. No one but you knows of my involvement, but the entire ring knows of yours." She pursed her lips when the heavens barked their fury again, drowning out anything else she may have said.

Freeman stepped close to her side. "We had better get back."

"Yes, you had better." Robbie edged away from the crates and tugged his hat a little lower. Then he paused at her side. "Winnie..."

She lifted her brows and waited.

The rain sluiced down, dripping off the corners of his hat. He bent down, eyes echoing the storm, and pressed his lips to her cheek. Then he stepped back. "Thank you for being the one to tell me."

Winter could only nod and watch him stride away as the rain washed his kiss from her cheek.

Twenty-One

Ben slid behind a taller man and peeked over his shoulder at the contingent of soldiers riding down the street. At the lead trotted the traitor himself, head held high and chest puffed out beneath his pristine red coat.

Perhaps it was his imagination that made him think the citizens around him all shrank back and hid their secrets behind their half-hearted cheers. In all likelihood that was his own frustration coloring his perception, for it seemed that ever since General Arnold arrived in New York, no honest thoughts ever found their way to lips—or, at least, no honest thought that breathed a word against the British establishment.

How in thunder was he supposed to discover whether certain parties had been involved in espionage when anyone with mixed loyalties was all of a sudden mute?

George, beside him, crossed his arms over his chest and glared with pursed lips at New York's newest person of infamy. 'Twas no great mystery why. His father, along with countless others, had been hauled in for questioning under Arnold's orders not two days ago.

It seemed the man was determined to earn his thirty pieces of silver by finding the spies that were operating in the city. As if arresting every man who had once spoken against the Crown would lead him to the elusive ring.

Blasted traitor. Mrs. Hampton had one thing right. No man could ever be trusted again after he turned on his cause for monetary gain. And now he was here scaring into silence everyone to whom Ben needed to talk to make the last connections in his own hunt.

One far more orderly than this willy-nilly arresting nonsense. Arnold had no idea how to go about the business Ben had been agonizing over for so long, and he would ruin all his efforts if he kept this up. Anyone who knew anything would be frightened underground.

George spun away and jerked a head in the direction of Rivington's. "Coffee?"

"I would like nothing more." He matched his stride to his morose friend's. "Is it me, or has everyone been looking askance at everyone else since Benedict Arnold came to town?"

With a snort, George shoved a hand into his pocket. "'Tisn't you. With a man of his ilk proving how fleeting loyalties can be, no one is willing to trust anyone. Every word ever spoken is being examined and judged." He sent Ben a sideways glance. "Not that *you* have anything to worry about, what with Archie in the army and your father in England. You could climb up on your rooftop and scream 'Down with tyranny!' and no one would mutter a word against you."

Ben echoed George's snort. "Somehow I doubt that, my friend. Were I to say such things, my brother and father may be the first to haul me in." He hesitated but a moment. "And speaking of fathers?"

His friend gritted his teeth. "They released him this morning, but with a threat to take all our military contracts from us." An unfortunate stone met George's shoe and went hurtling into the alley. "Blast it, Ben, I am sick to death of this supposed rule of the military. They are the most corrupt bunch of louts I have ever seen, and they are running roughshod over us all. Doesn't matter what side you are on, not really, only whose pockets you line."

Oh, how he hoped none of those louts were within earshot now. Ben did a quick check over his shoulder. "Valid as that complaint may be, do keep it quiet, George."

Shoulders hunched, his friend looked the part of a disgruntled delinquent ready to pick his next fight. "Or what? Will you turn me over to your saintly Colonel Fairchild? Or maybe your reprobate of a brother?"

It took all his willpower not to roll his eyes. "I realize you are frustrated and angry, but could you at least *try* not to be a complete dunderhead?"

George came to a halt and, when Ben followed suit, glowered at him. "What am I supposed to think?" His voice was low, tight as a throb. "Every time we meet lately, you are cautioning me not to say this, not to do that, lest you have to turn me in."

Ben took a step closer and returned the glower. Odd—had he always been so much taller than George? It had never struck him before. "Have you ever paused to consider why I only issue warnings and have not *done* it?"

George opened his mouth but then closed it again and lifted his brows.

"I thought not." Ben loosed an exasperated breath and shook his head. "You are my friend, George. My oldest, truest friend. I would never—but if *thinking* I would has a chance of getting you to halt activities that could get you killed, obviously I will issue the threat."

Not a muscle in George's face twitched. He just stared at him, no doubt trying to digest what exactly he meant by that.

Ben chuckled, though he felt far from amused. "Do you think me unaware of what you have been doing? That I have forgotten that night in my garden, that I am blind to the times I have seen you sneaking off somewhere or deaf to the warnings others have given me about you?"

Panic flashed through his friend's eyes. "I…that is…"

"Nay." He put on the same expression he used when a student decided, after a small explosion, to take his word for how two chemicals would react. "I am no fool. But neither am I fond of seeing my acquaintances, much less my friends, lynched."

George looked off into the distance, his freckles standing out as his face went pale. "I am in no such danger. They only hang spies."

And he was not *that*. Ben had verified as much months ago. "True. Arms smugglers they would simply shoot on the spot."

Now 'twas George who glanced over his shoulder to make sure no one overheard. "I don't know of what you speak, Ben old man."

"Mm-hmm." Ben motioned his friend onward. Once they were walking again, he shook his head. "One would think that, given recent events, everyone would see the dangers inherit in any clandestine work and cease at once." His, of course, was entirely different. He was trying to find the spies. He had not become one himself.

George shoved his hands into his pockets again. "You are all logic. I daresay there is nothing in this world you believe in enough to take a risk for it. Leastways, nothing you cannot grasp with your hands."

"That is not true." If it were, the accusation would not have sounded like one to his ears. "I believe that much in loyalty—if I did not, I wouldn't have spent the last months protecting you and trying to warn you against what might get you killed. I would have consigned you to the consequences."

"Loyalty." George spat the word like an oath. "The word has lost all meaning. If we side with the land in which we were born rather than some tyrannical monarch thousands of miles away, we are called disloyal. If, on the other hand, we offer lip service to the Crown while dancing through the war feasting on delicacies and tossing our sterling at the London Trade, then we are lauded as Loyalists. No Tory I know gives a whit about England or the king's right to rule us, Ben, and that's the honest truth. They simply lack the gumption to fight for what seems a losing cause."

A smile slithered its way around Ben's frustration and onto his lips. "But you don't care about blue coats or red, of course. Only about sterling."

George angled a grin his way too. "A story I intend to maintain, as no British officer can argue with it." His gaze went over Ben's shoulder, and sobriety won his face. "Well, *most* officers cannot."

Following George's gaze, he saw Colonel Fairchild striding down Broadway, probably having come either from the barracks or the jail. Ben sighed. Even from here, the weight on the man's shoulders was unmistakable. He looked as though the entire world pressed upon him, bending his spine and forcing his gaze down.

Poor fellow. Ben had tried to distract him on the second with a fishing trip, but Fairchild had only sat on the bank and stared at his line all morning. Not surprising, but it reminded Ben of why he hadn't attempted fishing since a boy by his father's side. If he was going to be surrounded by silence for so long, he would prefer to do it with a quill in hand and paper before him, if not his full laboratory.

George shook his head. "I have never much cared for Fairchild, but I feel badly for him. First he loses his ladylove to you, and now his best friend to the Patriot executioner."

"Thank you for grouping me with a hangman, George. Really."

"Well, I imagine it feels much the same to him."

Ben growled halfhearted agreement. He had been toying with the idea of proposing whenever the opportunity arose, but perhaps it would be best to wait, to give Fairchild time to heal. Or perhaps the merciful thing would be to do it now, so that the colonel wouldn't put too much hope in her, only to be let down once more.

"Toss the man a bone," George said, elbowing him. "Break things off with Miss Reeves."

He returned the jab in the side. "Perhaps I shall heed your advice when you heed mine."

Though Rivington's loomed directly ahead, George halted again. "Would you? Give up your foolish involvement if I did the same?"

Was that serious contemplation in his friend's eyes? Ben shook his head. "I was jesting. I cannot. I love her. I intend to ask her to marry me soon."

"And you call *me* a dunderhead." George looked off into the distance. "Ben, I know you cannot understand why I do what I do any more than I can understand your affection for that ninny. But if she will make you happy, you know I will wish you well. I hope you can offer me the same respect in spite of not agreeing with my position."

Ben could nod with no compunction. But as they moved on again, he couldn't help but wonder how someone who knew him so well could know him so little.

Perhaps he was better at this covert business than he had thought.

Rob headed for the apex of Queen Street, where it angled from northeast to east. His gaze locked on the sign for Hercules Mulligan's emporium, and he nearly bumped into two soldiers jogging across the busy thoroughfare.

"Pardon us, Mr. Townsend."

Rob offered a smile to the officers and gave way to them. "My fault, gentlemen. I was paying no heed. And where are you headed this fine autumn day?"

The soldiers exchanged a glance, and then one nodded toward the emporium. "About some business with Mr. Mulligan, is all."

"Ah, as am I." Rob motioned them to go on ahead of him. They were no doubt in search of some shiny epaulettes or gold buttons. Braid. Perhaps new scarlet coats altogether. All those things that officers considered of the utmost importance.

He hoped one of the tailors under Mulligan could help them. Rob had received a note from his old friend asking him to stop by, and it could very well be because he had information to pass along. Culper Junior had yet to send any intelligence out since General Arnold descended upon the city last week, but Roe was scheduled to come by tomorrow.

The very thought of putting a letter into the courier's hand made his nerves blaze. Yes, the dangers had always been there, but never like this. The entire military was still reeling from André's execution, thirsting for blood. And Benedict Arnold had made it known to everyone that his new life's purpose was to find Washington's ring of spies in the City of New York. Rob's ring of spies. Rob himself.

Every time he swallowed, he could feel the noose that awaited him.

The soldiers in front of him opened the door to Mulligan's and held it for him. He muttered his thanks and preceded them into the warm interior. A fire crackled cheerfully in the hearth, and an older man greeted them all with a smile. "Good afternoon, sirs. Do you have appointments?"

One of the officers stepped forward before Rob could answer with an affirmative. "Nay, but we are here on order of the general. We must see Mr. Mulligan at once."

Rob's throat closed a little more.

"Certainly. One moment while I fetch him." The assistant disappeared into the back. While he was gone, the soldiers did a great deal of sighing and shifting but indulged in none of the chatter Rob was used to hearing when in company with such men—and these men in particular.

He took a chair and picked up a newspaper, hoping the rustling of pages would keep them from hearing the raging beat of his heart.

After an interminable minute, Mulligan appeared. He was dressed with his usual impeccable style, his usual perfectly arranged wig, his usual smile. But Rob detected uncertainty in the eyes of his father's friend even as he clapped his hands together. "Good afternoon, gentlemen. What can I do to assist you today? Do you need to place an order?"

The men looked to each other as if silently urging the other to speak. Both shifted from foot to foot. At length, the same one who had spoken before stepped forward. "I am afraid such happy business is not what brings us here today, Mr. Mulligan. We have been given orders by General Arnold to arrest you."

Mulligan's only visible response was the arch of a single brow. "On what grounds, sir? Did I cut his new coat incorrectly? For I assure you, I have done nothing else that could possibly be of interest to him."

The second soldier drew in a long breath. "'Tis nothing you did—recently, anyway. The general wishes to question anyone who expressed loyalty to the rebels before we won the city. Your name came up."

"Did it now?" With a cool efficacy Rob could never hope to emulate, Mulligan folded his arms over his chest. "If he wishes to speak with me, then perhaps we ought to have a drink together."

"I am sorry, Mr. Mulligan." The first soldier put a hand on his saber and stepped toward the tailor. "I am sure you will be released after you have been questioned, but right now you must come with us."

It took all Rob's willpower not to fist the newspaper, but rather to lower it calmly. To make his face reflect curious concern rather than outright panic.

Hercules Mulligan, though, seemed determined to live up to the fortitude of the original bearer of his name. "If it is a matter of 'must,' then I suppose there is no point in arguing." He cleared his throat and glanced past them to Rob. "Mr. Townsend, my apologies. It seems I chose an inopportune day to ask you to come by for that list I need filled."

Rob set the *Royal Gazette* aside and stood, clasping his trembling hands behind his back. "'Tis hardly something *you* need to apologize for, Mr. Mulligan."

The elder man motioned toward his assistant. "Would you fetch me my cloak, please, Mr. Anders? I fear if I move to get it myself, these fine young men may think I am trying to escape."

The talkative soldier sighed. "Mr. Mulligan, please. We mean no disrespect—"

"You are following orders, I know. But your superior, good sir, most assuredly *does* mean disrespect." Mulligan tugged his coat into place and rolled back his shoulders. "Mr. Townsend?"

Rob drew in a breath meant to steady him. It failed, but he hoped it helped him look calmer than he felt. "Sir?"

Mulligan walked past the soldiers and stopped before him. He smiled, though a myriad messages clamored in his eyes. "You are still leaving for Long Island tomorrow?"

Though Rob wanted to frown—he had no trip planned until Christmastide—he forced a tight smile instead. Mulligan's meaning was clear. "I am, yes."

His friend nodded. "Do give your family my regards. And I must say again how glad I was to hear you planned to visit with them for a goodly while this time. Your parents will relish your company."

"And I theirs." He would hurry home as quickly as he could manage. Tell Oakham he had received a letter saying Mother had taken ill, and he wanted to care for her. Stop by Hampton Hall to let Winter and Freeman know he planned to lie low on Long Island until Arnold's spy hunt had relaxed.

And get out of town with the evening tide. If Arnold had discovered Mulligan's ties to the Patriots, Rob's would come to light soon too.

The assistant returned with Mulligan's cloak, and he donned it with chin held high. "Very well then, men. Let us be away. Mr. Anders, do go round my house and let Elizabeth know I won't be home for dinner, if you will."

Mr. Anders didn't look nearly so unflappable as his employer. His eyes bulged and looked suspiciously damp. "Yes, sir."

Rob shut his eyes rather than watch the Redcoats escort his compatriot away. He gave them a moment's lead, and then he fled the shop and headed for his own. All the way he attempted to turn his thoughts to prayer, to put a cork on the rising panic. A few more hours of calm 'twas all he had to manage. Just a bit longer to hold himself together.

He hurried into his shop and was grateful to find no one there but his partner. For that matter, he was grateful for the first time that he had brought Oakham into his business, because otherwise he wouldn't have been able to leave it for any length of time.

It took only a few quick exchanges to tell his false story and be assured that the store would be taken care of. A few minutes longer than that to hurry to his room and pack a bag with two changes of clothes and a few necessities. Then he walked to Hampton Hall, valise in hand, praying all the while he wouldn't find Winter in Lane's company as he seemed to do so regularly. If he did…well, he could make his meaning clear, as Mulligan had. But, oh, how he wanted to say farewell without modulating his every syllable.

Following his hopes, he headed not for the front of the house, but around to the back gardens. It was Winter's favorite spot, he knew, other than her secret lair. So long as the air had a hint of warmth, she would likely spend every moment she could manage out here.

And yes, praise the Lord, there she was kneeling amid the chrysanthemums. Alone.

A kernel of peace burrowed into the roiling ground of his spirit. "Winnie."

Jumping up, Winter turned wide eyes upon him and brushed the soil from her skirt. "Robbie! What are you…?" Her gaze landed on his valise. "Are you going somewhere?"

"Oyster Bay." He drew near, but not so near that he would be tempted to touch her. This vision of her, concern in her eyes and sweetness upon her lips, would have to suffice. "They arrested Mulligan."

She pulled in a quick breath and tugged at her cloak. "For…?"

A glance around him showed him no other listening ears, but at this moment he wanted no unnecessary risk. "So far as I could tell, just for questioning, as with so many others. But…"

"Yes." Her composure wavered for a moment, long enough to let him glimpse the fear before she replaced it with hope. "A trip to Long Island is an excellent idea. How long will you stay?"

The shake of his head felt strangely like defeat. "I don't know,

Winnie. As long as I must. You could…" He knew, even as the words formed on his tongue, that there was no use saying them. Yet he could not stop himself from making one last offer, one last attempt to remove her from this situation into which he had placed her. "You could come with me. Visit my sisters."

Her smile reflected serenity so perfect he knew it must be a mask. Yet he could not find a crack in it through which to glimpse her true heart. "I thank you for the offer, Robbie, but I cannot."

Pressing his lips together, he nodded. Part of him wanted to force the matter, to insist she remove herself from danger. If anything happened to her because of this, because of him—but he had always been cautious. No one else knew of her, not so much as a hint. Tallmadge thought he overheard all the useful gossip at Rivington's, at his shop, or through Mulligan.

She was safe.

"Robbie." The mask slipped, and she frowned. "The ring, then. Is it over?"

As her question swirled through his mind, he glanced beyond her to the horizon. Marred by buildings, crowded by man's invention, yet still the sun gleamed golden. Still it warmed, in spite of the chill of autumn's wind. Peace, in spite of the change of seasons. "For now there is no other choice. Perhaps Senior and I will speak on occasion, but circumstances being what they are, I cannot fathom risking a written message. I will in fact miss my meeting with seven-two-four tomorrow evening at my store, but it will not be the first time one of us did not show up."

She smiled, no doubt at his familiar complaint about Roe's lack of dependability. "I wish you well, Robbie. And thank you, over and again, for being the friend I needed."

Such a final-sounding goodbye. Realization pierced. Lane would no doubt propose soon, and they would leave New York once they were wed. After such a leisurely courtship, the betrothal would not last long. She could be gone by the time he deemed it safe to return.

He took a step backward and clutched the handle of his valise. "Be happy, Winnie. Safe and happy."

Waiting for no more than the graceful lift of her hand in a wave, he spun away. If he hoped to make the tide, he must hurry.

Twenty-Two

Winter picked up a spool of ribbon and pretended to care as she examined the width, the shade, the texture. The two other shoppers in Robbie's store, as well as Mr. Oakham, no doubt thought her about her usual, frivolous business.

Her nerves snapped with each footfall, each ring of the bell over the door.

Would he come? Would she know him if he did?

She replaced the spool, making sure her face reflected boredom as she reached for another. Robbie would be furious if he knew she was here hoping to intercept Austin Roe. Would no doubt wax long and poetic about the stupidity of inviting danger, with an eloquent addition about how he hadn't preserved her anonymity so long to have her destroy it now.

He seemed to have forgotten about that note in the Shirleys' bureau that went missing—or perhaps he had written it off as a servant moving it. But still it niggled, still it tormented her. What if she weren't as anonymous as she thought? What if someone already suspected her?

She could hear his voice in her head. *If someone already suspects you, then you must cease all activity at once and protect yourself.*

Perfectly logical. Yet now, more than ever, Washington needed to be aware of what went on in New York, what General Arnold was doing. And she was the only Culper agent left free in the city.

If someone was watching her closely enough to discover that note, then her other actions would already be known anyway. Certainly she would be as careful as possible, but she could get no guiltier of this particular crime. And she was more concerned with answering to the ultimate Authority, who had yet to release her from her calling.

The bell jingled. Winter looked up, as did everyone else in the store, and then back to her ribbon. Her heart pounded, pulse thumping in her head. Was that Roe? She thought so—middling height, dressed as a farmer, dark hair uncovered by a wig. 'Twas the same man she had spotted coming in here back in July, and she had later verified Roe had come by that day. Too big a coincidence to be one.

With the sigh she had learned from Grandmother that said nothing met with her satisfaction, Winter put the second spool of ribbon back and turned for the door. Roe had moved off, scanning the shop with a frown. Looking for Robbie, no doubt.

Chill air swept over her when she exited. Freeman straightened from the side of the building, brows arched. Tugging her gloves back on, she only nodded and started down the street. Once she was even with the same alley in which she had spoken to Robbie, she dropped the bracelet she had tucked, unfastened, into her sleeve, and then kicked it as if by accident.

Loosing an exasperated huff, just in case anyone was close enough to hear, she chased the beads into the alley. Then ducked behind the stack of crates and waited.

A few minutes later Freeman's voice carried toward her on the wind, along with an unfamiliar one. Though tempted to peek out from behind her blind, she waited instead for them to come to her.

Her lips quirked up as she considered how she must look. Decked out in the finery of a pampered gentlewoman, hair powdered, neck encircled with pearls, and slouching against the stained, sooty bricks in a back alley ready for a tête-à-tête about espionage.

How she longed for the day when duplicity was behind her.

Freeman stepped in front of her, Roe at his side. Winter tried not to laugh at the bulge of his eyes, but a smile escaped. She straightened and held out a hand. "Mr. Roe?"

The farmer-cum-soldier fumbled a moment before taking her hand and bowing over it. "At your service, Miss…? Your servant did not give me your name but only said that we have a mutual friend."

"Mr. Culper, yes. Junior, that is." She offered a confident, practiced smile, but otherwise did not guard her expression. She hoped he would see in her eyes that she knew what it meant. "If it is all the same to you, sir, I would like to remain nameless, as I have not been given an assignation that may safely fall on any ear."

After releasing her hand, Roe stared at her for a long moment. "What is it you wish to speak with me about, miss?"

Cool air gusted, and Winter drew in a long breath of it. "I grew up a neighbor to Junior, Mr. Roe. When I moved to the city as he began this business, he called upon me to provide information now and then. Which I was perfectly willing to do, considering that my father prefers the same style of coat as you."

Roe's brows lifted. "Junior never mentioned you."

Freeman snorted a laugh. "He has better sense than that, sir."

"Indeed he has. Which has led him back to Long Island in these dangerous times." Winter leaned forward a bit so she might pitch her voice low. "Fleeing is not an option for me, which means I am still here. Still privy to the information Junior would have passed along. If you think seven-one-one would still like to receive it, then I would be willing to impart it myself. Though I am running very low on the vial of medicine Junior entrusted to me."

"He gave you…?" Roe's face went contemplative, thoughts clicking away behind the sienna of his eyes. He was without doubt considering all the details she had shared that she couldn't have without knowledge of the inner workings of the ring. Evaluating her trustworthiness. At length he released a slow breath, then nodded. "Seven-one-one has great interest in what is happening in New York with Arnold here, though he is always wary when he discovers that the Culpers have invited others into the family without allowing him to know their histories first. So I will continue his tradition of secrecy when it comes to you, if that is acceptable."

"More than acceptable. It was going to be one of my terms." Winter's shoulders relaxed a bit. "Junior often passed along particular information seven-one-one sought. Have you such requests?"

Roe nodded and then jerked his head toward the street when a noisy group sauntered by. Winter slouched down again to be sure the crates covered her. The courier frowned. "I have a missive I had intended for Junior, with such instruction. Have you the counter liquor?"

"I do, yes."

He nodded but didn't turn her way again. "'Tis in my room. I will leave it in the usual location, if you know where that is."

Was he testing her, or did the passersby make him nervous? Either way, Winter nodded. "Junior has told me of it. In the hollow of the tree, correct?"

"'Twill be there within the hour. Have a response in the same place in exactly two weeks, when I next come to the city." Without another word, Roe repositioned his hat and headed out of the alley.

Winter turned raised brows on Freeman. Try as she might, she couldn't quite determine if that had gone as well as she had expected. He certainly hadn't welcomed her as eagerly as Robbie had—but then, he didn't know her. And the success of the ring was based entirely upon trust born of friendship. She was lucky he had accepted her history with Robbie as credentials enough.

Freeman pursed his lips and then motioned toward the street, empty once more. "Shall we?"

"Mm-hmm." Winter brushed at her skirt to make sure she had picked up no grime from the wall and then fell in beside Freeman. "You may have to be the one to check for that item later, Free. I will barely get back in time to prepare for our evening with the Lanes as it is."

"Of course." He paused at the mouth of the alley and looked down at her, long and intently. "This is a new risk, Winnie girl, in a time when everyone else is shying away from taking the old ones."

She knew well he didn't speak of the risk to him, fetching the letter. No, as always she was his concern. But there was little to do other than shrug. "Someone must take them, Free. I am the only one left."

Despite the proud light in his eyes, his face remained sober. "That is why I fear."

Ben drained the last drop of coffee from his mug and then glanced at his pocket watch. Blast—he had better hasten home if he intended to don appropriate attire before the Hamptons and Winter arrived for dinner. Shuffling his newsprint, papers, and books together, his mind still lingered on the theory he had just jotted down with a pencil. If only he had his laboratory at hand, he could do a quick experiment and see if the idea would prove itself.

His fingers itched for a beaker. He could all but feel the flame he would hold under it. And, oh, for that long-missed joy of watching a plume of vapor shoot from the top of a cylinder, frothing over onto his table.

How had eleven months gone by? This spy hunt was only supposed to take a few. And really, what did it matter anymore? For all he knew, the plan that brought him here had been long-since forgotten. Certainly all intentions had shifted when Arnold arrived. Who was he fooling, thinking he could do what no one else could and find the ring of spies the best military minds couldn't pinpoint?

Moreover, his prime suspect had just left town, so why bother staying himself? Ben was fairly certain Townsend was the linchpin of operations in the City of New York, but he would not be passing any more messages along for the foreseeable future.

Only one thing held him here at this point, and the thought of her made Ben smile. The obvious answer was to propose, to marry quickly, and to repair to Connecticut as soon as his house could be opened up.

Yes, indeed, that was the solution to everything. He would, in fact, speak with Mother the moment he got home and ask for one of the family rings to bestow upon Winter.

Blessed satisfaction coursing through his veins at long last, Ben slid his books into his satchel. Next came a stack of his papers. Included in them was the letter he had received from the president at Yale, begging for his return. Which, yes, was what had gotten him thinking of it, longing for it himself. And finally a few miscellaneous papers and the *Royal Gazette*.

Sliding those into his bag, though, revealed an unfamiliar envelope upon the table. Ben picked it up with a frown and glanced at the name inscribed. Well, bother. Fairchild must have left it. Ben couldn't be entirely sure what "it" was, but someone had written "urgent" under the colonel's name.

Perhaps tomorrow would be soon enough to satisfy the urgency? If he detoured to Fairchild's office, there was no way he would have time to talk with Mother about a ring for Winter. 'Twas dubious he would even then have time to put on a wig.

Shame, that.

Still. Stopping by either the barracks or the headquarters inevitably meant waiting. Often earning glares from soldiers who considered him nothing but an inconvenience who had no business being underfoot. And, really, he was in no mood to be surrounded by army men when his mind was occupied with Winter. And chemistry.

Haste unto the den of lions.

Tempted to growl like one himself, Ben shoved Fairchild's letter into his satchel and wished his mind would cease with the Bible quotations. Perhaps he ought to ignore it, solely to prove a point. Besides, if the verse from Daniel had struck correctly, it would have been complete: *Then the king arose very early in the morning, and went in haste unto the den of lions*.

See? Morning. Morning would be plenty of time.

He strode out of the coffee shop, hesitated, and then angled for Fairchild's office. Deuces. Ridiculous as the verses were, they had yet to lead him astray. And there had surely been a reason his first thought hadn't included the "morning" part. Probably because the colonel was already down, he needed no more kicks. Ben had no idea what kind of trouble might visit Fairchild if he lost something important, something that could *not* wait until morning, but he didn't intend to play a part in it when a simple detour would help his friend.

He nodded a greeting to a few gentlemen headed toward Rivington's and lengthened his stride. If Providence were with him, he would find Fairchild alone and unoccupied and be able to hand off the envelope without delay. Or better still, the colonel would be busy but his aide present and able to take it for him. Then he could rush directly home and find Mother. Perhaps they would even have time to sort through the jewels.

Did they have an emerald set? Ben had never paid the slightest attention to such details as what jewelry his mother wore, but emeralds would complement Winter's eyes. If it were such an easy decision, he would try to find a time to propose tonight. Take her out into the garden—no, that idea made him wince. That was where Fairchild had nearly made the same offer last winter. Perhaps the library.

That would do. Propose tonight, and the banns could be read beginning this Sunday. It may take some doing, but surely they could convince the Hamptons to forgo a large ordeal so they might have the nuptials as soon as possible, in three weeks. They could be back in Connecticut before November. Perhaps a goal of returning before the snow came would convince everyone that haste—and hence simplicity—was a fine plan.

'Twas worth trying, at any rate.

A few minutes later the house-turned-offices loomed before him, and Ben jogged up the steps with a whistle. Which died when he entered and saw both outer and inner desks empty. He could set the envelope in a place to be seen, he supposed, but he would rather make sure Fairchild knew it had been delivered so he didn't go off in search of it.

"I don't know, General." Fairchild's faint voice came from above stairs.

Ben, brows drawn, moved toward the staircase and then hesitated. He had made several visits to this building over the last near year, but he had never had cause to go up to the second floor and felt odd doing so now. Especially if the colonel were meeting with a superior. Better to wait.

"Not good enough, Colonel." This second voice was unfamiliar, though the accent was American—certainly not General Clinton. Arnold, perhaps? "According to André, it has been known for a year that there are spies in the city. A *year*, Colonel. Tell me, how have you gone so long without uncovering them?"

A floorboard squeaked overhead, and Ben could well imagine Fairchild shifting from foot to foot. "Well, sir, I suppose because we were not willing to arrest each and every person in New York with some distant tie to the rebels—lest our jails, as you have already discovered, become too full for us to manage."

Definitely Arnold.

"Careful, Fairchild. You may not yet be accustomed to answering to me, but I am nevertheless your superior."

Oh, how Ben would have liked to see the expression on Fairchild's face at that one. From what he had gleaned from the colonel's tight-lipped responses to recent events, he was one of many officers who greeted his new general dubiously.

"My apologies, sir. I am still a bit raw from André's untimely loss."

The general grunted, a sound that barely made it to Ben's ears. Loud footfalls sounded, then the slide of a turning heel, then foot-falls again. "Colonel, allow me to be blunt. For at least a year, perhaps more, General Washington has been operating an elite group of spies from this very place. A group that has fed him information that has allowed him to foil your every move, to counteract the covert steps *you* have taken. And your only reaction to this is that you feared making your jails too full?"

Though he could hear nothing but reverberating silence, Ben had a feeling Fairchild sighed. "We have long had a plan in place, sir, to ferret out the vile creatures and use them against the rebels who trust them."

Ah, yes, the plan. The very one that Archie had overheard André discussing with the infamous redhead he had stolen from him. The one he had then written Ben about. The very one that had brought him here.

"Then why has this plan not been enacted?"

"We have tried—several times. But we had apparently not found the spies you speak of, the ones with Washington's ear. And I know not how we could find them now. We have kept our eyes on several persons of interest, General, and they have all gone silent or disappeared since you arrived. Terrified, no doubt, that you are aware of their identities and will seek them out."

A valid fear, to Ben's way of thinking. And undoubtedly to the thinking of the spies in question too.

"Not all of them have gone silent." A pause.

Lighter footsteps. Fairchild's. "What is this? Some kind of letter?"

"Recovered not fifteen minutes ago. One of my scouts saw a man putting it in place, though he could not see enough of said man to be useful. Still. It is written in General Washington's hand, and though the legible message is benign, there is surely an invisible one. Look, see the 'A' in the corner?"

"I do." Rather than ringing with the excitement Ben would have expected, Fairchild's voice fell heavy and low down the staircase. "Have you any idea with what to develop it?"

"Nay. But if there are still secret messages being brought into the city from Washington, then there are still spies here to receive them. And *they* will know with what to develop it. Now, what I need from *you*, Colonel Fairchild, is for you to stop moping and go about avenging your friend's death rather than just mourning him. Do you understand me?"

Another slight pause. "Perfectly, General."

"Good."

Ben hurried away as quietly as he could from the stairs and into Fairchild's office, not relishing the idea of being caught eavesdropping on Benedict Arnold. After sinking into his usual chair across from the desk, he indulged in a frown. Was it possible that whomever left that letter didn't know that Townsend was gone? Or had Ben been wrong? Or, another possibility, were others in league with him still operating?

Blast it all. He was ready to be finished with this. He ought to have known better than to think he was, though. It had been far too convenient to be true.

A minute later Fairchild's slow steps came his way, and then his figure appeared in the doorway.

Not wanting to startle him, Ben stood up slowly. "There you are. You left this at Rivington's. I thought I had better drop it by." He fished out the letter.

"Lane." Rather than offering a smile, Fairchild swept his wig off his head and tossed the thing onto his chair.

Ben stared at it. Men aplenty treated their wigs like hats, doffing them whenever they came indoors, but Fairchild had never before removed his careful curls in Ben's company. A sign of comfort?

Nay. It smacked instead of defeat.

Loosing a blustery sigh, Fairchild passed a hand over his cropped hair and sank onto the corner of his desk. "Been here long?"

"Only a moment. Are you all right?"

With an unamused breath of laughter, the colonel scrubbed a hand over his face. "Do you ever wonder at the point of it all, Ben? Why we keep on when none of it makes sense anymore?"

Ben filled his lungs with a long, slow breath. In their months of growing friendship, that was the first time Fairchild had ever used his given name. A contemplated answer was called for. "I have wondered that, yes. I think, Isaac, that we keep on because there is comfort in routine. Because we do not want to shirk our duties. And because we trust that the decisions we made rationally are to be trusted above our emotions at a given time."

Fairchild met his gaze, shoulders still slumped. "But what of when our logically deduced duty tells us to do what our hearts scream is wrong?"

A frown burrowed into Ben's brow before he could stop it. Was it the business Arnold assigned that settled so ill, or simply answering to a man he didn't trust? "We do what we must, I suppose, after weighing the consequences of our decision. And, of course, reevaluating based upon that, for sometimes the best-laid plans must be changed along with the circumstances. The best theories revised when new facts are discovered."

Lips pursed, Fairchild nodded and held out a hand. "What is it I forgot?"

"Some kind of letter. Had it not said 'urgent,' I would have waited until morning, but…"

"Thank you." After staring at it for a moment, the colonel tossed it to his desk. "You had better get home, Ben. The Hamptons would probably appreciate it if you had time to dress."

Though he nodded, it seemed he should say something more. Something insightful and encouraging. If only he knew *what*. "I…" Ben sighed and turned toward the door. "I am no good with this sort of thing, Isaac. If you were an element in my laboratory, I would know exactly what to do, but…"

Fairchild chuckled. "You manage well enough."

Kind of him to say so, though Ben had his doubts. "Coffee tomorrow?"

"I will be there at the usual time."

"Until then, then." With another nod, Ben exited the office and the building. Would it be terribly unseemly to run all the way home? Probably. He should have brought his horse.

Walking as fast as he could without completely compromising his sense of propriety, Ben willed his brain to provide some handy advice on what to do for Fairchild. He would even welcome a Scripture, if it would help. Wasn't there a proverb about a friend's counsel being like ointment and perfume? That one would be good.

If it would then tell him what counsel he ought to offer.

No answers had struck him by the time he reached home, so he filed the concern away for later rumination and let his thoughts turn back to Winter as he walked in the door. If they had no emeralds, then rubies would complement her skin perfectly. Those were rubies that Mother used to wear every Christmas, weren't they? Or perhaps garnets?

"There you are, Bennet." Mother stepped into the doorway to the sitting room, a smile upon her face. "We received a letter from Clefton and were waiting on you to read it."

"Oh. Ah…" He put a hand on his satchel and glanced up the stairs.

Mother arched a regal gray brow. "Come and read it, and then you can take your things up and dress for the evening. You know your father is never verbose."

Nay, he always got his points across quite succinctly. *Bennet, you must come soon. There is much to learn, and you have played long enough at chemistry. Duty awaits.*

No doubt Mother was so eager to read the letter because she wanted him pondering Father's latest demand to cross the Atlantic all through dinner tonight. She would hope that entertaining such contemplations while in Winter's company would make him see the inaccurate point she insisted on—that Winter would not be a suitable mistress for Clefton.

Stubborn woman.

Well, 'twould be quicker to agree about the letter than to argue with her. He handed his hat and lightweight greatcoat to the waiting servant and strode into the sitting room. Archie was already sprawled over the settee, looking bored and impatient. He acknowledged Ben with a wave of his wrist. "Have at it, Benny old boy. Mother insisted, as usual, that we wait for you to read it to us."

Ben accepted the sealed envelope from his mother and sat in his usual armchair, near the fire. "Very well, then." He frowned a moment at the script on the outside. Not his father's hand. He must have had a servant post it again. He couldn't say why that bothered him so, but when one couldn't find the time to write a simple address on a letter…

Ah, well. No point getting irritated about something so trivial. He broke the seal and pulled the paper from inside it.

His frown deepened. *This* wasn't his father's hand either. "'Tis signed from Uncle Lane."

"Oh?" Mother's voice combined disappointment with curiosity. "I had assumed…well, we are all here. You might as well read it to us."

Ben cleared his throat. "Dated six weeks ago. 'My Dear Niece and Great-Nephews. It is with a heavy heart that I pen this missive, when surely you would rather receive one from your husband and father. If only such were possible. I regret to inform you that my nephew contracted a raging fever not two days ago and lost the battle to it this morning…'"

His throat closed off. He heard Mother's gasp and Archie's curse as his boots hit the floor. But he couldn't pull his gaze from the page and the words that swam together nonsensically.

Impossible. Father could not be gone. Ben hadn't even seen him for nearly two years. Their only correspondence had been short, emotionless things barely more than business transactions. And even before that, he had never made the effort to come home but had been content to have his parents visit him once a year.

How had he been content with that? *Why* had he been content with that? Certainly, his opinions had little in common with his father's, and their interests were as far removed as the east from the west. But he had always been a good father. Understanding yet indulging. Firm yet kind.

Gone. Never to visit him in New Haven again, never to send another letter demanding he come to England.

"No. *No!*" Mother's anguished cry jolted Ben to action. He let the letter fall and sprang up, reaching the couch just as she slid from the cushions to the floor.

Too late to catch her, he knelt at her side and wrapped his arms around her. "I know. I know, Mother."

"I was going to join him in the spring. Just a few more months." She covered her face with her hands and spilled a sob into them. "We had never been apart more than a month until this, and I…I missed him so. Oh, my darling Thaddeus. He cannot be gone. He cannot."

Archie took up a position on the floor at her other side, his expression a window into the splintering of his spirit. As he embraced her, he squeezed his eyes shut and pressed his lips together.

Ben murmured something, but he couldn't be certain what he said. Nothing with any meaning, to be sure. Why had he never thought to ask his mother how she fared, separated so long from Father? It hadn't occurred to him. *He* had gone so long without seeing them that it hardly struck him at all, and Mother had never complained. He had assumed her fine with the distance.

And why would he assume that? Why, when he had spent so many months courting Winter, had he never paused to wonder about his parents' marriage, his parents' hearts? Had he been asked about their relationship, he would have answered with a shrug and assumed them to be like any other couple, happy enough together but happy enough apart.

An assumption that looked stupid and ignorant in this moment, with Mother crumpled on the floor sobbing. And he too much an idiot to know how to help. Too numb to consider what this loss would mean to him when the fog lifted. All he could do was hold her and rub a hand over her back. Grip Archie's arm when it reached for him.

Useless.

But there was nothing he could do. Nothing to undo death. Nothing to lessen the blow for his mother. Nothing…*nothing*. So he just sat there, murmuring and holding and wishing he could do more.

Time lost all meaning. He couldn't have said how long he sat, hunched on the floor. But when a swath of silk swished into his vision, he became aware of the crick in his neck, and the fact that Mother had fallen silent, though she clung to him and Archie still. Winter crouched down, her face saturated with concern. "Bennet?" Her voice, not even loud enough to be called a whisper, soothed like honey.

He held out a hand and felt, when she gripped it, as though he breathed again for the first time since he read the letter. "'Tis my father. We just got word that he died of fever six weeks ago." He spoke softly, fearing the words would break his mother anew. But she made no response.

Movement behind Winter made him aware of the Hamptons hovering in the doorway. Mrs. Hampton urged her husband back a step. "We ought not intrude at such a time. Our condolences. We will go home and pray for you. Come, Winnie."

"Nay. I will stay here to pray for them. Bennet." She reached with her other hand to touch his cheek. Only then did he notice the dampness upon it. His own or Mother's? "My love, I am so sorry."

"I know." He turned his head enough to kiss her hand, the only thanks he could think to offer.

"I will return directly."

Ben closed his eyes as she vanished, ushering her grandparents out with her. He knew not where she would send them and didn't care a whit so long as she returned.

Archie shifted and scrubbed a hand over his face. Then he sat, arms propped on raised knees, and stared into the fire. Mother moved not an inch.

Some moments later Winter returned with a tea tray. She poured a steaming cup and pressed it into Archie's hand and then sank to the floor. With a few gentle motions she had Mother sitting up and sipping at a glass of water. Then she withdrew a soft-looking handkerchief and dabbed at his matron's face with the same care Mother had once used with him as a child.

And with so simple an action, composure returned. Mother sniffed, drew in a long breath, and straightened her spine. "My apologies, Miss Reeves. I should have—"

"Nonsense, Mrs. Lane." Winter offered that smile Ben so loved, the one free of pretense and filled with her heart. Her *true* heart. "'Tis I who am sorry. May I pour you some tea?"

Mother hesitated a moment and then nodded. "Thank you. I...'tis such a shock. I received a letter from him not a week ago, talking of when I would join him, the things we would do. The places he wanted to show me. Now to get this news, and to realize it happened so long ago and I knew nothing. How did I not know?"

Winter somehow managed to look graceful as she poured the tea from a kneeling position, adding two lumps of sugar and a splash of lemon, exactly as Mother preferred. After stirring, she eased back down and transferred the cup to his mother. "Such sudden loss is always a terrible blow, no matter when we learn of it."

"Yes. Even so…"

Winter looked from Mother to Bennet, her eyes full of love and shared sorrow. "Even so. We expect our heart to recognize when its other half ceases beating, but perhaps not knowing is one of the Lord's gifts to us. For how much worse would it be to feel such loss and yet have no answers as to why we do?"

Breath suddering, Mother leaned against the couch and cradled the cup in her hands. "Perhaps. Though I can see no gift in anything right now."

"Of course not." Winter reached up to smooth a few of Mother's curls back into place and straighten her necklace, quietly restoring her dignity. "There is no way to mitigate something like this. The only comfort to be found is in those who share our pain. As new facets of grief reveal themselves, you will cling to your sons and find solace in their devotion to you, and in offering the same to them as they mourn."

At that Mother reached for Ben's hand and gave it a desperate squeeze. "That much I have already seen, yes. Had I been alone when I read that letter…"

"Praise the Lord you were not." Winter moved from her place and motioned Archie into it, and then she settled by Ben's side.

He pulled her close with his free arm. Under normal circumstances he would never dare do such a thing in company, but at this moment it seemed necessary. "I love you," he murmured into her ear while Archie said something to Mother.

She nestled in and looked up into his eyes, her smile somehow full of both sorrow and joy. "And I love you, Bennet."

He tucked her in a little closer. "How did you know exactly what to say, what to do?"

"'Tis what Freeman did for me. And it only worked because you had already done what she needed first. Held her while she cried."

He pressed his lips to her forehead. "I'm glad you are here."

Mother leaned forward enough to look at them. For the first time, no hostility shone in her eyes when she gazed upon Winter. "As am I, Winnie dear. As am I."

Perhaps the family jewels would have to wait, but it seemed that Winter had earned a place in the family.

Ben nearly smiled, until he recalled that her addition was only due to the gaping absence of his father.

Twenty-Three

Winter stared at Freeman, praying she had heard him wrong. "What do you mean it wasn't there?"

Freeman leaned against the door to Canterbury's stall. "Just that. There was no letter in the tree. I checked the other locations Mr. Townsend had mentioned using, and those were all empty too. No letter, Winnie."

The scent of hay teased her nose, combining with that of rain and damp earth from outside. Soothing smells that imparted no comfort. "Did Mr. Roe not leave it? Robbie had always said he was undependable."

The arch of Freeman's brow highlighted the unlikelihood of that. "Undependable in coming to the city when he said he would, not in delivering the promised correspondence once here. Nay, Winnie. I fear something has happened. Either to Roe before he could leave it, or—"

"Or someone intercepted it." Winter let her eyes slide shut. It hardly mattered that no one would be able to read Washington's message. The fact that a second missive had gone missing—and heaven forbid anything had befallen the courier himself. "Unthinkable."

"Sorry I had to tell you such news." Freeman chucked her under the chin, bringing face and eyelids up. "You hardly need to be worrying about this right now. I shall check again, and in a few other places."

"Be careful, Free. They are obviously watching—"

"I only go when it's so dark no one could make me out even if they *are* watching. I know how to use the shadows, Winnie. Now, you go and take care of your Mr. Lane. I can take care of this."

Much as she hated to leave this question unanswered, she indeed had little choice. With news of the elder Lane's death making its way into the city, family and friends were all gathering at Bennet's house today. She must be there, and she must leave now. Still. "It seems unfair to burden you with this, when it is my—"

"'Tis *ours*, Winnie girl. Always has been. You know that." He tweaked her nose, offered the same grin he had given her since she was a tot swinging from his arms, and gave her a push toward the carriage waiting outside. "Go. And give your young man my sympathies if a time presents itself when you may."

"I will." But she paused when a groan sounded from one of the stalls. Her eyes went wide, her pulse thundered. Had someone heard them?

Freeman's jaw ticked. "Nothing for you to fret over. 'Tis just Percy."

"Percy?" She scurried to the stall the sound had come from and gasped when she saw the young man lying facedown in a pile of clean straw, his back a lattice of fresh, bloody welts. So far as she could tell, he was unconscious—undoubtedly a blessing. "What happened?"

Freeman urged her away from the stall. "He tried to run away last night. They brought him back. I thought I had talked him out of such a foolish—well, obviously I failed. He must have been simmering all these months. But I shall take care of him, Winnie. You take care of Mr. Lane."

Nostrils flaring, all she could do was nod and obey his gentle push toward the door, murmuring a prayer for Percy as she did so. When she moved to the stable's exit, the footman dashed into the rain and opened the carriage for her. She hastened up the pull-down steps and settled onto the seat.

If only she were making this trip alone, as she had the return drive last night, long after her grandparents left the Lanes'. But they would come too, and so the carriage rocked to a halt at the front of the house.

Grandfather alone climbed in, his face as stormy as the clouds above. "Your grandmother has a headache."

"Oh." Much as she disliked spending time with Grandmother, she had always been present since July to provide a buffer between her and Grandfather. Being alone with him now…had he been the one to wield the whip applied to Percy's back, or had he delegated that to another slave, as he had the blow to her head? "I am sorry to hear that."

He grunted and sent her a scathing look, and then he turned toward the window. Winter directed her gaze out the opposite one, trying not to think about the last time she had been alone in a carriage with her grandfather. Though she had no memory of it, the rough scar she felt every time she brushed her hair never allowed her to forget its results.

The drive passed in silence taut as fabric in a loom and seemed twice as long as usual. But then they were at the Lanes', and Winter could climb down and escape Grandfather's presence. She hastened inside to find Bennet.

His mother found her first and took her hands the moment they were free of gloves. "There you are, my dear. The guests will begin arriving any moment, and I had hoped you would read to me again first. It calmed me so last night."

Winter smiled and squeezed Mrs. Lane's fingers. "Of course. Did you get any sleep?"

"Directly after you read to me, yes. Though I awoke some hours later and could not sleep again." The lady sighed and rubbed at her shadowed eyes. "How I wish you and Bennet were already married so that you needn't leave us. Do you think your grandmother would consent to staying here with you for a few days?"

For a moment Winter could find no answer, no words at all. Not twenty-four hours ago, it would have been unthinkable to all involved that Mrs. Lane would be so eager for her presence. Perhaps she ought to have abandoned pretense around her months ago, despite Grandmother's insistence she shouldn't. Certainly *this* was not the way she had hoped to earn a place in the Lane family.

But then, yesterday was when the Lord had made it clear she was to be only herself. Rather than indulge in regrets, she would thank Him for using her to provide some measure of comfort.

"I cannot say of what Grandmother may approve, and unfortunately she remained at home with a headache." Winter offered a small smile. "But if she would agree to it, know I would come most willingly and remain as long as you wanted me here."

Mrs. Lane held her gaze long enough that Winter thought she might reference their less-than-amiable history, or make some comment about the change in her. Instead, the woman gave her a ghost of a smile and led her toward the sitting room. "The Bible you read from is in here."

Winter took a seat, accepted the hefty tome, and opened to the Psalms, where she had left off last night. 'Twasn't difficult to find some of David's words that sang of both heartbreak and joy, battles lost and faith won. After reading several chapters, she closed her eyes and succumbed to the urge to pray.

"O Lord, infinite and infallible, let us dwell in that secret place within Your shadow, where no fear nor malice nor strife can overcome Your safe protection. We can turn nowhere but to You for consolation, wisdom, and support." She drew in a deep breath when Mrs. Lane reached for her hand again and clung to it. "And so, God of our ends, we bow before You with spirits contrite and broken, ready for the salve of Your Spirit, so graciously offered us so that we might approach You when our own natures would forbid it. Breathe Your strength into us, Father of our fathers, and prepare our hearts to reflect Your glory, for only in You rests any victory in these times of lamentation. Amen."

"Amen." Bennet's voice came from the door, though Winter had no idea how long he had been there. She opened her eyes to find him regarding them with contented sobriety. "Not to interrupt, Mother, but your friends have begun to arrive."

"Thank you, Bennet." Mrs. Lane stood and pulled Winter up with her, though she transferred Winter's hand to Bennet's arm once they reached him. "Would the two of you handle the receiving for a moment? I am going to send a note to Mrs. Hampton straightaway."

"Certainly, Mrs. Lane."

Bennet waited until his mother had gone, and then he loosed a low groan. "I came in here hoping to avoid having to greet our visitors. They all arrived with their daughters, and I don't relish making a fool of myself today. I cannot bring myself to imagine them as young men in costume."

"As what?" Not sure whether to laugh or shake her head, Winter stared at him.

One corner of his mouth pulled up. "Just a little trick George recommended to help me speak to baffling females with some coherence. After observing, that is, that I have no trouble talking to our school chums with whom I have little more in common."

Leave it to George Knight. Winter pressed her lips together against a smile. "Now I am curious. Did you do this with me? Is that why in the beginning you would suddenly seem to find your tongue?"

He tucked her hand more securely into the crook of his arm and grinned down at her. "Nay, my love, not with you. All I needed was a glimpse at those mysterious secrets of yours, and I was too intrigued to be awkward."

Perhaps the intrigue had faded as he puzzled her out, but the love that replaced it was far more precious. As they headed toward the sounds of arriving guests, though, Winter knew the last of her secrets could not long be suffered. Not now. She could hardly stand beside him as he mourned his father's death and not confess that hers yet lived in the Patriot camp. And, from there, share that he had instilled the same beliefs of God and country in her.

But now was not the right moment to bare her soul. So she settled for speaking for him as they greeted their acquaintances and friends. More and more of New York society filled the house over the next half hour, and though Mrs. Lane returned soon to welcome everyone and thank them for coming, Winter stayed near at hand in case she needed her even after Bennet had mumbled something about checking on Archie and disappeared.

She was beginning to wonder where he had gone when two men came in bearing the equally spaced shoulder laces of a general. General Clinton she had met before, but the other...given the angle of his chin and the whispers that swept the room, it could only be Benedict Arnold.

Winter sucked in a breath and leaned close to Mrs. Lane. "Could you excuse me for a moment, ma'am? I must..."

Too late. The generals strode their way, and Clinton even now reached for Mrs. Lane's hand. "My condolences, madam. I remember your husband fondly from the one time we met before he left for England."

Mrs. Lane murmured something, but Winter paid no attention, given the way Arnold stared at her as if trying to place her face.

Never in her life had she wished she didn't take after her father, but in this moment it seemed more curse than blessing. She could only pray that her mask of oblivion covered any resemblance to her contemplative sire, if Arnold had indeed known him.

General Clinton motioned toward his companion. "Mrs. Lane, allow me to make introductions. This is Benedict Arnold, our newest general."

Mrs. Lane's smile was tight, though that was hardly unusual today. "Of course. How good to meet you, sir."

Arnold delivered the appropriate niceties as he bowed over her hand, but then his gaze arrowed Winter's way again. "And is this your daughter, Mrs. Lane?"

Now her smile went warm, and she slipped an arm around Winter's waist. "God willing, someday soon, General. But at the moment she is still Miss Winnie Reeves, under the charge of her grandparents, the Hamptons."

"Reeves." The arch of Arnold's brow eclipsed the dutiful clasp of her hand. "Are you by chance related to a Colonel Reeves, serving under Washington?"

The earth could have been shaking and the walls tumbling down around them for as solid as her footing felt right now. Tears wanted to burn her eyes, and her knees wanted to buckle. Her heart wanted to cry out "Yes! He is my father!"

But she could not. Certainly not to a traitor like Benedict Arnold. Even if it felt as though she must play the part of Peter denying Christ, she held any emotion back from her eyes and put on that practiced smile and empty-headed blink that settled on her face like a slap.

"Well now, General, I am afraid my memory for ranks is somewhat faulty. They are too bothersome. But I do have a second cousin thrice removed who sided with the Patriots, I believe. Though he was far too stupid to become a colonel. That *is* a higher rank, isn't it, in the Patriot army? Or do they do those backwards, as with so many other things?" She looked up, to the side, and pursed her lips. "Oh, and my—what was he? My great-uncle's second wife's older son. Whatever that makes him to me, I never was quite sure, as we share no blood. But this second wife was far too young for my great-uncle, everyone said so, and yet came to the marriage with a horde of children from *her* first marriage.

Mostly girls, though. Oh, but I suppose her son never took the last name of Reeves, so it can't be him of whom you think."

She couldn't tell if the narrowing of the general's eyes was an attempt to peel back all those layers of nonsense or if he simply disdained her. "Nay, Miss Reeves, I have no concern for such distant relatives. I was wondering more about who your father is."

"My father?" She allowed a portion of the pain to slip through as she drew back an inch.

And let Mrs. Lane step forward and all but push Benedict Arnold away with her chiding gaze. "Really, General, had you been in our city any true length of time, you would know not to ask such an insensitive question. Miss Reeves has lost both her parents and needs no extra reminder of her suffering. 'Tis hard enough on her, facing this loss with me and my sons."

"My apologies. I did not realize." He bowed to Winter, though no apology shone in his eyes. Only icy calculation. Then he repeated the motion toward Mrs. Lane. "And my condolences, ma'am. Though I am sure your family and Miss *Reeves* will deliver you through the grief with their support."

And people thought spies were dastardly creatures? Nay, not unless they combined it with treachery like this beast before her.

Winter put on her sweetest smile and added a few bats of her lashes. "'Twas nevertheless an honor to meet someone of such fame, General Arnold. And allow me to say that no matter what gossip may report, I find that the color red does indeed suit you." When his face mottled, she couldn't resist adding, "It complements your complexion so well."

The general spun around and stalked away, Clinton on his heels. Mrs. Lane leaned in. "I finally see what Bennet meant when he claimed your silliness covers a world of wit."

Her hostess smiled over it, no doubt having enjoyed seeing Arnold insulted, even if she may disagree about his new British jacket suiting him. But Winter could hardly manage to share in the mirth.

He knew. He knew who her father was, and while that did not necessarily mean he would suspect her of any covert activities beyond lying about her Patriot ties—something half of the city did—he was now aware of her. He would be paying attention. Perhaps poking and prying as with Hercules Mulligan and so many others.

She clasped her hands to keep them from shaking and wished she could go home and find Freeman.

They must be prepared to protect themselves.

What a miserable pair they must make. Ben stared into his mug of coffee and let his thoughts swirl along with the din of other patrons in Rivington's. For once he hadn't bothered bringing any texts or papers with him. He had been sitting as he was now ever since he took a seat ten minutes ago, rarely even sipping at his coffee.

When Fairchild came in, he hadn't said a word. He just sat down across from him with his own cup, which he proceeded to ignore as well.

Ben drew in a long breath and willed the black brew before him to reveal a few answers. A week had gone by since he read that life-shattering letter, and it had taken that long for the fog to lift, once the crowds cleared. For pain to take the place of disbelief. For the choices to weigh upon him.

The second half of Uncle Lane's letter repeated continually in his mind. *I am no better now than when my nephew arrived, and I have no greater expectation to last this next year. Bennet must come at once and acquaint himself with the estates. If he might depart before winter, that would be best, for I fear come spring that I will be too weak to be of any help to him.*

'Twasn't the responsibility that weighed so heavily when he read those words. 'Twasn't the thought of taking up Father's so recently vacated position. Nay, 'twas the realization that the only decision he could in good conscience make would disappoint—perhaps infuriate—what family he had left. Mother would suffer a fresh devastation. Uncle would surely not understand. And Archie...

It didn't bear thinking about.

Fairchild sighed as he lifted his mug, sipped, and eased it silently back down. "You look tired, Lane."

Ben snorted a laugh. "Pot and kettle, Fairchild."

His friend offered a crooked, halfhearted smile. "I have been kept quite busy. Still, I am sorry I have not been around more. You were there for me when André…"

A nod seemed acknowledgment enough, and encouragement besides. He knew well Fairchild would have come had he needed anything the man could offer. And surely he conveyed that knowledge with the movement of his head. He hoped so, for it was all he could muster.

Fairchild put a finger against his mug's handle and twirled his cup in a slow circle. "I did come around a few times, but you were with George Knight or Miss Reeves. I figured they could do as much good as I."

Except when both were there together, anyway. George had been more baffled than ever by Mother's sudden acceptance of Winter. Although, witnessing the veiled bickering between two of his favorite people had at least proven a distraction. "I am getting along. In a way I think the loss has not hit as it should, having been separated from Father so long. But then in other moments, that very fact haunts me."

"Understandable." Fairchild halted, and then let his hand fall. "I hear Miss Reeves and Mrs. Hampton stayed with you a few days upon your mother's request."

He wanted to smile but held it back for his friend's sake. That had truly been the one ray of light in the week, knowing Winter was there the moment he went below stairs. "She has been a great comfort to Mother."

Fairchild only nodded, his face bereft of feeling.

A lack that made discomfort wriggle in Ben's stomach. "Fairchild, are you all right?"

His friend's smile took on a note of self-deprecation. "I must look terrible indeed for you to ask me that in *your* current state. I am well enough, Lane. Simply tired. And fresh from a distasteful meeting."

Ben arched a brow.

As usual, 'twas all the invitation Fairchild needed. "A contact our new general secured to help in this task of ferreting out Washington's spies. A lowbred, sniveling…well, let us just say he is unsavory. I wouldn't trust the lout as far as I could throw him, but Arnold is convinced he knows on whom we must focus our attention and has hired this man to follow said person around." The curl of his lip spoke of true disgust. "His very meeting place of choice speaks to his character. He insisted I meet him in Holy Ground, and he will be meeting the general there to report on Monday next."

Arnold had someone in his sights, did he? Obviously not Townsend. Ben frowned. "That seems a rather odd place to meet someone if you want privacy." The very thought of all those crowds of women flaunting themselves, the bawdy talk…he shuddered.

Fairchild smirked. "My thought as well. Though as it happens, during daylight hours the place is quiet. Filthy and disturbing, but quiet. We met on the edge nearest Barclay Street, so I could escape quickly."

"Still, I don't envy you that meeting."

"And I am glad it will be Arnold meeting him next week."

Silence fell again, and for a long moment Ben held Fairchild's gaze. His mind drifted back to their first meeting here, when the tall officer had waltzed in with authority and confidence. Where had that gone? These days his rival-turned-friend seemed a mere shadow of the man Ben had been sure he could never measure up to.

His fault? Deuces, he hoped not. But then, if Ben had fallen deeper and deeper in love with Winter yet had to watch her fall for Fairchild…if he had then lost his best friend…if he found himself under the thumb of an authority he could not respect…

'Twas no wonder the colonel's infernal dimples rarely flashed, that his shoulders seldom seemed square.

Fairchild pressed his lips together for a moment. "You will ask her soon, will you not?"

Why did such happy news have to distress so many people he liked and admired? Why did everything he wanted, everything he worked for, have to delve into the complicated? "Soon, yes. It did not seem the time, with my family in such deep mourning, but as soon as it's appropriate."

The colonel nodded. "And then to England?"

His throat went dry. "Connecticut. I don't intend to go to England."

"You don't…" Eyes wide, Fairchild leaned forward. "What do you mean? You are the heir to a sizable estate. Responsible for the lives and livelihoods of your tenants. You cannot ignore that."

Yes, all was so complicated. "I don't intend to ignore it. I intend to send Archie in my place and have Uncle name him as heir instead. The estate is not entailed. He may make such a change."

Fairchild shook his head, his frown radiating from his eyes as much as his brows. "*May* perhaps, but it is simply not done. You are the eldest. You will inherit. And if you try to tell him otherwise, he will likely ignore you and force it upon you anyway, thinking—rightly—that you will step up by necessity."

Ben curled his hand around his cup, though the coffee had gone cold. Such may have been the case with Father, but the uncle who had never met Ben—who *had* met and liked Archie—was far more likely to relent.

Especially when Ben laid out his reasoning. A task for which he had yet to find the energy.

"If necessary, I will make the legal provisions myself when the time comes. Either way, I have no intention of leaving America. Archie will make the better master of Clefton."

"Your brother is a—" Fairchild cut himself off with gritted teeth. "Well, no matter my opinion of him. But I invite you to think long and hard about what it takes to be a good master of an estate like Clefton and evaluate well which of you possesses those traits. I believe we both know the answer."

Not when one considered that topping the list was dedication to said estate and all to which it owed its being. "I appreciate your advice. And I promise you, I *will* think long and hard before I make any decisions."

Had, in fact. For the past year, as he made the other decisions that in turn decided this for him. The decisions that dictated not only that he ought not to inherit Clefton, but that his uncle would not want him to do so. Not once Bennet admitted what he had spent these eleven months doing.

An estate like that one would never be entrusted to a man who had soiled his hands with espionage.

Fairchild's breath eased out in a slow leak. "Ben, go to England and take the good name your uncle is leaving you. Marry Winter as quickly as you can manage, and depart before you cannot any longer."

The words were rife with warning that made Ben frown. It could not be the approaching cold weather that made such urgency shadow his friend's tone. Did it have to do with Winter, perhaps? With Fairchild's need to know once and for all that she was out of his reach?

Again with the complication. All Ben could think to do was stand, nod again, and toss a coin onto the table to cover his coffee.

And wonder, as he strode back out under the low-hanging gray clouds, whether Fairchild had any intention of ever speaking to him again once he left New York.

Twenty-Four

A gust of wind sent the sign creaking on its hinges. *The Knight's Arms.* Winter barely glanced at it as she continued past, but the scrolling script burned into the wood remained fixed in her mind. As soon as they turned the corner, she held up so Freeman could draw even with her. "You are sure he is the only one inside?"

Not so much as a hint of a smile softened his features. "I'm sure. Are *you* sure this is the best idea?"

"Have you come up with a better one?"

Freeman's lips whitened, so hard did he press them together. "Only what you already dismissed."

Because stealing one of Grandfather's guns was unthinkable—if they were caught, Grandfather wouldn't hesitate to turn it on them. But purchasing one from George Knight...well, the worst he could do was laugh at them.

Or tell Bennet.

That could certainly be worse. She had every intention of confessing her loyalties to him soon, but she would rather no one else did it for her. Especially in a way that would reveal her covert involvement. Her loyalties she would make clear, but the Culper Ring's secrets were not hers to share, just hers to protect.

And so she must take what action she could to protect them as necessary. She could all but smell the hounds closing in, barking at her with every glance Benedict Arnold sent her way. And he had been present at far too many of the gatherings she had attended these past two weeks.

"Here, this one." Freeman steered her into a close, dark alley that presumably led to the back door of the Knights' shop. Given that he had been the one to explore these dank ways earlier, and to send the false messages to get the eldest and youngest Knights to leave, Winter happily gave him the lead.

"How far?"

"Not very. In fact…" He motioned toward an unmarked door that looked like every other in the alley. But just beyond it the space opened up, and she recognized the smells and shapes of a forge. Definitely the Knights'.

They had already discussed how they would enter—namely, without attracting any avoidable attention. So she forewent knocking and slid her hand around the iron ring, giving it a tug.

Freeman sidled in as soon as he could fit, Winter following quickly and easing the heavy door shut again. Whatever room they had entered was dark, but light poured through its open threshold leading to the inside of the building. Freeman nodded his head toward it.

She had chosen her shoes for their silence and now crept her way through the unfamiliar chamber and down the hall. At its end she paused and peered into the room beyond.

George Knight sat at a table, bending low over a half-formed rifle and doing something with a small, pointed tool. No one else was in sight.

Perfect. Winter took that final step inside and cleared a throat. "Do you have a moment, Mr. Knight?"

He started, swore, and spun. She tried not to smile as his eyes went wide. "Miss Reeves? What in the world are you doing here? Are you with Ben?" His gaze went past her, so she obliged him by stepping farther into the room, thereby allowing Freeman to fill the doorway.

Perhaps she took a grain too much pleasure in the wariness that darkened his expression when he caught sight of her companion.

For the first time in his presence, she let her smile flash without the filter of faux Winter. "Nay, I am not with Bennet. This has nothing to do with him."

His eyes narrowed now. "With what, then, has it to do? We have nothing else in common."

"That's not quite true." She turned to the wall and the weapons displayed upon it. "We have at least one other person in common—Silas Beech of Long Island."

Silence hummed for a moment, and then another muted curse slipped from his lips. "Blast it, you bring that up now, nearly a year later? Miss Reeves, I know it was trying for you to be held hostage, even briefly—"

"You misunderstand me." She faced him again, unable to tamp down the beginnings of a grin. "And if you thought for half a second, you would realize I couldn't have known his name had I been only a hostage. Mr. Knight, Silas Beech is a hand on my family's farm. When I came with my grandparents to the city, I left him in charge."

She watched the thoughts click away in his eyes and snap into place. Yet he shook his head. "That cannot be. 'Tis far too great a coincidence that you would be there. And the implications…"

Another awareness crept over his countenance too, one that made him stare at her as if he had never seen her before.

But then, he hadn't. Not really. Winter inclined her head. "Shall I spell it all out for you so nothing need be implied? My family is Patriot, Mr. Knight, and has always been so. *I* have always been so. But when my mother died, my grandparents would not allow anyone with Whig politics into their home—so they told me what I might say, how I might act, and revised any part of my history they did not like."

"Blast." Still as an unwound clock, he regarded her. "Ben was right."

She grinned. "'Tis an annoying trait of his."

He breathed a laugh, picked up his slender tool, and flipped it around his fingers. "Yet I cannot think you came here simply to confess your secrets. Nor do I know why you did so."

"You helped my man before, which means you either care nothing for loyalties or you are inclined in the same direction I am." She slid deeper into the room, nearer his work table. "Whichever it may be, I am here because I now need the same assistance. I need to purchase a weapon."

The tool clanged to the table. "Tell me you jest. *Please* tell me you jest. Does Ben know you are here? Nay, a stupid question. He couldn't because he would bash me in the head if I even *considered* selling his sweetheart a gun."

She folded her arms over her chest. "He would *not*. He would simply devise a particularly nasty chemical compound with which to threaten you."

Again he stared at her, agape, before loosing another breath of laughter. "Miss Reeves, surely you understand that he is my dearest friend. I will not sell a weapon to the woman he intends to marry without his knowledge. Yet given that you did not bring him with you, I must therefore assume you don't want him to know. But I cannot keep such a thing from him."

She shrugged, praying the action covered her panic. "Very well, tell him. I did not come in secrecy to keep *him* from knowing, but rather the rest of the city. Given how my grandfather has treated me in the past, I daresay Bennet would applaud me taking a step to protect myself, if it comes to that."

His eyes bulged all the more, and his freckles seemed to darken as his face went pale. "You intend to shoot your grandfather?"

"What?" She looked to the ceiling and shook her head. "Don't be daft, Mr. Knight. I *intend* to shoot no one, and certainly not Grandfather. But neither do I intend to quietly fold my hands and acquiesce when my life is threatened."

"Why would your life be...?" His voice faded away when she settled her gaze on his again and held it. "Your grandfather?"

She said nothing. But neither did she shutter the thoughts rampaging through her mind.

Without moving his eyes, Mr. Knight slowly shook his head. "You can be in no other danger. You are all but engaged to Ben, arguably the wealthiest man in the city, not to mention having enjoyed the suit of Fairchild, one of the most connected officers..." His eyes went wide again. "Nay."

Not knowing exactly what thought he couldn't accept, she nevertheless figured it could be no more dangerous than the truth. So she again made no response.

A long exhale left him deflated. "I have no weapon suitable for a lady."

"How fortunate, then, that I am not one. Have you anything suitable for a farm girl whose father taught her everything he would have a son?"

A corner of his mouth pulled up. "I may have a pistol that would interest you. Have you ever shot one before?"

"With better aim than my father."

He shook his head, but he pushed up from the table and went over to a cupboard against the far wall. Withdrawing a key from his pocket, he unlocked it. "Ben is going to have an interesting future with you at his side. Here, see what you think of this one."

She waited as he withdrew a pistol and strode across the room, holding it out to her stock first. But when she gripped it, he didn't let go.

His brows were raised. "You love him?"

How could she help but smile? "I tried my best not to. I failed miserably."

Grinning, he released the barrel. "All right, then. Does it suit?"

Winter weighed the weapon in her hand, tried the cock, and examined the fittings. "Very nice. My father had a flintlock much like this— wait. Is this barrel rifled?"

Mr. Knight shrugged. "The British remain uninterested in the design, but I fail to see why we should eschew accuracy."

"Amazing. The cost?" She'd been putting back pin money since she arrived, and had what silver had been left at the farm besides, stored all this time with her forbidden books and pamphlets. It would surely be enough. If not for this one, then certainly for a traditional smoothbore barrel.

Mr. Knight sighed. "Take it."

She halted her examination, gaze flying to him. "What?"

"You heard me." He shoved his hands in his pockets and looked every bit as irritated as he had upon their first introduction. "I always give a reduced price to…certain sectors. Combine that with the discount I would make Ben, and it's hardly worth drawing out your purse."

She handed the pistol to Freeman so that she might slide over to George, push up on her toes, and place a kiss on his cheek. Then she grinned at the shade of scarlet his fair face turned. "You are a good man, George Knight."

"Well." He cleared his throat and rubbed a hand to the back of his neck. "I don't know about all that. I have, after all, spent nigh unto a year trying to convince Ben to forget about you."

She chuckled and backed away until she stood beside Freeman. "Given the picture I presented you, that too speaks to your character, though I am glad he did not listen."

He nodded, and then he cast a glance toward the door opposite the one she had come in. "My father will return soon. And while he wouldn't begrudge a fine Patriot lady her right to protection, I would rather not have to explain the situation."

"Certainly. Thank you for your help, Mr. Knight."

He sat upon his bench once more. "May it keep you safe, your lady-ship. Or may heaven help any of us in Ben's path."

She turned and then paused. "Mr. Knight, I'm sorry for the opin-ion I know you thought I held of you. It was never my own, but I regret it nonetheless."

"Think nothing of it. I never let it bother me." He waved a hand and picked up the would-be weapon from the table.

Winter exchanged a smile with Freeman. "Bennet said you call me 'Lady of Oh' because of the word I dismissed you with when we first met."

"He *told* you that?" Mr. Knight snapped his head up again, though then his face creased in a smile. "All right. Perhaps it bothered me a little. But no more. So long as you make Ben happy, my lady, we have no quarrel remaining."

She wanted to ask what he thought Bennet might do if he discov-ered her secrets, wanted to ask if he thought his loyalty to the Crown might weaken, or at least if he might grow more accepting of those of them with opposite views. She wanted some assurance that the last remaining barriers between her and Bennet wouldn't crush them when they fell.

But Mr. Knight wouldn't be able to give her that. So she murmured a farewell and followed Freeman out the back entrance, down the dank

alley, and into the blustery October day. It took them only a few minutes to walk to the carriage they had left a few streets over, twenty more
for him to drive her home.

Eyes shut, she let the motion of the carriage lull her, the bump of
wheels wake her, and her mind drift to that place halfway between
thought and dream. The place where both the greatest fears and greatest hopes seemed equally possible.

*Blessed God, support me by the strength of heaven, that I may never
turn back.*

The carriage rolled to a halt, and Freeman jumped down to help
her out. The moment her slippers touched the ground, she spotted the
familiar horse in the stable before her. Colonel Fairchild must be here.

Freeman followed her gaze and frowned. "Haven't seen much of
the colonel lately. I began to think he must have resigned himself to
losing you to Mr. Lane."

"I suppose he has been too busy to call, and with me gone so much
at the Lanes'…"

"Mmm." He patted his waist, where he must have secured the flintlock. "I shall find some ammunition for this after I check on Percy. Say
a prayer for the boy, Winnie. Infection has set in."

Poor Percy. "I will. And thank you." Having no idea how long
Fairchild had already been waiting, she hurried through the house's
kitchen entrance and handed her cloak to a servant. "Am I needed?"

The man offered a tight smile. "In the drawing room, Miss Reeves.
The colonel only arrived a few minutes ago, however, so you needn't
rush overmuch."

She saw no reason to dawdle though, so headed toward the receiving rooms. Because the door stood open, she could see Grandmother
and the colonel within. Her arrival drew the attention of both, and
Fairchild surged to his feet.

"There you are, Winnie dear." Grandmother indicated Winter's
usual seat. "Now you can entertain the colonel for a few moments
while I attend a pressing matter. I will return shortly."

Winter dipped her knees a bit. "Certainly, Grandmother. And good
day, Colonel."

"Good day." Fairchild motioned to the place beside him on the
couch as Grandmother left the room. "Will you sit with me, my dear?"

"Of course." She settled on the cushion and smoothed out her skirt. She noted that handsome Isaac Fairchild seemed to have aged a decade since she had seen him last. "Have you been unwell, Colonel? You look peaked."

His smile came off sad. "Nay, my dear, 'tis only…everything. Here. I brought these for you." He pulled a pot of daffodils off the table and handed it to her.

She blinked at the cheerful yellow heads and wanted to cry. Fairchild's flower gifts always reflected their meaning. These stood for unrequited love as well as bright respect. "Some of my favorites. However did you find them this time of year?"

His smile went lopsided. "A hothouse. I probably should have chosen cyclamen, but these never fail to remind me of you."

"Cyclamen?" She lowered the pot and frowned. "Why would you be saying goodbye, Colonel? Are you going somewhere?"

His gaze fell to his clasped hands and stayed there as he drew in a long breath. "Nay. But I expect you soon will be, with Ben."

Ben. How strange it sounded to hear them call each other by their given names, to realize it was a testament to their unlikely friendship. It would all be so much simpler without admiration and respect. If Fairchild weren't such a genuinely good man.

He ought to have given her clematis—the flower to accuse her of artifice.

"Colonel, I…" But she knew not what to say.

He shook his head. "You needn't try to make me feel better. I at least have the comfort of knowing you will marry a good man, one who loves you with all his heart. I only wish…I only wish I had spoken earlier, before you ever met him. I cannot think why I dragged my heels, except that I was so enjoying the courtship itself."

Twice now she had heard that sentiment, first from Robbie and now Fairchild. And how could she possibly respond? Perhaps, had it happened that way, she never would have known the love she would have missed with Bennet, but as it stood now, she could not share in their regrets. And yet she could not help but regret their pain.

"I have always enjoyed your company, Colonel." It seemed a paltry offering, but what more could she give?

His smile went a degree brighter. "And I yours. I cannot tell you how precious it has been to have someone that would listen, who could offer sunshine and smiles in a world otherwise gray. But there is no reason we cannot all still be amiable."

She pasted pleasant confusion on her face. "Oh, you know I am terrible with anything requiring good aim. You surely remember that time Dosia recommended an archery competition." It had taken all her skill to hit the hat another officer had left on a table while seeming to aim at the target. "But at any rate, we can remain friendly."

"Indeed." As always, his smile was indulgent. "I am blessed to have such friends. But I had better not tarry long now. I left rather pressing business. A few of the whaleboaters sympathetic to the Crown have kidnapped...well, I had better not say who, but Washington will feel the loss quite acutely."

She stood when he did, though she made sure to pay more attention to the daffodils she set upon the table than the words pounding through her mind. "Grandmother says those whaleboaters are scoundrels, the lot of them."

"Usually, yes, though in this case we owe them a debt of gratitude." Fairchild picked up his hat and held it at the ready to put on. "They managed to capture a particular friend of Washington's who is known to be on an assignment that would keep him away from the general's camps for months, though certainly he didn't intend to pass the time at Fort St. George. We plan to send false information of our movements using his name, with none the wiser."

Winter turned from the flowers to smile at Fairchild. "How clever you are." And how she prayed that information would be enough for Washington to discern who it was they had captured. Perhaps an operation would be mounted to rescue the poor man from the Long Island fort, and at the least they would know to look suspiciously on any correspondence.

"Well." He slid his fingers along the rim of his hat. "I will let you get on with your day. And I do expect an invitation to the wedding when the time comes."

Again, tears threatened to well. "Of course. And I thank you, Isaac, for the faithful friend you have always been."

He only nodded, put his hat upon his head, and strode out.

What a dreadful situation. She headed out too, toward the stable

and her room beneath it. But, oh, how she hated to send this information, even as she knew she must. Roe would be in the city again
tomorrow, and though she couldn't pass along the particulars she never
learned, she must share this.

Still, it felt as though a giant hand squeezed her chest. Perhaps
because she knew Bennet would propose soon and they would head
to Connecticut, which would mean this may be her last missive as a
Culper agent. Or perhaps it was because she couldn't stand knowing
how she had hurt Fairchild, all because of this.

She pushed the sensation aside as she gained the stable, checked to
be sure no one watched, and descended into the darkness. Duty must
be done. And if she could perhaps save a life, save a cause in the process...

Nerves jangled against nerves when she got out the stain. Would
she have enough? She would just have to be concise. Because the message must be sent, and it could not possibly be done with any other ink.
Not given how tight security was these days, and missives already gone
missing. If she dared write anything with a heat-developed...

The idea bloomed full and brought a measure of peace. She put the
stain upon the table for the message to Tallmadge. And she got out her
lemon water for a second one.

Twenty-Five

Never in his life had Ben dreaded a meeting with a lawyer as he did this one. He glanced from the bespectacled man to the clock in the corner of what had been Father's study and willed the man to get started. He had a meeting in Holy Ground to eavesdrop on in just a few hours.

Mr. Carroll cleared his throat as he studied the document before him. A moment later he looked up at Bennet, then Mother, and finally Archie. "Thank you for your patience with me. I do regret I was out of town when you received this dreadful news. I am especially sorry to hear of it because I had a communication from Mr. Lane not two weeks ago addressing the issue of his will, and the fact that he wanted to wait to change it until he was in possession of Clefton after his uncle's expected demise."

Ben winced—first at the casual mention of death and then at the implications—and darted a glance at Archie. He sat stone still, his jaw clenched.

The lawyer sighed. "I understand there had been some discussion in recent months about leaving all the family holdings in New York to Archibald, since all the English property would go to Bennet. Unfortunately, as I said, this change was never made, as Mr. Lane was never the official possessor of Clefton."

Another glance showed Ben the whitening of Archie's knuckles.

Mr. Carroll held up a hand. "Do allow me to stress, Archibald, that your father was fully in favor of this proposed change. He had every intention of leaving the American property to you. And as I under-stand it was your brother's suggestion to begin with, if he wishes I can assist in the transference of deeds from Bennet to you—though again, wisdom dictates we wait until Bennet is the master of Clefton."

Archie jerked his head in what he probably meant to be a nod.

Ben pressed his lips together. "I certainly intend to rectify this, yes."

"I imagined you would." The lawyer smiled and focused on Mother. "You, of course, receive your widow's portion, Mrs. Lane. And as stated in the will as it was written before Clefton was ever at issue, Archibald receives the house and property you brought with you to the marriage, as well as a sum of money I will specify in a few moments, and the investments in several businesses. Everything else—the house here in New York, the one he occupies in New Haven, his family's businesses, and the greatest portion of sterling—goes to Bennet."

Ben drew in a long breath. If one didn't consider Clefton, then Father had made every attempt to divide the property fairly. Mother would be cared for, and both he and Archie received enough money and interests in businesses to ensure their continued well-being.

But Clefton still must be considered, and 'twas obviously on Archie's mind. Perhaps they had received nearly equal portions in the will now, but when one added the expansive holdings in England into the mix...well, a volatile reaction was inevitable.

Ben paid careful attention to the details Father had laid out, espe-cially as concerned his portion and Mother's, because providing for her would largely fall to him. Assuming she would allow it after his plan was carried out.

When Mr. Carroll finally left, Ben stopped his brother with a hand upon his shoulder and looked him in the eye. "I will make this right. You know that, don't you?"

Archie turned his head toward the door and shrugged Ben's hand off. "Of course you will. Perfect Benny always does what he must."

Nay. All he could do now was sigh as his brother stormed out say-ing something about the work awaiting him at the barracks.

Mother stepped to his side. "He will come around, Bennet."

"I know." But not in time. Not before the truth came out. Though they barely tolerated one another in person, he hated to think that a wedge would come permanently between them. Friends or not, they were brothers. Perhaps Clefton would be enough to secure peace. "Will you excuse me, Mother? I need to write to Uncle Lane."

"Of course, dear. And then will you go see Winnie? If so, ask the Hamptons to dinner tomorrow night." She took a step away but then paused, brows arched. "For that matter, when are you going to ask her to join us as your wife? Have you need of an engagement gift? I have been pondering it, and I think the emerald ring your father gave me would be perfect."

Those thoughts were far sweeter than the others clamoring around his mind. "I intend to ask soon, yes. Actually, I had planned to speak with you about jewelry the day we received the letter from my uncle. Now...well, as soon as the time is right."

"The time is right whenever you make it so, Bennet. Given the way she has stood beside us through all this, I daresay no one will be surprised if an engagement follows quickly on the heels of this loss, especially given your need to hurry to England."

That again. "You have an emerald, you say?"

"Come."

He followed her up the stairs, into her room, and waited while she sorted through a mix of shining, sparkling pieces. She straightened a minute later and held out a large, rectangular emerald clasped in a circle of gold.

"The fit should be good. Her hands seem much the size mine were when I could still wear it."

Ben studied its green depths a moment more and then slid it into his waistcoat's inner pocket. "I thank you, Mother."

Her grin was indulgent, and the brightest he had seen from her in weeks. "The only thanks I need is a daughter and then a few grandchildren to dote on."

He managed a smile around the heaviness in his chest. "I am glad you finally see in her what I do."

Her laughter shed light on the whole house, it seemed. "As am I, Bennet. I had begun to think you quite daft."

She may think him so again shortly. Murmuring another thanks and a farewell, he left her room and headed to his own. At his desk he uncapped his inkwell and then chose a quill and the best paper he had. He heaved a long breath and began.

> *Dear Uncle Lane,*
>
> *News of my father's unexpected death has hit us all as a severe blow. I know it must have been painful for you as well, and we all send our love and respect. And while I appreciate your need for an heir to teach in his stead, I urge you to consider my brother as that heir rather than me.*
>
> *I am not who you think me.*

It took him several minutes to pen his reasons, to expose his heart for the first time since he left Yale. To immortalize what would make him an exile to those who shared his blood.

He squeezed his eyes shut after he signed his name. If he sent this, if he held to it, he could lose it all. Everything that mattered. Mother, Archie...Winter. What if she refused him when she discovered the truth?

Nay, she would forgive it. He knew in the depths of his heart she would. But with his family he hadn't the same certainty. So though he may have the woman he loved, he could very well be asking her to join a family fractured, one who had thrust him away. He would be able to provide for her needs, even her comforts, but he knew what she most wanted was love and understanding.

Well. He would confess before he proposed. And if she accepted him, then they would build the family her heart so needed.

He scattered sand over the ink to dry it, poured it off again, and folded the paper. Then he slid it into an envelope. A dab of wax provided a seal, and he penned the direction. A moment later he left his room, caught the servant headed out with the day's post, and sent his fate on its way.

Then he grabbed his cloak and whipped it around his shoulders. He would go see Winter. If he were going to lose her too, he would just as soon know it before he followed Benedict Arnold to Holy Ground.

Winter tilted her face up to receive the kiss of warm sunshine and smiled into the cool whisper of air. Soon enough she would be trapped inside while snow and ice overtook her world, but today was a beautiful promise of what awaited her in spring.

A few more weeks and they would reach the anniversary of when Bennet first stumbled into her life. Thinking of it now, she could scarcely remember the panic his penetrating gaze had inspired, the determination to stay away from him at all costs.

How far they had come—and how twisted a road they had traveled to get here.

Perhaps they could marry on that date. A late November wedding, before winter gripped them too wholly. Then they would still have ample time to settle into his home in Connecticut before classes resumed after Christmas. She could hardly wait to see him in that paradise he had told her about so many times, the laboratory with all his favorite equipment.

Footfalls interrupted her reverie, but she didn't mind it when she saw Bennet turn the corner and step into the garden. What she *did* mind was the concern that saturated his eyes. She stood from her bench and held out her hands. "Did the reading of the will not go well?"

Rather than clasp her fingers, he walked into her embrace and gathered her close. She probably ought to pull away for the sake of propriety, but instead she wrapped her arms around his neck and enjoyed it as he buried his face in her shoulder.

"It went as expected."

"I'm sorry." She stroked a hand over the unpowdered hair gathered below his hat and shivered in delight when he pressed his lips to the base of her throat.

An "ahem" alerted them to Freeman's presence nearby, but Bennet didn't pull away. "I love you." He kissed his way up her neck and over her jaw.

Heaven. Perhaps they could marry sooner than she had been thinking, if ever he decided to ask. "And I love you."

"*Ahem.*"

Bennet grinned even as his lips met hers for another of those brief, tantalizing kisses that he so rarely found the chance to give her. Then he put a bit of space between them. "For your sake, Freeman."

"I do appreciate it, Mr. Lane."

Winter heard the note of laughter in Freeman's voice but focused instead on Bennet and the desperation that seemed to radiate from his gaze. For her? No, she didn't think so. She lifted a hand and settled it against his cheek. "I don't like seeing you like this."

Amusement softened the edge of his expression. He lifted a brow. "Like what? Amorous?"

A laugh tickled its way out. "Nay, that I like quite well. But you seem...unhappy. Distressed."

He removed a hand from her waist to rub at his neck. "'Tis thoughts of my family and all the changes to it."

"I assumed as much. I have been praying."

"I assumed as much. You generally are." He dropped his other hand and took a seat on the bench.

Why was that always, *always* his response to the topic of prayer? Deflect or retreat. Winter turned to face him but held her place and folded her arms over her middle. "You know, Bennet, the Lord may be more apt to answer said prayers with an affirmative if *you* were the one to offer them up."

His face went hard, though he seemed to try, unsuccessfully, to soften it again. "Can we discuss that later? Come, sit. I have more pressing things to speak with you about."

"There is nothing more pressing." The words seemed to lodge in her throat and felt like a mere murmur on her lips. "Nothing else will be resolved so long as you keep such distance between you and the Lord."

Even the attempt at softness disappeared. "There *is* distance between me and the Lord—a universe of it. I fail to see how addressing myself to the Creator will change a jot or tittle of my life. He set it in motion long ago, but the future is up to us."

Her fingers curled into her sides. "How can you say that?"

"How can you say otherwise?" He surged to his feet again and paced to a dormant rose bush and back again. "Do you think I have never uttered a prayer? That, had I seen some response, I would think as I do?"

Ever the scientist. Winter raised her chin. "You have recited prayers, I am certain. But unless they came from your heart, my love, 'tis like pouring two elements into beakers beside each other and then claiming they had no reaction when mixed. How could you possibly judge such a thing if not done properly? Just so, prayers mean nothing unless they are *meant*."

He halted before her, amusement lighting his eyes again. "I appreciate you trying to put it in terms I understand, but the analogy is feeble, my love."

Then she would try again. She caught his hands and clasped them. "Then look at me, at us. Before July I spoke to you many a time, but how often did I ever say anything with meaning?"

His answer was an indrawn breath.

She squeezed his fingers. "I gave you words but kept all feeling, all honest thought from them. Was that enough for you?"

"Nay," he said on his exhale, low and near silent.

"And so our words, if nothing but empty syllables recited by rote, mean nothing to God. Just as you could not force me to draw near, so the Lord will respect your decision when that is all you offer Him. But He wants to know you, my love, to hear the agony of your heart so He might soothe it. Just as you have soothed mine."

"Winter." He leaned down until their foreheads touched in that way that never failed to wring her heart. "Compelling words, but logic forbids I accept them so easily."

She smiled and held his hands even tighter. "Does logic alone tell you that you love me?"

His glare was at least playful. "You know it does not. And so you will say that if I will admit the heart plays a factor in my dealings with you, so I ought to try utilizing it in my dealings with Providence."

She straightened when he did. "More, I'm saying you are no scientist at all if you do not do so, because it will mean you have judged without properly experimenting first. You will be no better than Descartes, laying out rules of motion that can be proven false with a simple demonstration."

His chuckle seemed to combine appreciation with brooding. "And if I conduct this experiment and *my* hypothesis is proven rather than yours, what then? Will you relent, and leave me to my prayerful contemplation while you go about your contemplative prayer?"

She could respect that he made no suggestion that if his theory were supposedly proven, she ought to change her views. "I cannot fathom such an outcome. When we earnestly seek the Lord, He faithfully answers."

Bennet pulled away and regarded her for a long moment. "We shall see. I have an appointment to keep, but we will have the conversation I intended soon."

Did he mean the conversation she thought he did? Presumably, which made her smile. And if regret pulsed for a moment that she hadn't let him initiate a proposal when he arrived, she pushed it aside. This needed to be resolved first. "I will be waiting." And praying.

He nodded and stepped away, lifting a hand in farewell to her and then Freeman, and then he disappeared back around the corner of the house.

Winter watched him go, and then she glanced at Freeman when he came to her side. "How is Percy today?"

"Bad, Winnie. Real bad. I daresay he shan't make it another day. The infection..." Her friend cleared his throat. "I checked on the second letter, with the heat-developed ink. It's gone."

Her heart threatened to pound from her chest. Freeman had at least made sure her missive to Washington had gone directly into Roe's hand, but the fact that the one she had left as bait had been taken...

She had better hasten to her knees.

Twenty-Six

Ben had a feeling his expression was every bit as stubborn and indignant as Archie's had been a couple of hours earlier. He hadn't been angry when he left Winter, but with each step her words chafed a bit more.

What made her presume to know whether his prayers had always stopped at his lips? What made her so certain he had not prayed earnestly at one point, and through *that* had come to his conclusions? She made assumptions. Wrong assumptions.

Of course he had prayed from his heart before. What child didn't? There was that time he had asked for a new wooden horse…which, granted, had been a purely selfish prayer, so he suspected it didn't count. The same could undoubtedly be said of all the others from childhood. But then, when fourteen…no, that had contained a definite note of newly born cynicism. He had dared the Lord, but Winter would argue it was testament to His merciful nature that He had ignored him.

She may have a point. Both in his imagination and the one she had actually made.

Blast it all.

Ben turned the corner and wished it were as easy to turn one in his thoughts. How was he to simply engage his heart when he was none too convinced doing so, if he could manage it, would achieve any-thing? He could not make himself believe. Could not make faith spring up as Winter so obviously desired. Could not rewrite his perception of God to be one of a loving Father when the only evidence he had ever seen was of a distant Creator.

He sidestepped a slow-moving couple ambling past the shops and frowned. Winter would say that if he wanted evidence, he must con-duct an experiment through which he had a hope to glean some. That was something, he must admit, he had never really done. He hadn't seen the point. 'Twas illogical. It relied more on what one felt than on what one saw.

But then, had it not infuriated him that everyone dismissed Win-ter simply because of what they saw with their eyes, having never dug deeper?

He grumbled and scowled at the injustice of having something turned on him like that.

So be it. He would not be a hypocrite. He would at least try, and try genuinely. The worst that could happen was nothing.

Ducking into an alley, Ben turned his back on the passersby and leaned a shoulder into the brick wall nearest at hand. He felt a bit ridic-ulous and more than a bit at a loss, but he was trying. Perhaps that, in the celestial scheme, counted for something.

How to even begin? All the prayers he had memorized, had heard in chapel, seemed an unwise example to follow right now because he would fall into habit and neglect to include his heart.

But he had heard Winter pray several times. *God of my end.* That seemed to be her favorite salutation. It had a pretty ring to it, but that could not be what he focused on. What did it really mean?

God of my end. His end. Even Bennet believed that. That at the beginning and at the end was the Creator.

He could leap off from that. *God of my end, I know You are omni-scient. And so You know how difficult this is for me. Winter would have me believe that is of interest to You, and though I find it difficult to believe...if it is true, I want to believe it.*

The sun intensified upon his shoulders. That was something he had never considered. There was a possibility Winter was right. And if so, of course he would want to know it. Had he not spent his entire adult life seeking the truths of his world?

He squeezed his eyes shut. *Lord, I do indeed want to know who You are. If I am wrong, please show me. If she is right, then reveal it in a way I cannot mistake. And while I am beseeching You…well, this business that brought me here has reached a tipping point. Lead me to the spy, Almighty Lord, before it is too late.*

Unable to think of anything else to say, he rested his back against the wall and stared at the one across from him.

A wise man's heart is at his right hand.

Ben frowned. Was it coincidence that another obscure verse came to mind, or, as Winter suggested, could it be the Lord speaking to him? Either way, he turned his head to the right.

Benedict Arnold hurried past, his attention on something in his hands. A rectangle of white fluttered to the ground, but he didn't seem to notice. His gait didn't so much as hitch.

Interesting. Ben moved toward the street even as a gust of wind blew the paper his way. An envelope of some kind. He picked it up, looked at both front and back, but it was unmarked.

Had he the leisure, he would have opened it. But it seemed the wiser course to pocket it and follow Arnold. He knew where he was going in general terms, but he had dreaded the thought of wandering through Holy Ground searching him out. His hope had indeed been to intercept him on his way from the barracks.

The Lord's guidance? He wouldn't dismiss the possibility, but he also wouldn't be convinced by something he had already made steps to achieve himself.

He made sure to stay a goodly distance behind the general, just close enough to see at what point he turned into Holy Ground. As Fairchild had said, the chosen spot seemed to be off Barclay Street. Good. Perhaps he could hover on the outskirts and still be close enough to overhear.

Though he obviously had to be on the correct side of the street. And once across, there was no way to remain outside the village of harlots. Their tents and lean-tos and hovels crowded the church's land. On the rare wall of brick, blackened trails still marked where the fire had rampaged through this section of town some four years ago now.

Odd how this was the one place that had been quickly rebuilt, while the rest of the city crowded into too little housing, the charred remains empty and forlorn.

At least he spotted no women displaying their wares. The few figures he saw moving seemed to be headed out of Holy Ground in the direction of the vendues and their bargains.

Arnold's scarlet coat stood out like a cardinal among pigeons against the weather-stained canvas. The general stepped out from between two tents and surveyed the area, presumably looking for his contact.

Get thee behind me, Satan.

Ben sent a glare heavenward even as he stumbled backward. If it *was* the Lord sending him these verses, then the Almighty had an unexpected sense of humor.

A flap of canvas enveloped him, sending him into a dim chamber lit by a single lamp. A cough made him spin around—but the figure sitting on the pallet looked to be no threat. Indeed, she looked like little more than a child, innocent eyes fixed on him with curiosity and a strange luminosity.

Which, of course, made him realize he had intruded upon this waif's home. "Ah…" He passed a hand over his hair, sending his tricorn tumbling to the ground. He retrieved it quickly. "So sorry to… that is I…" He motioned outside. "I am eavesdropping on someone."

The girl's lips turned up in the corners. "I was making tea. Would you like some while you…listen?"

He glanced from her to the one tin cup beside a dented kettle. "I thank you, miss, but no." Instead he strained toward the wall nearest where Arnold was. Or had been. Had he left? If not, he was silent.

"As you like, sir." The girl sprinkled a few leaves into the cup and poured steaming water over it. "I am Viney."

He nodded but said nothing. His attention was snatched by Arnold's low voice outside.

"You are late."

"Mayhap you are early," said a second voice, rough and reedy. "What is it to you, so long as I come bearing the news ye seek?"

A grumble sounded that Ben could not make out, and then, "So you have evidence enough?"

"Evidence…" The lout made it sound like a vile thing, an instrument with which to torture rather than prove truth. "I saw her man handing a note to a farmer what quickly left the city, not long after that high-bred officer of yours visited her. Otherwise the chit spent most her time with that other gent's family."

Arnold hummed. "'Tis hardly enough to prove anything. She has ties to many a farmer on Long Island, having grown up there. But then, if my man did his job and she *is* the one we seek, then that letter will prove Washington's undoing."

Ben squeezed his eyes shut. The words, the similarities…nay. Unthinkable. Better to focus on the other terrible realization.

He was too late. The plan had been enacted. The agent, if truly discovered, had been used against the Patriots.

"And I retrieved the other letter she had left," Arnold went on. "I have not yet had a chance…blast. Where did I put it?"

Ben pulled it out of his pocket and stared at it for a long moment. Was there any point in looking now? Arnold had already negated his whole purpose for coming here, but perhaps there was still some hope. Somewhere.

And at the very least, curiosity got the best of him. Yet even as he broke the seal, his limbs seemed to double in weight. His chest went tight. And his eyes, after glimpsing the script on the page, slid closed. He needn't read it to know. 'Twas Winter's hand.

"No." The denial slipped out on a quiet moan. All this time, he had been seeking her on two fronts without even realizing it. And why hadn't he seen it? He knew Robert Townsend was involved, and as close as they were…all those strange glances between them he hadn't known how to interpret…but it made no sense. Perhaps Arnold was wrong. Perhaps…

Even as he hoped it, dread certainty iced over him. He had prayed the Lord would lead him to answers. If this was the one he got, he ought never beseech Providence again.

He stroked a finger over the condemning paper while the miscreant outside made some suggestion about where Arnold may have put it. "Not you, Winter," Ben murmured. "You cannot have put yourself in such a position."

"Winter?" Viney's eyes were wide in her sunken face, though she kept her voice to a whisper. "Winter Reeves?"

And why did it surprise him that his beloved was acquainted with harlots when he had just learned she was a spy? Yet he was. So much so that he could only blink at the girl.

Viney smiled. "I met her in July, when her grandfather had her struck o'er the head and dumped her here. I saw her before anyone else did and nursed her until she awoke, and then I helped her leave again before more ill could befall her."

When her grandfather *what*? For a long moment he stared, agape. "He…she…July…Of course, that head injury." And why had she not told him while she confessed her inability to live without him?

That answer was obvious enough. She didn't trust him. Not enough.

"You must be her beau." Viney sank down to her knees again. "The way you say her name…"

"I intend to marry her." Or did. Assuming she could avoid the noose long enough to walk up the aisle.

Blast. He looked around, wishing for a sturdy post to lean on. Or strike. He had to make do with rubbing at the back of his neck. "How could she be so stupid as to get involved in something like this? She knows the consequences."

Viney folded her hands in her lap and regarded him evenly. "I know not what 'this' you mean, sir, but she would have had valid reasons. She is a good soul. One of the only people I have met in years who cared for the heart beneath the grime."

Ben raised the letter he held, but the words were empty. Nothing but the prattle of the pseudo Winter and an odd little *H* in the corner. "Yes, she is all that is good. Which is why I cannot fathom this." But then, he had not come to New York thinking the spy he sought would be a base creature like the one mumbling to Arnold outside. He had known he—and she, apparently—would be someone trustworthy and trusted if they indeed put their hands to such vital information. And Winter, through Fairchild, had overheard plenty.

But *Winter*. Stooping to such levels, putting herself in a position to be hanged. For a cause in which she had never given the slightest hint that she believed, not even to him.

He could not be angry over the secrets, not when he had plenty of them himself. But to think of the danger she was in, the general outside determined to see her undone…

When he suspected George of being involved, there had been fear. But not like this.

"Never mind. I will find it later," Arnold said outside. "It hardly matters. We will know soon enough if she is guilty. And if so, she will pay the price for it."

The second man grunted. "Seems to me, sir, that 'tis obvious she is not working alone. And given what I have seen of her, 'tis equally obvious she has no part in the brains of it."

"We will keep an eye on her. Perhaps she will lead us to whomever else she is working with."

"Now see here, General, I told you from the start that I have business taking me out of town this afternoon. I'm happy to pick it up again when I come back next week, but—"

"Fine, fine. Their letters are never closer together than a fortnight anyway."

Ben paid no heed to their farewells. His gaze snagged on that unobtrusive H again. What in thunder?

Heat—the primary developer for invisible inks. Of course. He turned to Viney and motioned toward her lamp. "Do you mind if I borrow your flame for a moment?"

She lifted her brows but waved her acquiescence.

Ben slid over to it and held the paper up. Close, then closer to the open flame. Closer still until the smell of scorching paper filled his nostrils, until a faint sizzle reached his ears. Until the invisible ink filling the space between the lines of nonsense turned a golden brown.

> *What fun it has been to be part of your experiment! I did so enjoy helping you create the stain and acid. But alas, the current climate being what it is, we had better call a halt to our game before someone thinks us really involved in espionage. 'Tis a shame we never found a reliable formula, but perhaps you can try again after this dreadful war is over, when it will not seem such a suspicious hobby.*

Perhaps he would have smiled at what was an obvious attempt to explain away the evidence of her involvement, had it not spoken to the fact that she must know someone was closing in. Must be frightened. What if she did something foolish? Something that got her killed?

Blast it all, this was precisely why he had hoped no one he knew was involved in this.

And she wondered at his lack of faith. How could he have faith, the substance of what one hoped for, when his hopes had shattered so fully?

"Is it as bad as all that?" Viney cradled her cup in her hands and regarded him with a solemnity strangely colored with cheer.

"Worse." He lowered the singed paper and let his shoulders droop. "Winter is involved in something that could get her killed. For months I have been trying to determine who—and it was her all along."

The girl, for some reason he could not fathom, smiled. "How fortunate you discovered it, then, so you can help her while those men outside are about other business and so paying no attention to her."

His frown felt harsh on his brow. "Fortunate? Are you daft? The very hour I accept her challenge to pray about all that is going wrong in my life, I learn this about the woman I love—and you call it *fortunate?*"

She traced a finger around the dented edge of her cup. "Perhaps this seems like a blow to you, whatever it is. But would it have been better if you had *not* found it out and those men out there got ahold of her?"

He folded his arms over his chest. "It would have better had she not been guilty of it at all."

"So you will blame the Lord for the decisions she has made? Decisions that I suspect run deeper than anyone else could know?" She turned her head away to cough in a handkerchief. It came away stained red.

Decisions no one else could know…another something he could well understand. "Then if Providence were leading me to it, He could have led me sooner so I could help her before she was discovered and removed her from the city entirely."

Again she smiled. "When would you have done this, sir? Three months ago? Six? A year? And yet if you had, I never would have met her. And so she would not have given me the gift that allowed me to survive these last few months without inviting anyone into my tent."

Though she stated that last part with calm, he shuddered on her behalf. She was a mere child. She ought not have to suffer such things.

But Winter, somehow, had helped save her from it. "You are saying that the Lord sees what I cannot."

"More, sir. I am saying that this very day is the right and proper time for whatever is unfolding. That every step you have taken until now has led you here according to His perfect will."

Led him here? Ben frowned. To get to this particular place, at this particular time—to meet this particular girl who, against all odds, knew Winter—he had followed Arnold, thanks to that verse, and he had found the letter that fluttered his way. Only because he had paused to pray, as Winter urged him. To which he would not have been receptive had he not been contemplating all he stood to lose.

A reality that would not have been so forceful had the news of Father's death not reached them when it did, had he not been at Rivington's that day after Fairchild had met with Arnold's unsavory contact.

Yet he may not have believed all this possible of Winter had he not first discovered Townsend's involvement, which certainly would not have happened had he not stumbled upon the right information connecting him to Woodhull, Brewster, and Tallmadge. Information all made clear by those verses.

And how much information had come from Fairchild? Yet he never would have known the man had they not been pursuing the same woman. He never would have dared approach Winter, though, had he not needed a well-connected courtship as an excuse to enter the society he had long shunned.

Winter. A woman he had only met because of an urge to go to that first party, where he saw the dichotomy in her behavior. But he had gone because he had a mission—one he had never questioned, yet which had come to him by what he had deemed an accident.

One random line in a letter Archie had sent. One random piece of gossip about a man named John André, who had whispered a plan to a young woman who Archie then charmed.

His head swam. "If every step leading here was orchestrated by God..."

She smiled and clutched her cup close. "Then He must love you very much to have planned such an intricate journey. Correct?"

A breath of a laugh escaped his lips as all his knowledge, all the memorized Scriptures stored in his mind, at last coalesced into a picture. One of a God involved in His creation. Of a Father who had steered him to this very spot in ways Ben never could have imagined, no matter how long he contemplated it. *"Quad erat demonstratum.* And so it is proven."

Viney placed the cup on her rickety table and stood. "I feel you must hasten to Winter, sir. But before you go..." She moved a rug and then a broken shingle covering a hole, out of which she drew a small velvet bag. After untying it, she poured three pearls into her palm and held it out to him. "This is what remains of the necklace Winter gave me. Would you return them to her?"

He studied the gleaming spheres and then her pale face. "Do you not need them?"

How could a smile seem at once to be peaceful and yet no more than a ghost? "Nay. I know enough of consumption to realize this burst of energy I have felt these past few days will be my last. The provisions I just purchased will keep me until the end. It will come soon, and I am ready for it. Please." She held her hand closer to him.

His throat tight, Ben reached out and plucked the pearls from her palm.

She seemed to relax. "Thank you. I pray they will serve as a reminder of His provision, of His plan for us all. Will you tell her I send my greetings? And assure her I have prayed for her daily, as I. promised I would?"

His fingers curled around the gems. The lustrous promises. He had to squeeze shut his eyes for a moment. What was that verse about casting pearls before swine? That was what he felt like now—unworthy. All his life he had not only doubted, he had reasoned his way into rebellion against the Lord. Yet still He had guided him, had blessed him, and had, so quickly after being asked, demonstrated Himself to him. "I will tell her."

"Thank you. And what hours I have left will be spent in prayer for the two of you." She pulled tight the shawl around her shoulders. "Go now. Quickly."

Her command lit an urgency in the very core of his spirit. He nodded, pocketed the pearls along with the brittle, burnt letter sure to
crumble around them, and flew out. Over Holy Ground. In search of
the promise still waiting to be grasped.

Twenty-Seven

Winter watched Freeman disappear up the steps to the stable and heard his footfalls lead him to the far corner, where Percy lay so near death.

Her gaze swept the room. Everything was in its place. The inks, the quills, the paper, her books. The silver had been returned to its hiding spot. The gun rested on the table before her, loaded and ready.

Unease burned her stomach. No matter how much she prayed, she couldn't shake the feeling she had made a mistake. Taken a misstep. That the enemy was closing in.

She ought to return to the house, but her limbs froze when she considered distancing herself from her sanctuary right now. Something was happening. Some scale had been tipped.

God of my end, help me to know Your will for me.

More footsteps sounded above her, entering from the main doors. Her gaze flew to the narrow, steep staircase. Was that light from above slivering through? Surely Freeman had closed the trap door carefully, hadn't he? He always did.

But when Percy had screamed in such pain…

Well, there was no need to fear the worst. She clamped down on the instinct to panic, to rush to blow out her lamp. As jittery as she felt, she might knock it over and thereby draw unwanted attention on herself—not to mention ignite all her most precious belongings.

Instead she held her breath and closed her eyes. *Father in heaven, protect me.*

The footsteps came directly overhead. Paused. Shuffled. That bar of light went dark.

Winter's arm stole out of its own accord, and her fingers wrapped around the handle of the flintlock.

A creak, far too familiar—the sound of the trapdoor being raised. Knees shaking, she rose too. Her arm lifted until it extended the gun before her. She aimed at the stairs and whoever would come down them.

She recognized the boots, scuffed and worn as they were, and the shape of the legs that followed them. He descended quickly, pulling the door closed above him. "Bennet?" Her voice shook to match her hand.

He didn't seem surprised to see her down here—until his gaze landed on the gun. Hands flying upward, his eyes bulged. "Blast it, Winter, put that down! You could ki—wait. Is that one of George's?"

She tried to calm her racing heart, but in vain. Though she did lower the weapon. "Yes."

"How in thunder did you—never mind." Lowering his arms back to his sides, he stepped from the final stair onto the packed dirt of the floor and looked around. "I suppose I should simply accept that you find ways to procure things, be they weapons or information, that I never suspected. You have everything you could need down here, I see. I must say, when I saw that trap door open, I did not expect to discover this."

As her heart lurched into her throat, he wandered over to her shelf and picked up the vial once filled with stain. Only a drop remained—he shook it. "The infamous invisible ink, I presume? Have you the formula? I toyed with a few myself, back at Yale, but I was never satisfied with their darkness when developed."

She tried to tell her fingers to relax, to direct her hand to set down the weapon. They wouldn't budge. "No, I...Bennet."

He put down the vial and strode to the scarred desk, lifting her code book and flipping it open. "Ah, the next level of protection." His brows knit. "Why did Tallmadge assign numbers to words like 'a' and 'an'? They are used so often it all but guarantees the code can be broken by anyone who intercepts it."

Her eyes slid shut. He knew the code was Tallmadge's. What else did he know? "Bennet…"

"Really, even I know that much, and I have certainly bumbled my way through the rest of it."

"The…you…" She opened her eyes again. "How long have you known?"

He put the book down, but not where she had kept it. Instead, he set it in a crate. Gathering the evidence with which to hang her? Yet he grinned. "Oh, about an hour now, I suppose. Though I am embarrassed to have missed it this long. I grant I had no idea for whom I was looking when I came to the city seeking Washington's spies, but I never suspected you. Townsend, yes—but not you."

When he came to the city seeking Washington's spies? She raised the pistol a few inches, though she knew even as she clung to it that she couldn't use it. Not against him. Even if he were the enemy, even if he would drag her to the hangman himself, she could never hurt him.

Though he probably didn't realize that when he turned to her again and saw her defensive pose. Which was probably why a mild curse slipped from his tongue. "Will you *please* put that thing down?" Obviously not trusting her to do so, he closed the distance between them, pried it from her grip, and set it on the table.

Never in her life had she felt so exposed. "I'm sorry. I wouldn't… but you…"

He framed her face with his hands, and the love shining from his eyes blanketed her. "Do you really think I would hurt you? Or let you be hurt?"

Surety descended, smothering the doubt and stilling the fear. "No."

"Good." He brushed a stray hair from her face and feathered a kiss over her lips. "Even were I your enemy, my love, I would do all in my power to protect you. But the truth is that I did not seek the spies so I might turn you in. I sought you so I might warn you."

She gripped his wrists, looking from one eye to the other. And still she could not comprehend how those words could be true. "Warn us of what? And why?"

His second kiss lingered a fraction longer. "Why? Well, I'm afraid your grandfather was right—Yale is a hotbed of Whiggish sentiment. I may have gone there a fine, loyal young man, but one of the primary reasons I had never come home was because I could no longer believe the politics my family held dear."

"You mean you are…" Dare she hope it? "…a Patriot?"

He grinned. "Call me whatever you like. A Patriot. A rebel. A man very relieved to have realized that I need not beg your forgiveness for it, if nevertheless terrified at the danger you have put yourself in with these actions of yours." He slid his hands down her arms and locked her hands in his. "Why, Winter? Why would you do something so perilous?"

She gripped his fingers and forced a swallow. "My father is not dead, Bennet. He is in Washington's army."

His eyes widened, and his fingers tightened around hers. "Alive?"

She pressed her lips together. "Are you angry?"

A small smile bloomed. "How could such good news anger me?" He leaned a little closer. "I rejoice for you. Now, please. Continue."

She drew in a deep breath. "When Robbie asked me if I would pass along information, I knew I had to do whatever I could to help Father's cause—my cause. To bring him back safe and whole. Can you understand that?"

His smile was crooked, his gaze sad. "When I consider that your precious life could be extinguished…nay. And yet obviously I do, because I came to New York for a similar reason. My brother shared a plan I could not bear to see come to be, and so I took actions that will separate me from my family. Already I have written my uncle, confessing my politics and my part in stopping the plan to betray Washington through his most trusted men."

Her brows knit. "You mean Arnold? But how could your brother have known so long ago—"

"You, Winter. And Townsend and Woodhull and all the rest."

Her blood ran cold. "I don't understand. There is no treachery among us. We were chosen and bound by trust formed from the deepest of friendships."

"I know." His thumb stroked over her knuckles. "'Tis exactly what they intended to use against you. The plan was to feed you false information, with the certainty that you would pass it along and be believed. And that when Washington acted on it, he would walk directly into General Clinton's—and now Arnold's—trap."

Fear pounced, clawed, gnashed. "What information?"

Bennet drew in a long breath and held both pairs of joined hands together between them. "Archie's original letter said only that they would use the whaleboaters' reputations as kidnapping pirates to make Washington think someone dear to him had been captured."

Dear Lord above, let it not be so. The Spirit had tried to warn her even as she came down here to write that letter, but she had ignored Him. She thought the impression on her heart nothing but her own fears and dismissed it because it contradicted her more rational thoughts.

She shook her head. "No. Bennet, Fairchild told me that just the other day." New pain pierced. "He must know."

"'Tis Arnold who suspected it. He undoubtedly told Fairchild to give you the information so they could see if you would pass it on. And if so, plan their ambush for when Washington mounts a rescue." He leaned closer. "But surely you could not have sent it. Townsend is not here to receive it from you."

If only that had been enough to silence her. If only she hadn't taken matters into her own hands when Robbie had told her to lie low. "I had Freeman give it directly to Roe not two days ago."

His eyes slid shut. "Winter."

"I know." She rested her forehead on his shoulder, but his comforting presence could not still the quavering that overtook her. "What have I done, Bennet?"

He released her hands and encircled her with his arms. "Nothing that cannot be undone."

"I cannot send another message. I have no more stain, and Roe will not return for weeks at any rate." By that time it would be too late. Washington would have already walked into a trap. All because of her.

His arms tightened around her. "Then we will not send a written message. I will deliver one myself. Take the truth straight to Tallmadge."

She tilted her face up so she might see the determination shining in his eyes. The squeeze of her heart changed in pressure, sweet rather than scared. "You are wonderful for offering, but they will never believe you. You are a Manhattan Lane, with a brother in the British army and strong ties to England. I will have to go or send Freeman."

"No. I will not let you remain unprotected in this house. 'Twould be best, in fact, to get you out of the city at the first possible moment." He held her close, as if he feared she would vanish otherwise. "Together, then. The three of us."

That made more sense than any other idea. As Woodhull had discovered long ago, a couple traveling together—and a supposed servant would help the image—were not halted nearly as often as a man alone. Woodhull had enlisted his neighbor's wife to ride with him when he must get a message to Brewster. Just as it worked for Culper Senior, Winter's presence with Bennet and Freeman would make their business seem legitimate to both British and Patriot guards. "Yes. We must leave at once. I will go fetch Freeman."

He held her tight. "One moment more. When I left here earlier, I followed Arnold to a meeting in Holy Ground. That is how I discovered the final pieces of my puzzle. And I met Viney."

"Viney!" She gripped his cloak. "Is she well? I have prayed for her daily—"

"And she for you. She is nearing the end, my love, convinced she will not last more than a few days. She asked me to give you these."

He pulled away enough to reach into his pocket, and then he dropped three pearls from her necklace into her hand.

Tears stung her eyes as she closed her fingers over them. "It was sufficient, then. I prayed it would be."

"The Lord answered your prayer, as He answered mine today." He tipped her chin up. "You were right. He has been speaking to me all along. Guiding me and directing me. To you. Winter, this is not how I envisioned asking you, but will you be my wife?"

How could hope so quickly replace the panic? She nodded and blinked away her tears, even as he slid something onto her finger. "You know I will."

He bent down and touched his lips to hers. Then he tightened his hold and angled his head. Hers swam as the kiss moved from the gentle touch he had given her before to one deeper. More demanding, yet more giving. Filled with the promise of a future together full to bursting with all she had begun to think out of her grasp. Companionship and passion. Love and understanding. A sharing of all the things that mattered.

Winter wrapped her arms around his neck and held on, accepting every drop of feeling he offered. Her knees went weak, but it hardly mattered. Gravity could have no effect, not as light as she felt. The ground seemed to fall away, the heavens to lift her up. His strong arms were surely all the world she needed. His embrace could chase away any chill. Lips against lips, heart against heart, whispers and pulses matched.

Together.

When finally he broke away, she clung a little longer, nestled in a little closer. If only the pleasant haze could remain forever, but already reality intruded. She sighed. "I suppose we had better hurry. You can explain it all to Freeman, and I will gather what I need from the house."

"No. While I explain it to Freeman, you must gather up anything incriminating from this room. Then the house."

Of course. Which was why he had put the code book into the crate.

A creak sounded behind them. "What is he explaining to me?" Freeman said from behind her. "Why he is where he ought not to be, perhaps, with my little girl in his arms?"

She spun with a smile, though it was fleeting. "That is legitimate enough. He just proposed."

Freeman arched a dark brow. "Here?"

"Well, he…that is…" She huffed and looked to Bennet. "Explain. I will pack."

She dashed about as Bennet went quickly through what had brought him there and the solution they had agreed upon. Inks and quills and papers, into the crate. Books and pamphlets and coin. All into the crate. Each of the little touches she had put here rather than her room in the house—into the crate.

Freeman's face was sober when she faced him again. He nodded. "I can think of no sounder plan. No one will look twice at the three of us together. I wish we could follow the Hudson straight north, but we haven't the British passes. We will have to try to make Patriot territory as quickly as we can. Not to mention that if Arnold gets wind that Winter has disappeared…"

Bennet nodded. "Do you still have your homespun, darling?"

"In my room in the house. I will change before we go."

"We can take Old Canterbury." Freeman pursed his lips. "I hesitate to try to liberate the Hamptons' wagon, though."

Bennet grinned. "No need for that. I stopped at my house on my way here and brought mine, along with a capable horse to pair with Canterbury. Mother and Archie will never miss them." He turned to her. "Get what you need. We will pack all this into the wagon. Bring only what you must, and you too, Freeman. I already have my belongings."

"All right." She paused on her way by to hug Freeman and then to toss her arms around Bennet and gave him a kiss as warm as she could manage in a few seconds. Then she darted up into the stable, through the gardens, and into the house. Thankfully, her grandparents should be out for a while yet.

Once in her room, she threw open the drawers and cabinets and dug her way to the backs of them, where her clothing from Long Island had been pushed. As she bypassed silks and satins and put her fingers to cotton and wool, it seemed she was grasping hold of rightness.

She packed what she needed in a simple bag, including one finer dress for her wedding, and managed to wriggle her way out of the complicated gown she wore. Getting into her homespun required no assistance, thank the Lord. Once dressed, she paused in front of her mirror and smirked at the strange creature reflected. With a few quick motions, she jerked the pins from her hair, shook out the elaborate style, and put it up again in a simple chignon.

There, that was the Winter she had missed so long. The only piece of wealth remaining on her person was the emerald ring she had scarcely looked at yet.

But one more was called for. She fished the pearls out of the pocket of the discarded dress, and then withdrew a box buried under all the meaningless trinkets Grandmother had provided. Inside lay a delicate strand of gold that had once encircled Mother's throat on the most special of occasions. The clasp was not secure, which was why Winter never wore it. But now it allowed her to remove the barrier so she might slip on the pearls and then replace it. It would hold enough for now, and she would have it fixed later.

Her Bible was the only other thing she wanted, and its addition filled out the bag. Perfect.

Ought she to have written a note to Grandmother? No. Better to post one once they were out of the city, letting her know she was well, betrothed, and...what? There would be no returning. Wherever they went after they found Tallmadge, it could not be here, at least not for her.

Did Bennet realize...? Of course he did. He had come with a wagon, his own things already on it. He would not mourn the City of New York, and perhaps he could mend things with his mother and brother once they were settled in Connecticut.

Father of fathers, knit tight the bonds of blood and love.

She bade a silent, happy farewell to this prison of a room and flew downstairs toward freedom.

Ben slid the bag of Freeman's belongings into the wagon and then accepted the stack of blankets the man handed over. Part of him wanted to leap on his horse and go on his own—'twould be faster by far—but he couldn't. Winter must be taken out of this situation as quickly as possible.

Not to mention that she was right about his chances of being believed.

He halted at the sound of approaching hoofbeats and moaned when Archie vaulted off his mount and strode his way.

He did not need this right now.

Archie wore a thundercloud on his face and waved a rolled paper in the air as he neared. "What in blazes is this, Benny?"

Oh, deuces—one of his maps. He thought for sure he had grabbed them all. But no, his bottom drawer. He had forgotten to clear it out. He had become distracted when Mother had walked by on her way out for the afternoon.

"Ah..."

Archie stopped a step away, rage in the gaze he moved from his brother to the wagon behind him. "Going somewhere, are you?"

Ben sighed. "If you would have rifled through your *own* things instead of mine, you would have found the letter I left for you." Left among Archie's shaving supplies so he wouldn't find it until tomorrow, that is.

"In which you would say what? Why, perchance, you have maps laying out where the militaries are and the spots in the city where officers gather?" Archie shook his head, sparks all but spitting from his eyes. "Is it not enough you have received every worldly good that should be mine? Will you take my standing in the army away from me too?"

Ben slid the blankets into the back of the wagon. "Don't be ridiculous, Archie. I have taken nothing from you. In fact, I—"

"Taken nothing?" Archie hurled the map at him. "You've taken everything, absolutely everything. And now I learn you are…what is it you are exactly, Benny? A spy?"

Freeman stepped to Ben's side and somehow packed a world of encouragement in a glance, a message he was there if needed.

Oh, how he prayed he wouldn't need him. "Archie—"

"And what are you doing here now? Has Miss Reeves actually forgiven you your loyalties and agreed to run off with you? An idiotic move. You know her grandparents will hunt you down."

"Oh, I doubt that." Winter appeared in the barn's doorway, her face peaceful, dress simple, hair sleek and dark. An image that made him think, *There you are.* The woman he had always hoped hid beneath the gloss. The woman he loved, and with whom he could build a future. She smiled at his brother. "They will not miss me. Especially when they realize I have taken your brother to meet my father. In the Patriot camp."

"Your…?" Archie's face mottled red. "Quite a pair the two of you are. Well, I'm sorry, Benny, but I can't let you do this."

In that infinite second he had in which to consider what was happening, he wondered if Archie would draw out a gun or perhaps his sword. If he would maybe even make some signal that would draw an entire squadron of soldiers out of hiding, ready to arrest them all.

When he realized that Archie instead charged him as he had done a thousand times before, arms out ready to tackle him, he nearly laughed.

Nearly. Instead, he bade farewell to the luxury of protecting his little brother and prayed that the Lord would do it for him.

When the impact came, he didn't go placidly wherever Archie pushed, as he usually did. He didn't succumb or pretend to be weak. He crouched and absorbed. Then he struck back. One mighty push that both freed him of Archie's grip and sent his brother tumbling to the ground.

Archie's eyes were glazed with shock as he landed on his back. Though he surely could have leaped back up, he stayed put and stared up at him. "Since when can you—?"

"I always could. I chose not to." Ben swept a hand over his damp forehead. A hand that shook. "I wanted to protect you, Archie. To keep you from being hurt. That was always my goal, always my reasoning. That was why I never told you I was a Patriot."

Archie slumped a little more into the ground. "You are my enemy."

"Nay. I am your brother. That is why I never took up the colors, Archie. I could not risk fighting you." He knelt down beside him and prayed the truth would shine through. "I am sorry we cannot agree about so many things, but please don't doubt that I did all I could to protect you."

"I don't understand you, Benny. I never did, and apparently I never will." He pushed onto his elbows but moved no farther. "Please rethink this. If you go to the Patriot camp, if word gets out where your loyalties lie—"

"Freedom is worth sacrifice." A hint of a smile found its way onto his lips. "I already wrote to Uncle Lane, explaining my position. I have no doubt he will name you his heir, as I suggested. You should, in fact, resign your commission as quickly as you can and hasten to England."

A light sprang up in Archie's eyes, one that made peace swell within Ben. Not a light of greed, nor of gladness to get what he thought he deserved. Nay, 'twas a light of respect. Archie sat up the rest of the way and gripped his arm. "But then what of you, Ben? You will not be able to return to New York for the foreseeable future. Without Clefton, you will have only your house in Connecticut."

"Which is all I need." Ben hauled them to their feet. "If Mother by chance is not ready to go with you and doesn't wish to remain alone in New York, tell her she is welcome in New Haven with Winter and me."

"I will tell her." Archie dusted off his rear as he set his jaw. "And I will have the property from her family transferred to you. Perhaps it will help see you through the war, since it seems you will soon have a wife to support, after all."

Winter stepped to Ben's side and leaned into him. "At the first possible—"

"Winter!"

Winter's fingers bit into his arm. Ben bit back a curse. "Hampton is home, and no doubt his servants reported that I arrived with a wagon. Archie, get out of here. *Now.* It will do you only harm to be seen with us."

Archie lifted a brow. "Still protecting me?"

"Just *go.*"

His shoulders went back, his chin up. "I could help."

"Nay." Ben pushed him toward his horse. "Mother needs at least one of us to be at her side. You must be that one."

"Ben—"

"Please, Archie. Do this for me."

Archie muttered something unintelligible, but he whistled for his mount. "If you get yourself hurt, I shan't readily forgive it."

In spite of the anxiety mounting with each second, Ben smiled. "I'll keep that in mind. Godspeed, Archie. To home and then to England."

"The same to you, brother." He swung up onto his horse. "Write me?"

The smile begot a chuckle. "We always did make better correspondents than companions. Of course I will."

Freeman grasped the horse's bridle. "I'll show you out the back, Major."

Glad when his brother disappeared, Ben looked down at Winter. "Perhaps if we meet him in the garden and act as though nothing is out of the ordinary…"

She glanced down at her modest gown. Doubt crowded her brows, but as he watched she pushed it away and dropped her mask into place. "'Tis worth a try."

Twenty-Eight

Why now? Of all the times for Grandfather to arrive home early, to seek her out, to call her name with such venom, why must it be now? Another five minutes and they could have been gone. Away from Hampton Hall and on the road out of New York. Free.

Winter gripped Bennet's arm and stepped from the stable into the warm sunshine of the October afternoon. They moved a few steps into the garden before she saw him.

She swore her heart stopped.

Grandfather, standing with arms crossed. And Hank, his favorite slave, behind him with a musket in hand.

Bennet sucked in a breath. "'Hide me under the shadow of thy wings,'" he murmured, "'from the wicked that oppress me, from my deadly enemies, who compass me about.'"

She put her free hand on his arm. "'He shall cover thee with his feathers, and under his wings shalt thou trust: his truth shall be thy shield and buckler.'"

Grandfather sliced a gaze over her. She knew that sneer well. She had seen it for the first time when he and Grandmother arrived on the farm in Oyster Bay. On that day they had finally deigned to see the place their only living child had chosen over the wretched mansion before Winter now, and they had judged it a disgrace. Judged *her* a disgrace.

But she was not. She may never be what they wanted, but they would not be her judges. Winter lifted her chin and glared right back at him. "You called?"

"Going back to your filthy roots, are you?" Grandfather took a casual, menacing step toward her. "We never should have raised you from them. I said from the moment Phillippa read Amelia's letter that we ought to leave you to your swine and their muck. You could never be anything but a shame to us."

O my God, I trust in thee: let me not be ashamed, let not mine enemies triumph over me.

Bennet's arm went taut under her fingers, and he too took a step forward. "You will not speak of her so."

"And why not?" Grandfather slashed a hand through the air. "She is no better than her whore of a mother, and you are no one to defend her. Or did you plan to marry her before you load her into that wagon you drove up?"

Many a time she had seen Bennet's face flush, but never with fury as it did now. "Marry her I most certainly will, once I have the permission of a family member whose word I can actually esteem. We are going to her father."

For a moment she thought Grandfather would succumb to apoplexy. She could see his veins bulge in his forehead from where she stood. But rather than fall, he barked, "You will *not*!" and motioned Hank forward.

A shuffling sounded from the door at the opposite end of the stable. Freeman? She didn't know whether to hope it or fear it. The last thing she wanted was for him to be in danger too.

Percy stepped out, his face contorted with pain. He leveled what looked suspiciously like her pistol at Grandfather. "You might want to rethink obeying him right about now, Hank. I haven't a whole lot to lose at this point."

Winter drew in a sharp breath as the slave advanced a few wobbling steps. He wore no shirt, and the angry, oozing welts on his back screamed for justice. Even from here she could see beads of sweat on his forehead despite the cool breeze. No doubt his eyes would be as glazed and feverish as when she had looked in on him earlier. Poor man. She put one foot forward.

Bennet pulled her back.

Hank transferred his aim to the injured slave. "Think about this, Percy. You put that weapon down now before you get yourself in more trouble."

"More trouble?" Percy's lips curled up, his chest heaving. "There is no more trouble. This fever is eating me up. But if I'm going to die, I'm going to take that devil with me."

Freeman stepped out from the same door Percy had, but his usual steadiness seemed to snap and crack. Dark dread pulled at his features. "Percy, don't. You would be no better than him."

"So be it." He took another step toward Grandfather, who stared with bulging eyes. "Get yourselves gone, Free. I'll not let him chase after you."

Bennet gripped Winter's arm and pulled her toward the stable.

Freeman held out a hand toward Percy, imploring and cautious. "Don't kill him, Percy. You don't need that guilt on your shoulders."

"Where lies the guilt in slaying a monster?" Another step.

Winter stumbled backward, but she couldn't turn, couldn't take her eyes off the scene, even when Grandfather lunged for Hank's weapon. When he raised it up. When he pointed it, not at the slave threatening his life, but at her.

Save me from the hand which hates me, God my God. Redeem me from the hand of my enemy.

The world slowed and then shifted. 'Twas as if she saw the breeze dance around her and felt the touch of a flower's scent. Heard the music of fire's spark as she tasted the motion of the ones she loved.

Bennet pulled, tugged, and lifted. She went where he willed, but her gaze remained locked on Grandfather's musket.

Hammer, released.

Frizzen, stricken.

A spark. A puff of powder from the pan.

She closed her eyes and felt the darkness cover her. Heard the crack of coming death, wood splintering nearby.

Then another shot, of a different tone. A scream. She opened her eyes to see Grandfather clutching his leg, falling.

"Hurry!" Freeman shouted from somewhere out of sight.

Bennet hoisted her into the wagon, jumped up after her, and grabbed the reins. The world came back into startling alignment. The post of the stable door was absent a hunk, but she was whole.

"He missed." The whispered words felt like a miracle upon her tongue as she burrowed into Bennet's side. "He missed."

"'Tis what he gets for buying a weapon from the Knights' rivals." Bennet pressed a kiss to the top of her head. "Let us get Freeman. Yah!"

The horses jolted forward, following the same path Major Lane had taken a few short minutes earlier. As they swung near the garden, Freeman vaulted into the wagon, the pistol in his belt. Winter turned to him. "What of Percy?"

He shook his head, his mouth pulled down, and reached across Winter to take the reins from Bennet. "He collapsed the moment he fired the shot. He's gone. 'Tis only by a miracle he managed to stand long enough to save us. God rest his soul."

A shudder overtook her as a tear slid down her cheek. "We owe him everything."

"Indeed." Bennet craned around as the wagon turned toward the alley. "Your Grandfather is writhing as much as he is screaming. Depending on where the ball lodged…"

She drew in a shaky breath. "I give him to Thee, Mighty God. If it be Your will, preserve His life."

Bennet put his arms around her and tucked her in close to his side. "I was rather hoping He would rain His vengeance down. But then, I have not been about this faith business as long as you."

Freeman chuckled and set the horses to a reasonable pace as they hit the street. "You two keep your faces concealed as much as you can. And pray we can get out of the city without anyone recognizing you."

Her hand still trembling, Winter reached behind her for the bonnet she had tossed in with her bag. A few years out of date and inexpensive to begin with, it had seen better days—but then, that alone should make anyone looking dismiss her. She tied it on and lowered her face as if studying her hands.

Bennet pulled his tricorn low and his cloak up. "We should be fairly safe once out of the city."

Winter sighed. "May the Lord grant us wings as well as guardians. Otherwise, there is no way we will catch up with Roe."

"Maybe not, but that does not mean his letter will go straight to seven-one-one. Tallmadge could be out on campaign and not there to forward it." Freeman reached over to pat her shoulder. "The Lord's will shall be done regardless, Winter."

"I know." She gripped Bennet's hand, closed her eyes, and prayed with all her might that the Lord's will would be merciful to the Patriots.

Minutes rumbled past, slow and steady, as Freeman navigated them through the streets. Her stomach clenched more and more the closer they drew to the city's limits, where soldiers were sure to be checking passes. What if Grandfather had dispatched a messenger to the authorities? Or if General Arnold had instructed them to be on the lookout for her?

Bennet slipped an arm around her again. "We will get out, my love. I have passes enough for that, if not to take us all the way through New York."

She nodded, but the anxiety didn't abate. And so she closed her eyes again and stormed heaven with her prayers for safety, hardly paying any attention to the rate at which they rolled on or the soft words Bennet and Freeman occasionally exchanged.

"You can look up now, Winnie girl."

She did and saw they had left New York behind them. Through the copse of trees they now moved through, she could hardly see the city she had never wanted to call home. "We were not stopped at all?"

"Praise the Lord, the guards did not even look up from their cards." Bennet glanced over his shoulder, smiling as he faced forward again. Then his grin faded all the way into a scowl. "Oh, blast."

Winter followed his gaze and groaned. A lone rider had stopped his horse in the middle of the road ahead of them. One with a brilliant red coat and gleaming black boots. And a posture she would know anywhere. "Fairchild."

Freeman hissed out a breath and pulled the horses up. Bennet grumbled.

Winter watched as the colonel urged his mount to where they stopped and drew alongside them, on Bennet's side. His face was sober, his brows arched as he glanced from one of them to the other. "This does not look to me like the way to England, Ben. Nor do you look dressed for Clefton, my dear."

Bennet cleared his throat. "Isaac—"

"Don't." Fairchild lifted a hand, palm toward Bennet, though his gaze locked on her. "Did you know, Winter? Did you have any idea the gossip you shared was being used to aid the Patriots?"

Was he truly willing to think her innocent? An inadvertent player in this game?

Pain pulsed from his eyes. "General Arnold is convinced you knew. He is convinced you passed it along with full understanding of what you did, but I…I cannot fathom it. Tell me you were unaware, at least until recently. Tell me you had no idea. That it was Ben who…"

He would believe her, if she said as much, if she once more played the empty-headed chit. Perhaps would let them go if she came up with a convincing enough story.

No. The time for truth had come. She reached across Bennet to take the hand Fairchild gave her so willingly. "Isaac, I'm sorry. It was never Bennet. He didn't even know until today. It was me. It was always me."

He squeezed her fingers and closed his eyes.

"I never wanted to hurt you. Please know that. At the start, I hardly knew you, so it seemed like nothing to send along whatever you shared. But then…you are a good man." She swallowed back a sob that threatened. "You deserve better than what I gave, and I pray the Lord you will someday forgive me. That you will find happiness far beyond what I could have given you."

"Impossible. There *is* no happiness beyond what you gave." His Adam's apple bobbed. "The Colonel Reeves that Arnold mentioned, in Washington's army?"

"My father."

He nodded. "Then it makes sense, I suppose. Though when Arnold laid out all the evidence, I was sure it was you, Ben. Here from Yale, having arrived in the city a bit after we first suspected a spy, but with so many plausible connections."

Bennet lifted his brows. "And so you told me to leave town, quickly."

"You should have gone. I cannot stand to see another friend killed for this." He let go of Winter's fingers, his shoulders slumped. "Certainly not the woman I love."

How could her heart twist so within her and yet continue beating? Winter swiped tears from her eyes. "I was never the woman you thought me, Isaac. I am sorry to have deceived you, even if it began only as my attempt to be what my grandparents demanded. But if you loved the Winter you thought you knew, you would not have loved the real one."

"This one I see now? With her eloquence and humility, and the fire of passion in her eyes?" He offered a sorrowful, lopsided smile. "Do not be so sure. But it is irrelevant. You are on your way to try to stop that letter, I suppose. The one bearing the news I was forced to give you."

She glanced at Bennet, hope struggling with fear in her eyes.

"You will never catch it, not traveling by wagon, not if you intend to go through Patriot territory." Fairchild heaved a sigh and reached into an inner pocket. A moment later he handed a few papers to Bennet.

Bennet's eyes went wide. "British Passes? Isaac, you could be court-martialed."

"Only if you get caught and confess from whence you procured them." He cocked a brow. "So don't."

Even as he shook his head, Bennet tucked the passes into his own pocket. "But why?"

Fairchild shrugged and looked off into the distance, toward the city. "Perhaps because I admire you for letting your hearts, rather than your families, decide your loyalty. Perhaps because I want to see you both safe and happy. Perhaps because nothing means what it once did." He met Bennet's gaze again. "Just go. There are Patriot passes there too, that we had confiscated. They should be sufficient to get you up the Hudson and into rebel territory."

Winter blinked as he sucked in a breath. "We are forever in your debt."

He gave her a small, fleeting smile and clapped Bennet on the shoulder. "Nay. The two of you are the dearest friends I have left, no matter your politics. Just swear to me you will keep her safe, Ben."

"You know I will. And when this war is over, one way or the other..."

Fairchild nodded and backed his horse up a few steps. "We will meet again. Until then, go with God. And pray for me, as I will for you."

They nodded, and with one last jerk of his chin, Fairchild cantered back the way they had come, a streak of bold red against the brittle brown leaves.

Winter leaned into Bennet's arm. "If Arnold gets wind of what he did…"

"He will not. I daresay Fairchild covered his tracks before he ever ventured out here."

"I pray so. If anything were to happen to him because of us…" She shook her head and drew in a long breath. Surely she had done nothing to deserve such devotion. 'Twas without doubt a testament to Fairchild's character rather than hers that he held her in such esteem.

"I know. We will pray, and we will trust that when this war is over, friendships need not be determined by the color of our coats." Bennet looked over her head and nodded to Freeman. "Straight up the Hudson, good man. We haven't a minute to spare."

True enough. They still must put all possible distance between them and New York before the darkness closed in.

Twenty-Nine

The fire snapped and danced, sending a few sparks heavenward. Ben let it lull him, let the cool night air soothe him, let himself bask in the beauty of God's creation and the quiet that allowed him to revel in it.

"One more day." Winter snuggled close to his side, a tin mug of weak coffee in her hand. Through these last few days of grueling travel, she hadn't once complained. She seemed, in fact, happier than he had ever seen her, in spite of them only risking an inn once, when it rained. "I hope we will be able to find Father. That at the very least someone will be able to tell us in which regiment he is."

"I hope so too." He rubbed a hand up her arm and glanced at the other side of the fire, where Freeman had laid out his bedroll. A soft snore rose over the crackling of the flames. Ben grinned and cupped her cheek, and then he leaned down to capture her lips in a warm, lingering kiss. There had been little time for such stolen embraces these past four days, but Lord willing they would soon be wed and snuggled up in their home in New Haven, set to make the future theirs. "Will he give us his blessing, do you think?"

Her grin had a note of mischief in it. "I should think so, unless he gets wind of how you kiss me the moment our chaperone is asleep."

"I have been a perfect gentleman." But he kissed her again for good measure. "I love you. I cannot think why the Lord blessed me so as to give me you, but I will never cease thanking Him for it."

"Nor I, for you. I still cannot believe that all this time we were working for the same goal and failed to realize it." She pressed her lips to his jaw. "You were entirely too convincing a Loyalist."

Ben chuckled. "I always did excel at debate, so long as there were no ladies present. And I suspect you would have too, had you been a fellow at Yale."

Her gaze went serious, intense. "No more secrets. Not from each other."

"Agreed."

She nodded, settled against his side again, and took another sip of her coffee. For a long moment only the pop of fire, the settling wood, and the next quiet snore from Freeman disturbed the silence of the night. Winter hummed out a breath. "Would you really have taken up the colors?"

He breathed a soft laugh. "Do I seem an unlikely soldier? I confess I had a few moments of doubt as to whether I would be an asset or a liability to my country, but I fully intended to follow my friends into the army, yes. Until I got a letter from Archie saying he had bought a commission."

The same feeling settled over him now that had four years ago—the realization that he was the only one in his family who believed so firmly in America's right to be free. That they would never see eye to eye.

And that he could never risk meeting Archie on a battlefield. Never.

"I'm glad you did not. Who knows if we ever would have met had you done so."

"A possibility I cannot bear to entertain." He held her close, considering yet again how the Lord had arranged his every step. "We ought to get some sleep. We still have half a day of travel before we reach the army and many prayers for safety to offer up."

Winter straightened and poured out the dregs from her cup. "I will never tire of hearing you talk of praying, Bennet Lane."

"Don't be so sure. When I get excited about a topic, I can drone on about it endlessly."

She grinned and leaned over to kiss him, soft and sweet. "Drone away, my love. Drone all you like."

"I will remind you that you said so one cold winter night when I have been talking for hours already about some minuscule philosophical point whose importance you cannot fathom." Smiling, he stood, stretched, and took the three steps to his bedding.

"If it becomes unbearable, I will return the torture by lapsing into talk of hats and dresses and shoes."

He chuckled and settled upon his hard, cold blanket. "Which would be as tortuous for you as for me."

"How fortunate, then, that I enjoy minuscule philosophical points." She took her place opposite the fire. "Good night, Bennet. I love you."

"And I you."

Freeman shifted and groaned. "Will you two please go to sleep?"

They exchanged one last smile over the orange flames before settling in. Ben sighed as he tried to find a comfortable position on the unforgiving ground, and he turned his thoughts toward the galaxies above him and the hand that had shaped them.

Creator, yes. One of such artistry and comprehension that Bennet could never hope to appreciate the full depths. So many things shone now to be grateful for. All that had brought them here. The safe travel they had been given straight through British territory, thanks to Fairchild's passes.

But one of the greatest challenges lay before them tomorrow.

Father above, let them believe us.

Winter could only stare at the sea of blue with tears in her eyes. Not a red coat in sight. Nay, just the deep, beautiful color of home. Her people. And somewhere out there, she hoped, Father.

Their wagon rumbled into the Patriot camp near Passaic Falls, New Jersey, and headed for the tent they had been told belonged to Tallmadge.

She twisted her handkerchief between her fingers. *Let him believe us,
Lord my God. Let him be here, and let him recognize the truth in our words.*

Winter caught a few curious glances sweeping over her, but no one
said anything as they drew to a halt and Bennet helped her down. Freeman set the brake on the wagon, and they moved together to the open
flap of the tent. Inside a cluster of men bent over a table strewn with
maps, and another sat at a field desk, quill in hand.

Tallmadge. She didn't know how she was so sure, but it must be him.
He had pale skin, with features surprisingly delicate until he cocked
his head and so displayed a prominent nose. Handsome, without question, as she had heard him rumored to be. And a demeanor that put
her at ease, though he had not so much as looked up at them. Something calm and sure. Something straight from heaven.

Of course. Robbie had mentioned once that Tallmadge was a man
of deep faith.

She stepped forward and drew in a long breath. Bennet had tried
to convince her that he ought to handle this, but she had insisted. She
was, after all, the one who had been involved in it so long. "Excuse me,
Colonel Tallmadge."

Tallmadge jolted and looked up, no doubt surprised to hear a female
voice. A second later he surged to his feet. "Good day, miss. Sir. May
I help you?"

"I hope so, yes." She moved forward, flanked by both Freeman and
Bennet. Her throat closed as she neared his desk and spotted a familiar
envelope upon it, one bearing her script. The seal was broken. Clasping her hands to keep them from shaking, she darted a glance at the
other soldiers. "May we beg a private audience with you, Colonel? I
have a matter to discuss of a very sensitive nature."

Tallmadge's brows knit. "May I ask who begs such an audience?"

She dipped a polite curtsy. "Miss Winter Reeves of Long Island, sir,
daughter of Colonel Hezekiah Reeves."

"Reeves, you say." Tallmadge looked beyond her and nodded to the
soldiers. "Certainly I will grant an audience to the daughter of Colonel
Reeves, though I wonder why you seek me rather than him."

"Oh, I hope to find him next." Winter motioned to Bennet. "This
is my betrothed, Mr. Bennet Lane of New Haven."

"New Haven—Yale, perhaps?" Tallmadge brightened as he smiled at Bennet. "I went there myself."

Bennet inclined his head. "I am aware, sir. You were a couple years ahead of me, I believe, but I was acquainted with Nathan Hale, who I understand was a particular friend of yours."

"Yes. Yes, he was." Tallmadge's voice went quiet. As the other men filed out, he motioned them to a few chairs. "How may I assist you today?"

Winter checked to make sure the others had all gone and caught Freeman's fortifying nod as she looked back to Tallmadge. Another deep breath was in order. "I must speak with you about the latest Culper letter, sir."

Tallmadge only blinked, though she thought she detected a twitch in his fingers. "I am very sorry, Miss Reeves, but I am unaware of what you reference."

Of course he would say so. She leaned forward. "Sir, are you aware that we Reeves are from Oyster Bay, neighbors with the Townsends?"

Tallmadge's brows lifted, and his finger twitched again. Then he folded his hands in his lap when he sat, out of her view. "I cannot say as I recall from where your father hails, no. But should your acquaintance with said family have special meaning to me?"

"You know well it does." She kept her voice calm, she hoped, though she wanted to shout at him to abandon the pretense. She had had enough of pretense. "What you probably do not know is that I have spent these last two years in the City of the New York with my grandparents, where I was in regular communication with Robbie Townsend. And where I learned of the Culpers."

He gave her a tight, empty smile. "And who are the Culpers? Friends of the Townsends?"

Her eyes slid shut long enough for her heart to cry to the Lord. "Please, Colonel. I know he never mentioned me. He swore he would not, did not, for my protection, but it was I who gave him the news of the paper stolen from the mint in Philadelphia. I who, more recently, let him know that the British were aware of Rochambeau's arrival in Rhode Island. I who foolishly sent that letter on your desk when Robbie fled to Long Island to avoid General Arnold."

Tallmadge folded his arms and blinked. "I apologize, miss, but we seem to be speaking different languages."

How exasperating! What must she do, recite verbatim the words she had penned? She hoped not, for with all that had happened since, she could hardly recall the exact words she had used. But otherwise, how could she convince him she was on his side and not merely a spy who had learned too much?

Bennet made a motion that caught her eyes. His lips hinted at a grin as he splayed both hands over his chest, right hand above his left, moved them out. Then put his palms together and opened them as if they were pages. *Interesting book.*

What in the world…? She followed his gaze toward Tallmadge's desk. Papers abounded, but only one book sat upon it. The code book.

Father above, send Your whisper. Be my truth and buckler.

She looked again at the letter. "I pray you have not sent the information in that letter to seven-one-one, Mr. *Bolton*. For it was fed to me by General Arnold, who recognized my father in me and suspected that I was involved in the Culper Ring. If seven-one-one goes in search of the three-seven-one supposedly captured and taken to the one-nine-two on seven-two-eight, he will be ambushed."

Tallmadge cleared his throat and reached for the letter. "Who supposedly captured this three-seven-one?"

A bit of calm edged out the desperation. "Whaleboaters. You haven't that in the code, and it isn't pronounceable in the coded alphabet, but it would be spelled out *y-b-e—*"

"All right, all right." He held up a hand, contemplation thinning his lips. "You obviously know much. The question is, are you an enemy who knows *too* much or a friend of whom I have been unaware?"

Running footsteps interrupted before she could form an answer, and Winter spun on her seat as a tall form entered, one with a face more lined, hair more gray, but so blessedly familiar. Father's eyes went wide. "Freeman? Winter!"

She flew from her chair and threw herself into his arms, tears tangling with laughter in her throat when he caught her and spun her in a circle as he had done when she was a child. "Father! Oh, how I missed you. I prayed for you every day. Every single day."

"And I for you, Winnie girl." He put her down and framed her face in his hands. His green eyes gleamed, and his smile shone brighter than the sun. "Look at you. All grown up and so beautiful. You are the very image of your mother."

"Am I?" Her smile wobbled. "General Arnold thought rather that I looked like you."

Sobriety dimmed his eyes. "Is that why you are here? I wanted to think you safe in the city. I told myself you were well cared for with the Hamptons. I tried to write you but received a curt note from your grandfather saying no letters would be shared with you." He sucked in a breath and shook his head. "I am so sorry I was not there, Winnie, when your mother died. By the time I received word of it, you were already gone."

She could only manage a tremulous smile that she prayed had some encouragement in it, and a soft "I know."

Tallmadge cleared his throat and stepped out from behind his desk. Bennet and Freeman had risen as well. The colonel motioned toward her. "This obviously *is* your daughter, then, Reeves? And can you verify that your family is familiar with the Townsends of Oyster Bay?"

"Acquainted?" Father grinned and tucked her into his side. "Of course we are. My Winnie played with the Townsend girls since they were in their cradles, and young Robert was the one who let her know I was still alive and well while they were both in the city."

'Twas relief, if she weren't mistaken, that overtook Tallmadge's eyes. "Well, then. I am sorry to have doubted your word, Miss Reeves."

"You need not apologize, sir. 'Tis a wise man who doubts such things."

Father cocked a brow. "I have missed something."

"Nothing to worry about, Hez." Freeman stepped forward, his smile bright and sure. "Just news we brought with us from New York."

Father released her to clap his friend in an embrace. Winter smiled over it, but more so over the fact that Tallmadge slid over to his desk, picked up her letter, and ripped it in two. Then he ripped it again and again, until it was nothing but shreds. Once finished, he held up the paper he had been writing upon when they came in and repeated the process—presumably his letter to Washington.

Praise the Lord, they had not been too late. She motioned Bennet to join her and gripped his hand, resting her forehead against his arm. Not too late.

Father laughed at something and then said, "Thank you, Free, for watching over our girl."

"No thanks needed, as you well know. Though this young man here would like to take over the task."

"What?" Perhaps he hadn't even noticed Bennet's presence, for Father looked startled when he noted him by Winter's side. "And who is this?"

Winter tugged him forward a step. "Father, this is Bennet Lane. Originally of Manhattan, though he is now a professor at Yale. We plan to marry."

When Father straightened, his eyes glinting steel, she feared for a moment that Bennet would shrink. Perhaps if it had been her mother he would have—terrifying as females apparently were. But now he squared his shoulders and bowed his head in respect. "With your permission, of course, Colonel Reeves."

"My permission." Father folded his arms over his chest. "Are you a God-fearing man, Mr. Lane?"

Bennet smiled, at peace. "I am, sir."

"And a Patriot?"

The smile turned to a grin. "Much to my family's dismay."

The steel softened a bit. "You love my daughter?"

Bennet looked down at her and held her hand the tighter. "With all my being."

"Hmm." Father's lips began to twitch. He glanced at Freeman. "You obviously have Free's blessing, otherwise he would not have brought you here. And my Winnie's heart—which is good enough for me."

He held out a hand, and Bennet released hers so he might shake it. Father grinned. "A professor, you say? Of what?"

"Philosophy and chemistry, sir."

As she had known they would, Father's eyes lit up. "Chemistry? Have you ever read any of the papers by a Frenchman named Lavoisier?"

Oh, dear. Words to guarantee a long, animated conversation. Winter slid over to Freeman as she smiled at them. "They will be fast friends."

He chuckled and rested a hand on her shoulder. "That they will. And it's glad I am to be back where we belong. But I believe Colonel Tallmadge would like another word with you, Winter."

"Oh." She turned and saw that Tallmadge made a motion with his head. She moved over to where he stood by his desk, removed from the reunion. "Colonel?"

He held her gaze, measuring her not as he should the daughter of a fellow officer, but as he might a colleague. "You are really the one who provided Townsend with that information?"

"That which I mentioned, yes, and smaller details besides, though of course he had other sources."

He glanced beyond her. "Your Mr. Lane?"

"Nay." She looked his way too and smiled at the way he gestured as he spoke, completely at home in the conversation with her father. "But he is the one who realized I had been found out. His brother is in the British army and let slip their plot to undermine us. Bennet was determined not to let it happen, so he came on his own to the city to seek us out and prevent it."

Tallmadge's eyes went hard. "And he found you?"

"By the grace of God."

He sighed as he clasped his hands behind his back. "Praise the Lord for that, then. Dare I guess you are not returning to the City of New York?"

The very thought made her shudder. "'Tisn't possible, thanks to Benedict Arnold."

"And Townsend and Woodhull refuse to put quill to paper." The colonel shook his head. "I fear the Culpers may have run their course. Yet we owe so much to them. To you."

She drew in a long breath and slowly let it out. Praise had certainly never been a part of why she did what she did, but it was nevertheless a blessing to be thanked. "It was our honor, sir. The Lord did not put us in a position to help so that we might shy away from it."

"If only everyone thought that way." He held out a hand. Not palm up, as a gentleman usually did when seeking to greet a lady, but sideways, as if to shake the hand of an equal.

Forcing a swallow, Winter put hers against his and tamped down a smile at the strangeness of it when he clasped her hand and then shook it firmly. "I am glad I was able to meet you, sir."

"And I you, Miss Reeves."

"Winnie!" Father waved her over, and she nodded again to Tallmadge before rejoining her family.

"Father?"

He put an arm around her, and the other around Bennet as he led them out into the brilliant sunshine. "Come. We have a wedding to plan."

Epilogue

The City of Washington
1811, 31 years later

Ben put a hand on the small of Winter's back and guided her into the office, looking around with interest. It was his first time in their nation's capital, certainly his first time visiting the domain of a congressman. From what he could tell, the city was little more than a town, rather eclipsed by nearby Baltimore. But they had enjoyed strolling past the White House, and Winter had even exchanged a few words with the First Lady.

She drew in a deep breath now and glanced over her shoulder at him. He nodded and approached the desk of the secretary. "Excuse me, sir."

The man looked up with a distracted smile. "May I help you?"

"Could you please see if the congressman has time for a brief audience? We are Mr. and Mrs. Lane, formerly of New Haven."

"Ah." The man's smile brightened in sincerity. He stood. "The congressman is always happy to speak with his constituents. One moment, please."

While the secretary slipped through another door, Winter tucked her hand into its place in the crook of Ben's elbow. "I can hardly believe it has been five years since we have last seen him."

"I know. We need to plan another trip home to Connecticut soon. Before…"

She nodded and rubbed a hand over the soft fabric of his new great-coat's sleeve, the only indication she gave of her anxiousness.

The door to the inner office opened again, and the secretary smiled and waved them in.

Benjamin Tallmadge stood to greet them, his smile large and bright. "The Lanes! What a pleasant surprise. I had hoped to make my way to Annapolis at some point, but it seems there is never enough time. And since you are no longer within forty miles of me in Connecticut…"

Ben grinned and held out a hand to be shaken. "We are as guilty as you, never making the trip here. I blame it on how busy they keep me at the college. How have you been, Ben?"

"Quite well, Ben."

Winter rolled her eyes at the long-standing joke, though she grinned. "Will you two never tire of that?"

Tallmadge laughed and motioned them into plush chairs. "Please, have a seat, Winnie. How are the children?"

"As undauntable as ever." Her emerald eyes gleamed as she sat. "Philly is bound and determined to achieve the same education at her home that she was denied through a college—an ambition her husband supports, thankfully. Amelia and Jacob are in raptures over their twins."

Tallmadge grinned and perched on the edge of his desk. "And Thad? Is he still based in Baltimore and getting his fill of adventure on the high seas?"

Ben cleared his throat. "That is why we are here, indirectly."

His tone must have spoken far more than his words, for Tallmadge straightened again, concern lining his mouth. "Tell me he has not been impressed by the British."

"No, praise the Lord. But the tales he tells us when he comes home…" Ben sighed and shook his head. "We are headed to war again, Tallmadge. I trust you realize that. The British have never accepted our independence."

Tallmadge echoed his sigh and pinched at the bridge of his nose. "I would be a fool not to know it. Though there are fools aplenty in this city who refuse to acknowledge its coming."

Winter scooted to the edge of her chair. "Do you also know that they never ceased in their intelligence gathering? While we have all focused on growing our country and establishing a government, they have been perfecting what we abandoned."

For a moment, the congressman was silent. He just stood there, toying with a button. "I have suspected as much. Have, in fact, urged the president to dedicate more funds and manpower to establishing an organization to gather intelligence. But no one listens."

"They don't have to. Not if you will." Winter looked at Ben and gave him a worried smile.

He put encouragement into the one he returned. So long they had talked of this eventuality. They had even tried to speak with Townsend about it, but the man never wanted to be reminded of those days in New York, and he refused to speak of the business except to say that Washington had never given him a bit of the acknowledgment he had been promised. No position in the government. No thanks.

Ben suspected it was more than that. More that he had never quite resigned himself to losing Winter and so shunned any reminder of the days when he worked with her. But that was supposition.

This was fact. He faced Tallmadge again and drew in a deep breath. "We think it is time for the Culpers to get to work again."

Tallmadge looked first at Winter, undoubtedly noting that she was still so beautiful, still so sure of what she must do. Then to him. Would he think of all the talks they had had over the years in Connecticut on everything from science to politics to banking? Conversations that may have never brought up the old business, but which had proven him of sound mind. Of solid loyalty. Of dutiful determination.

The congressman leaned against his desk once more, arms folded and eyes shrewd. A smile tugged up half his mouth. "What exactly do you propose?"

Discussion Questions

1. In a time when intelligence work was considered filthy as well as dangerous, Winter risked working with the Culper Ring out of obedience to the Lord and to help her father's cause. Has the Lord or your family ever asked you to do something dangerous or questionable?

2. One of the primary themes in *Ring of Secrets* is truth— man's version versus God's version. How do you see these playing out in the book, and what are your thoughts on "truth" and truth? Are there ever times when we must hide something from others in order to obey the Lord?

3. Who is your favorite character and why?

4. Bennet and his brother have a complicated relationship— loving but not always friendly. How would you react to a brother like Archie? How do you feel about how Ben treats him?

5. When Winter meets Viney in the ironically named Holy Ground, she comes to a realization about innocence. What are your thoughts on this?

6. Do you feel Winter behaves fairly regarding Colonel Fair-
    child? What would you have done the same or differently?

7. In a society where appearance is very important and style
    very extravagant, both Winter and Bennet have a fond-
    ness for simplicity that sets them apart. What similari-
    ties do you see between society in 1780 and society today?
    Where do you fall in the spectrum and why?

8. As George Knight observes, many Americans during the
    Revolution based their loyalties not on what cause they
    believed in, but on which side they believed would be vic-
    torious. What do you think you would have done if you
    were alive at the time? Would you risk your life or liveli-
    hood for a cause that seemed destined for failure?

9. By the end of the book, Bennet can review the events of
    the year and see the Lord's guidance. Do you have a story
    from your life of when all seemed confusion or coinci-
    dence at the time, but upon looking back you could dis-
    cern God's hand?

10. At the end, Fairchild says that "nothing means what it
    once did." How has he changed through the book, and
    how do you feel about him by the conclusion?

Author's Note

When I decided to explore the world of American's first spy ring, I had the expected visions of cloaks and daggers, grand adventure and cutthroat suspense. Invisible ink and drop locations, cover stories and daring men. As I sat down with my sources, especially *Washington's Spies* by Alexander Rose, I instead learned about the reality of a group of people determined to do what they could in spite of a common hatred for the work, getting little thanks and no money for their efforts. America's first spies were just people. Untrained, common people who wanted to do the right thing, who rose to the challenge. And who went through each day afraid their next letter to Washington might be their last.

I love little more than redefining history through fictional characters who interact with historical figures, which is what I did in this story. Winter, Bennet, Fairchild, and all their family members live only in our imaginations. But Robert Townsend and Austin Roe, Benjamin Tallmadge, Abraham Woodhull, and Caleb Brewster were real members of the Culper Ring. Tallmadge moved from espionage to banking, and then to politics in the years leading up to and during the War of 1812. Woodhull hung up his spy cloak for family life on his Long Island farm. Austin Roe owned an inn and joined a militia after the

Revolutionary War, where he had the privilege of continuing to serve with his friends.

Robert Townsend was an enigma. A Quaker who was greatly influenced by *Common Sense* by fellow-Friend Thomas Payne, he was plagued all his life by black moods that seem counterintuitive for a spy. His anxious spells are well documented, but it's also recorded that he attempted to offset them by being well read and able to converse on many topics. Still, he had few friends and died a bachelor in 1838, embittered by the hand life had dealt him, though he was arguably the most trusted source of information Washington had during the war.

Benedict Arnold was in many ways the undoing of the Culper Ring, his arrival in New York having scared its agents underground. There is conjecture that the Culpers took a more active role in uncovering his plot to hand West Point to the British, but the facts don't bear that out. What is well recorded, however, is that the much-beloved John André was mourned by both Patriots and Loyalists, and his death remained a mark against Arnold, who never gained the respect of either side again.

Another historical tidbit I'd like to note is my use of sign language. Though American Sign Language was still many years from being developed, the foundation had been laid by this time. There existed no universal sign language in our country, but that which eventually came about most likely bears a strong resemblance to the systems in place in the late eighteenth century. And so when I describe a sign, it is a simplified version of the modern word. I had a great deal of fun giving Winter a history that included a language no one but her family could understand—the foundation for espionage, mwa ha ha ha.

If you were moved by some of the prayers Winter prayed, especially those her father had supposedly transcribed, then you may be interested in a beautiful little book of compiled Puritan prayers called *Valley of Vision*, compiled by Arthur Bennet from the prayers of seventeenth- and eighteenth-century theologians. The sections of prayers Winter remembers or reads from her father are taken directly from this book.

I had a blast getting to know the Culpers as I worked on *Ring of Secrets* and hope you enjoyed reading about them. They have the distinction of being the only spy ring made solely of friends, of civilians. What became of them after the end of the Revolutionary War can only be wondered about. But in a recent interview, the CIA said, "The Culper Ring may or may not still exist." You see, a group so very secretive, so very unknown could pass along its mantle for years, decades, and centuries without ever being discovered.

Which, of course, breeds all sorts of stories in the mind of a novelist. Oh, the possibilities...

About the Author

Roseanna M. White grew up in the mountains of West Virginia, the beauty of which inspired her to begin writing as soon as she learned to pair subjects with verbs. She spent her middle and high school days penning novels in class, and her love of books took her to a school renowned for them. After graduating from St. John's College in Annapolis, Maryland, she and her husband moved back to the Maryland side of the same mountains they equate with home. Roseanna is the author of two biblical novels as well as several American historical romances. She is the senior reviewer at the Christian Review of Books, which she and her husband founded, the senior editor at WhiteFire Publishing, and a member of ACFW, HisWriters, and Colonial Christian Fiction Writers.

Roseanna loves little more than talking to her readers! You can reach her at: roseanna@roseannawhite.com

Be sure to visit her blog at www.RoseannaMWhite.blogspot.com and her website at www.RoseannaMWhite.com, where you can sign up for her newsletter to receive news about upcoming books.

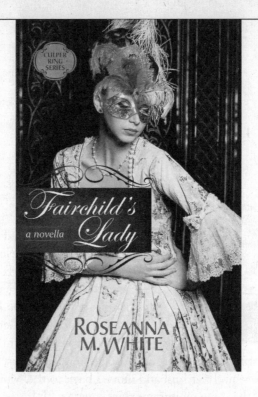

Fairchild's Lady

Roseanna M. White

(FREE eBook novella)

This bonus romantic eBook novella is set in the intervening years between *Ring of Secrets* and *Whispers from the Shadows* by Roseanna M. White. In 1789 General Isaac Fairchild travels across the Channel on a very special assignment. After surviving the American Revolution, he is now gathering information on life at King Louis XVI's court. But he must also locate a countess and her grown daughter and escort them back to England before revolution explodes in France. He knows danger is in the task set before him, but when he meets the beautiful Julienne, a new peril beckons him deeper into the intrigue of Versailles.

Don't miss the Culper Ring's continuing adventures in
Book 2 of The Culper Ring Series
by Roseanna M. White

Whispers from the Shadows

❦

One

London, England
April 1814

The servants hefting her trunks onto the carriage might as well
have been loading her coffin. Gwyneth Fairchild pulled her pelisse
close and looked out over Hanover Square with a sick feeling in her
stomach. Surely, any moment now, she would awaken from this nightmare, walk down to the breakfast room, and find Papa smiling at her.
He would speak and say something that actually made sense.

Not like yesterday, when he'd thrown her world into tumult.

She shuttered her eyes against the image of all that was familiar, all
that she might never see again. What if the *Scribe* went down? What
if it were attacked by a French ship that had not yet heard of Napo-
leon's surrender or those dreadful American pirates? What if, assuming she made it to Annapolis, they killed her the moment she stepped
foot ashore?

Annapolis. Had Papa not looked so very sorrowful, so very determined when he said that word yesterday, she would have thought he
had gone mad.

His hand settled on her shoulder now, warm and large. Those hands
had steadied her all her life. Capable, that was what General Isaac

Fairchild had always been. Capable and steady and so very noble. All that was good, all that was worthy of love and respect. So surely, surely she could trust him now when all logic and reason said she couldn't.

"I know it makes little sense to you, dear heart." He touched her chin, a silent bid for her to look at him. She obeyed and found his eyes gleaming with moisture he would never shed. Not, at least, when anyone could see him, though she had heard his heartrending sobs when Mama died last fall. "I wish there were another way, but there is not."

Another way *for what*? He wouldn't say. Gwyneth drew in a tremulous breath and tried to stand tall and proud. Like Mama had taught her, like Papa himself had instilled. To convey with her posture that she was the great-granddaughter of a duke, the granddaughter of two earls, the daughter of a general.

A daughter sent into exile for no apparent reason. Separated from all those she loved, the only people left in the world who mattered. "Papa—"

"I know." He leaned in and pressed a kiss to her forehead. "I do. But I cannot entrust you to anyone but the Lanes."

A light mist descended, heavier than fog but too tame to be called rain. At this moment, a thunderstorm would have better matched the confusion roiling within. "Please, Papa, tell me what is happening. Why must you entrust me to anyone? And if you must, why not Aunt Poole or Aunt Gates?"

His jaw moved for a moment, but no words came. Nay, he simply looked past her, his eyes searching for something she suspected was well beyond the corporeal. Then he sighed. "The Lanes will welcome you and take care of you. I will follow quickly as I can. A month at the outside. No more."

That was all the information he had volunteered yesterday too. He would give no explanation as to why he was sending her to a nation with whom they were at war, across the Atlantic to a family she had met only once when she was too young to remember them.

"Papa, your words hint at danger, but what could possibly threaten me here more than the sea and the pirates upon it? The French, the Americans?"

"The French ought to pose no threat now that we've subdued them. But…" He reached inside his coat of blazing red and pulled out an envelope. "In all likelihood you will not need this, and your ship will reach harbor safely. But if by chance you do encounter American privateers, offer them this."

She frowned as she took the envelope. It was too thin to contain anything but a single sheet of paper. Surely not some sort of bribe. "What—"

"Trust me. 'Twill suffice." Chatter from the house grew louder, and Papa looked away again, to the approaching housekeeper and gardener. "There are the Wesleys. Time for you to go."

A million arguments sprang to her tongue. She didn't want to leave. Not her home, not him, not all she held dear. Not her first Season, the one that had been put off because of Mama's illness last year. Not her friends and all their plans.

And Sir Arthur. What about Sir Arthur? She hadn't spoken to him to tell him she was leaving; she hadn't even dared send a note. Much as she hoped he would propose someday, he had made no declaration, and she could not take such liberties as to contact him. "Papa...Sir Arthur..."

"It isn't to be, Gwyn. Not now, at any rate. Perhaps when this has passed, when it is safe for you to return."

Tears burned, begging to be set loose, but she clenched her teeth against them. How had it come to this? Promise had finally shone its light again. Shopping with Aunt Gates and preparing for her debut had made it feel as though Mama were with her still. Making the rounds with her friends had finally distracted her from the loss. Getting vouchers for Almack's, and then Sir Arthur's court—she had already been called the darling of society. Had been termed a Great Beauty. Had, at long last, looked forward to the future.

"Please don't cry, dear heart." Papa thumbed away a wily tear that escaped her blockade and kissed her forehead again. "Up with you now. You must be at the docks soon."

Instead, she surged forward, wrapping her arms around him and burying her face in his chest. "I don't want to leave you, Papa. I can't. Don't make me go. Or if I must, then come with me."

He held her close. "Would that I could. Would that I didn't have to bid goodbye, yet again, to the one who matters most." He gave her another squeeze, another kiss, and then he set her back. His eyes were rimmed with red. "I love you, Gwyneth. Go with God."

And with that he let go of her and pivoted on his heel, all but charging back into the house. She almost wished she could be angry with him, that she could resent him. But how could she, seeing how he struggled with this decision? Whatever his reasons were, they must be valid.

And whatever his reasons were, they must be dire. A shiver coursed up her spine and made the mist seem colder. Isaac Fairchild was a respected general, a man loved by all. A man of considerable sway in London and beyond. If there were something frightening enough that he must send her away, was planning on leaving himself—

For America, no less. Why? Would he be going there to take command of troops? Possibly. Though why would he be secretive about it? But then, there was much about Papa's work he could not discuss. Secrets, always secrets.

"All's secure, Miss Fairchild," the driver called down from the bench.

She slipped the envelope into her reticule and took a step toward the Wesleys, who seemed to be double-checking their supplies. They, at least, would provide familiar faces for the journey. They would be an anchor on foreign seas.

Quick hoofbeats drew her attention to the drive. "Miss Fairchild!"

Her eyes went wide when she saw the dashing figure astride the horse. Sir Arthur reined to a halt beside the carriage and leaped down, fervor ablaze in his eyes.

"Miss Fairchild." He gripped her hands as he searched her face with his gaze. He had the loveliest brown eyes, so warm and beckoning, the perfect fit to his straight nose and perfectly sculpted mouth. "Is it true, then? Broffield just told me that Miss Wills said you informed her yesterday you were leaving Town."

"I…" He was holding her hands. Sir Arthur Hart, Knight of the Order of Saint Patrick, presumed heir to a viscountcy, the most sought-after bachelor in all of London, grasped her fingers as if he never intended to let go. He looked at her as if her leaving might indeed cause his demise. The mass of confusion inside didn't unravel so much as twist. "Yes, it is true. My father…"

He eased closer, his gaze so compelling she feared she might drown in it. "Something to do with military business, then? You will return soon?"

"I don't know. I don't think Papa knows."

"Dear Miss Fairchild. Gwyneth." His fingers tightened around hers, but not so much as the band around her chest squeezed tight. Never before had he spoken her given name. Hearing it in his rich tenor, spoken with such affection, made her fear her tears would overcome her again. "Why must you go with him? Can you not stay here with your aunt?"

Her attempt at swallowing got stuck in her throat. "I am all Papa has since my mother passed away, and so he is loath to send me anywhere without him." True, so true. Why, then, was he sending her an ocean away, to a hostile land?

"But surely there is a way to convince him. What if…" He paused and then swallowed before pulling her closer. "What if you were betrothed? Surely then he would not expect you to pick up and follow him?"

Her heart quickened inside her, beating a desperate tattoo against her rib cage. *Would* that change anything? Could it? "I…I don't know."

"Gwyneth." Oh, he made her name into music. The breeze toyed with his honey-colored hair under the brim of his hat and made her itch to touch the curls. "My darling, I have such a great love and admiration for you. If you would feel inclined toward accepting my hand, I will gladly seek your father out this very moment to attain his permission."

For a long moment all she could think was *He proposed!* Then she drew in a quick breath and nodded with too much enthusiasm, sending a flower falling from the brim of her bonnet. "Of course I am so inclined. Only…" She drew away when he moved closer still, recalling Papa's discomposure mere minutes before. "Let me speak with him first, as he was a bit out of countenance."

"Certainly. Yes. Anything." He laughed and raised her hands to kiss her knuckles, as if surprised she had said yes. Indeed, relief joined the joy sparkling in his eyes. "I will take a turn through your garden to try and calm myself while you go in."

"Perfect." If only she could be sure it would make any difference to Papa. If only she could be sure that, if not, Sir Arthur would wait for her. She pulled away, but he snagged her hand again.

"Gwyneth. Darling." He smiled, so bright and handsome it made her doubt any trouble could exist in their world. "I will make you very happy."

A smile stole onto her lips. It melted away again in a moment, but he had turned toward the garden by then.

Mrs. Wesley, eyes wide, held her place at the carriage but made a shooing motion toward the door. "You had better hurry, love. If the general does *not* change his mind, we had best hasten on our way."

Gwyneth flew up the steps to the door and back into the house. For a moment she paused just to breathe in home, the home she'd already resigned herself not to enter again. But she hadn't time to savor it— and if her mission went well, she needn't say goodbye to it at all.

Please, Lord. Please let him relent.

She sped down the hallway and around the corner toward Papa's study. He always ended up there, either busy at work or else, lately, just staring at the picture of Mama she'd painted for him. A professional portrait hung in the drawing room, but he said she had done the better job. Praise which always made her heart expand.

The study door was before her by the time she realized voices spilled from within it. Two of them—though when had anyone else arrived? And surely no servant would dare speak over Papa like that.

"Isaac, listen to yourself!"

Gwyneth froze a step away from the door. It was open a crack, letting her look in, though only the corner of the desk was visible, and just behind it, where Papa stood. But she needn't see the other man to realize it was Uncle Gates who spoke.

"'Isaac' now, is it?" Papa's laugh sounded devoid of humor. "Odd how you only remember our familial ties when you disagree with my decisions. Otherwise it's always my rank to which you appeal."

A loud bang made Gwyneth jump. Uncle's fist connecting with wood, perhaps? "Blast it, Fairchild, it's your rank you are abusing!"

"No! 'Tis my rank I am trying to honor. Someone, Gates, must do what is right. Someone must stand for justice rather than hatred. Someone must—"

"Oh, hang all that noble rot." A nasty curse spilled from Uncle Gate's lips even as the sound of shattering glass echoed. Gwyneth recoiled, staring in horror at that sliver of the room she could see.

What precious keepsake had he destroyed? The vase Mama had chosen two years ago? The small porcelain figure Gwyneth had given Papa for his birthday when she was fifteen? Something precious, for only the precious gained a place of honor on Papa's shelves.

And why? Why would her uncle, Mama's own brother, do such a thing?

He sent something else toppling. "You are undermining *years* of careful work! The Home Office—"

"The Home Office, you say?" Papa leaned forward onto his desk, that look of deathly calm upon his face. The one that sent underlings scurrying away with the terrible dread that they had disappointed the best man in all England. "Nay. The Home Office has decent men in it yet. A few at least, though you are not one of them. This evil must be stopped, Gates. *You* must be stopped."

There came a shuffling sound, one Gwyneth couldn't fathom the meaning of, but which made Papa snap upright. Made him lift his hands, palms out, and make a placating motion. "Gates—"

"I am through reasoning with you, Fairchild. Tell me where they are. *Now.*"

One of Papa's hands lowered toward his desk drawer, but another shuffle made him pause. "I am only—"

"You think me so great a fool? I already removed *that*, dear brother."

Papa's swallow looked painful. "I cannot help you."

More curses exploded from Uncle Gates. Closer now, as though he were rounding the desk, just out of her view. "Like thunder you can't! Tell me where they are!"

Papa's sharp inhalation was clearly audible, even in the hall. "Gone."

"Gone? Gone? What do you mean, *gone?*"

"Just that. Out of my hands and on their way to those who can put a stop to this before you destroy two nations in the name of avarice."

A cry tore through the room, guttural and animalistic. Light flashed on something metallic as her uncle charged into view, the gleaming length held before him. Still, she had no idea what it was he wielded until she saw the silver stained red.

She pressed her hands to her mouth to hold back the scream, hold back the horror. But it didn't help. Uncle still hissed words of hatred.

Papa still staggered back, away from the blade. Then he crumpled and fell.

Gates followed him down, muttering, "You couldn't have, not yet. You must have it." And his hands shoved into Papa's jacket and searched.

Papa, fight back! But he didn't. He gasped, seemed to struggle for a moment, but then he went lax. *No. No, no, no, no, no!*

Did she bleed too? She must. She felt no life, no heat, nothing. Couldn't move, couldn't make a sound, couldn't *be*. Not anymore. Not without them both. Mama, and now Papa too.

His head lolled to the side and he blinked. And his gaze focused on her. There was life yet in those familiar depths, but it seemed to flicker. To sputter. "Gwyneth."

She didn't hear it, not really. Just saw the movement of his lips. But her uncle, tossing Papa's case of calling cards into the wall, snarled. "*Now* you worry about your darling daughter? Oh, have no fear, Fairchild. Dear Uncle Gates will take care of our precious girl."

He had called her that before, and always she had accepted it as an affectionate gesture. Now, though, it sounded filthy. Threatening.

Papa blinked again, tried to pull in a breath that choked him. Again his gaze sharpened, caught hers. This time when his lips moved, she knew that he made no sound whatsoever. *Run.*

Then it was gone, all light in his eyes. Extinguished like a flame left before an open window.

And she ran. She turned on her silent slippers and fled back around the corner and down the hall. Out the doors and straight into the waiting carriage.

"Gwyneth? Miss Fairchild?"

All she noted of the voice from the garden was that it wasn't Uncle Gates's—nothing else mattered. Seeing that the Wesleys were already seated, their eyes now wide, Gwyneth pulled the door shut herself. "Drive!"

An eternal second later, the driver's "Yah!" reached her ears and the carriage jolted forward. When she closed her eyes, all she could see was darkness yawning before her.

To learn more about Harvest House books and
to read sample chapters, log on to our website:

www.harvesthousepublishers.com

HARVEST HOUSE PUBLISHERS
EUGENE, OREGON